Kate came up b̶e̶s̶i̶d̶e̶ ̶h̶e̶r̶.̶ ̶'̶W̶h̶a̶t̶'̶s̶ ̶t̶h̶e̶ matter with Maxine? She l̶o̶o̶k̶e̶d̶ ̶a̶s̶ ̶i̶f̶ ̶s̶h̶e̶'̶d̶ ̶g̶i̶v̶e̶n̶ you a real mouthful.'

'She was.' Elsie turned and looked at her, still dazed. 'She said she was getting engaged at the week-end, and then getting married. I didn't even know she was going out with anyone special. Did you know about it, Kate? Who is it?'

'Engaged!' Kate echoed in astonishment. 'Married! Well, I supppose she must mean Joey Hutton, but they've only been going out together for a few weeks. I never realised it was that serious.' There was no reason why it shouldn't be, though, she thought. She'd known Brad only a few weeks and she was deeply, hopelessly in love with him.

Elsie shook her head. 'I hope she's not going to do anything silly. It's not worth getting married to the wrong bloke, just to leave home. I dunno, Kate, everything seems to be falling to bits lately. This war's getting us all down, that's what it is, and with this invasion hanging over our heads we're all starting to feel the strain.'

'We've got to carry on though,' Kate said. 'We can't crack up now, not if it's getting as close as they say.' She thought of Brad again and shivered. 'If our boys are going over to France, they're going to need all the munitions they can get.'

Lilian Harry grew up close to Portsmouth Harbour, where her earliest memories are of nights spent in an air-raid shelter listening to the drone of enemy aircraft and the thunder of exploding bombs. But her memories are also those of a warm family life shared with two brothers and a sister in a tiny backstreet house where hard work, love and laughter went hand in hand. Lilian Harry now lives on the edge of Dartmoor where she has two ginger cats to love and laugh at. She has a son and daughter and two grandchildren and, as well as gardening, country dancing, amateur dramatics and church bellringing, she loves to walk on the moors and – whenever possible – to go skiing in the mountains of Europe. She has written a number of books under other names, including historical novels and contemporary romances. Visit her website at www.lilianharry.co.uk.

By Lilian Harry

Goodbye Sweetheart
The Girls They Left Behind
Keep Smiling Through
Moonlight & Lovesongs
Love & Laughter
Wives & Sweethearts
Corner House Girls
Kiss the Girls Goodbye
PS I Love You
A Girl Called Thursday
Tuppence to Spend
A Promise to Keep
Under the Apple Tree
Dance Little Lady
A Farthing Will Do

Dance Little Lady

LILIAN HARRY

ORION

An Orion paperback

First published in Great Britain in 2004
by Orion
This paperback edition published in 2005
by Orion Books Ltd,
Orion House, 5 Upper St Martin's Lane,
London WC2H 9EA

A CIP catalogue record for this book
is available from the British Library.

ISBN 0 75286 420 3

Typeset at The Spartan Press Ltd,
Lymington, Hants

Printed and bound in Great Britain by
Clays Ltd, St Ives plc

www.orionbooks.co.uk

To all the ladies (and the gentlemen!) of Priddy's Hard, Gosport, and other Armament and Munitions Depots throughout the country, who worked throughout World War Two to supply our troops, ships and aircraft with the equipment they needed.

Special thanks to the wonderful *Explosion!* exhibitions situated at Priddy's Hard itself and to the ladies who came there one afternoon to reminisce on my behalf, together with that fount of knowledge, Bill Mansfield. And special thanks as well to fellow-author Julia Bryant, who so generously shared her own research with me.

With such a complex subject as armaments, I feel sure that I have made some mistakes. I hope that my readers will forgive these and understand that I did try hard to get everything right – and enjoy the story of Kate, Maxine and the others as a fair portrayal of life at that time and the people who lived it.

Chapter One

'No! Don't! You mustn't!'

The man just about to lower a sack into the choppy waters of Portsmouth Harbour turned in surprise as a girl rushed towards him, her dark curls flying out from under the scarf she wore around her head. With half a dozen others, she had been walking through the Naval Armament Depot of Priddy's Hard, on her way to the shifting room, when through the dim morning mist she had seen Sam Reece stride past, carrying the sack. From the size and shape of it, and the way something inside wriggled, she knew just what he was about to do.

'He's drowning the kittens!' Forgetting all about work, she pushed past the other girls and rushed across to the Camber. Sam was almost at the quayside now, a shadowy figure bending to find a space between the barges where he could drop his burden into the waves that slapped against the wall. Kate screamed at the top of her voice, and several men, at work loading the lighters to take munitions across the harbour, straightened up and stared at her. Sam Reece himself jumped like a naughty boy caught in the act of mischief, and then flushed a dark, angry red. He was a squat, swarthy man with small, permanently bloodshot eyes and a surly scowl, and he'd never approved of bringing women in to work at Priddy's Hard.

I

'You yelling at me, girl?'

'Yes, I am!' Kate was beside him now, breathless, her eyes spitting blue fire. She snatched at the bag and tried to pull it away from him. 'You're going to drop them in, aren't you? Our Tibby's kittens – you're going to drop them in the water.'

'Yeah. What of it?' He dragged the sack back and a chorus of faint mewing sounds rose from inside. Kate's eyes filled with tears. 'You know we can't keep all the bloody kittens that are born here. Leave go, and get over to the shifting room, or you'll be late clocking on.'

'I don't care if I am!' It would mean a dock in her pay but Kate ignored that. 'You're not drowning these kittens.'

'For cripes' sake—' Sam was beginning, when another voice broke in and they both turned to see the office manager bearing down upon them. Thank goodness, Kate thought, seeing the tall, broad figure. It's Mr Milner – he'll understand. She let go of the sack and stepped towards him.

'What's going on here?' Arthur Milner stopped and stared at them both. 'I could hear the shouting back in the office. Why aren't you getting ready for work, young lady, and what's in that bag?'

'It's the kittens, Mr Milner,' Kate began, but Sam's voice overrode hers, taking on an indignant whine. 'I'm just trying to carry out orders, sir. It's nothing to do with this young woman. She just flew at me, started on about how I mustn't do this, can't do that – if you ask me, it's a pity they ever brought women into the yard. Nothing but trouble, they bin, ever since they first walked in the gates!'

'Well, that's a matter of opinion,' Mr Milner said, cutting in on the flow. 'We'd be in a poor way without them. Anyway, you haven't answered my question. What's in the bag and what were you going to do with it?'

'It's the *kittens*,' Kate began again, but the manager lifted his hand to silence her and looked at Sam.

'Well?'

The workman thrust out his lower lip. 'All right, so it's kittens. I was going to drop 'em over the side – it's what we always do when there's too many. Blooming cats bin popping off all over the place the past few weeks; we can't let 'em all live, now can we?' He appealed to Mr Milner, as man to man. 'I mean, I likes animals as much as the next bloke – got a cat of me own at home, Ginger he's called and soft as butter 'cept when another tom comes sniffing round – but anyone with any sense'd see that we can't just let 'em breed willy-nilly. Wouldn't be able to move for the little perishers, now would we? So when we gets a new litter, we just puts 'em in an old sack with a couple of stones and drops 'em over the side, nice and tidy. It's the best way. They don't know nothing about it.'

'Of course they know about it!' Kate burst out. 'They're *drowning*! It must be horrible for them. It's *cruel*.'

Arthur Milner looked uncomfortable. 'Yes, but Reece has got a point,' he said. 'We'd be overrun with cats if we let them all live. We need a few to keep down rats, and if anyone wants to give a kitten a home they're welcome to take them, but apart from that they've got to be put down. And they don't suffer much, not if it's done almost as soon as they're born.'

Kate stared at him. 'You mean you're going to let him *do* it?' She snatched the bag and Sam, taken unawares, released his grip. Kate untied the bit of string that was knotted around its neck and peered inside. 'I knew it! *These* haven't just been born – they're nearly six weeks old! They're Tibby's kittens, from our hut. We've been helping her look after them.' She cradled the bag against her and looked fiercely at the two men. 'You're not drowning Tibby's kittens.'

There was a moment's silence. Kate was suddenly aware of the clatter going on around her – the noise of the munitions factory at work, the clanging and shouting as the lighters were loaded with crates of shells, the sounds of the great harbour that lay beyond the jetties of the little dock. In a few moments she should be clocking on, and even one minute late would mean the loss of half a day's pay. She stood her ground, meeting the manager's eye, and he sighed.

'These kittens ought to have been dealt with before,' he told Reece. 'Five weeks is too late – they're almost ready to leave their mother. Why wasn't this done sooner?'

'It's them bleeding girls,' the man grumbled. 'You heard what she said. Bin looking after them, they have. Hiding them in a locker, I dare say, bringing in food for 'em, giving the mother milk. You knows what girls are.'

Mr Milner glanced at Kate and she felt her face colour. 'We were going to find homes for them all,' she said defensively. 'And they're so pretty. One of them's a tortoiseshell – look – and one's black with a white bib and paws, just as if he was going to a posh party. And this one's pure white. Look, see how fluffy—'

'Yes, yes, all right,' Mr Milner said hastily as she drew out the tiny creatures, one after another, to display their charms. 'They're pretty little mites, but they still ought to have been dealt with sooner.' He sighed. 'You say you've found homes for them all?'

'Well, I'm having the tortoiseshell,' Kate said eagerly, seeing victory within her grasp. 'Maxine Fowler wants the white one, Elsie Philpotts says she'll have the fluffy ginger one, and I'm sure someone will have the black and white one.' She looked up at him, opening her dark blue eyes very wide. '*You* wouldn't like him, would you, Mr Milner? He's got ever such a sweet face. And they're almost ready to go – we were going to take them home on

4

Friday.' She put her head on one side. 'Don't let him drown them, Mr Milner. Please don't let him drown them.'

The office manager hesitated. Sam Reece heaved a loud, heavy sigh. Kate cuddled the tortoiseshell kitten against her breast and kissed the top of its head, then looked up at Mr Milner from under her lashes. He pursed his lips in resignation.

'All right. You can take them back. So long as they're not in a dangerous place – dangerous to the job and the workers, I mean. They've got to be out on Friday, mind – and if the mother cat gives birth again you must let your supervisor know at once, and leave them to be disposed of. Understood?'

For a moment, Kate struggled with her feelings. Then she nodded. 'Yes, sir.'

Mr Milner glanced at Sam Reece. 'Right. You'd better both get back to work. The whistle will be going at any minute and we've got a big job on. Nobody's going to have time to worry about kittens for the next few weeks, I can tell you that.'

He turned and strode away. Kate and the workman looked at each other.

'Bleedin' kittens!' he said disgustedly. 'Bleedin' *girls*!'

The other girls looked at Kate as she strode towards the shifting room, triumphantly holding up the sack of wriggling, mewing kittens. 'You did it! You stopped him! What did Mr Milner say?'

'He said they were too old to drown. But next time Tibby has kittens, we've got to let someone know, so they can be "disposed of".' She snorted. 'Disposed of! He means drowned, just like these would've been. It's cruel.'

'My dad always drowns our Micky's kittens,' one of the

5

girls said sadly. 'He says they don't feel it when they're so young. He leaves her one though, otherwise she's got nothing to take the milk, see.'

'Well, I don't believe it. Of course they feel it.' Kate carried the sack over to the corner just outside the long shed, where the mother cat had a nest made of old rags in a disused wooden bomb crate. Tibby wasn't there – she'd probably gone hunting – and wouldn't even know that her babies had been missing. Kate opened the sack and tipped the kittens gently into the crate, watching them as they scrambled about in a heap of fur.

'Come on, Kate.' Maxine Fowler, Kate's best friend, was at her elbow. 'The whistle will be going any minute and you're nowhere near ready. They'll be all right now.'

Kate nodded and opened her locker. Each girl had one, a green-painted metal cupboard where she could put her outdoor clothes and valuables while she was at work. Not that anyone had anything of real value, except for wedding or engagement rings, but even these must be put into the locker. Anything made of metal could cause a spark and blow the entire site sky-high. It had happened years ago – her grandfather, who had also worked here, still talked about the men who had been killed then – and again, in 1921, when her father had been here. Four men had been killed then, all Gosport chaps, and it had brought home to everyone on the site the dangers of the materials they worked with.

The shriek of the whistle broke into her thoughts. She closed the locker door and followed the others into the shifting room. They had five minutes now, to take off their jumpers and skirts and hang them up, then step across the painted red line in their underclothes into the 'clean' area and put on their magazine clothing – loose brown overalls and a cloth cap. Some of the caps bore a red spot, denoting that its wearer worked with gunpowder, while those who worked with more modern explosives were marked by a black spot.

'I feel like Blind Pew,' Kate observed when she was first given her cap, and when the others looked blank she explained, 'You know. The old pirate in *Treasure Island*,' They nodded then. The story had been read to most of them at school and they remembered the sinister tap-tap-tap of the blind man's stick, and the horror of having the 'black spot' laid on you. It had haunted Kate for a week, and she'd been unable to sleep at nights, certain that every little tapping sound was Blind Pew coming for her. Her brother Ian had discovered this and stood outside her bedroom door when she was in bed, tapping on the stairs and driving her into nightmares from which she woke screaming, but she'd never told her mother what was frightening her so much. She didn't want her complaining to the teacher who read the story to them, in case he stopped.

From the shifting room, the girls trooped through to the laboratory and took their places at the benches where they would spend the next twelve hours inspecting and putting together ammunition. As soon as the chargehand's back was turned, Kate ducked down and lifted a section of floorboard to reveal her tea can. She pushed in the paper bag of sandwiches she had brought with her, replaced the board swiftly and stood up, winking at Maxine. 'That's for tea-break. We'll make a cuppa from the outlet pipe when old Fred goes up to the office.'

'You'll get caught one of these days,' Maxine said, but Kate shrugged.

'Everyone does it – reckon they know, anyway. They never search us for food. A couple of Marmite sandwiches won't set the cordite off – and I haven't noticed you turning your nose up when I offer you one!'

Maxine grinned. 'Matter of fact, I've got a bit of cake

7

this morning. Mum found a packet of sultanas at the back of the cupboard and made one at the weekend.' She didn't add that she'd deliberately refused a piece when it was offered her at Sunday tea-time, just to upset her mother, Clarrie, and only grudgingly accepted it for her lunch-box.

'*Fruit* cake!' Kate rolled her eyes. 'You'll share it around, naturally.'

'Only with my best friend,' Maxine said, and then turned hastily to her work as the chargehand bore down upon them.

They worked steadily through the morning, stopping only for the illicit tea-break when the supervisor was out of the way, and then for their official lunchtime at twelve. By then, Kate's legs were aching from having stood for nearly six hours, and she was glad to push her way out with the rest of the girls and get a bit of fresh air.

Set on a peninsula of land on the western shores of Portsmouth Harbour, the armament depot covered a large area of what had once been wasteground, a 'hard' area of solid mud, its channels washed twice a day by the tide, and covered with tough grass and furze bushes which burst into golden flowers every spring. Until it had been taken over by the government nearly two hundred years ago, the area had been more or less wild, with the grassy ramparts of Gosport Lines – the earthen fortifications once constructed to ward off possible invasion by the French – forming a long low hill across its neck.

Before then, Naval munitions had been made and loaded at the Gunwharf, on the Portsmouth side of the harbour, but that had been considered too dangerous for the fleet of ships coming through the narrow entrance and mooring at the jetties, so the work had been transferred to Gosport. By 1777, the huge Magazine had been built and munitions were being shipped across the harbour by barge, or lighter, just as they were now.

The ramparts were still there, making a good buffer against possible explosions, and other hillocks had been pushed up between the sheds so that each was protected from the others. What with these and the old moats that ran between the Lines, with blackberry bushes growing along their banks, and the groves of walnut trees that had been planted to provide wood for rifle butts and pistol grips, it was almost like being out in the country.

'They say you can't see Priddy's from the air at all, with all the roofs being painted green to match the grass,' Maxine observed. 'That's why we don't get bombed. Makes you wonder why they don't paint everyone's roofs green, doesn't it.' She looked up at the sky and unbuttoned her brown herringbone tweed coat. 'Look – sunshine!'

'Don't blink, it'll be gone in a minute,' Kate advised. 'It's only the first of March, you know, not Midsummer Day.' She grinned as a chilly wind sprang up and Maxine hurriedly pulled her coat around her again. 'Not a bad day really, though: in like a lion, out like a lamb, they say, don't they? Don't really know what today is like, it's just sort of grey and draughty. Like a seagull, perhaps,' she added as half a dozen birds flew over, cackling.

'It'd be quite nice if you pushed away the clouds and switched off the wind,' Hazel Jackman remarked. 'At least it's not raining.' She gazed across the harbour at the warships that lay at the jetties, awaiting their load of ammunition. 'Did you hear Mr Churchill was in Pompey last Monday? My Uncle Joe came round last night for a game of cards, and he said heaps of people saw him walking round looking at the bomb damage. He was smoking a cigar and he gave them the V-sign and everything.'

'Well, *I'm* more interested in all those Canadians who arrived at the weekend,' Maxine declared with a wink.

'Reckon it'll be worth taking a trip over the water on Saturday? I bet there'll be quite a few on the lookout for a nice girl to show them the sights, and they'll have plenty of money to spend as well.'

'Maxine! You're awful.' Kate poked her friend in the ribs. 'You'll get into trouble one of these days, the way you go on.'

'Not me! I may not always be good, but I'm *always* careful.' Maxine tossed her blonde curls and giggled. 'Why don't you come too? It's only a bit of fun – they're decent blokes, most of them.'

'Sad to say,' another girl put in, and they all laughed. 'Let's all go. Safety in numbers and all that. What about it?'

Maxine nodded vigorously. 'I'm on! Hazel? Janice? Val? Kate, you'll come, won't you?'

'I don't know,' Kate said, and the others stared at her in surprise. 'I'll be taking Topsy home on Friday. She'll be lonely – I can't really leave her to Mum.'

'For goodness' sake, you can't stay in all weekend for a *kitten*! She'll be all right – probably sleep most of the time anyway. Look, you'll have all Saturday afternoon to play nursemaid, and you can come out with us in the evening – what about that? We'll go over to South Parade Pier, there's bound to be a dance on and they always have a good band. You don't even need to *talk* to a boy if you don't want to.'

'Well, that sounds like a really good night out,' Kate said. 'I can sit on a chair being a wallflower and not open my mouth all evening, while the rest of you get off with rich Canadians. Thanks a lot!'

Maxine laughed. 'I can't really see you doing that! You talk more than all the rest of us put together. Anyway, I thought maybe we could get some of them to take us to the pictures on Sunday. That new Bob Hope and Bing Crosby film's on at the Gaiety – *Road to Zanzibar*. They say it's ever so good. It's got Dorothy Lamour in it as well, she's really glamorous. But if you're not interested . . .'

Kate clutched her arm. 'I didn't mean it! I was only joking. I'll come. Only – I don't want to come home on my own, all right? No malarkey – you'll have to promise to catch the last boat with me.'

'Well, what else d'you think we're going to do? Of course we'll catch the last boat, dope!' The irrepressible blue eyes gleamed. 'There's plenty of time for a bit of malarkey before then.' Maxine grinned. 'Don't worry, Kate, *we'll* be good. Won't we, girls? The question is – will *you*?'

The others giggled and nudged each other. Val said, 'We might find ourselves a nice rich husband, what about that? I wouldn't mind going to live in Canada.'

'Gosh, yes! That'd be nearly as good as America – better, because they're still British. Part of the Empire, anyway.' Maxine stretched her arms above her head. 'Just think of it, no food rationing, plenty of nylons, plenty of *everything*.'

'That's just greed,' Kate protested. 'You wouldn't marry someone just for nylons. You'd have to love him.'

'Well, I would love him,' Maxine said. 'I'd love anyone who could give me a new pair of nylons every day!'

They screamed with laughter, and Kate gave them a reproving look. 'Well, *I'm* not going to look for a rich Canadian to marry. I'm not looking for a steady boy at all. Not till the war's over, and maybe not even then.'

'We'll all be old by the time the war's over,' Hazel told her. 'Nobody will look at us. You've got to take your chances when they come, Kate. There's a Mr Right for all of us. You never know when you might meet him. Anyway, I'm just looking for a bit of fun – a good dance, and a nice kiss and cuddle at the end of it.'

'And that's all?' Janice asked slyly, and they laughed again.

Kate shrugged but joined in their laughter, while privately making up her mind that although she was happy to dance with boys, British *or* Canadian, and even go to the pictures with them, any goodnight kisses would be just that – a kiss and no more. And there would be no question of finding 'Mr Right'.

I wish I *could* be like the others, she thought, eating her sandwiches and gazing out across the grey, choppy waters. I wish I *could* believe that there's a boy out there who's meant for me. But I just can't. I can't forget what happened before, and I can't believe it won't happen again.

It would take one very special man to make her believe in love again. Perhaps there really was one somewhere, and one day she would meet him.

Perhaps.

Chapter Two

Friday was payday. At twelve o'clock prompt, everyone gathered outside the pay office. They sorted themselves into queues – one for the store and factory, one for the laboratory. The supervisors and men were paid first and the girls waited until it was their turn, then walked one by one into the office and came out, feeling the lumps in their little brown pay packets. It was rather like feeling the lumps in your Christmas stocking when you were little.

Pay for working in munitions was good for the girls and women. Kate was taking home four pounds a week now, a handy addition to the family income. She gave her mother two pounds ten shillings, put ten shillings into National Savings and had a pound left over for pocket money.

'Well, girls, we're rich again,' she declared as they strolled back to eat their sandwiches. It was raining today, a cold, spiteful rain that tasted of salt from the wind which was blowing across the harbour and whipping the tops off the waves. 'What shall we spend it on?'

The others laughed sarcastically. 'What *is* there to spend money on these days?' Janice Watson asked, turning back from the scrap of spotted mirror that hung on the wall, where she had been trying to twist her straight, light brown hair into some sort of curl. 'Boxes of chocolates? Frilly petticoats? Gravy browning for your legs, to make out you're wearing stockings? It's not even worth going round the shops now. Not that there's many shops to go round,' she added, gazing with dislike at the row of brown overalls hanging like gloomy ghosts on their pegs. 'I tell you what, I'd give a month's wages for a pretty frock. A *new* one, not one I'd cobbled together from something else.'

The others grimaced in agreement. So many of the big Portsmouth shops had been bombed, some of them scattered into different small departments all over the city, that an afternoon's shopping was more like a hunting expedition, and when you did get there you couldn't find much worth buying. What there was would be on ration anyway, and most of the girls had used up their clothing coupons on winter clothes. It was no fun going shopping when you couldn't buy anything.

'We'll have a real fling when it's all over,' Val Drayton said. She was a tall, thin girl with glossy brown hair that fell as straight as rainwater down her back, and which she never even attempted to curl but usually twisted into a single thick plait. She and Hazel Jackman were close friends and often referred to as 'the long and the short of it', for small, chubby Hazel barely came up to Val's shoulder. She opened her pay packet and counted the contents. 'If we save up hard, we'll have enough to buy our own houses!'

'Don't make me laugh. Girls can't buy their own houses.' Maxine stretched her arms above her head. 'Why should we, anyway? We'll stay at home with our mums and dads till we get married, and then it'll be our husbands who pay for the house. We buy the crockery and bedlinen and stuff. I wouldn't mind buying some furniture too,' she added thoughtfully. 'I want a nice home. But there's only utility now, and that's horrible. Anyway, I'm not getting married for ages.'

'You'll be on the shelf then,' Janice warned her. 'If you haven't got a boy by the time you're twenty-one, no one will look at you, that's what my mum says.' She glanced at her left hand. Janice was engaged to a soldier but couldn't wear her ring at work because of the danger of sparks. You weren't allowed to wear any jewellery or anything inflammable, not even nail varnish. Janice didn't always wear her ring at weekends either, particularly if they were going to a dance. She said she didn't see any reason why she couldn't have a bit of fun while Wally was away, so long as she kept her promise when he came home.

'Go on, Maxine'll never be on the shelf,' Hazel said. 'She could have any boy she likes, any time.' She looked enviously at the blonde hair, freed from its turban and shaken out into curls. 'You know, you could be a film star with those looks, Max. You look just like Anna Neagle.'

'I certainly wouldn't mind having Michael Wilding as my sweetheart,' Maxine said. 'But as it is, I suppose I'll probably have to settle for someone like . . . like . . .' She grinned wickedly at their expectant faces. 'Sam Reece!'

The girls howled with laughter. 'Sam Reece! Gosport's answer to the Hunchback of Notre Dame! You'll be telling us next you're going out with Blobber Norman, or Bogey Pinner!'

'Or Spud Murphy!' They were all joining in now, the name of each male worker or chargehand producing a fresh gale of mirth. 'Or Wiggly Bennet, or Onion Bailey, or Jumper Collins!'

'You're all having a good laugh.' An older woman, plump and ginger-haired, came over to them. 'What's the joke?'

'It's Maxie,' Hazel said, still giggling. 'She wants to go out with all the blokes in Priddy's.'

'I never said anything of the kind!' Maxine protested. 'Don't you believe a word of it, Elsie. They're just a lot of silly girls.'

'Oh, teasing you about your boyfriends, are they?' Elsie Philpotts found a space on the bench and settled her broad bottom between Hazel and Val. 'Well, don't you take no notice of them, Maxine. You have your fun while you can. There's too much sorrow in this world to pass up any chance of a good time.' Her cheery face saddened for a moment and then she shrugged and gave them a large wink. 'So are you all off to Pompey tomorrow to see what the Canadians have got to offer? Much the same as British boys, I wouldn't wonder, only with a bit more cash to go with it! They'll be glad of a few girls to help them spend it.'

'Elsie!' Val Drayton protested. 'You make us sound like a lot of gold-diggers. I'm not going looking for a boy, anyway – I've already got my Jack. I don't mind having a bit of fun, a dance and a giggle, but that's as far as it goes.'

'That's all any of us want, isn't it,' Maxine said demurely, and the other girls hooted. The whistle blew, making them all jump, and they gathered up their things hastily and hastened back to the shifting room, stuffing empty paper bags and greaseproof paper back into their lockers to take home, and hurrying to change from out-door 'dirty' clothing to 'clean' brown overalls.

Friday afternoon was everyone's favourite. Not only did they get paid, but they also knocked off work early, the rest of the time being given over to cleaning the magazines. Everyone had their own task: while Val and Hazel helped pack up the boxes and stack them against the wall, Kate and Maxine worked at clearing the tables and benches. Then they set to work with cans of lacquer, rubbing it into the wood until it shone, and the charge-hand – the very 'Jumper' Collins they'd been laughing about over their sandwiches – got out his can of shellac to spread over the floor. By the time they had finished, you would have thought it was a new magazine that had never been used before.

'Well, that's that,' Kate said, surveying it with satisfaction. 'All nice and smart for Monday morning. Now I'm going to get the kittens.'

She returned to the shifting room. Tibby was in her box just outside the door, with all her kittens around her. She was washing them industriously, and the girls looked down at them with softened faces.

'It's almost as if she knows what's going to happen,' Hazel said. 'She's saying goodbye – having a last cuddle and making sure they're all clean and smart to leave home. She's going to miss them, isn't she?'

'I don't think so – not much, anyway.' Kate bent and lifted out the tortoiseshell that she had chosen for herself. 'She's got fed up with them this week, been off hunting for hours and only come back to give them the odd feed. And they're used to drinking out of a saucer and eating scraps now, so they haven't been needing her much. They're ready to go.'

She had brought a cardboard box for each kitten, and now she began to lift them inside, tying a bit of string round each one so that they couldn't force their way out. There were holes punched in the sides to let them breathe and the girls laughed as a tiny black and orange paw tried to push out. She gave the white kitten to Maxine and the fluffy ginger one to Elsie Philpotts. 'There – it matches your hair!' Then she put the black and white one into a box and glanced around.

'I'll take this one to the office. Mr Milner's having it.' In truth, she wasn't absolutely sure of this – he hadn't exactly said he would take the kitten – but she was certain that if she took it along, he wouldn't refuse. She set off, carrying the two boxes.

Arthur Milner was in his office, filling in forms. Priddy's Hard was very strict about keeping track of all the explosives and the munitions that were made with them. Gunpowder, cordite, shells, cartridges – all had to be accounted for. They also kept figures for the number of shells produced each week, and the different huts and magazines would compete for the honour of having made the most.

As Kate knocked on the door, he looked up, frowning for a moment until he recognised her.

'Hello, Kate. What can I do for you?'

Kate held out the box. 'It's your kitten – the black and white one. They're seven weeks old now, and we're taking them away. I'm having the tortoiseshell one and Maxine's having—'

'Yes, yes, I remember.' He looked at the box. 'But I didn't say I'd have one, Kate. Whatever made you think I did?'

'Well,' she stared at him in dismay, 'you didn't say you wouldn't. When we were down on the quay, when Mr Reece was going to drown them, I showed them to you, and you said they were pretty, and I said the only one that hadn't got a home was the black and white one, and I looked at you, and I thought . . .'

'I see.' He remembered very well the way Kate had looked at him, her dark head tilted to one side and her blue eyes peeping up at him through long, black lashes. 'But I didn't say I'd have one, Kate. I can't.'

'Oh.' She gazed at him, her lips trembling a little. 'But what am I going to do? The others will have gone home now and I've got to take it somewhere. Can't you really have one, Mr Milner? He's very small.'

He smiled a little. 'But he will get bigger,' he pointed out. 'However, that's not the point here. I can't have one because I've got a dog – a big one – and he hates cats. He'd eat this little fellow for breakfast, he really would. It wouldn't last five minutes.'

'Oh,' she said in a deflated tone. 'That's that, then. I'm sorry, Mr Milner.'

'I'm sorry too,' he said. 'Are you sure there's no one else who will have it?'

'I've asked,' she said despondently. 'I asked weeks ago, when we decided to help Tibby keep them. They've all got cats already, and some of them are having kittens too.' She lifted a corner of the lid and looked inside. The tiny black face, with a smudge of white on its nose, peered up at her and opened a pink mouth to emit a loud miaow. Mr Milner laughed.

'I think you'd better take him home with you, Kate. He obviously holds you responsible. And you're having one already – will another one make so much difference?'

'Not to me,' Kate admitted. 'But my mum might have something to say about it – she wasn't all that keen on having one at all. We've got a dog, too, but he's a daft thing, he'll probably be terrified of them.' She lifted the two boxes and prepared to leave. 'Well, I don't see what else I can do. Maybe I'll find someone over the weekend. I'm sorry, Mr Milner.'

'I'm sorry too, Kate. I'd have taken one willingly if it weren't for Rajah.' He smiled at her, then added as she opened the door, 'But I think the next time Tibby has kittens, you'd better let Reece deal with them, all right? I know it seems harsh, but it really is the best way. It's very quick, and they can't suffer for more than a second or two. And we really can't have the place overrun with cats, now can we? We need a few to keep the rats down, but they do have to be controlled.'

'I suppose so. All right, Mr Milner, Goodnight.' She made her way out into the yard, still unconvinced that kittens did not suffer when they were drowned at birth. But at least Tibby wouldn't be having any more for a while. The big ginger tom responsible for most of the litters that had been born this spring had been caught and dealt with by one of the men in the Proof House, who had once worked in a chemist's shop and had got to know a vet. The ginger tom had been released from his ministrations furious, snarling and no longer a true tom. He prowled around the yards as if looking for something he had lost and spat viciously at anyone who came close.

Kate walked to the gates. She was almost the last to leave and the duty policeman came out of the search hut and looked suspiciously at the boxes. 'What you got in there, then?'

'Kittens.' She lifted the corner of the boxes to show him. 'You wouldn't like one, would you? It's ever so pretty – black and white, look.'

He shook his head. 'We've already got a cat, love. How d'you manage to rear these, then? I thought they all got drowned at birth.'

'Well, these didn't.' Kate was tired of people assuming that it was all right to drown kittens as soon as they were born. 'And I'm taking them home – both of them. *I* won't drown them.' She marched out through the gate, her head held high to prevent the tears from slipping down her cheeks. Nobody cares, she thought, nobody. They just think newborn kittens are lumps of meat to be chucked away. They don't realise that animals have feelings like anyone else. They don't realise what Tibby feels when her litters get taken away. It must be every bit as bad as a mother losing her children in the war.

'Kate! Is that you?'

She turned swiftly. In the gathering darkness, she could see a tall, shambling figure. She waited, feeling a mixture of relief and mild exasperation as the young man caught up with her.

'Ned, for goodness sake, you nearly made me jump out of my skin.' She regarded him with disapproval. 'When are you going to get your hair cut? It's sticking out all round your head – you look like a flipping scarecrow.'

'I thought it was you,' he said, coming to her side. 'I've been waiting by the gate. Why're you late coming out?'

'I had to collect the kittens.' She showed him the boxes and he peered at them in the darkness. 'I couldn't leave them any longer. Old Pig-Eye Reece would have drowned them over the weekend, I know he would.' Her voice rose indignantly. 'He won't get the chance now.'

'That's two boxes,' he informed her. 'I thought you were only going to have one kitty.'

'I know it's two. I *can* count, you know!' Immediately, she felt ashamed of her sharpness, and added more gently, 'I couldn't find anyone to have the other one. Can't you really have him, Ned?'

He shook his head. 'Cats bring on my mum's chest. It's the hairs. What are you going to do with him, Kate?'

'Take him home, I suppose. I don't know what Mum will say – it took me a fortnight to talk her into having one. She thinks Tyke won't like it, but Tyke's so daft he's frightened of his own shadow. Anyway, two will be able to gang up on him. Here,' she held the boxes out towards him, 'you can carry one for me.'

Ned took the box and they walked along the road together. Priddy's Hard was bordered on two sides by creeks that ran deep into the streets around the yard. Like Foxbury Point, a little way to the north, it was still covered with gorse bushes, which the local people called 'furze'. Some people said that was where Gosport had got its name – 'Gorse Port' – but Kate preferred the other explanation, that a one-time Bishop of Winchester had been caught in a storm at sea and found refuge in the little settlement, calling it 'God's Port'.

Ned loped along beside Kate, talking in his rambling way about the week at work, what was on at the pictures, and the latest *ITMA* programme on the wireless. Tommy Handley was a great favourite of his and he refused to go out on the evenings when it was broadcast. He also liked Arthur Askey and Richard Murdoch, and chuntered on, repeating the jokes in their recent wireless programme, until Kate thought she would scream.

'I *know* what the barmaid said, Ned. I heard it too. And you told me all about it yesterday as well.'

'Oh.' He was silent for a moment, then went on cheerfully, 'Will you come to the pictures with me tomorrow, Kate? There's a Roy Rogers on at the Cri. I like Roy Rogers, he's good. And Trigger, I like him as well.'

'You like any cowboy picture.' Kate quite liked Roy Rogers and his horse Trigger as well, but she always pretended reluctance, knowing that if she didn't, Ned would want to take her to every cowboy film that came along. 'Anyway, I can't, I'm going over to Pompey with the girls. We're going to the Pier.'

'Dancing? I could come too,' he said a shade doubtfully. Dancing was something Ned did not do well. He was too lanky and awkward, never sure what to do with his feet, and he didn't even know how to hold a girl. He seemed to need an extra pair of elbows in his long arms.

'No, you couldn't. We're just going together, all girls.' She didn't say they were hoping to pal up with some of the Canadians who had arrived last week. Not that it mattered, she told herself. Ned wasn't her boyfriend, she just went out with him sometimes because she felt sorry for him, and she had no intention of getting off with a Canadian anyway. But there was no point in upsetting him.

'Oh. Well, I'll go anyway,' he said, returning to the subject of Roy Rogers, and then added hopefully, 'It's on all week. We could go on Wednesday.'

'You'll have seen it by then, you dope.'

'I don't mind seeing it again.'

She could feel him gazing at her with the eyes that

always reminded her of Tyke when he wanted a titbit. 'Oh, all right. We'll go on Wednesday.'

They had arrived at the corner of Kate's street. She took the box back from him. 'Thanks, Ned.'

'Come for a walk, Sunday afternoon?' he suggested, and she hesitated.

'I don't know. I've got a lot to do – mending, and things. I ought to stop in and help Mum. And there's the kittens – they'll need to settle in.'

'Oh. All right then, Kate. I'll see you on Monday.' Ned worked in one of the other magazines and they encountered each other frequently around the yard, or going to and coming home from work. He shambled off into the darkness and Kate turned to walk down Cider Lane to number 12.

The Fisher family had lived in Cider Lane ever since Kate had been born. Before that, they'd lived in a two-up, two-down terraced house in one of the streets off Whitworth Road, but with Kate's arrival Win and George had decided to move to a larger house in Elson. They now had three bedrooms – one for themselves, one that Kate shared with her sister Sally, and one for the boys: Ian, who was now away in the Navy, and Pete, who was out in the country, leaving the room for Barney, the baby of the family, to have all to himself. There was also a small room described as a 'boxroom' where Barney had had his cot at first and where he'd have to sleep again when the family was together once more.

Barney wasn't really a baby any more, he would be five in September, but Win always called the youngest 'the baby', and would probably go on doing so until Barney objected, or another one came along to take his place – not that that seemed very likely. Five was enough, she said. Barney himself was an 'afterthought', and anyway she was forty-seven now and too old to have babies.

'My friend Pam knows a woman in her street who had a baby when she was fifty. She didn't even know it was coming till it was born,' Sally had remarked once when Win had said this, and her mother had turned on her sharply.

'Well, *I'm* not going to, and I'll thank you not to talk about such things, young lady. It's not decent.'

'I only said—'

'I know what you said. It's what you and your friends talk about that bothers me. Babies, at your age! It's nothing to do with you.'

Sally scowled and glared at her plate. Kate felt sorry for her sister. Ever since she'd come home from the village where she'd been evacuated, she seemed to be forever in trouble for saying the wrong thing, and Kate sometimes wondered if she'd rather have stayed with the Spriggs, who had fostered her. But when she'd suggested this once, Sally had made a face and shaken her head.

'No! I wouldn't go back there for a fortune. I wanted to come home.'

Sally had come home because she was fourteen and old enough to leave school. She'd got a job in Woolworths at the bottom of the High Street, serving on the hardware counter and living in hope of being moved to cosmetics, but she'd been there nearly a year now and was beginning to give up hope.

Kate pushed open the gate leading into the tiny front garden. George was proud of the tiny strip of lawn there and Win grew a few flowers in a little border round it in summer. The back garden was given over to vegetables and soft fruit – currants, gooseberries, a few raspberry canes and two or three rows of strawberries. The family was allowed one serving for Sunday tea when they were picked, and the rest were bottled or made into jam.

Kate rang the doorbell and waited, shivering in the cold

24

night air, until her mother came to open it. Then she hurried in, pulling the blackout curtain tightly behind her. Tyke, the spaniel, came rushing to meet her and then backed off, growling at Kate's burden.

'What's that you've got?' Win Fisher was a small, bird-like woman who did everything quickly. She would have died for any member of her family, but treated them as if they were permanently on probation for some misdeed. Her bright brown eyes scanned the boxes keenly. 'Is that the kitten?'

'Yes. Mum. Well, as a matter of fact, there's two of them.'

'*Two*? You mean you've brought *two* of the blessed things home with you!'

'I had to. I couldn't find anyone to take the black and white one and he's ever so sweet. Look.' They were in the back room now and Barney, who had been on the floor playing with tin soldiers, scrambled up and tried to grab the boxes from her hands. She held them away and then set them on the square dining table that stood in the middle of the room. 'Wait a minute, Barney. Don't frighten them.'

She opened the first box and a tiny black face, smudged with white, appeared, looking questioningly with wide eyes at the two humans. Tyke stood on his hind legs to sniff, and when the kitten moved towards him he jerked his head back as if he'd been stung.

'Look at that! He wants to be friendly.' Kate lifted the tiny scrap into her arms and nuzzled the hard little head. 'Here, Mum, you hold him.'

Win Fisher gave her a look and held out her hand. 'Are you sure they're big enough to leave their mother? He's no bigger than a mouse.' The kitten sat on the palm of her hand, gazing into her face, and Win sighed. Kate hid a smile and opened the second box.

25

'This is the one we're having. I've been calling her Topsy. Isn't she lovely?' The second kitten was no bigger than the first, a jumbled mass of black and white and orange with a black patch over one eye that gave her a rather rakish appearance. She mewed and burrowed her nose into Kate's coat.

'Let me hold one! Let me!' Barney hopped up and down, stretching out his hands, and Win handed him the black and white kitten.

'Take care now, don't squeeze him. They're only babies.' She watched him for a moment and then gave her daughter an ironic glance. 'I suppose you think I'll be soft-hearted enough to say we can keep them both.'

'Oh, can we, Mum, can we?' Barney was jumping up and down, the kitten clutched to his chest. 'Please can we keep them both? I want this one. Look, he likes me.' Kate saw that he was holding the kitten carefully, despite his eagerness. 'He wants to stay with me, Mum, he *does*.'

Win sighed again. 'Well, I suppose we'll have to. But you've got to look after them, mind,' she warned them both. 'I've got too much to do to clear up after kittens. And I'm not buying fish and special stuff for them. They'll have to live on scraps, same as Tyke does.'

'I'll buy them fish heads,' Kate said, 'and they can have some of my milk. We'll look after them, won't we, Barney? What are you going to call yours?'

'Turvey,' he said at once. 'They'll be Topsy and Turvey. Oh, listen – he's *purring*!' A grin of delight spread over his face and he held the tiny animal to his cheek. 'He likes me, he really does.'

Kate cuddled the tortoiseshell kitten against her and looked at her mother. She didn't bother to tilt her head or peep up through her lashes – she knew very well that those little tricks would get her nowhere – but she glanced down at Barney and gave a small, mischievous grin.

Win shook her head. 'As if I hadn't got enough to do! There's to be no cats on beds, understand? Or on the chairs. They'll sleep downstairs in their box. And it won't be my fault if they get trodden on. You know what your father's like with those great boots of his.'

'Let's put them on the floor,' Kate said to Barney, and the two kittens were set down on the rag rug. They sniffed about cautiously, and Turvey put out a paw the size of a sixpence to touch one of the toy soldiers. Barney laughed uproariously and both kittens fled to hide beneath Win's armchair. Tyke, who had already crept there when they were put down, scrambled out and ran whining to Kate.

'You coward!' She rubbed his ears. 'Call yourself a dog! I can see who's going to be in charge in this house.'

'It'll be Turvey,' Barney said. 'He's a man. He'll help me play with my soldiers and we'll have wars.' Barney had never known anything but war in his life. He had been born on 3 September 1939, only minutes before war had been declared, and the first sound in his ears had been the wail of the siren. It didn't seem to bother him but then, as Win said, he didn't really understand. Going down to the air-raid shelter was part of his life, something the family did so often it wasn't worth asking about, and since he had never been taken to the pictures (except once, to see *Snow White and the Seven Dwarfs*) and never looked at newspapers or listened to the news on the wireless, he knew almost nothing about the war. The battles he fought on the rug in front of the fire were with soldiers on horseback, wearing old-fashioned uniforms, or with cowboys and Indians in feathered head-dresses.

Win went out to the kitchen and Kate followed her. 'You don't really mind me bringing two home, do you, Mum? Only no one else wanted him, and old Pig-Eye would have drowned him.'

'Kate, I've told you before about calling the charge-hands names!'

'Mr Reece, then. But it's what everyone calls him – and he *is* a pig, Mum. He was going to drown them all the other day. I only just caught him in time. Anyway, you can see Barney loves him already,' she added wheedlingly.

'It doesn't make much difference whether I do mind or not, does it,' her mother retorted. 'I've said we'll keep them, and that's that. Now, take off your coat and give me a hand with these vegetables. Your dad'll be in any minute and tea's nowhere near ready. I'm all behind like a duck's tail this afternoon.'

Kate did as she was told and began rinsing chopped cabbage under the tap. The potatoes and carrots were already simmering and an appetising aroma filled the kitchen. 'What are we having?'

'Steak and kidney pudding without the steak and kidney. Well, more or less – I managed to get a bit of stewing steak this morning and one kidney, so it should have the flavour but you'll have to look hard for the meat. It'll fill us up though, and that's as much as we can expect these days. There's stewed apple and custard for afters.'

'I can feel my tummy rumbling already.' Kate shook the cabbage in its colander and tipped it into the saucepan of boiling water. Win put a cup of tea at her elbow and she sipped it gratefully, feeling the warmth trickle down into her stomach. The day had been a cold one, with a scouring wind and sudden showers. She was tired after the week's work – twelve hours a day standing at the table working on heavy ammunition, with only the short lunch-break and whatever time they could snatch for a cup of tea or a snooze when the chargehand wasn't looking. Her legs ached so she returned to the back room and sat down in her father's armchair to drink her tea and watch Barney playing with the kittens.

They were exploring more boldly now, creeping about the room, pausing to sniff at each new object and starting back in surprise at smells they'd never encountered before. They found Tyke, now crouched under another chair, and climbed up on his back before he knew they were there. He jumped and almost tipped the chair over, and the kittens scampered away.

Win, laying the table, looked at them and then at Barney and Kate. 'If they start getting destructive . . .'

'They won't. It was Tyke being stupid. Come here, Tyke.' The dog crept to Kate on his stomach, rolling his eyes, and she laughed at him. 'You're a terrible coward! They're only kittens, they're not going to hurt you. Dogs are supposed to chase cats, don't you know that?' She rubbed his silky ears. 'Bring one of them over here, Barney.'

Barney caught the black and white kitten and carried him across the room. Kate took Turvey from him and held the tiny animal under the dog's nose, keeping his head firmly in her other hand so that he couldn't squirm away. He whined and the kitten patted his nose with its paw, causing his whimpers to grow even more frantic.

'Stop it!' Kate commanded. 'You're being silly. Look at him. *Look* at him. Why, he's hardly as big as one of your ears. Now be friendly. Come on. No, not *that* friendly,' she added with a laugh as Tyke, gathering up his courage, put out a large pink tongue and licked the kitten's fur. 'You'll drown him!' She thought of the kitten's fate if she hadn't saved him from the chargehand, and cuddled him against her. 'Poor little kitten. Poor little Turvey.'

Barney regarded his kitten with pride. 'Turvey,' he said, in a tone of deep satisfaction. 'Turvey.' He looked up at his mother. 'Now we're a *proper* family.'

Chapter Three

Elsie Philpotts took her kitten home to the little cul-de-sac off Carnarvon Road and let it out on to the floor in the back room. Her husband Charlie wasn't in yet, and she was able to give the newcomer her full attention, watching it pick its way cautiously across the rug, pausing every few seconds to sniff at something.

There was plenty to sniff at. Elsie's housekeeping was of the tidy-up-when-you've-got-to school, and she hadn't felt the need for at least a fortnight. There were two weeks' worth of the *Daily Mirror* piled beside Charlie's armchair, a similar heap of *Woman's Weekly* magazines beside Elsie's with some navy-blue knitting perched on top, a wicker basket full of socks, shirts and jumpers waiting to be mended, and a pile of washing on the table waiting to be ironed. On the mantelpiece was a jumble of old letters, bills and Christmas cards that Elsie liked too much to throw away, all mixed up with cigarette packets and pipe-cleaners in a mug with a picture of King George VI and Queen Elizabeth at their Coronation. The walls were covered with gaudy pictures of seaside resorts and gloomy representations of Highland cattle up to their knees in bogs, waiting hopelessly for impending thunderstorms. Elsie had bought these in the junk shop in September Street, over in Portsmouth, where she and Charlie had lived before the war. She'd carried them home in triumph. 'I like a bit of art,' she'd declared, making Charlie hammer nails into the wall to hang them on. 'The seaside pictures are more cheerful, mind, but these show you've got taste.'

There was also a small bureau, tucked into an alcove beside the fireplace, but the top of this was given over to photographs of one person – Graham – Elsie and Charlie's son. There were snaps of him as a baby, held awkwardly by Charlie, and at his christening, in a long white frock that Elsie had made herself. You couldn't see the cobbled stitches at all, in the photo. There were a couple of pictures that had been taken at school in September Street, with Graham and his friend Bob Shaw in the front row, grinning to show the gaps in their teeth, and there was one of him and Betty Chapman, the girl from the bottom of March Street that he'd gone out with for a while. Elsie's pride and joy was the one showing Graham in his Naval uniform when he'd first joined up, back at the beginning of the war, his face beaming and his lanyards carefully knotted. Elsie always laughed when she thought of Graham and his lanyards. He'd got in such a tangle with them, he'd been like Houdini trying to escape from a straitjacket.

She didn't laugh for long, though. The pain of losing her only child was still too sharp and raw, even after three years. You don't expect your children to die before you, she thought, watching the kitten trying to scramble up onto the pile of newspapers. You don't expect it – but a hell of a lot do, these days.

The kitten had reached the top of the pile and perched there looking startled, as if it had never been so high before and didn't know what to do next. It mewed, then noticed Charlie's chair. Encouraged by its achievements, it started to clamber up the cover that Elsie had made for it, pulling out some of her big, untidy stitches and loosening the frayed ends.

'Well, you're going to be a proper treasure, I can see

that,' Elsie said, scooping it into her arms. It turned towards her body and nuzzled into her big, cushiony bosom and she smiled and pressed her cheek against its fur. At that moment, a slam of the back door announced that Charlie was home, and a minute later he was in the kitchen, taking off his coat and hanging it behind the door.

'Blimey, it's freezing brass monkeys out there,' he said, coming in and rubbing his cold hands together. 'Ain't you got the fire alight yet, Else? Crikey, what's that?'

Charlie's voice was dry and rustly, like old sandpaper. Next to his wife, he looked small and grey, a wispy little man with pale blue eyes and a wary manner, as if he'd gone through life expecting something to fall on him and squash him. Bob Shaw had once said he was probably scared of being squashed by Elsie, but Graham had given him a black eye for it and he'd never said it again.

'What's it look like? It's a kitten, of course. Here, you hold her for a bit while I puts a match to the fire.' She'd cleared the fireplace and laid the fire before going out that morning. She thrust the kitten into Charlie's arms and fished about amongst the cigarette packets for a box of matches. 'I told you I was bringing her home today,' she added, sinking to her knees on the rug and rearing up her broad bottom as she blew at the flames.

'So you did. I'd forgot all about it.' Charlie held the kitten as awkwardly as he'd held the baby Graham in the photograph. 'Tell you the truth, I didn't think you'd do it. You always said we'd never have another cat.'

'Well, that was because of old Sooty, wasn't it? He was always our Graham's cat, and when he died I never had the heart to get another one. But when Tibby, down the Hard, had these kittens and young Kate Fisher said she was going to keep them out of the chargehand's way and let them grow, I thought – well, why not? It's nice to have an animal around the place. Pretty little thing, ain't she?'

'She is, now you mention it.' Charlie held the kitten up and peered at her. 'Got nice long fur. What are you going to call her, then?'

'Fluffy.' Elsie got up stiffly, leaning her hand on the arm of the chair, and took the animal back. Charlie laughed.

'Know what? Her fur's the same colour as your hair! You'll know where to come if you ever need a wig, Else.'

'That's enough of your cheek, Charlie Philpotts,' she said. 'Look, I'll put her on the floor again while I make a cuppa. You watch where you're putting your feet, mind, I don't want her trod on. Just let her find her way about, get used to things. And don't let that fire go out.'

Charlie sat down in his chair and watched the kitten continue its explorations. Perhaps this was what Elsie needed, he thought. For all her loud cheerful manner, Charlie knew she was miserable, so miserable she hardly knew what to do with herself. He'd come in more than once and found her hunched over the dining table, crying her heart out, and there was nothing he could do but sit down beside her and lay his skinny arm over her shoulders. Nothing could ever bring back what she so desperately wanted – least of all a cat. But having something to look after might help.

Charlie and Elsie had lost Graham, when the Royal Hospital in Portsmouth had had a mine dropped right in front of the entrance. He'd been helping Gladys Shaw, who was a volunteer ambulance driver, to bring in patients, and by rights he shouldn't even have been there. It seemed especially cruel, somehow, when he'd got through all those battles at sea, to come home and be killed in Pompey. But that was war for you – cruel and unfair. There was no sense in expecting anything else. As Elsie said, there were plenty who'd lost their sons, and their daughters too. And there'd be plenty more too, before this lot was over.

The kitten had approached him and started sniffing at his boots. It took one of the laces between its tiny white teeth and began to pull. The lace started to come undone, and Charlie gave a rueful chuckle.

'So now I got two women after me to take me boots off the minute I come through the door! Talk about a man being master in his own house.'

Elsie came in with a tray of tea. She set it on the table on top of a knitting pattern and said, 'What's that about being master in your own house? I hope you're not getting ideas above your station, Charlie Philpotts.'

He looked at her. 'Not likely, after all this time. I knows me place, Elsie. I knows who's top dog.'

Elsie paused. Her face softened and she came over to stand beside him, her plump hand on his bony shoulder. She bent and kissed his bald patch.

'You're an old fool,' she said, 'but you knows I couldn't do without you, don't you, Charlie? You knows I'd fall to bits if it wasn't for you.'

There was a moment's silence, and then he looked up at her and said, '*You* fall to bits, Else? That'll be the day. It's *you* what keeps *me* going – didn't you know that?' His voice was gruff and he cleared his throat and said as brusquely as he could manage, 'What does a bloke have to do to get a cuppa tea round here? Come on, girl – pour it out, will you? I'm bloody parched.'

Clarrie Fowler had just arrived home from the dairy when Maxine came in. She was leaning back in her chair, a cup of tea beside her, greying hair straggling round her face, her eyes closed. The fire had only just been lit and the room was still cold. It was a comfortable enough room, with two armchairs and a small settee in front of the fireplace and the dining table pushed against one wall. The gramophone that Maxine's brother Matthew had

34

built stood in one alcove, with the wireless on a shelf above it, and the other was taken up by a built-in cupboard which housed crockery and groceries. It wasn't very convenient, because Bert Fowler's armchair was right beside it and when the cupboard was being used he was forever having to move or duck his head but, as he remarked philosophically, he didn't get much time to sit in a chair these days so it didn't really matter.

Clarrie opened her eyes as her daughter entered, and looked without much interest at the box.

'What's that you've got?'

Maxine set the box on the table and lifted the white kitten into her arms. Clarrie gave a little scream.

'It's a rat! Take it out, take it out of here, get it away!' Her voice rose and she flapped her hands. 'Take it *out*!'

'Don't be daft, Mum. Of course it's not a rat. It's a kitten – look. I told you I was bringing it home.' Maxine held the little creature out and Clarrie looked at it nervously. Her lips twitched in a faint smile.

'So it is, I can see that now. But when you picked it up, it looked . . .' She shuddered and stared at the kitten more closely. 'Here, it's quite pretty, isn't it? Sweet.'

'Of course it is. Best of the bunch.' Maxine held the small, furry body up to her cheek. Her hair fell against it and it reached up a paw to pat at the yellow curls. 'I'm calling it Snowy.'

'That's a nice name, love.' Clarrie levered herself up out of her chair. 'I'll get you a cup of tea, shall I?'

Maxine nodded and sat down in the chair her mother had just vacated. She cuddled the kitten on her lap, murmuring to it. Clarrie came back with the tea and sat down on one of the upright dining chairs watching her daughter.

'It's a pity we never had a cat before,' she said at last. 'I

35

expect you'd have liked one when you were little, wouldn't you?'

'I expect I would,' Maxine said briefly. 'Not that that would have made any difference.'

'Don't say that, love! Of course it would've made a difference. It's just that, what with me out at work all day, and your dad having Rex . . .'

'Well, that's it, isn't it? Dad had Rex, so there was never any question of us having a cat. *Some* people have cats as well as dogs, but we couldn't. But then *some* people have dads who—'

'Maxine! Don't start that again – please.' Clarrie gave her a pleading look. 'Rex is gone now and you've got your kitten, and there's nothing any of us can do about the rest of it. Why can't you just let – let—'

'Let sleeping dogs lie?' Maxine said caustically, but her mother shook her head.

'Let bygones be bygones. That's what I was going to say.' She stretched out a hand, but Maxine turned away. 'You know we've always done our best for you and Matt.'

'Yes, but it was different for Matt, wasn't it!' Maxine burst out. 'He's younger, and he's Dad's *son*. Of course you've always done your best for him – you *would*.'

'It's nothing to do with that,' Clarrie said quietly. 'We've treated you both equal. You know we have.'

Maxine stared at her. She opened her mouth to make a sharp retort, then closed it again abruptly as the kitten began to climb up her front. With tears stinging her eyes, she bent and rubbed her nose against the hard round head. I didn't mean to start arguing the minute I came in, she thought miserably. I meant to try to be nice, but somehow it never seems to work. Somehow, it's as if just *seeing* her sets me off.

'So it's all right if I keep Snowy, then?' she asked, trying not to sound too ungracious.

'Of course it is, love. Only you'll have to see to it, mind. What with me having to be out early in the morning and your dad over in the Dockyard . . .'

'I'm not asking anyone else to do it. It'll be my cat.' Maxine bent her head and nuzzled the furry body again. 'Something of my own. Something I *know* is mine.'

Clarrie looked at her daughter and sighed. She opened her mouth to speak, then thought better of it. Instead, she levered herself out of her chair again and started to lay the table for supper.

'It's sausages and mash tonight. I managed to go round the butcher's at dinnertime and get two each. We'll have a tin of peas with them too.'

Maxine nodded. She didn't offer to help her mother. She sat in the chair, playing with the kitten, and then put it on the floor and rolled up a sheet of newspaper into a ball for it to play with. When she went upstairs to wash in the tiny bathroom she took the kitten with her and put it on her bed, then stroked its fur until it fell asleep.

Something of her own. Something that was really hers.

Chapter Four

Friday night was bath night. Some houses, like the one Maxine lived in, had a bathroom – a tiny slip of a room, with just enough space to stand beside the big bath and a huge geyser – known as the Monster – taking up the wall at one end. Others, like Kate's, hadn't been built with such facilities and although George Fisher had talked about turning the boxroom into a bathroom, Barney's arrival and the start of the war had put paid to that idea so the family still had to lug in the tin bath from the yard and fill it up with buckets of hot water from the Ascot.

On Friday nights the whole family took turns to have a bath. It was a long drawn-out process, with Kate and Sally having first go, then Barney because he was the smallest – though not necessarily the cleanest – and then Win, and lastly George. There were frequent top-ups of hot water, but you couldn't use too much because of the necessity to save both gas and water. You weren't supposed to have more than five inches anyway, although as Sally pointed out, if they all had their own five inches, George would be up to his neck by the time his turn came so she didn't see why she should have to make do with the least. Win dismissed this, as she did most of Sally's pronouncements, saying that since she got the cleanest water she must be satisfied with that. And if George objected to the perfume of Sally's 'English Rose' bath salts, *he* must make do as well – although by the time Barney'd been in the water it didn't smell of anything much, other than the general grubbiness of a small boy and coal tar soap.

Hair-washing had to be done on a different day. George and Barney did theirs in the bath but Win and the girls refused to do this, saying that it spoilt their hair. You couldn't rinse it properly and it wouldn't shine. They did it on Saturday afternoons when they came home from shopping, each leaning over the sink with her head under the tap of the Ascot, the water adjusted so that it was just the right temperature, with the cup of shampoo powder mixed with water beside them. Afterwards, they knelt in front of the fire to dry it.

Sally's hair was long and more or less straight. She'd worn it in plaits when she was at school but refused now that she was out at work, and was trying it out in a French pleat. Win disapproved of this, saying it made her look too old, and now Sally was thinking of having it cut. That meant having a perm, but Win wouldn't hear of it. 'At fifteen! I never heard of such a thing. A nice bob's all a girl needs at your age.'

'A nice bob!' Sally said in disgust. 'It's too straight, Mum. It'll never keep a curl, not just with setting lotion. It'll look awful.'

'Well, you're not having a perm and that's that. And you can wipe that lipstick off your mouth. You know your father doesn't like young girls wearing make-up.' Win sat down in her armchair to do her knitting. She had unpicked an old jumper and was turning it into a sleeveless pullover for George.

'I'm only trying it out,' Sally muttered, and knelt down again beside Kate. 'I don't see why I can't have a perm. Our Kate's hair looks as if it has one.'

'Kate's hair's naturally curly.' Win looked at Kate's mass of dark curls, so like her father's. 'She doesn't even need setting lotion.'

'Yes, but it *looks* as if it's permed,' Sally argued. 'It did when she was fifteen too, so what's the difference? It's not fair. Why should she have all that curly hair and me not have a single wave?'

'You could have some of my curls and welcome,' Kate said. 'I'd quite like to be able to do it different sometimes.'

'We all have to make do with what we get,' Win said, tiring of the argument. 'Are you going out tonight, Kate?'

'Yes, we thought we'd go over the Savoy or Kimball's, or maybe the Pier. There's a good band on tonight.'

'Can I come too?' Sally asked instantly, and her mother turned on her.

'No, you can't go too! How often do I have to tell you, Sally? The local church hop's all the dancing you're going to get for the next few years. A girl of fifteen, wanting to go to South Parade Pier and the Savoy – I never heard the like!'

Sally pushed out her lips. 'Brenda Sellaway goes to dances. *Her* mum doesn't mind.'

'What Brenda Sellaway does is nothing to do with it. *You* won't go until you're seventeen at least, and that's an end of it.'

'*Seventeen*? But that's nearly two years away. What am I supposed to do in the meantime? How will I ever get a boyfriend?'

'I told you. Go to the church dances. Go to the pictures with your friends. *Girls*,' Win added emphatically. 'Boyfriends, indeed! You shouldn't even be thinking about such things. I don't know what girls are coming to, I really don't.'

'Juliet was only fourteen when she got *married*.'

'Juliet? I don't know any Juliets. Is she that girl with yellow hair that's just come to live up the top of Perry Street? Anyway, she can't be married. You're not allowed to get married till you're sixteen.'

'In *Romeo and Juliet*,' Sally explained with heavy sarcasm. 'You know – by Shakespeare. Our teacher told us about it at school. She read bits out to us.'

'Well, she shouldn't have. Putting ideas into young girls' heads – she should have read you something out of the Bible, or a nice story like *Jane Eyre*. I've always liked that book.'

'Oh yes,' Sally said. 'The mad wife locked up in the attic and setting fire to the house. A really nice, family story.'

Win sighed with exasperation. 'I've dropped a stitch now, with all this argufying.' She peered at her knitting, then turned back to Kate. 'You won't be late, will you? You know I worry when you're over in Pompey.'

'We'll catch the last ferry, don't fret.' Kate ran her fingers through her tight, dark curls. 'There, I'm dry. You can have the fire to yourself now, Sal.' She got up and looked in the mirror that hung over the fireplace. Dark blue eyes looked back at her but she grimaced at the sallowness of her skin. It was working with gunpowder that did it. Kate was luckier than most, and Maxine too had managed to keep her English rose complexion, but some of the girls at Priddy's had gone a real yellow. You had to keep scrubbing away, and putting on plenty of Pond's cold cream to protect it. They were all looking forward to the summer, when they could sunbathe and get a bit of a tan.

Topsy and Turvey had been asleep all afternoon, curled up on a cushion in George's armchair. The rule that they'd stay in their box had very quickly gone by the board and they'd miaowed so piteously – and loudly – yesterday evening that Kate had crept down again and taken them both up to bed with her. They were missing their mother and brother and sister, she said when Win discovered them in the morning, and it was cruel to leave them alone in a strange place. They'd probably be all right tonight, once they'd got used to their new home.

'They'd better be,' Win said grimly. 'I mean it, Kate, they're not to sleep on the beds. Especially Barney's. It's not healthy.' She rolled up her knitting and got up. 'Your dad and Barney'll be home soon. I'll start getting the tea ready.'

As Kate put the finishing touches to her curls – pushing them into place with her fingers – the two kittens woke and stretched, yawning pinkly. Tyke, who was still suspicious of them, crept over and sniffed, and Topsy patted him on the nose, causing him to jump back as if he'd been stung. Kate and Sally laughed.

'You're just a coward,' Sally told him, scooping Topsy down on to the rug with her. 'What are you wearing tonight, Kate?'

'My black check skirt and red blouse. Just right for jitterbugging.' Kate twisted about in time to imaginary music. 'I bet there'll be lots of that sort of music tonight—' She stopped abruptly, glancing towards the kitchen door. Win could be heard getting out cups and saucers, and putting the kettle on. Kate made a face at her sister and put a finger to her lips.

'You mean you think there'll be Canadians there?' Sally whispered. 'Ooh, Kate, d'you think they'll have nylon stockings and chocolate?'

'Not with them,' Kate retorted. 'And don't get any ideas – I'm not interested in what I can get out of them. In fact, I'm not interested at all. I'm just going to keep the others company – and to have a good dance, of course.'

'Come on, Kate, wouldn't you like a nice handsome Canadian boyfriend? I know I would.' Sally felt her hair to see if it was dry yet. 'I'm fed up kneeling here. Long hair takes too long to dry – I'm definitely having it cut, as short as I can.' She sat up, still cuddling the kitten. 'Tell you what, if you meet anyone nice, make a date with him and I'll go!'

Kate stared at her. 'Don't be daft. They're all much too old for you. And what would Mum say?'

'She wouldn't have to know. Please, Kate. I've never been out with a boy, not properly. Or if you won't do that, make a date and ask him to bring a friend along, and we can both go. That would be okay, wouldn't it? You'd be there to see that I was all right. *Please*, Kate.'

'I told you, I'm not interested in boys. I don't *want* to make a date.'

'In that case I'll just have to go and wait outside the Dockyard gate then,' Sally said off-handedly, and Kate snapped at her angrily.

'Oh no you won't! It's only – you know – *bad* girls who do that. Honestly, Sal, Mum's right, you're too young.'

'Too young for what?' Win said sharply, coming back into the room. 'What's she trying to talk you into now?'

'Too young for anything,' Sally grumbled. 'Too young for *everything*. Too young to have any fun at all. I'm fed up, I am really. I can leave school and go out to work and earn money – not that *I* get much, once I've given most of it to you, Mum – but I can't *do* any more than when I was at school. And everyone else is going to dances and the pictures and getting boyfriends, and I've got to stay in and *knit*. It isn't fair!' She jumped up, still holding the kitten, and glared at them both. 'It just isn't *fair*!'

She ran out of the room and up the stairs. Kate and Win looked at each other.

'She's right in a way, Mum,' Kate said. 'She doesn't get much fun. And it's not the same being fifteen now as it was when I was that age. I mean, that's five years ago, and it's been wartime ever since then. Things are different. People grow up more quickly. Sally's more like I was at seventeen.'

'She still can't go to dances at places like South Parade Pier,' Win said. 'Not with all these servicemen about from who knows where. Canadians it is now, isn't it? Only be here for a matter of weeks, and then they'll be gone and we'll never see or hear from them again. It's bad enough you going dancing with them, Kate, but a girl like Sally, not even sixteen years old – well, it's asking for trouble. I know it's hard for her, what with the blackout and everything, but that's just the way it is. It's hard for everyone in wartime.'

Kate nodded. She picked up Turvey, who was pulling at her shoelaces, and put him on the cushion. Then she started to help her mother get tea ready.

Perhaps she'd think about Sally's suggestion. Only if she met someone she thought could be trusted, of course, and only if he had a mate who was nearer Sally's age. Some of them were only seventeen or eighteen, after all. And she'd make sure Sally didn't go out with him on her own.

It did seem a shame that her sister had to stay at home so much. As for Kate herself, she had spoken the truth when she said she wasn't interested in finding a steady boyfriend. She had made up her mind two years ago that she couldn't take the risk – not after what had happened to Godfrey.

Maxine was getting ready too. She had spent the afternoon in the bath and she'd washed and set her yellow hair, and painted her nails bright red. She was wearing a blue dressing-gown made out of an old winter coat and her red frock hung on the wardrobe door, newly pressed and waiting to be put on.

The white kitten was asleep on the bed. Maxine put out her hand and gently touched its head. Since bringing it home last night, she'd hardly been parted from it, but tonight she'd have to leave it with her parents. A twist of undefined emotion tightened in her stomach – anger or jealousy, she didn't know which and didn't bother to try to identify it. It was always there these days, whenever she thought of either her mother or her father. They were both, in Maxine's view, at fault.

'Tea's ready, Maxine,' her mother called up the stairs, and she put the cap back on the bottle of nail varnish and waved her hands in the air to dry them. The kitten hadn't moved. It had spent most of the afternoon charging round the bedroom, leaping on and off the bed, chasing small objects and hiding from imaginary enemies, and now it was exhausted. Maxine left it there and went downstairs.

'Sardines on toast *again*,' she said, wrinkling her nose. 'You know I don't like sardines, Mum.'

'I'm sorry, love. It's all there is. I've made a few rock cakes as well, you like them.' Clarrie Fowler looked at her anxiously. 'Eat up, love, it's good for you, you know that.'

Maxine sat down, looking grumpy. In truth, she didn't dislike sardines as much as all that, but she rarely came to the table these days without some sort of complaint. It wasn't that she'd made up her mind to grumble about whatever her mother put in front of her, she told herself guiltily, it was just that there always seemed to be something she didn't like. Once, she'd have put up with it, like you had to put up with so much these days, but now she just didn't feel like doing what the old song said and 'smile, smile, smile'. There didn't seem to be much to smile about these days – not at home.

'Your father said he'd be a bit late,' Clarrie said nervously. 'We might as well start. I've left his ready to do when he comes in.'

Maxine made no comment. She ate in silence. Clarrie looked at her once or twice and then said, 'Going dancing, love?'

'Yes, can't you see I'm all dressed up?' Maxine indicated her dressing-gown scornfully, and Clarrie bit her lip. Tears came into her eyes and the girl felt another stab of guilt. I can't help it, she thought angrily. I can't help it, and it's her fault anyway. All of it's her fault.

'I'm going to wear my red frock,' she said curtly. 'It's been hung up in the bathroom to get the creases out.'

'I'd have ironed it for you, love.'

'I didn't want you to! I don't want you doing *anything* for me.' Maxine pushed away her empty plate. She'd eaten the sardines almost without noticing them. She jumped up and made for the door, her whole body trembling. 'I'm going upstairs.'

'Oh, *Maxine*!' Clarrie started to get up too, holding out both hands. She was crying now, tears coursing down her face, getting trapped in the creases that had come too soon, dripping from her chin. She looked ugly, Maxine thought, looking at her with disgust, old and ugly. 'Don't dash off. Stop down here a bit, by the fire, there's a good girl. Your dad'll be in soon and you know he likes to see you.'

'My *dad*?' Maxine's voice rose in bitter scorn. She jerked the door open so viciously that the crockery in the cupboard next to it rattled. 'My *dad* likes to see me? Don't be so stupid, Mum. Don't be so bloody, bloody *stupid*!' She slammed the door behind her and rushed upstairs. Clarrie stared after her, and then sank back into the chair, laid her arms on the table and buried her face in them. Her shoulders shook.

Up in her room, Maxine sat down on her bed and pulled the kitten onto her lap. Still worn out by its afternoon, it barely opened its eyes, but snuggled down against her. She picked it up, cuddling it against her face until her own tears came, and then she laid it down again and stroked its fur.

'Oh Snowy,' she said, her voice breaking. 'Oh *Snowy . . .*'

The girls crossed the harbour to Portsmouth on the ferry – a succession of small boats which plied from Gosport to Portsmouth and back every eight minutes. The journey itself took five minutes, and you could either stay up on deck, sitting on broad seats or standing up, or go down below. Kate hated the dark, stuffy cabin and only used it in the worst weather, so when the others made for the narrow companionway she shook her head, wrapped her old coat more firmly around her and stood in a sheltered spot beside the funnel, leaning against it for its warmth.

The boat forged its way across the darkened harbour. It must have been horrible doing this journey during the Blitz, she thought, remembering the terror of 1941 and 1942 when the sirens had wailed night after night and the German planes had swarmed above their heads in the black sky, dropping bombs in thousands. She remembered the night of 10 January, the first of the three worst raids, when Portsmouth Guildhall had been gutted and people in Gosport could read a newspaper by the light of the flames. She remembered too the dread that Priddy's Hard itself would be hit, and the terrible devastation that this would have produced.

The raids had diminished at last as Hitler turned his attention to other areas of war, although there was always the danger that they might start again, and always the rumour of some terrible new 'secret weapon'. But although the memories of Dunkirk and Dieppe were always present, there was now a growing confidence in the air. The war was still a long way from being over, but there was a sense that Hitler was being gradually pushed into retreat. One last, mighty effort and he might be beaten.

The wind was still blowing but the sky had cleared and stars could be seen between the flying clouds. The bulk of Portsdown Hill showed as a solid black bulk to the north, and Kate could see the dim shapes of ships moored in the harbour and against the dockyard jetties. Some of them, she knew, were the Canadian ships that had arrived last week, bringing hundreds of soldiers and sailors. Some were British ships, come into harbour for repairs or to be loaded with ammunition before setting out again. The ammunition we make at Priddy's, she thought proudly, going out to win the war.

'Come on,' Maxine said, digging her elbow into Kate's ribs. 'Stop dreaming – we've arrived. I don't know how you can stay up here in the cold.'

'I don't know how you can go down there by the engine,' Kate retorted, detaching herself from her warm funnel. 'Anyway, it's not cold – it's nice and cosy, and the air's fresh.' She followed the others onto the floating pontoon and then up the long wooden ramp. The tide was low, so it was steep and you could peer between the great staves that supported the harbour railway station. During the first bitter winters of the war there had been gigantic icicles hanging under there. Kate had once brought Barney across just to see them.

'Come on,' Hazel said, breaking into a run. 'There's a bus just about to go!' They hurried after her, racing across the road in front of the trolley-bus so that it couldn't leave them standing, and flung themselves aboard, laughing. They scrambled up to the top deck and the clippie follow-ed them, frowning.

'You'll get yourselves killed one day, dashing across in front like that. Where are you going, then?'

'Southsea.' They fished out their pennies. 'Five singles, please.'

'Returns,' Kate said. 'Well, mine is, anyway.'

48

'Don't be daft! We'll get brought back, won't we! We won't need to pay.'

'I'd rather have my ticket,' Kate said. She handed over her pennies and folded the return half safely away in her coat pocket. The others shrugged and Maxine said off-handedly, 'You're getting a bit prissy, Kate, you know that? It's like going out with my mum, having you along.'

Kate flushed a deep red. She could feel the tears coming to her eyes and turned away to stare out of the window at the darkened streets. Maxine touched her arm and said in a remorseful tone, 'Sorry, Kate. I didn't mean that. It's just that you never really seem to have any fun these days. You used to be such a happy person, always making us laugh. Now it's as if a light's gone out or some-thing.'

Kate said nothing for a moment. Then she turned back and looked at her friend. The others were in front of them, laughing and chattering, taking no notice. She bit her lip. The tears were still in her eyes but her flush had subsided and, after a minute or two, she said quietly, 'That's just the way I feel, Maxie. As if a light's gone out. Everything seems sort of dim. I feel as if I'm looking at the world through – I dunno, a net curtain, or a veil. A grey veil.'

'But why? Look, we've all got problems – there's a war on, it's hard for everyone. Most of us have lost someone we loved. But that doesn't mean we've got to stop living and having fun. The way I see it, it means we've *got* to have fun. Or there's just no point in it all.'

'I know.' Kate looked at her again. 'But I can't. At least, it's not that I can't enjoy things – it's just that when you meet a boy, and you go out with him a few times and then he goes away and gets killed – well, you start to wonder if it's your fault. As if you're jinxed or something. And once you've thought that, you just can't risk it any more.'

Maxine stared at her. 'That's daft. How can you be jinxed? And how many boys have you gone out with that have been killed?'

'Six – no, seven.' Kate held up her hands, counting them off on her fingers. 'There was Jack Benson at school. He took me to the pictures two or three times, and then he was at Dunkirk and never came back. Next there was Sam Smart who was in the RAF and got killed when the airfield was bombed. And those twins, Freddy and Mike Tompkins, who went down on the same ship. We used to go swimming together out at Stokes Bay. And there were those two Canadian soldiers we met over at the Savoy that time – they were killed at Dieppe, at least we think they must have been, as we never heard from them again. And there was Godfrey.'

Maxine didn't speak. Then she said, 'But Godfrey was the only one you were serious about. Those others – well, Jack Benson was before the war, and so were the Tompkins twins – anyway, they weren't exactly boyfriends, if all you did was go swimming with them. And those Canadians are probably perfectly OK, they just haven't bothered to get in touch. And I don't see how it could have been *your* fault that Sam Smart got caught by a bomb miles away from here.'

'No, but I went out with all of them, didn't I, one way or another. And it doesn't make any difference whether I was serious about them or not – they're *dead*. The Canadians too – you know how many were killed at Dieppe, thousands.' Kate sighed as she struggled to explain her feelings. 'I know it sounds daft, Maxie, but it's just how I feel. I can't let a boy get close to me any more. A few dances are all right, even a goodnight kiss, but I can't let it go any further than that because he might go off and get killed too, and I couldn't bear it.'

There was a little silence. Maxine touched her arm.

'Kate, I'm really sorry. But you've got to try to stop feeling like that. It'll drive you mad.'

'It is,' Kate said quietly. 'Sometimes, I really believe it is.'

There was a scream of laughter from the girls in front. Janice had been telling the others a joke and they were convulsed with mirth. She turned to recount it to Maxine and Kate, but the trolley-bus had arrived at Southsea front and was drawing to a halt outside the Royal Beach Hotel so they got up hastily and piled down the stairs, still giggling. Kate and Maxine got off last.

'Try to forget about it,' Maxine urged in a low tone as they waited for some of the downstairs passengers to alight. 'Put it behind you and have some fun, Kate.'

'Oh, I will.' Kate grinned at her and tossed her head so that her curls bounced. 'I'll have fun dancing, but that's all. No more boyfriends for me – not until the war's well and truly over.'

South Parade Pier jutted out into the sea immediately opposite the Royal Beach. It was long and white, with a dance hall and theatre at the end, and there were amusement arcade machines along its sides. The girls drifted by, putting pennies into the machines and trying to fish out prizes. Hazel had her fortune told by a threatening-looking effigy of a gypsy woman, whose black eyes flashed as the penny dropped into the slot. The fortune came out on a piece of card the size of a bus ticket and Hazel read it eagerly.

'*The path of true love does not always run smooth, but in your case it will,*' she declaimed. 'Coo! Does that mean I'll meet Mr Right tonight? A tall handsome Canadian who'll sweep me off my feet and take me back to America with him?' She rolled her eyes dramatically and pretended to faint. Val caught her.

51

'More likely you'll meet a garage mechanic from Forton Road. Anyway, Canada's not in America, twerp.'

'It is. It's North America. Well, it's not *south*, is it!' Hazel straightened up and gave her friend a disdainful look. 'Anyway, I'm not throwing myself away on a garage mechanic – especially not one from Forton Road! Tell you what, I'm not going to take any chances. If anyone asks me to dance with an English accent I shall pretend I don't understand.'

'How do you dance with an English accent?' Kate enquired innocently, and Hazel slanted her an exasperated look.

'For that, you can buy me a squash at the interval.' They were at the door now and holding out their money to go in. There were a number of people already there – girls like themselves, wearing frocks that had seen more than one alteration during the past four years, and a sprinkling of British servicemen. To their disappointment, there were no Canadians in evidence and not many people were dancing yet. The girls were sitting round the walls on upright chairs, chatting, and the men were over by the bar, talking and laughing loudly. The Priddy's Hard girls glanced at each other and shrugged.

'I suppose they'll be along later,' Janice said. 'Perhaps they're not allowed ashore until a certain time.'

'Perhaps they're not allowed ashore at all,' Val said gloomily. 'Remember there was a ship once that came in and the sailors weren't allowed off in case they deserted or didn't get back in time?'

'Yes, but that one was sailing again in a few hours,' Maxine pointed out. 'Perhaps they've gone somewhere else – Kimball's, or the Savoy.'

'Well, we can't afford to trek all round the Pompey dance halls looking for them,' Janice said with decision. 'Might as well make the best of it, I suppose.' She glanced around until her eye caught that of a tall young sailor with blond curly hair, standing a little way off with some mates. A brief smile, a tiny lift of the eyebrows and he was strolling across the floor towards her. Janice half-turned so that she wasn't quite facing him, but certainly hadn't turned her back, and he stopped and said, 'Like a dance?'

'Oh!' Janice said in a surprised tone. 'Yes, all right.' She flashed him a smile and moved into his arms as the band struck up a quickstep. The others watched them glide away, and then turned to grin at each other.

'She's got it down to a fine art,' Val said. 'I don't know what her fiancé's going to say when he gets home.'

'You don't imagine she's going to tell him, do you?' Maxine said scornfully, and followed Janice's example. This time it was a dark-haired boy who had come over, followed by his mates, and one by one the girls disappeared in the arms of dancers of varying expertise. Kate was left alone, studiously gazing at the floor.

'Don't you want to dance?'

She looked up quickly. The speaker was tall, with short, crisp black curls and thick dark brows above bright blue eyes. He was smiling at her, showing very white teeth, and was wearing the uniform of a Canadian airman. As Kate stared at him, he lifted one of his eyebrows enquiringly. 'I guess it *is* why you're here?'

Kate's heart skipped a beat. She glanced hastily from side to side, but could see no one she knew. The hall was now filling with Canadians. 'Y-yes,' she stammered, feeling her skin colour. 'At least, I just came with my friends really . . .'

'But you came to dance. *They're* dancing, unless they're invisible?' He pretended to look around for them. 'And I'll bet you're a good dancer, so why waste the music?' He grinned invitingly. 'C'mon.'

Almost as if mesmerised, Kate took his hands. They felt

53

dry and warm, not hot and sweaty like some men's hands. She let him draw her into his arms and smelled a mixture of soap and faint perspiration and uniform. Uncertainly, she looked up at him and he grinned down at her.

'There. Not too bad, is it?' He was a good dancer, quick and light on his feet, and as he guided her round the floor his hand pressed firmly, but not too hard, in the small of her back. Kate began to relax. He's right, she thought. This is what I came for – to dance. And her love of dancing flooded over her, so that she forgot to feel anxious and let her feet answer the music, melting into his arms, twirling in increasingly complex steps, and swinging with him into and out of the corners.

The music ended and they stopped reluctantly and looked at each other.

'Say,' he said slowly, his eyes on her flushed cheeks and sparkling eyes, 'you're some dancer. Will you dance with me again?'

Kate nodded. 'Yes, if you like.' The band was striking up again already – a foxtrot this time – and once again they were off. This time the steps were even faster, the band swinging out the rhythm, and when he led her back to her seat Kate was breathless and laughing.

'I'll come for you again,' he told her as she sat down. 'We make a good couple.'

Janice, Hazel and Val were already there. They watched as he walked across the floor to rejoin his mates, and then turned on Kate.

'Whoo! What a smasher! And what did he mean, you make a good couple? What have you been keeping secret, Kate Fisher?'

'Nothing! I've never seen him before in my life – how could I?' She thought fleetingly of the Canadians who had come to Portsmouth before, and gone to Dieppe, never to return. 'He just meant we dance well together, that's all.'

'Well, it *might* be all,' Janice said, her eyes on Kate's pink cheeks. 'And then again, it might not. Anyway, you'll soon find out – he's on his way back already.'

'No!' Suddenly, Kate felt scared. The quickstep and foxtrot had been glorious, but the bandleader was now announcing a tango, and that was the most intimate dance of all. I don't want to do a tango with him, she thought, and got up, meaning to slip out to the Ladies' before he reached her.

It was too late. His long legs had brought him swiftly to her side and he was holding out his hands and smiling. A second later, Kate found herself in his arms, and then the band punched out the dramatic notes of 'Jealousy' and they began the staccato movements of the dance.

As Kate had known it would, the dance grew more and more daring as the music played, and the Canadian was clearly enjoying it. He held her firmly, guiding her into ever more flamboyant steps until, as the tune reached its climax, she found herself bent back over his arm so low that her head almost touched the floor. She stared up into his eyes, feeling a shock run through her, and for a second or two they remained perfectly still. With a final flourish, he brought her up against him and held her close for a moment before letting her go.

'That was amazing,' he drawled, his eyes still holding hers. '*You're* amazing. Hey, I don't even know your name!'

'Kate,' she said, putting her hands up to her burning cheeks. She was breathless, almost dizzy.

'And I'm Brad. Let me buy you a drink – we need one after that.' He led her across the floor to her chair and deposited her there. 'What would you like?'

'A – a lemonade, please.'

He nodded and grinned. 'Don't go away.'

Once again, the other girls looked at her. Kate looked

back defensively. 'It's just a dance, that's all. He just likes dancing with me.'

'He looks as if he likes a lot more than that,' Janice said. 'And you're not exactly having a miserable time yourself, Kate.'

'I enjoy dancing,' she said with dignity. 'And we came to dance, didn't we? So that's what I'm doing. What about the rest of you, anyway? Have you met some nice boys?'

'Hazel and Val have,' Janice said. 'I'm engaged, so of course I won't be—'

The others hooted with laughter. 'It's never stopped you before! And that redheaded sailor said he'd be back. Have you told *him* you're engaged?'

'It's none of his business. Look, the only reason I take off my ring is so that I'll get a few dances. Boys won't ask you to dance at all if they think there's a fiancé hanging about somewhere. It doesn't mean I'll take it any further.'

'We'll believe you,' Val said with a grin. 'Thousands wouldn't . . . Here comes your beau, Kate.'

'He's not my beau,' Kate began, then looked up as Brad sat down beside her and handed her a glass of lemonade. 'Oh, thanks.' Suddenly feeling awkward, she fell silent.

Brad glanced past her at the other girls. They were watching and smiled at him, Janice coquettishly, the other two with a mixture of friendliness and frank curiosity. 'Going to introduce me to your pals?' he asked finally.

'Oh, yes. This is Janice, this is Hazel and that's Val at the end. There's another one too, Maxine, but I don't know where she is just now. We all work together.'

'Work together and play together, hey? That's good.' He nodded pleasantly at them all. 'So, what sort of work do you do?'

Kate hesitated. 'We – we don't talk about our work.'

Brad nodded again. 'War on, eh?' He indicated Kate's drink. 'Lemonade OK?'

'Yes, it's lovely, thanks.' The band was striking up again, the jazzy tune of a jitterbug, and she glanced at him inquiringly. He put his drink on the floor under his chair and stood up, holding out his hands.

'Come on, Kate. I bet you're a great boogie dancer.' The floor was filling fast, partners arriving for the other girls, and Kate felt herself caught up again by the lights, the laughter, but most of all the music and the need to move in time to its thrilling beat. She put her own drink down and jumped up, taking Brad's hands eagerly, and they moved to find a space where they could dance.

The jitterbug was quick, jerky and smooth by turns, and Kate was so caught up in the rhythm that she forgot everything but the sheer joy of being able to respond to it. Laughing and tossing back her dark curls, she challenged the tall young Canadian with her eyes, and he answered by whirling her about, the merest flick of his fingers telling her what to do next, the slightest pull on her hand bringing her close, then urging her away, twisting her at arm's length before twitching her into his arms, sliding her down between his knees and then, with one swift movement, swinging her high above his shoulder. Kate gave a little scream of surprise and delight and, as quickly as she had been lifted off her feet, found herself back on the floor and between his knees again. The music came to an end and he drew her upright and grinned at her.

'Say, little lady, you're some mover.' There was a ripple of applause and Kate glanced up to find that a circle of people had formed around them, clearing a space as they had danced. She felt herself colour and gave him a frantic, pleading glance, but Brad just laughed and shook his head. 'There's no way out now.' The music began again, another jazz tune, and he gripped her hands once more. 'Dance, little lady!' And once again, she was whirled into the exciting, dangerous world of the jitterbug, where anything could happen and probably would, where your body took over in inescapable response to the music and catapulted you into realms you would never dare enter at other times – and yet it was safe as well, for you knew that when the music ended you could come back to earth, and nothing would have changed.

This time, however, something *had* changed. And when the second dance was over and Kate stood still, catching her breath and looking into Brad's eyes, she knew it.

'Say . . .' he began, a new, deeper note in his voice, and panic flared inside her.

'I'm sorry, I've got to go.' She turned and ran back to her chair, snatching up her bag. The others hadn't come back yet and she hadn't seen Maxine since the first dance. There wasn't time to search for them now. All she wanted was to get away.

Brad followed more slowly, his eyes half-concerned, half-amused. 'Say, are you OK? You'll be back, won't you? I'll hang on here. Don't be too long – things are just starting to hot up.'

Kate looked at him wildly and then ran for the door. Probably he thought she needed the lavatory and would be back in a few minutes. She scuttled through to the cloak-room, fished in her bag for her ticket and grabbed her coat. The girl looked at her in surprise. 'Are you all right? Not poorly, are you? Only it sounds really good from here. They're a smashing band.'

'Yes. No. Yes, I'm all right.' Kate shrugged into her coat, desperate to get away before Brad came looking for her. 'Look, if my friends ask about me, just say I went home early, would you? I haven't got time to find them now.' Then she was outside in the cold night air. The wind was snatching the tops of the waves, sending spray up over the deck of the Pier, and the salty breeze whipped her hair around her face. She ran the length of the Pier to the pavement, and then stood breathing quickly for a moment before turning right to the nearest bus stop.

No, she thought, if he comes to look for me he'll look there. She turned left instead and walked briskly down the darkened seafront to the next stop, terrified all the time that Brad would follow her. Reason told her that he wouldn't – why should he, when there were so many other girls to dance with? But she knew that something had happened during that last dance – something that might last only an evening but might last longer, could even last a lifetime if given the chance. Something she didn't dare let happen.

I should never have come, she thought, her heart aching. I knew I should never have come.

Chapter Five

Sally had spent the evening listening to the wireless and playing with Barney and the kittens. They'd quickly got used to their new surroundings and came to life in the evening, racing around the room, hiding behind chairs and leaping out on each other and rolling around together on the rag rug, locked in combat. Topsy found that she could get underneath the rug and taunted Turvey, who crouched to watch the moving lump in disbelief before pouncing on it, and the rug was screwed up as the two kittens fought. Sally and Barney, delighted by their games, sat on the floor and found themselves part of an obstacle course, and even Win laughed, while Tyke retreated under a chair and watched in amazement.

'They're a proper entertainment,' Win declared, picking up her ball of wool and tucking it down the side of her chair so that the kittens wouldn't find it. 'Pity our Kate's missing it.'

'I bet she's having a smashing time,' Sally said, reminded of her own complaints. 'Honest, Mum, I don't see why—'

'I've *told* you.' Win's good humour vanished. 'I'm not having you out late at night. Not till you're seventeen, and maybe not even then if this war's still on.'

'But that's not fair! The war was on when Kate was seventeen.'

'Yes, but she never went over to Pompey. There was all the bombing, if you remember.'

'And I was out in the country, evacuated – *if* you remember.'

'There's no call to be cheeky,' Win said sharply. 'You were out there for your own safety. Anyway, you can take it from me that Kate wasn't going out dancing, not then. We spent most of our nights down the air-raid shelter.' She looked at Barney, who was cuddling the black and white kitten. 'You'd better put that animal down now, Barney, it's time for bed.'

'Oh, *Mu-um* . . .'

'You heard me. Put him in his box, there's a good boy, and I'll get your milk.' Win finished her row and poked the knitting needles through the ball of wool. 'And don't try sneaking him upstairs like you did last night.'

'He was lonely. And anyway, they both slept on our Kate's bed.'

'Yes, and they're not doing it again. They're no more lonely here than when they were down the Hard. They've got each other.' The two kittens had now fallen asleep, one in Barney's arms and one curled up between Tyke's front paws. 'Tyke'll look after them,' she added, smiling at the sight. 'Pity we haven't got any film for your dad's camera, it would make a good picture, that would.'

She went out to the kitchen and opened the back door. The milk was kept in a meat safe on a wooden bench just outside, so that it wouldn't turn sour overnight – not that it was very likely at this time of the year and the kitchen wasn't exactly warm unless there was cooking going on, but Win believed it was better out in the fresh air than indoors. In summer, she boiled it every night to keep it from going off, and then the children would squabble over who was going to have the cream on their cornflakes. There was nothing quite so delicious as the top of boiled milk.

It was quiet outside. Win could hear the low hum that

was the sound of Portsmouth – a hum compounded of the noise of ships' generators, buses and the few cars that were on the streets, and places like Dockyard workshops, the Gunwharf and Priddy's Hard itself that were working nights. She was thankful that Kate wasn't on nights – it was hard enough as it was, twelve hours at a stretch day or night, and night workers never seemed to sleep properly. It made it difficult for the rest of the family too, when one member needed peace and quiet during the day. All right if the rest were out too, but not so easy when you had a kiddy like Barney at home. You couldn't keep an active five-year-old quiet for long.

Barney made his cup of milk last as long as possible and slowly ate the biscuit he had been given to go with it. It was one of those that had little knobs sticking out all round the edges, which he always thought looked like toes. He nibbled them off, one by one, until Win thought she would scream with impatience. 'Come on, Barney, for goodness sake,' she said at last. 'I never knew a boy like you for spinning things out. How you can take ten minutes to eat one little biscuit I just don't know.'

'I like eating it this way.'

'Well, now try another way. Quicker. And if you don't drink that milk soon it'll turn sour. Come on, it's past your bedtime. Daddy'll be in from the shed soon and he'll expect to see you in your pyjamas and ready to go up-stairs.'

The shed was at the bottom of the garden, just past the Anderson shelter, and George always took himself down there in the evenings, unless it was light enough to work on the allotment. There was always something for him to do – shoes to be mended, a bit of woodwork, seeds to be checked and watered. He could mend electrical things too and had built his own wireless before the war, with Ian's help. It stood on a shelf in the back room now and you could tune it to both the Home Service, for serious things like the news, and the Light Programme for *Music While You Work* or comedies like *Much Binding in the Marsh* and *Stand Easy*. You could probably get the Third Programme too, but that was all highbrow stuff and the Fishers had never bothered with it.

George's shed was his own domain, as the kitchen was Win's. As they grew older, the boys were allowed to join him there, to learn woodwork and how to mend shoes, useful things that every man needed to know, but with Ian at sea, Barney too young to be trusted with sharp tools and Pete in the country, there was no one for him to teach. That was something Win wanted to talk to George about, and the reason why she wanted Barney to be ready for bed.

At last he was in his pyjamas. George could be heard coming up the path and stamping his boots at the door before coming in and taking them off on the mat. Win wouldn't have dirty shoes on her kitchen floor, especially on a Saturday night when everything was clean for Sunday. They heard him wash his hands at the sink and then he came in, looking approvingly at Barney.

'I thought I might go down the Queen's Head for a game of darts,' he began, but Win shook her head firmly.

'I want to have a bit of a talk.'

'Oh? What's that about, then?' He sat down in his armchair and lifted Barney on to his knee. The little boy snuggled against him, much as the kitten had snuggled on his own lap earlier. 'This young man been playing up, has he?'

'Barney? No, he's been good as gold, playing with the cats. I must say, they're a comical pair. And Tyke's getting accustomed to them now. Look at him, with Topsy asleep on his front paws. They've been like that for half an hour or more.' She wrapped up her knitting

63

again and got up. 'Come on, young man, say goodnight to your dad now, it's bedtime. No, no more arguing,' as Barney opened his mouth, 'and don't even bother to ask if you can take Turvey with you. It's stuffed animals only on beds, and that's all there is to it.' She watched as Barney gave his father a goodnight kiss and scrambled down from his lap. 'Come on, up the wooden hill.'

'To Bedfordshire,' Barney said, as he always did. 'Night-night, Daddy. Night-night, Sally.' He wound his arms round Sally's neck and gave her a smacking kiss. 'Night-night, Tyke. Night-night, Turvey. Night-night, Topsy. Night-night, chair, night-night—'

'All right, that's enough. You don't have to say night-night to every piece of furniture.' Win hustled him out of the room and up the stairs. Sally and her father heard the soft chant of Barney's prayers ('*God bless Mummy and Daddy and Ian and Kate, and Sally, and Pete, and me, and Tyke, and Topsy, and Turvey, and everyone we know . . .*') and then the squeak as he got into the lower bunk and the murmur of his mother giving him a last kiss, and Barney's entreaties for her to stay a little longer . . . and then, at last, the closing of the bedroom door and Win's footsteps coming downstairs again.

'Honestly!' she said, coming in. 'That boy spins it out longer and longer every night. I thought we were going to ask God to bless everything in the house before we'd finished.'

'Just sing "Bless This House" then,' Sally suggested. 'That ought to cover everything.'

Her mother looked at her. 'Well, maybe that's not such a bad idea at that. Now then,' she sat down and picked up her knitting again, 'me and your dad want to have a talk, so you find something to do. Read your library book. You did change it today, didn't you?'

Sally turned down the corners of her mouth. 'But

I wanted to listen to the wireless. There's dance music on.'

'Dance music! Don't you never think about nothing else?' Win turned off the wireless. 'You read your book quietly, and you don't need to bother about what me and your dad are talking about neither.'

Sally picked up her book grumpily. It was a story about a family in Scotland and she'd chosen it because there was a girl of her own age in it. But the girl didn't seem to play a very big part in the story, and her concentration soon drifted. In any case, she was more interested in what her mother wanted to discuss with her father so, although she kept turning the pages over, in truth she wasn't reading a word.

'. . . so it seems to me he'd be better off at home,' Win was saying, her needles clicking away as she talked. Like most women, Win could never feel easy sitting down unless she was doing something as well. 'He's not doing any good at that school, you can tell that, and from what Mrs Baldwin says he just runs wild when he's not in class. They can't get him to help around the farm or anything. All he wants to do is play that blessed mouth organ we gave him last Christmas.'

George was filling his pipe. Tobacco was scarce and he kept it for evenings – you weren't allowed to smoke at the Hard anyway, it was far too dangerous. He'd known men get the sack just for having a cigarette in their pockets, and nobody would dare go in with matches. 'Well, but what do you reckon we'd do with him if he did come home? He's not of an age to leave school.'

Win snorted. 'Leave school? Seems to me they've all left school already! You can't say they're getting an education, not when they're only there half the day and all crowded together in one classroom. Look, our Pete's got a good brain, he ought to have got through the scholarship exam to the County School, you know that. If you ask me, that's half the trouble with him now. *He* knows it too, and he's turned off school because he didn't pass.'

'And what good would that have done him? Learning a lot of fancy subjects. French and Latin -- what use are they to people like us? And chemistry and physics and algebra and such – *I've* never needed them. Not to mention the cost of it all, the uniform and satchel and everything. I tell you, Win, I wasn't sorry he didn't pass. I wasn't sorry at all. He's better off where he is. At least they teach 'em sensible things like a bit of woodwork and metalwork – things that'll be *useful* to a boy.'

Win shook her head. 'I don't know. He doesn't seem to me to be the sort of boy who's ever going to be any good with his hands. You've said yourself, often enough, he seems to have ten thumbs.'

'He'd get over that. He'd have to, if he was going to get an apprenticeship.'

'That's just it, George.' Win leaned forward. 'I don't think an apprenticeship's what our Pete wants. I really don't.'

'So what do you want him to do, then? Just get some dead-end job that'll never take him anywhere? Look, Win, you know as well as I do that a boy who's got a trade at his fingertips'll always be able to get work. I don't care what it is – in the Dockyard, or down Priddy's, or round with Bob Gibson learning to be a plumber – so long as he does a proper apprenticeship that'll set him on his feet. And when this war's over, you mark my words, it's good workers that this country'll need. Look at all the bomb damage. Look at all the rebuilding. They'll be crying out for young men who can do that, and there'll be good money to be made for any bloke that's qualified to do it. If he doesn't do a decent apprenticeship, he'll end up carry-ing bricks for a living, and I don't want a boy of mine doing that.' He sat back in his chair and took a long pull at his pipe.

Win was silent for a moment. Then she said, 'But he won't be happy, George. It won't suit him. He'll be miserable all his life.'

Her husband snorted. 'Not happy? Miserable all his life? Don't talk so far back, Win! Where does *being happy* come in? We're talking about working for a living. You don't expect to be happy, not at work. *Home's* where you expect to be happy – and not there, all the time,' he added under his breath.

'I don't know what you mean by that,' Win began in an offended tone, but he held up his hand.

'I was only joking! But all this talk about being happy – well, it's daft, Win, for people like us, anyway. People like us has to take what we can get and put up with it. It might be different if you've got money, if you're a doctor or a teacher or something like that, but people like us, we just has to get our satisfaction from doing a decent job and doing it well. And Pete'll get more satisfaction if he does an apprenticeship first and gets work he can take a pride in doing. That's what people like me gets from their work. Pride and satisfaction. Happiness!' he snorted, tamping down the tobacco in his pipe. '*Happiness!*'

'And if he isn't any good at what he's doing? If he can't do it well? What sort of pride could he take in it then? I tell you, George, he'll be miserable. And I don't want him to be miserable, I really don't.'

'Well, that's up to him, isn't it. Anybody can be miserable if they sets their mind to it. Don't you think I could've been miserable all these years, slaving away down Priddy's? Shoving barrels of gunpowder up and down the rollway, stacking it up on lighters day in, day out? Taking torpedoes to bits and putting them together again? Dismantling bloody – sorry, blooming – big guns to see why

67

they didn't go off when they were supposed to? Don't you think I'd rather have been out fishing or working on the allotment or down the shed, almost anything but shut up in those great brick buildings with all that noise and the stink of cordite and the rattle and crash of machinery all the time? Don't you think *I* could've been miserable? Of course I could!' He paused, then added as if he'd never properly realised it before, 'And I was, too. I tell you, I've been *bloody* miserable at times—' this time he didn't apologise for the swear word, '—but have I come home moaning about it or said I wanted to do something different? No, I haven't. Because I knew there *wasn't* anything different, that's why. Because that's what people like us, working people, *do*. We don't moan and gripe about our lot. We don't talk about being happy. We just get on with it.'

The silence this time was longer. Sally had given up all pretence of reading and was staring at her father. Win was looking at him too, with an odd expression on her face, a mixture of compassion, exasperation and more than a tinge of admiration.

'I know, love,' she said after a while, 'but that's just what I'm getting at. You *have* been miserable, a lot of the time. I know you have. You'd rather have been a – a gardener or a carpenter, or something like that. And I reckon you'd have been good at that – and happy as well. But you were sent to work at the Hard when you were thirteen, and then the First War came along and you went into the Army, and when that was over you didn't have no choice but to go back to Priddy's. And you've never liked it. You've just got on with it.' She dropped her knitting in her lap and leaned over again. 'But that's not what I want for our Pete. He's right at the beginning of his life; what he does now will stay with him for the next fifty years. Just because you didn't have no choice, does that mean he can't have one neither? Can't we at least *think* about what might be better for him?'

George looked at her. He looked into the fire and then he looked at his pipe. He tamped down the tobacco again, sighed with exasperation and took a spill of thin wood from the jar on the mantelpiece. He poked it into the fire and then put the burning end into the bowl of his pipe, drawing on the stem until it glowed once more. Then he pinched out the glow of the spill, stuck it back in the jar, took a long pull at the pipe and blew out a huge cloud of smoke.

'All right, then, Win. What do you think *would* be better for him? What do *you* think he ought to do?'

'Music,' Sally said from her corner. 'That's what he wants to do. Music.'

Her parents turned and stared as if they had forgotten she was there. '*Music*? Whatever are you talking about, girl?'

Sally gestured at the piano standing against the wall. She had never been taught to play, but Kate and Ian had had lessons and Pete had often leaned against the instrument, watching as they'd practised, before the war. He'd been not much older than Barney then, but Sally could remember Ian showing him how to play 'Chopsticks' and where to find middle C. 'You know he's always liked music,' she said. 'You've just said how much he likes that mouth-organ you gave him.'

'A mouth-organ's not going to bring him much of a living!' her father said scornfully.

Sally shook her head. 'I didn't say it would. I just said he likes music. But he's learned to play the church organ in the village, and Mr Edison, the headmaster out there, he's given him a few lessons on the violin. And there's an old man who used to be a bandmaster in the Royal Marines; he's still got a trumpet and Pete's had a go on that as well. He really likes it.'

'A go on a trumpet? A few lessons on the violin? Playing the church organ?' George looked at his daughter as if she'd taken leave of her senses. 'You'd better get on with your book, our Sally, and stop butting in on your mother's and my conversations. We're trying to have a serious talk here.'

'I know you are. I'm trying to help, that's all. You wanted to know what Pete's good at and I'm telling you. He's good at music and he'd like to do it properly.'

'But people like us *don't*—' George was beginning when Sally butted in again.

'Don't what? Don't ever do anything we want to? Don't ever better ourselves? Don't ever get out of the rut of apprenticeships, and horrible jobs in factories? Don't ever win scholarships and go to grammar schools and get a good education, and do something *interesting* with our lives? Why not?' She stared at them, challenging them with her brown eyes, so like her mother's. 'Why *shouldn't* we? We're just as clever as people who've got money. All we need is a start – and Pete could have it, he could do music if you'd only let him have a start. And then you wouldn't have to worry about him being miserable or not having a trade because he'd be doing something he enjoyed and was good at. He'd be happy at *work*, as well as at home!' Her book slid from her lap and she bent to pick it up.

Win and George looked at each other. George folded his lips together and shook his head again, but Win said, 'But what *could* he do? I mean, how does anyone make a living out of music? How do they get started?'

'I don't know,' Sally said, straightening up again. 'Perhaps he could play in a band – a dance band, like Joe Loss or Billy Ternent.'

'A *dance* band?' George broke in, starting to get angry again. 'A boy of mine, playing in a *dance* band?'

'Well, there's nothing wrong with that. They earn a good living and make a lot of people happy. Or he could do what old Mr Dean did and be in a Royal Marine band. They're really good. *You* like the Marine bands, Dad.'

George had to admit that was true. The family had often watched the Marines parade through the streets of Gosport or Portsmouth, and had gone to some of the open-air concerts. They were the smartest of the lot, George had said proudly, remembering his own days in the Marines. The idea of his son following him into the Service wasn't a bad one.

'I don't want Pete going in the Army,' Win said flatly. 'Not at his age. If he waits, by the time he's old enough to be called up the war could be over. He could think about it then.'

'But it's now we're talking about,' her husband pointed out. 'And if he joined up as a boy at thirteen, he wouldn't be sent away anywhere. I don't suppose they go into action till they're seventeen at least.'

'And if he was in the band,' Sally said, 'he probably wouldn't go on active service for years and years.'

Win looked at her. 'Have you talked to him about this, Sal? Is it what he wants to do – go into the Marines?'

Sally shrugged. 'He's never mentioned it. I just know he wants to do music, that's all. I think he'd jump at the idea if he could do music in the Marines. A lot of dance-band players have been in the Services – look at the Squadronaires.'

'I don't like the idea of him being in a dance band—' George began again, but he was interrupted this time by the sudden shrill of the doorbell. Tyke leaped up from his position in front of the fire and began barking hysterically and both kittens woke with a start and fled under the sideboard. Sally answered the door and came back with Kate. They all stared at her.

'Kate! Whatever are you doing home so early? It's barely nine o'clock.' Win looked at her closely. 'Are you all right? What's happened?'

Kate shrugged off her coat and dropped her bag on a chair. 'Nothing. Nothing's happened. I'm perfectly all right. I just got fed up, that's all.'

'Fed up? Wasn't it a good dance, then? Did the others come home early too?'

'Nope. Just me. You don't have to look at me like that, Mum. I've told you, I'm just tired, that's all – I've been working like a dog all week. All right?' She made for the kitchen door. 'I'm going to make a cup of cocoa and take it up to bed. I'll make you one too, if you like, Sal.'

'Thanks.' The fire had gone out of Sally now, and the subject of Pete and his future was dropped. Win picked up her knitting and George glanced at the clock on the mantelpiece.

'There's still an hour before closing time. I might as well go and have that game of darts.' He knocked out his pipe and got up. 'If that's all right with you, Win?'

'Yes, you go on. I want to finish this armhole before I go to bed.' But Win spoke abstractedly, and when Sally had left the room to help Kate make the cocoa she spoke in a low voice. 'There's something the matter with that girl, George. It's the first time she's been to a dance in Pompey for months and she's back home before nine o'clock. Something's upset her. Something's upset her badly.'

Elsie too had spent the evening listening to the wireless and playing with her kitten. Fluffy seemed to know that her fur matched her ginger hair, and kept putting up her minute paws and getting them tangled in the frizzy curls. Elsie laughed and cuddled the kitten, enjoying the feel of the warm little body against her bosom. It was almost like cuddling a tiny baby.

I hope those girls are going to be all right over in Pompey, she thought. There's plenty of others who've already got cause to regret going out with the sailors who come here. It's all very well to sing, '*Every nice girl loves a sailor*', but you've got to remember a few other sayings too. Like, '*A wife in every port*' and '*Here today, gone tomorrow*'. I wouldn't like to see young Kate or Maxine or any of the others go the way of poor little Jackie Prentice . . .

Jackie had been one of Graham's old girlfriends. He'd gone out with her for several months soon after they'd moved to Gosport from Portsmouth, and before he'd met Betty Chapman again and started courting her, Elsie had thought he and Jackie might have been getting serious. Jackie was a bright, bubbly girl and just the sort Elsie would have liked having about, but it wasn't to be. Once he'd seen Betty again, Graham hadn't had eyes for anyone else.

Jackie had had a lot of bad luck since then. Her mum had been killed in an air raid, while Jackie was firewatching at the shop where she worked in Stoke Road, and her dad had been badly hurt. The house had been patched up and Jackie had had to stop at home to look after him instead of joining the Wrens as she'd intended. Then Elsie had seen her going around with a GI and looking really happy, so maybe her luck was turning.

She lived a couple of streets away with her invalid father, and Elsie often bumped into her in Carnarvon Road or down town, and sometimes invited her in for a cup of tea and a chinwag. She had come across her soon after Christmas, wandering along the street looking as if the world was about to end. Elsie had stopped in concern, afraid that something had happened to her father, but Jackie had just looked at her and burst into tears. Elsie had put her arms around the girl and brought her indoors at

73

once. She told Charlie to go down to his shed for half an hour and Charlie, who always got embarrassed when girls started to pipe their eye, departed at once, taking the sports pages of the *Daily Mirror* with him.

'Now, tell me what it's all about,' Elsie said, sitting the sobbing girl down in Charlie's armchair and putting a cup of tea beside her. Elsie's kettle was always on the boil. 'I thought you were getting along better now. Is it your dad?'

Jackie sniffed and shook her head. She was small and slim, with her fair hair cut into a bob that just touched her shoulders. Elsie looked at her with some regret, thinking that if only Graham had stuck with her she could have been her daughter-in-law by now, and the mother of Elsie's grandchildren . . . But she'd thought that about Betty Chapman too, and Gladys Shaw. And there were probably half a dozen other girls that Graham had never told her about, any of whom could also have been her daughter-in-law and the mother of her grandchildren. She would never have any grandchildren now. It was best not to let her thoughts run in that direction.

'Dad's all right – well, as all right as he'll ever be. The doctor says he's got to be careful of his heart, but as long as he doesn't do too much . . .' She sighed and Elsie felt sorry for her. It was no life for a girl having to look after an invalid father, especially one that grumbled as much as Herbert Prentice did. 'It's not that,' Jackie went on, her eyes filling with tears. 'It's Wilbur.'

'Wilbur?' Elsie searched her mind and then light dawned. 'Oh, you mean that GI you've been knocking about with? Why, what's happened to him?'

'I don't know,' Jackie said, beginning to sob. 'I don't know *what's* happened to him. He's just – he's just *gone*. All his friends have too, the whole unit, they've just disappeared. And I don't know where they are. I don't know how to get in touch with him. Oh, Mrs Philpotts, what am I going to do?' She lifted her face and stared at Elsie with woebegone eyes.

Elsie looked at her. 'You haven't been doing anything you shouldn't, have you, Jackie?' she asked. 'You know what I mean.'

Jackie's face coloured. 'No! I mean, well . . .' Her cheeks were in flames and she avoided Elsie's eyes. 'He said he *loved* me,' she cried piteously. 'He said he wanted to marry me. He's going to take me back to America after the war and we'll live in a big house on a farm, with horses and everything. He meant it, I know he did. And now . . .' Her face crumpled again. 'Now I don't know where he is. I haven't heard from him for over a week!'

'A week's not long,' Elsie said bracingly. 'You know what men are, Jackie, they get interested in what they're doing and they forget everything else. My Charlie's just the same. And what with things as they are just now, I dare say he's not had time to write. You'll get a letter soon, I'm sure.' She gave Jackie another look. The slim figure was bundled in a thick coat which Jackie hadn't unbuttoned. 'There's nothing else bothering you, is there?'

Jackie caught her look and flushed scarlet again. 'No! No, of course there isn't. There's nothing like that, Mrs Philpotts.' She got up quickly, leaving her tea only half drunk. 'I'll have to go now – I'm sorry I bothered you.'

'You haven't bothered me at all,' Elsie said, watching the girl struggle with the doorknob. 'You come round any time you like, and welcome. If there's anything you want to talk to me about – *anything* – you just knock on the door. You're no bother to me, Jackie, you know that.'

The girl's lips twisted in a wry smile. Tears still on her cheeks, she nodded and pulled the door open, keeping the blackout curtain pulled across. 'Thanks, Mrs Philpotts,' she said, her voice still thick with tears. 'Thanks, but I'll be okay. I expect he'll write soon. I'll probably get a letter tomorrow.' She slipped out through the curtain and was gone. 'Goodbye.'

'Cheerio,' Elsie said, and shut the door. She returned thoughtfully to her own chair and sat looking at the one Jackie had just vacated.

Slim as a reed you might be, my girl, she thought, and it's not easy to tell with that thick coat wrapped round you, but I wouldn't be a bit surprised if you weren't carrying that young man's baby. And I'll be *very* surprised if you hear from him again. A big house on a farm in America! Horses! That's what they all say, isn't it?

All the same, not all the Americans had taken advantage of the English girls. Some of them, she knew, had kept in touch and seemed to mean their promises. Perhaps Jackie's young man would be one of these.

Only time would tell.

Chapter Six

'Where did you go? What on earth happened? We were really worried.'

Kate shrugged. She was sitting on her bed cuddling the tortoiseshell kitten. Maxine, who had come round straight after church, stared at her accusingly. 'Come on, Kate. What went wrong?'

'What d'you think?' Kate pressed her face against the kitten and spoke into its fur. 'How's Snowy?'

'Snowy's all right,' Maxine said impatiently. 'It's you I'm worried about. We all were when you shoved off like that. That poor bloke, he wondered what on earth he'd done to upset you. He didn't make a pass, did he? I don't see how he had the time.'

'No, he didn't make a pass.' Kate spoke wearily. 'We just danced, that's all. Don't go on about it, Max.'

'But I want to *know*. You carried on and on about us all coming back together and then you just charged off without even saying goodbye. Suppose the rest of us had done that and left you all by yourself. How would you feel then?'

'I didn't leave anyone by themselves. You were all together. At least, the others were – I didn't see you from the moment you got up for the first dance.'

'No, but I came back after, and we did all go home together. *After* we'd waited about for you, and then asked the cloakroom girl.' Maxine pushed back her hair. 'It's not fair, Kate, going off like that. *Anything* could've happened.'

'Well, it didn't, did it. I got on a bus and caught the ferry and then got a bus up this side. I was perfectly all right. I'm not a baby, Max.'

'Well, you're behaving like one.' Maxine glowered at her. 'And what about the chap you were dancing with? He was really upset. He liked you. And from the way you were dancing, I'd have said you liked him.'

'Oh, so you did take a bit of notice of me, then,' Kate snapped, then bit her lip and scowled.

Maxine stared at her in surprise. 'What d'you mean? Of course I took notice of you. Everyone was watching – you were dancing really well. Look, what *is* all this about? Surely you weren't jealous of me. You didn't fancy my partner, did you?'

'No, of course I didn't!' Kate sighed, then said more quietly, 'If you want to know, I fancied the one I was with. And I could tell he liked me too. And – well, that's all, really.' She concentrated on the kitten again.

Maxie shook her head. 'I don't get it, Kate. You liked him, you clicked, so you ran away as if the devil was after you. It doesn't make sense.'

'No, I don't suppose it does.' Kate looked up at her friend, meeting her eyes at last, and gave a rueful smile. 'It doesn't make all that much sense to me, to tell you the truth. But – well, when I looked at him and I saw what he was thinking – and knew I was thinking it too – I just sort of panicked. I had to get away. I just couldn't stay there, Max, I *couldn't*.'

'But why on earth not? He seemed so nice.'

'I know. And that's just it.' Kate glanced around the little bedroom as if looking for help, then said, 'Maxie, you know what's happened before. The boys I've been out with. Godfrey. They've all been killed. I told you – it's as if I'm jinxed. And I can't take the chance any more. It's why I don't like going out – because I might meet someone and like them, and start it all over again. I thought – I thought perhaps if I went last night, and we all promised to stick together, and it was just dancing, well, maybe it would be all right. But I met Brad, and we liked each other – *really* liked each other. And I thought of what they're over here for. They're going to France, Max. They're going to be in the invasion when it comes. He'll get killed, just like those others, just like Godfrey and it will be all my fault.' Her voice trembled and broke. 'I couldn't let it happen. I had to get away.' She fished desperately for a hanky and blew her nose.

Maxie tutted in dismay. At last she said, 'But you don't *know* he's going to get killed, Kate. And even if he does – how could it be your fault?'

'I keep *telling* you, Max – because I'm *jinxed*. Some girls are. I've heard about it. At least if he does now, it won't be because of me. At least he's got a fair chance now.'

Maxine passed a hand across her forehead. 'This is daft. I know you've said things like this before, but I didn't think you were that serious. I thought you were still upset about Godfrey—'

'I *am*!'

'Yes, I know, but that's ages ago now, you've got to start living again sometime. And going on like this – well, it's daft, it really is. How can you be jinxed?'

'I don't know,' Kate said, 'but I know it happens. I've heard about it. There was a bit in the paper the other day about girls who had lost all their boyfriends and thought they were jinxed. I knew, as soon as I read it, that I was like that. I'm one of those girls.' She met Maxine's eyes again. 'I can't go out with anyone until this war's over, Max. I just can't. And it doesn't matter how upset Brad was last night, because at least he won't die because of me. *Nobody else* is going to die just because of me.'

*

Maxine didn't go straight home; instead, she walked to Brockhurst and down to the recreation ground. She was disturbed, not only by what Kate had told her but by her friend's appearance – white as a sheet, with great dark shadows under her eyes. She didn't look as if she'd slept a wink, yet she must have been home by nine.

Maxine thought she looked almost as distraught as she had when Godfrey had died.

Godfrey had been Kate's first serious boyfriend. All those others, they'd just been schoolmates or first 'sweethearts' – a boy and a girl announcing that they were 'going out' together but not actually doing much about it. A trip or two to the pictures, a walk out to Stokes Bay, a fumbling goodnight kiss at the front door – that was about it. Sometimes it wasn't even that much. Maxine could remember one boy who'd asked her to be his girlfriend and wait for him after school, and then virtually ignored her, coming out with a group of his mates and just giving her a casual nod as she tagged along. After three days she hadn't bothered to wait any more.

But Kate and Godfrey had been different. Godfrey lived in the next street to Kate and was three years older, so although he had always been around and had been a friend of her brother's, they hadn't had much to do with each other as children. Godfrey and Ian had their own gang who played cricket or football against a wall, or tramped down to Hardway to potter along the muddy tideline looking for washed-up treasures, while Kate and her cronies clustered around their front doors with dolls and an old toy pram, or played complicated games with fivestones, tennis balls (two at a time) or skipping ropes.

They hadn't met properly until two years ago, when Kate and Maxine were seventeen and had gone to a church dance at the Crossways Hall, just across the road from the Criterion cinema. Maxine being Roman

Catholic, it wasn't her church but, like all the young people in Gosport, she and Kate attended every one they could. At that age, like Kate's sister Sally now, they weren't allowed to go 'over the water' to the Portsmouth dance halls, especially after a year of bombing and with the sirens still liable to go off at any time.

There were several boys they knew there, and quite a few that they didn't. Neither of them had recognised Godfrey at first. He was tall and broad, his brown hair crisply cut and his face tanned. He was wearing Army uniform, his belt and shoes so highly polished that you could see your face in them. When Kate said this, Maxine giggled and said she wouldn't dare dance with him because of what else you might be able to see, and they'd both collapsed in giggles. Godfrey had come over then, grinning.

'Hello. You're Kate Fisher.'

Kate stared at him. 'Yes, I am. How d'you know?' Recognition dawned. 'You're never Godfrey Walker! You used to go to Elson School.'

He nodded. 'I remember you – Ian Fisher's sister. I used to muck about with Ian.' He hesitated. 'How is he these days?'

The girls understood his hesitation. You never knew quite whether to ask after anyone in case they'd been killed. Kate said, 'He's OK. His ship's in Singapore.'

Godfrey nodded and held out his hand. 'Want to dance?'

Maxine remembered how Kate had gone into his arms and how Godfrey had held her, not awkwardly as so many boys did, holding a girl as if she were a sack of coal and lumbering round the floor as if he had two left feet, but firmly and confidently, guiding her in perfect time to the music. Maxine had watched a little jealously, not because she'd wanted Godfrey for herself, although she certainly wouldn't have said no, but because it looked so good to dance like that and she knew it was unlikely there'd be another partner as accomplished there that evening.

Kate and Godfrey had danced every dance together and then Godfrey had walked the girls home. They'd dropped Maxine at her door first and then gone on together, leaving Maxine to go inside feeling a little lonely. It wasn't that she hadn't had plenty of partners, it wasn't even that she hadn't made a date to go to the pictures with another boy the following week, it was the radiance in Kate's eyes that had left her feeling out of it. Kate, she knew, was feeling something Maxine hadn't yet experienced. Kate was in love.

It had become more and more obvious during the weeks that followed. Godfrey had been slightly injured and was home for nearly a month to recuperate, and in that time they saw each other almost every day. He'd be waiting at the gate for her to come out of work, walk her home and then come and pick her up to go to the pictures, or another dance, or for a walk out to Stokes Bay before they'd closed it off with barbed wire – or just to sit in the Fishers' front room together holding hands. Nobody was surprised when Kate started to talk about getting engaged, and even married. But before they could do anything, he'd gone away again – and that was that. Only a few weeks later, the news had come of his death at Dunkirk. The radiance had vanished from Kate's face, her eyes had dimmed and she'd stopped going out at all. Then, when she'd agreed to go out again they'd met the Canadians who had gone to Dieppe. Last night was the first time they'd managed to get her out since then, and look what had happened.

It was nearly one o'clock – time for dinner. Maxine walked home, dragging her feet a little. She was hungry but not keen to go home, where she would be expected to sit at the table with her mother and father eating whatever meat her mother had been able to get at the butcher's shop and pretending to be part of a happy family. Once, I'd have believed it, she thought bitterly, but that was before I knew the truth . . . There was nothing else she could do, however. If she'd been in an ordinary job she could have volunteered for one of the women's Services and got away like that. But if you worked in armaments you were in a reserved occupation, and had to stay there until the war was over, and there was nowhere to live but at home.

She let herself in at the front door and took off her coat to hang it in the tiny porch her father had made when they'd taken down the partition wall between the front room and the narrow passage. It was much nicer, she had to admit, but Clarrie hadn't liked the front door opening straight into the room so he'd left a bit of the wall and added another door. It made the front room more private.

It was still the 'best' room, and Clarrie's pride and joy, with white lace antimacassars carefully arranged on the backs of the chairs and settee and a large china dog placed exactly in the centre of a small table in front of the window. Maxine had liked it once, thinking it showed that they had a bit of class, and had always taken pleasure in coming through the front door to linger here for a moment, enjoying the wallpaper her father had put up before the war had started and the curtains her mother had made. Now, however, she marched through without a second glance and even the thought of the antimacassars filled her with scorn. She walked through the back room, the table laid for dinner, and into the kitchen.

Clarrie was standing by the bandy-legged gas oven. She looked up from the roasting pan, her grey hair straggling over her flushed face, and gave her daughter a timid smile. 'Had a nice walk, love?'

'All right,' Maxine said shortly. 'I went round to see Kate.'

'To see Kate?' her father echoed, coming in from the garden and rolling up his sleeves to wash at the sink. 'I'd have thought you saw enough of Kate already. You see her every day at work and you were out dancing till all hours last night.'

'She's my friend. Anyway, it's my business how often I see her. Not hurting you, is it?'

Bert Fowler reddened and seemed about to swell up. 'Now you look here, my girl . . .'

'Don't call me that!' Maxine turned on him. 'And it's no business of yours what I do or who I see. I'm twenty-one now.'

'And still living under my roof! And that gives me the right to know—'

'It doesn't give you any rights at all. I pay my board, just as if I was a lodger. You wouldn't go on at me like this if I was a man. If I was *Matthew*.'

They glared at each other. Clarrie looked as if she were about to cry and said pleadingly, 'Don't start arguing. It's Sunday.'

'Well, we don't get time to argue during the week,' Maxine said bitterly. 'And he started it. Like he always does.'

'That's rich, coming from you! Nobody can speak in this house but what you bites off their head!'

'*Please*, Bert,' Clarrie begged, and he looked at her and sighed.

'All right, love. I won't say no more. But if she starts giving me lip again . . .'

'Let's just sit down and eat our dinner.' Clarrie squeezed past him, carrying a plate with slices of meat spread over it. 'I got this nice bit of brisket, see, it's done lovely in a slow oven, and there's our own cabbage and potatoes and carrots to go with it. Let's sit down and enjoy it. We can listen to *Forces' Favourites* on the wireless at the same time.'

'Good idea.' Maxine picked up the dish of carrots. 'It'll save us having to talk to each other.'

Bert started to swell again but caught his wife's eye and subsided. They sat down round the table and began to help themselves to the food. Maxine, who had been ravenously hungry twenty minutes earlier, found she had lost her appetite. She pushed the food round her plate until Bert said, 'If you're not going to eat that, you might as well pass it over here. Can't waste good food.'

'Oh no, Bert, she ought to eat it herself,' Clarrie said. 'She needs to keep up her strength.'

'Oh, let him have it.' Maxine shoved her plate towards him. It rucked up the tablecloth and she pushed it a bit harder, whereupon it tipped off the edge of the table and deposited its contents over Bert's lap. He jumped up, swearing, and lunged at Maxine who thrust back her chair and jumped up to face him.

'Bert! Maxine!' But Clarrie's pleas fell on deaf ears. The big man and the girl glared at each other, their eyes equally furious. Maxine tossed back her yellow hair in defiance, and Bert clenched his big fists and breathed heavily.

'You done that deliberate! Gravy and stuff all over me trousers, and good food wasted. Your mother gave you the best bits of meat and all. You oughter know better, girl of your age!'

'Go on then,' she taunted him. 'Teach me a lesson! Hit me, go on! You know it's what you want to do.'

'*Maxine!*' Clarrie's voice rose in panic. Tears were rolling down her face and her lips shook. 'Don't talk like that. Your dad doesn't want to hit you – he wouldn't ever do that – but you mustn't talk to him like that, you mustn't.'

85

'Oh, for Christ's sake!' Maxine exploded. '*Stop calling him my dad! He isn't* my dad. It's all just a big lie, a lie you've been telling me for years. He's just a man who lives here and *pretends* to be my dad!' She turned the full force of her fury on her mother. 'Isn't he? *Isn't* he?'

'Maxine, don't – please. You don't understand!'

'I don't want to understand!' Maxine raked them both with scornful eyes. 'You're disgusting, the pair of you. Disgusting! And I have to live here with you whether I want to or not, because there's a bloody *war* on. Because *you* made me go into Priddy's Hard when I could have gone into the Services, and now I can't get away. *I can't get away!*' Her voice broke and she began to cry, great noisy sobs forcing their way up from the depths of her chest into her throat. 'I've got to stay here with you and pretend to be a happy family, pretend he's my dad, pretend that – that – oh, it's all *pretend*. I hate it, I *hate* it!' Her words were lost in sobs and she covered her face with her hands, the tears running between her fingers and her shoulders shaking.

Clarrie moved towards her. 'Maxine, don't upset yourself like this. I can't bear it. It's not like you think.' She raised one hand but stopped an inch short of touching her daughter's shoulder. 'We used to be a happy family, didn't we? Why can't we be like that again?'

Maxine lifted her face and stared at her. 'Why? Well, of *course*, we can't. We can't *ever* be like that again – because it wasn't ever true. Was it? *Was it?* It was all *pretending* – you and *him*, pretending.' She caught sight of her mother's hand, about to touch her, and jerked away. 'Don't touch me! I don't want you to ever, *ever* touch me again! Not *ever*!'

She thrust her way violently past her mother, pushing Clarrie down into her chair, and made for the door. A moment later they heard her footsteps on the stairs and then the slam of her bedroom door. Clarrie and Bert looked at each other.

'One of these days,' Bert said heavily, 'I'm going to do that girl an injury. I'm warning you, Clarrie. I'm not going to be able to help meself.'

'Oh Bert,' she said, sinking her head into her hands. 'I don't know what to do. I just don't know what to do. She's so upset – but I don't know what else we could have done. Do you?'

He shook his head and sat down again. 'I don't, love. Seems to me we always done our best by the girl. We've never made any difference between her and Matt, not as far as I can see. I dunno what she's got to complain about. All I know is, I don't like the way she's treating you. You're her mother, and she ought to have a bit more respect.'

'That's just it,' Clarrie said sadly. 'She doesn't have no respect for me, none at all. She hasn't had, not since she first found out.' She looked at the table with its rucked-up cloth, at the plates of congealing food, at the mess of gravy and meat and vegetables on the floor. 'Eat up your dinner, Bert, do, while I clear this up. There's no sense in letting any more of it go to waste.'

He sighed and picked up his knife and fork, poking at the food in very much the same way as Maxine had done earlier. It was cold and unappetising, but he pushed it into his mouth, chewed and swallowed. Clarrie fetched a dustpan and began to scoop the remains of Maxine's dinner into it. She took it outside and then came back to sit at the table and pick at her own meal. After a moment or two she laid down her cutlery, leant her elbows on the table and covered her face with her hands. Her shoulders shook and the tears ran between her fingers and dropped onto her plate.

'I'm sorry, Bert,' she choked as he stared at her in

dismay. 'I'm sorry. It's all my fault, this is. I brought all this trouble on you. You shouldn't ever have married me. You shouldn't *ever* have married me . . .'

Chapter Seven

'Mind you,' Albert Fisher said, blowing on his tea to cool it, 'the Hard ain't what it used to be in my day. Twelve years old, I were when I was first took on, twelve years old. Youngsters these days don't know they're born.' He sucked tea noisily through his dentures.

'Stop it, Albert,' his wife said, reaching for another fish-paste sandwich. 'They don't want to hear all those old stories again.'

Kate looked at her grandparents. They'd come round for Sunday tea as usual, sitting side by side at the table, her grandad with his whiskers freshly trimmed yet still managing to look as shaggy as his eyebrows, her grand-mother a tiny wisp of a woman but with a back like an iron rod and a will that was every bit as strong. She had borne eight children, four were still living, had suffered several miscarriages and at least one stillbirth; had lived through two great wars – the Boer War and the First World War (losing two sons at the Somme) as well as countless other lesser conflicts – and was now facing up to the hardships of yet another. When she had been born, in 1868, there had been no telephone, no electric light, no motor cars or aeroplanes, and no elementary schools for the children of poor families. She'd lived in a differ-ent world, Kate thought, a world we can barely imagine now.

'I like hearing the stories,' she said. 'I like hearing about what Gosport used to be like, and about the Hard. You were there when they had the big explosion, weren't you, Grandad?'

Hilda Fisher sighed, but her husband looked pleased and put down his cup. 'I was. I was only an apprentice, mind you – eighteen, I was, been at the Hard six years but you couldn't start your apprenticeship till you were four-teen and I had another year or two to go before I got my indentures . . . Anyway, it was in 1883, a Saturday early in May, and six Artillerymen had been took over by ferry to fill shells in number 2 Filling Room. Old Bill Giles was the ferryman, I remember – he'd been there nigh on a quarter of a century. Him and my dad were mates, used to go fishing together. He had to give evidence at the inquest, of course.'

'What sort of evidence?' Sally asked. Having been evacuated for the past five years, she hadn't properly heard the story before. 'He wasn't in the explosion, was he?'

'No, but he had to say whether he'd taken any strangers over that morning, and whether the soldiers had any pipes or matches with them – Priddy's has always been strict about that, you've got to be when there's gunpowder about. And he had to say what they were wearing too, because some sorts of cloth can be dangerous, and metals too, like brass buttons – anything that can strike a spark, see.'

'That was one of the things that come out,' George put in. 'They had on their regimental clothes, and when they put on the overalls, they kept their trousers on. They weren't supposed to do that really, but it was common practice because the overalls weren't thick enough to keep them warm. The jury said that the regulations had got to be observed in future, but magazine clothes had got to be warmer, and that's what happened after that.'

'Anyway,' Albert continued, frowning at his son, 'to go back to what I was saying . . . Bill rowed the soldiers over at half-past six, soon after the magazine men and the laboratory men, and they went into the magazine and that was the last he saw of them till the explosion just after nine. He said it was like a long heavy roll, like thunder might be, or drums, only it wasn't the weather for thunder and there wasn't no band about, and he knew right away it was one of the magazines gone up. And the next second he saw a cloud of smoke and dust going up in the air like a huge great toadstool, and he saw the sentry run over to the building – and stop for a minute – and then run back. He said he'd never seen anyone look so afeared, and Bill had been through the Crimean War and seen plenty to be feared of there.'

'Go on, he must have seen worse at the Crimea,' Hilda objected. 'It was a cruel war, that was.'

'All wars are cruel,' Win said, coming in from the kitchen with a fresh pot of tea.

'I'm just telling you what Bill Giles told my dad,' Albert said. 'I can't say whether it's right or not, can I? I'm just telling you, that's all.' He waited a moment, then continued with the story. 'Well, then they got Josiah New in to give evidence. He worked in the laboratory and he'd been there as long as Bill, so he knew what was what. They asked him all about the procedures – how the shells were filled, and what about the fuzes, and whether they was greased before they was put in the shells, and so on – and he told 'em that the right procedures was always followed, he'd never known a fuze to be put in without being properly greased and whenever even a grain or two of gunpowder fell on the floor it'd be swept up straight away and thrown into the water barrel. They all knew what they were working with, see; they all knew the dangers. There was never no risks taken.'

'So what happened that day?' Sally asked. '*Something* must have gone wrong.'

'Someone was skylarking about,' Hilda said grimly. 'That's what I heard. My Uncle Reuben worked down there too and he reckoned—'

'Now look,' Albert interrupted, frowning again, 'there wasn't no skylarking, Hilda, you know that. We've had all this out before and what your Uncle Reuben said was just hearsay, and tavern hearsay at that. Hearsay don't count in a court of law. It's got to be proper eyewitness evidence.'

'So what was the eyewitness evidence?' Sally demanded. 'Did anyone actually see what happened?'

'Not to say *saw*, no,' her grandfather admitted. 'But the coroner complimented the men what gave evidence, he said he'd never heard evidence given better and they ought to be promoted for it . . . That was the two soldiers, a corporal and a bombardier, not Bill Giles and Josiah New, though I reckon he meant it for them as well only there wasn't no promotion for them . . . Anyway, they told all about how the Gunners were took to the shifting room where they changed into magazine clothes and then started to fill the shells. They'd taken three truckloads along the tramway to the store and they were just coming back for another load when the magazine blew up. They were right by the door when it happened and saw just where all the men were.'

'Where were they? What had happened?'

'Well, it was Mr Osborne who give the evidence about what happened, and it come out that one of the Gunners, Sewell by name – no, I tell a lie, it was Sewett, that's it, I remember because it always makes me think of pudding – anyway, he reckoned he knew more about filling shells than the blokes who'd worked at Priddy's all their lives. Not that he'd ever done it before, mind you, all the Gunners there that morning were there to learn – never done it before in their lives. Harry Osborne told the court he'd explained all the proper procedures. He'd used models to show 'em how the shells had bags inside – that was to prevent sparks striking inside, see, the shells being made of metal – and made sure the shell was clean as a whistle before you put the bag in. There was a button rod in the shell, to help push it down. Then you took out the rod and poured two or three pound of gunpowder in through a funnel, and rammed it in with the copper rod – only gently, mind, you never forgets it's gunpowder you're handling, never. Then, when the bag's full, you puts in the fuze.' He paused, waiting while Win filled his teacup, then stirred in two saccharin tablets and took a noisy sip. 'That's better,' he said, wiping his moustache. 'It's thirsty work, talking.'

'Well, maybe you've talked enough,' his wife said tartly. 'I'm sure these girls don't want to hear all this. Kate spends every day down the Hard filling shells, and Sally—'

'No, I want to hear it. I really do. Go on, Grandad.' Sally leaned her chin on her hand and gazed at her grandfather. Hilda sighed again, noisily, and rolled her eyes at the ceiling.

'Well, having done all that, this man Sewett was put on to filling shells what *didn't* have bags inside. Now, in these, as anyone with any common sense would know, you wouldn't want to go ramming it in with a copper rod, but no sooner was Harry Osborne's back turned than that's just what the fool started to do. Harry saw him and told him off for it, and took the rod away and put it in the corner. He said that in evidence – took it away and put it in the corner – and he gave Sewett the proper rod for the job and told him it was only to be used for pressing the powder down gently when the shell was full, and not for anything else. He had a look round, saw that all the rest were working as they should, and just then he was called out of the room. And it was at *that precise minute*,' he said dramatically, 'that the place blew up.'

He stopped and took another drink. The room was quiet, everyone watching him and waiting for him to continue. Even Hilda, who had heard the story so many times before, had her eyes fixed on his face – reliving her own memories, perhaps, Kate thought, for she knew that her grandparents had already been sweethearts at that time, and that when Hilda had heard of the explosion at Priddy's Hard she must immediately have been afraid that Albert had been involved.

'When they found that rod,' Albert said, turning his head to meet the gaze of each person in turn, 'it was blackened with the heat, and twisted almost out of all recognition. What's more, it had bloodstains and bits of skin still on it. It couldn't have got into that state if it had been over in the corner, where Harry Osborne threw it. It must have been right in amongst the shells, being *used*. And that's what the jury decided. They reckoned Sewett caused the explosion himself, by using too much force with the rod – a rod he never ought to have been using in the first place, a rod he'd been expressly told *not* to use.' Albert Fisher's voice rose with indignation as he spoke. 'Six men died. Six men! And Priddy's Hard's safety record ruined. All through one man thinking he knew best.' He shook his head. 'One of them was my best mate, Jimmy Jones, what lived up Hardway. His ma wasn't never the same again after that, never the same. He was all she had, see.'

'But wasn't there really any other way it could have happened?' Sally asked after a moment. 'I mean, it did look bad for him, I can see that – but couldn't it have been a fuze going wrong or – or something?'

'Don't you think they thought of that? Don't you think they tried every way they could to think what else could have gone wrong?' her grandfather demanded. 'Why, they called in an expert – a *Sir* he was, Knight of the Realm –

94

to come down specially to Gosport to see the Hard and try to get to the bottom of it. He did experiments himself up at Waltham Abbey where the gunpowder comes from, tried all ways to get fuzes to explode, banged 'em on the heads with mallets, chucked 'em against brick walls, everything you could think of, and in the end he reckoned there was no other way it could've happened than by that Gunner Sewett ramming it down with the copper rod. And the jury agreed.'

'Where were you when it happened, Grandad?' Kate asked. 'Were you anywhere near?'

'I was over in one of the other magazines. We heard it, of course – shook us up, I don't mind telling you. You hear a bang like that in a place what's full up with gunpowder, and you don't know what's going to happen next. We all had to get out, quick as we could, just in case anything else was set off.' He shook his head again. 'We saw what it was, soon as we come outside. Number 2 was no more than a wreck. The roof was blowed off, just a few struts and beams left, the windows all blowed out – proper mess it was. And the poor buggers – sorry, the poor blokes – what died, well, they was in bits, some of 'em, just *bits*.' He caught his wife's eye and stopped. 'I'm sorry, Hilda, I know you don't like to hear me say that, but it's true. We all know it's true.'

Hilda put her hand on his arm, 'I know, Albert. There's been enough of it in this war, with the Blitzes. It's just – well, hearing you talk about it brings it all back. I was working down Ratsey and Lapthorn's, making sails,' she said to Sally, 'and we heard the explosion so loud we thought it was the sail loft going up. Then, as soon as I heard it was Priddy's, I thought of your grandad. I didn't think I was ever going to see him again. You always think that, don't you, when something like that happens? You always think the worst.'

'Well, *I* think it's time we all cheered up a bit,' Win declared. 'We've heard the story now and if you've all had enough tea I think we ought to clear away and have a nice game of cards before Mum and Dad have to go home. And that dog could do with a walk, too,' she added, seeing Tyke go to the door. 'You men can take him up the road while the rest of us get the tea-things washed up. Barney can go along too. Come on, Sal, move yourself. Nobody can get past with your chair blocking the way.'

The family did as they were told. As Sally and Kate began to do the washing up, Sally looked at her sister.

'Aren't you ever scared, working at the Hard? Don't you ever worry that there'll be another explosion?'

'Not really.' Kate stood with a plate and a teacloth in her hand, thinking about her early days, the awe she'd felt on seeing the rows of huge shells, guns and torpedoes. 'Not any more, anyway. After all, you can get blown up these days just by staying at home.' She sighed. 'It's other people I worry about now. Some of them I just can't get out of my mind.'

People like Godfrey, she thought. And Jacky Benson. And Sam Smart and the Tompkins twins. And, after last night, the tall Canadian who had swung her over his shoulder in the jitterbug and whose eyes had met hers in mutual attraction.

Chapter Eight

Elsie Philpotts had had a visitor for tea too. It was Gladys Shaw, from April Grove, over in Portsmouth where Elsie and Charlie had lived before moving to Gosport. Gladys had been with Graham the night he was killed – it was her ambulance he'd been helping with during the Blitz – and she still popped over now and then, just to keep in touch. Privately, Elsie thought it was out of guilt. She knew that Gladys had blamed herself for months after Graham's death, but she was pleased to see the girl and hear a bit of gossip from April Grove. She was pleased, too, with the bag of biscuits Gladys had brought with her. Thoughtful, that was.

'So what's going on, then?' she enquired, bringing in a tin tray with a pot of tea and two cups. 'I suppose Ethel Glaister's still mincing about like Lady Muck? What about her Carol, how's she getting on?'

'Much the same as usual. I feel sorry for her – everyone knows she had a baby and had to let it be adopted, and you can see she's really miserable, looks like a ghost sometimes. It must be awful, having to give up your own baby.'

'There wasn't nothing else she could do though, was there?' Elsie said, pouring the tea. 'A young girl like Carol Glaister can't have a baby, all on her own, and you can bet your bottom dollar that mother of hers wouldn't help. Chuck her out as soon as look at her, that stuck-up old besom would.'

'Well, I don't know,' Gladys said. 'There's been a bit of

talk about her, so old Granny Kinch says. You know she works up at Airspeed these days, picking up rivets and stuff off the floor . . .'

'What, old Granny Kinch? I didn't know they were taking old women.'

'No, not Granny Kinch – Mrs Glaister. Apparently she's been dropping in at the Coach and Horses on her way home and bringing a Marine back for supper.'

'Well, it's better than the meat ration,' Elsie said, and squawked with laughter. 'Here, that's a good one, I must remember to tell my Charlie that when he comes in.'

For a long time after Graham had died, the sight of Gladys had reminded Elsie of her loss. Yet she had still wanted to see the girl, as if she was a link with the son she would never see again. Their friendship hadn't been serious, but Elsie had hoped it would develop.

'Fancy Ethel Glaister getting herself a fancy man,' she said, taking one of Gladys's biscuits. 'It just shows, doesn't it!' She didn't explain what it showed, but Gladys nodded in agreement, and Elsie continued, 'And what about you, love? Still like working up Fort Southwick, do you?'

Gladys had joined the Wrens, partly to make up for the Navy losing Graham, and had been posted to the big fort on the slopes of Portsdown Hill. Nobody knew quite what happened behind those earth ramparts and deep in the maze of tunnels that had been dug through the chalk, but at Priddy's Hard it was believed that they had secret radio transmitters and could plot the movements of all the ships in the Channel and perhaps even the North Sea. Gladys would never say what went on and Elsie knew better than to ask.

'It's all right,' Gladys said noncommittally. She hesitated, then said, 'I have got something to tell you though.'

'What's that, then, love?'

'It's Cliff – you know, Cliff Weeks that's been stopping with Mr and Mrs Vickers at the end of April Grove since his mum and dad were killed in the bombing. Mrs Vickers is his auntie. I've been seeing a bit of him when he's been home on leave, and writing to him and that, and – well . . .' She looked down at her lap and began pleating the navy-blue material of her skirt between her fingers. Elsie watched her and felt a strange twist to her heart. Gladys looked up at her again. 'He's – he's asked me to get engaged.'

'Engaged!' It shouldn't really come as a surprise, Elsie thought. You couldn't expect a girl like Gladys not to have a boyfriend. And she'd been through enough herself – seeing Graham blown to bits in front of her, and then losing her own mother when the two of them had been strafed in the street by that German plane. She deserved a bit of happiness. 'Congratulations,' she said, swallowing her own feelings. 'When's the happy day?'

'Oh, there isn't going to be one,' Gladys said at once. 'Not yet, anyway. I haven't said yes. I told him I wanted to wait – I didn't want to get married in a hurry, like some people, and then wish I hadn't.'

'Marry in haste, repent at leisure,' Elsie nodded. 'Well, perhaps that's sensible. But you don't want to wait too long, neither. Plenty of girls have lived to regret that, too.' She meant that plenty of young men had gone away and never come back, their sweethearts left to mourn the chance they had lost. 'And Cliff's a nice chap, from what I remember.'

'I know. I just want to be sure.'

There was a short silence. Elsie felt the teapot and went out to boil the kettle again. She came back and poured more tea before asking casually, 'How's that young Betty Chapman getting along now? Still out on the farm, is she?'

'Yes, and happy as a lark.' Gladys remembered that

99

Graham had been keen on Betty and bit her lip, but there was no point in trying to pretend it wasn't true. 'It seems funny, her marrying a conchie, and a Quaker too, but their wedding was lovely. And nobody can call him a coward. Working in Bomb Disposal the way he did – he was lucky not to be killed. As it is, he'll never see again.'

'Well, I'm pleased for her. She's a nice girl and it was all over between her and Graham long before she took up with him.' Elsie changed the subject. 'Your Diane, she all right?'

'Yes, she's having a whale of a time in the WAAFs. Goes out to crashed aircraft and helps salvage them.' They continued to chat about Gladys's family – how her father was managing without his wife, how her brother Bob was getting on in the Army – and about the other residents of April Grove, until at last Charlie came in from the garden and Elsie put the kettle on again and laid the table with bread and margarine, a pot of fish paste and a jar of jam. They all sat down at the table.

'I don't think much of this jam, Elsie,' Charlie remarked in his dry, sandpapery voice. 'What's it supposed to be? It's all full of bits.'

'Raspberry. That's the pips – always got a lot of pips, raspberry has.' She picked something out from between her teeth and laid it on her plate. 'Mind you, I reckon half of them are little bits of wood, put in to make you *think* that's what it is. They're up to all sorts of tricks like that these days.'

'Mr Budd, next door to us, grows his own raspberries,' Gladys said. 'All his own fruit and veg – Mrs Budd makes jam and bottles a lot of stuff too. She showed me her cupboard once – full of jars, it was. I wish our dad would grow things, but since Mum died he doesn't seem to have much interest.'

She helped Elsie to wash up and then left, saying she

had to get home to spend a bit of time with her dad before going back to Fort Southwick. After she'd gone, Elsie came into the back room and sat down, staring into the fire. Once or twice she sniffed a little and put one finger to her face to rub her eyes. Charlie watched her for a few minutes and then said quietly, 'It still brings it back, don't it, Else? Seeing that girl – it still brings our Graham back.'

She nodded and sighed. 'It's a funny thing, Charlie. I always have a little cry after she's gone – but I want her to come, just the same.' She looked at him and gave him a queer, twisted smile. 'And it makes me glad I'm working at Priddy's, too. I'm doing my bit to get my own back for what those Jerries have done to us. I'm doing my bit for my country – for the whole world. Just like Gladys is. Just like our Graham did. And I'll carry on doing it until we've won.' There was no laughter in her face now, only a tight, hard bitterness that sounded too in her voice. 'I'll carry on doing it until we've beaten that bastard Hitler and put him where he belongs – burning in bloody Hell.'

There was a long silence. Then Charlie said, 'I know how you feel, love. But you don't want to let it make you turn hard. Our Graham wouldn't have wanted that. He liked you jolly and laughing, you know that.'

'How can I be jolly and laughing, when I've lost my only son, my only *child*?' she demanded. 'It was bad enough knowing that there wouldn't never be another kiddy after our Graham was born. I always wanted a houseful of youngsters, you know that. And then I thought, well, maybe he'll marry some nice girl who'll have a big family of her own, grandchildren that we could have running in and out – and now even that's been took away from us, and we've got no one at all.' She looked at Fluffy, curled up asleep on one of the chairs. 'Just a kitten,' she said, her voice trembling. 'All I've got to love now is a *kitten*.'

'Well, you've got me, for what that's worth,' he pointed out. 'I know I ain't up to much, but—'

'Oh, I know I've got you, you old silly,' she said, giving him a shaky grin. 'You're part of the furniture.' She got up, giving herself a little shake. 'Well, this won't buy the baby a new bonnet. I thought I might unpick that old jumper of yours, the one that's gone at the elbows and got that big hole in the front. I ought to be able to knit some socks from it. You can help me wind it if you like.'

They had just begun this task, Charlie holding his hands up in front of him so that Elsie could wind the crinkly wool into a skein, when the doorbell rang. Elsie sighed and pursed her mouth in annoyance and Charlie let his hands rest in his lap, still held carefully apart so that the wool wouldn't get tangled.

'Who can that be? I bet it's that Mrs Jarvis wanting to borrow a cup of sugar again. We haven't had the last one back yet . . .' She plodded through to the front door. 'Well, Jackie Prentice! Where have you been hiding yourself? I haven't seen you around for weeks.'

'Can I come in for a minute, Mrs Philpotts?' the girl asked. 'I – I need someone to talk to.'

'Why, of course you can.' Elsie gave her a swift glance and knew at once what she wanted to talk about. The small body was still wrapped in the winter coat Jackie had been wearing when Elsie had last seen her, back in January, but the buttons were straining at their buttonholes and the belt was stretched almost to its fullest length.

Elsie popped her head round the back room door. 'Charlie, you can put that wool down and go down the shed for a while. Jackie's here and we wants to be private.' She went out to the kitchen and put on the kettle, then returned to the back room and settled the girl in Charlie's armchair. Already, tears were trickling down Jackie's cheeks. 'Now you just sit there, my duck, while I makes a cuppa. And take off that coat or you won't feel the benefit when you goes out again. It's all right – I can see what the trouble is. You don't need to be embarrassed.'

'Oh, Mrs Philpotts,' Jackie began tremulously, and broke into sobs. Elsie patted her shoulder and murmured something comforting, then slipped out to make the tea. By the time she returned with two cups and the remains of the biscuits Gladys had brought, Jackie was sniffing and wiping her eyes.

'I'm sorry. I can't seem to help it.'

'Course you can't.' Elsie handed her the cup. 'Drink that, it'll do you good, and look, there's a few custard creams here in these broken biscuits. You've got to take care of yourself, you know, you're eating for two now.'

'Oh, Mrs *Philpotts* . . .'

'Blimey, trust me to start you off again,' Elsie said ruefully. 'Come on, Jackie, have a good blow and drink your tea and then we'll have a talk.' She waited a moment while the girl found a hanky and gulped down some tea. 'Now, tell me all about it. It's that GI you were going round with, I suppose.'

Jackie nodded. 'Wilbur. I don't know where he is, Mrs Philpotts. I keep writing but I never get any answer. I don't know what to do.'

'Well, if you want my opinion,' Elsie said grimly, 'you might as well give up trying. You're not going to hear from him again, ever. You've got to make up your mind to that. I'm sorry, love, but it's true and there's no use in keeping up your hopes. You've got to think about yourself now – yourself and the baby.'

Jackie's face took on a look of terror. 'But what am I going to do? I *can't* have a baby, Mrs Philpotts – I just *can't*! Dad will throw me out, I'll have nowhere to go, and how am I going to manage? I just don't know *what* I'm going to do.' She was shaking now, her whole body shuddering. 'I've thought and thought about it, I can't *sleep* for thinking about it. I didn't even know for months – I couldn't believe it, I kept hoping it wasn't true, and waiting and waiting for my – for my – and it never came – and there doesn't seem to be anything I can *do* about it. I've tried hot baths and everything – someone told me that castor oil would stop it and I drank a whole cupful in hot milk but it didn't work, it just made me poorly for a day – and I don't know what else to do. I don't know which way to turn, I really *don't*.'

The words poured out in a jerky, only half-intelligible stream, and Elsie sat beside her, her arm around the girl's shoulders, listening compassionately. Funny, she thought, me and Gladys were only talking this afternoon about young Carol Glaister and her trouble, and now here's Jackie in the same case. Neither of them's the first, and neither'll be the last, but it's just as bad for each and every one of them. It crossed her mind for a moment that there might have been some young woman carrying Graham's baby when he died – that she might actually have a grandchild somewhere, a grandchild she would never know – but she swiftly brushed the thought aside. It did no good thinking like that, not when poor young Jackie was here needing help and comfort.

'Well, I'm sorry, love,' she said at last, 'but it looks as if you *are* going to have a baby, and like you say, there's nothing you can do to stop that.' She hoped that Jackie's naïve efforts to stop it wouldn't result in any damage, but didn't say so; no sense in putting fresh fears into the girl's mind. 'When d'you reckon it's due?'

'I don't really know. I found a book at the library but someone saw me looking so I couldn't really read much. It takes nine months, doesn't it? But I don't know when – when it happened.' She gazed up at Elsie with huge, piteous eyes. 'I mean, me and Wilbur . . .'

For the umpteenth time, Elsie wondered why girls weren't told the facts of life before it was too late. She knew of several who'd known nothing, nothing at all, until the day before their wedding when their mothers had stumbled through a halting, embarrassed explanation, and at least two who'd known nothing until the wedding night itself. One had never got over the shock . . . Elsie had always been open about the whole thing, thoroughly enjoying her own initiation, and she'd given Graham a straight talk as soon as he was sixteen; and when she'd suspected he was starting to get extra friendly with his first girlfriend she'd bought him a packet of rubbers and told him to make sure and always use them. So probably I haven't got any unknown grandchildren after all, she thought with a little sigh.

'All right,' she said to Jackie, 'let's see if we can work it out. When did you and Wilbur start to go all the way?'

Jackie blushed. 'Last September. It was on my birthday. He took me out for a meal – it was ever so nice, in that hotel in Pompey, the one by Clarence Pier – and we had a bottle of wine. I'd never had wine before. And then we went for a walk on Southsea Common and – and . . .' She faltered and her blush deepened. 'He said it would be all right. He used a – a French letter and he said nothing would happen. He said we were engaged and as good as married, and he'd be going away soon and wanted to have something to remember.'

'And now it's you who's got something to remember,' Elsie said wryly. 'And was that the only time?' She looked doubtfully at Jackie's stomach. It was swelling, certainly, but Elsie wouldn't have thought the girl was as much as seven months' gone. 'Was that the end of September?'

'No, the beginning. And we did it again.' The girl looked down and whispered, 'Lots of times.'

'And he always used a rubber?'

'Well, nearly always. Once, we – we wanted to do it again and he didn't have another one, and we couldn't stop, somehow.' Jackie's cheeks were so hot Elsie thought she could probably warm her hands on them. 'You don't know what it was like,' she finished desperately.

'Oh, you'd be surprised,' Elsie said drily. 'I haven't always been an old married woman, you know.' In fact, she could recall all too well a number of occasions on which she had been in a very similar situation, and there had been one or two scares afterwards, too. She was lucky, she knew, not to have been in the same position as Jackie was now. That had been before Charlie came along and swept her off her feet.

'So when was the last time?' she asked, still trying to work out Jackie's dates. 'And when did you last see blood?'

'I can't remember. But it must have been before Wilbur went away, mustn't it? And that was in December. So it must have happened before then.'

'I should think that's pretty likely,' Elsie agreed. 'I don't suppose he sent it through the post . . . I'm sorry, love, I'm not really making a joke of it, I'm trying to think . . . It seems to me you're probably about five or six months. So it would be due around . . . let's see . . . July, or maybe even August. It's a shame you can't remember.'

'Well, I know I came on the week after my birthday,' Jackie said. 'Because I had really bad cramps and had to go home from work. But I can't remember at all after that.'

'So perhaps you didn't come on at all? Didn't you worry about it?'

'No, I never even thought about it. I was quite pleased because it meant – you know.' She blushed again and Elsie sighed. Didn't the girl know anything at all? Hadn't it even occurred to her that she might be in the family way? 'Anyway, I've never been all that regular,' Jackie continued. 'I often miss a month. I never thought anything of it.'

'So we're thinking about July or August,' Elsie said. 'And the first thing you ought to do is see a doctor.'

'I can't do that! He'd tell Dad! He comes round every week to see him.'

'And hasn't he noticed anything?'

'Well, I'm usually at work when he comes. Anyway, I don't feel ill or anything. You don't *have* to go to a doctor, do you?'

'I suppose not. But you need to see the midwife and get her booked up.' Elsie broke off. 'That's if you're going to have it at home, anyway. Your dad's going to have to know, Jackie.'

The look of terror returned. 'I can't tell him! It would kill him – he'd kill *me*! Oh, Mrs Philpotts, isn't there anything else I can do? Isn't there somewhere I can go?'

'Well, there's homes for unmarried mothers, but I don't know much about them. Wait a minute, though – Gladys Shaw was round here this afternoon, and she was telling me about a girl in her street that got into trouble like you, and she went away for a while so that no one would know, and came back after the baby was born. She gave it up for adoption.'

Jackie gazed at her. 'But if she went away so no one would know, how did this Gladys Shaw hear about it?'

'Well, I suppose everyone did know, really. You can't keep things like that secret. But they could pretend *not* to know, couldn't they – those that didn't want to be nasty about it. There's always some who like to be spiteful. Mind you, it takes a lot of living down, even then.' She realised that this line of thought wasn't helping Jackie. 'Anyway, that's neither here nor there. It's what *you're* going to do that we've got to think about.'

'But how do you find out about these places? How do

you get there? And what about the baby – do you really think it could be adopted? I wouldn't like it to be in a Children's Home, like the one out at Alverstoke.' She touched her stomach and Elsie recognised the familiar gesture of a young woman on the brink of realising what it would mean to be a mother. At the same moment, a look of dread came over her face and she whispered, 'What's it *like* to have a baby, Mrs Philpotts? What happens? Does it – does it hurt much? I mean, I've heard of people *dying*—'

'Well, *you're* not going to die,' Elsie said briskly. 'And yes, I'd be telling a lie if I said it didn't hurt, but most people think it's worth it.' But perhaps not, if you had to give up your baby as soon as it was born, she thought, and wondered how anyone could do that. She could never have given up her Graham . . . She looked at Jackie and shook her head. The poor kid was going to have to go through such a lot. If only it could have been Graham's baby she was carrying. I'd never have let her give that up, never, she thought fiercely.

'Jackie, you've got to tell your dad sometime,' she said. 'And it might not be a bad idea to ask the doctor to do it. You don't want to upset him too much, not with his heart the way it is. Go and see the doctor, and get him to check you over, make sure everything's all right, and then ask him to tell your dad. He'll know the way to do it.' A fresh thought struck her. 'He'll probably have the address of one of these homes too, if you want it.'

'I don't know.' Jackie looked miserably at the fireplace. 'I don't know that I'd want to go anywhere like that. I've never been away from home – and I might not like the other girls there. I was at a Girl Guide camp once and they all made fun of me. I was ever so miserable. And it costs enough already, having the doctor for Dad. I don't know what to do.'

Elsie looked at her with a touch of exasperation. She wanted to *tell* the girl to do as she was suggesting, but it really wasn't any of her business. It was for Herbert Prentice to say what she'd got to do, but Elsie didn't hold out much hope for him showing any understanding. He'd always been a miserable so-and-so, in Elsie's opinion, and he'd got worse since his wife had been killed and he'd been injured. Well, that was understandable but it wasn't much help to Jackie now.

'Go and see the doctor,' she said gently. 'He'll help you. Come and tell me what he says. And if you need money, I can give you something to help out a bit.' She fetched her purse and pressed a half-crown into Jackie's hand, then watched as Jackie started to pull her coat around her. 'And you can come round here any time, any time at all. Me and Mr Philpotts'll help you however we can. Don't you forget that, now. I mean it.'

'Thanks, Mrs Philpotts,' Jackie said gratefully. 'I'll do what you say. I'll see Dr Berry, and come and tell you what he says. And I'll pay back the money.'

'Don't you dare! That's a present, that is. Charlie and me aren't hard up, not with his wage and my money from Priddy's Hard. Now, you try not to worry. We'll think of something, and you pop in whenever you like.' She felt a sudden ache in her throat and put her arms around the girl's slight shoulders. 'I always hoped you and my Graham would make a go of it,' she said gruffly. 'If you had – well, no use thinking about that now. But you just remember, you're always welcome here, whatever happens.'

She let the girl out and watched her go along the street. Poor kiddy, she thought. She's only just beginning to realise how hard it's going to be for her. If only things had been different. If only Graham hadn't been killed. He might even have taken her on, baby and all.

He'd always been fond of Jackie, even after they'd parted brass rags.

If only it could have been her grandchild that Jackie was expecting.

Chapter Nine

The Canadians were the first of a great wave of soldiers, sailors and airmen who flooded over from North America. All seemed to be heading for the South Coast, and most of all for Portsmouth and the beaches of Dorset, Devon, Sussex and Kent. There were enough, Maxine remarked wickedly, for every girl to have half a dozen or more all to herself.

'You'd need more energy than I've got then,' Hazel remarked as the girls changed into their clean overalls. 'One's enough for me. Gene's got more go in him than any bloke I've ever met.'

'It's because they're so well-fed,' Janice said, a little sourly. 'Don't know the meaning of the word *rationing*. Not that I'm complaining,' she added hastily. 'Erwin brought me a huge bar of chocolate last night. I could hardly lift it, it was so big.'

'Are you sure that was the chocolate?' Maxine asked, giving her a sideways look, and Janice lifted her nose haughtily.

'*I* know that,' Maxine grinned as the others laughed, 'but does *Erwin* know that? That's the question. And does it make any difference anyway? I'm sure he expects *some* special treatment in return for all that chocolate he's giving you.'

'Chocolate!' Hazel chortled. 'That's a new name for it! The only sort of chocolate that's not on ration, if you ask me!'

Janice tossed her head. 'I'm not listening to this. You've all got filthy minds. I don't know why I go around with you.'

'Because you love us, that's why,' Kate said, putting her arm round Janice's shoulders. 'And because nobody else will put up with you like we do – ouch!' as Janice poked a sharp elbow into her ribs. 'Well, if that's what you think of our friendship—'

The whistle sounded for the start of work and they hastily bundled their hair under the calico turbans. There was an air of even greater urgency about the Hard now: a sense that something big was in the offing, some new, even more powerful thrust that demanded an increased effort from Priddy's Hard – from everyone in Gosport, in Portsmouth, in the entire country, if this war that had dragged on for five long years were ever to be won; if life in Britain were ever to return to the way it had been before it all began, even though that time seemed to be so far in the past you could barely remember what it had been like.

For Kate, watching the endless stream of bombs and torpedoes leave the magazine, ready to be loaded on to the lighters and transported across the harbour, it seemed like the build-up of an ominous cloud in the sky, the threat of a storm that would envelop the world in thunder and its fury. Every one of those bombs is full of death, she thought, the deaths of dozens, perhaps hundreds, of people. Young men like Godfrey and Jack, young women like me and Maxine, mothers and fathers, children like Sally and Barney . . .

She turned her mind away. You couldn't think like that. You mustn't. It would stop you working, drive you mad. Worse, it was unpatriotic. You had to forget the Germans were people like yourself. They were the enemy, to be defeated, and everyone in the country had a part to play in that defeat.

Afterwards, perhaps, you could begin to think of them as human beings once more.

'Oh, I forgot to tell you,' Janice said suddenly. 'That Canadian's still after you – he asked Erwin to get me to give you a message.'

Kate's heart gave a leap, but she said nothing. She hadn't seen Brad since the night of the dance, but she'd thought about him a lot. There had been something special about him – not just that he was a Canadian, but the look in his eyes, the way he touched her hand and held her in his arms for the dance. She lay in bed at night, imagining herself doing the tango with him, bent backwards over his arm and gazing up into his eyes . . .

'He's dead keen to see you again,' Janice continued. 'You're the best dancer he's ever met, he thinks you're lovely and he wants to take you out.' She rolled her eyes. 'You lucky blighter! Wish it was me – he's a smasher.'

'And you're engaged,' Kate said automatically. 'Anyway, it doesn't matter whether he's a smasher or not, I'm not going out with him.'

'Why on earth not? Look, we could go as a foursome – you and him, and me and Erwin. Go to the pictures one night, perhaps. Or for a walk along Southsea front. Or if you won't do that, he says he'll come over to Gosport, you can show him the sights.'

'Sights!' Kate snorted. 'In Gosport? Like the old moat, all full of weed, or the gasometer going up and down? That'd give him something to write home about, I don't think!'

'Don't be daft. He's not really interested in "sights". It's you he wants to see, Kate.' Janice gave her a coaxing smile. 'Why don't you say yes? He's a really nice chap. They all are.'

Kate shrugged. She longed to say yes, but her fears held her back. Brad *was* a nice chap and that made it all the more important that she should have nothing to do with him. She looked at the long conveyor belts of bombs, slowly moving past, and shuddered. It would be like signing his death warrant.

Gosport High Street was always busy on Saturday mornings. People who were at work all week went 'down town' to do their shopping, browse around Woolworths and run into friends. When Kate wandered in, she made for the hardware counter where Sally was presiding grumpily over an array of screwdrivers and hammers. Not that it was much of an array – like everything else, tools were in short supply. It was a wonder, Kate thought as she gazed at the dismal collection, that they hadn't been put on ration, like clothes and food.

'You look fed up,' she said to her sister, and Sally nodded.

'Not for much longer, though. I'm giving in my notice this afternoon.'

Kate stared at her. 'Giving in your notice? Why? What are you going to do?'

'I'm going to work at Priddy's Hard,' Sally said with a grin. 'I nipped round in my lunch-hour on Tuesday and they took me on. One more week in here and then I'll be clocking on with you, earning good money *and* having Saturdays off. And I tell you what, I can't wait to get out of this dump.' She glanced disparagingly round the big shop with its throng of customers. 'I wouldn't have minded so much if they'd put me on a decent counter, selling something interesting like lipsticks, but *hardware* . . .' She made a face.

'I don't see that you'll find munitions any more interesting,' Kate said. 'Filling shells with cordite. Stencilling numbers on torpedoes. And at least screwdrivers don't explode.'

'No, but I'll be with more people, won't I? You can talk and sing while you're working, and you have concerts and things in your lunch-hour. And I'll be getting better money – I'll be able to come in here and buy as many lipsticks as I want. I'll never come near the hardware counter again in my whole life.'

'But you're not old enough,' Kate objected. 'You've got to be sixteen to work at Priddy's. You won't be sixteen till October. They won't let you start till then, Sal.'

'Well, they are. So there.' Sally tossed her head triumphantly. 'Didn't even ask how old I was, anyway.'

Kate looked at her sister. With make-up and the jumper she'd knitted during the winter, Sally could easily pass for sixteen, even eighteen. And Kate remembered her own words to their mother, that girls grew up more quickly now and that Sally was more like she herself had been at seventeen. She could see how the manager at Priddy's Hard would have thought she was old enough.

'They didn't even want to see your birth certificate?'

'I told you, they never asked. Anyway, I'm starting on Monday week and that's all there is to it.' Sally gave her a wheedling glance. 'You won't say anything, will you? You won't give me away? It's only a few months to my birthday anyway.'

'I won't,' Kate said grimly, 'but I wouldn't bank on our dad keeping quiet about it. He'll be down there the minute he finds out.' A thought struck her. 'You *are* going to tell him and Mum, aren't you? You weren't going to just change jobs without saying anything?'

'Well, I'll have to tell them, won't I, because of it being longer hours. They'd wonder why I wasn't getting home till eight o'clock if they thought I was still at Woolworths. And not having to go in on Saturdays . . . You don't really think they'll stop me, do you? I mean, I'll be able to give Mum more money. And it *is* for the war.'

Kate sighed. 'I suppose it'll be all right. I wouldn't want to be in your shoes when you tell them, though. You know what Dad'll say – you're underage, you're under his jurisdiction, you're not old enough . . .'

'Not old enough to make up my own mind,' Sally joined in bitterly. 'Not old enough to go to dances, not old enough to wear lipstick, not old enough to do this, not old enough to do that . . . Not old enough to do *anything* I might enjoy! But I'm old enough when it suits them – old enough to help round the house, and do the ration books and the shopping, old enough to *be sensible*. Well, I can be sensible at Priddy's Hard, and if they try to stop me I won't have a job at all, because I'll have handed in my notice here and it'll be too late!'

She glowered at her sister, and Kate recognised the determined, pugnacious toddler, who had thrown her little enamel chamberpot across the room rather than use it, who as a five-year-old had refused to go to school and clung to the playground railings so tightly that her fingers couldn't be prised away without breaking them, and who had then (having been coaxed in at last) refused to come home, so that the whole procedure had been reversed. This was the Sally who had been so determined to go to the Central School and learn shorthand and typing that she'd forged her father's signature on the form to allow her to take the examination, and the Sally who had wanted so badly to come home from evacuation in the first year of the war that she'd saved her few pennies' pocket-money for weeks to pay the bus fare as far as Fareham, and then walked the rest of the way.

She hadn't always won her battles. Eventually, she had learned to sit on her chamber-pot, accepted that she had to go to school every day and sit in class until it was time to come home, and returned to her foster home. But the first minute she could leave school and come home, she had done so, ignoring her mother's objections, and now she had got herself a job at Priddy's Hard and would give in her notice at Woolworths. This, Kate suspected, was a battle she was going to win.

'Well, it's up to you,' she said, 'but you're not going to find it as easy as you think. It's hard work, standing twelve hours a day filling shells or whatever job they give you. You'll be wishing you were back at Woolworths before you've been there five minutes.'

'I shan't,' Sally said. 'I'll be glad.' She turned her head as a young man approached the counter. 'If you want nails, we haven't got any, not till next Wednesday. And we've only got one saw in the whole place and it's too big for you.'

Kate grinned and moved away. It was obvious that the youth, who looked about seventeen, wasn't interested in hardware but in Sally, and that Sally knew it. She left them exchanging banter and strolled over to the cosmetics counter, where she found Maxine sorting through the few perfumes on offer.

'It's either *Soir de Paris* or *Ashes of Roses*,' she said gloomily. 'That's all they ever seem to have. I'd like something really elegant – a proper French scent. Have you bought anything, Kate?'

Kate shook her head. 'I'm saving up for a summer frock. Mum said she'd help me make it and I want to get some really pretty material. We're going over the water this afternoon to see what we can find. Seen any of the others?'

'Janice was here a few minutes ago. She said she was meeting Val and Hazel in the Dive – want to go along?' Maxine dropped the little dark blue and silver perfume bottle back on the counter and moved towards the door. Kate followed her and they crossed the High Street and ducked down the steps of the narrow tunnel of a cellar beneath the old Market House. It had continued to function as a café even though the Market House itself had been bombed and was now an empty shell, and it was a popular meeting-place. As usual, it was crowded but Kate saw Janice's arm waving from the very end of the tunnel and they made their way through the tables.

'I wonder why it always smells of old tea in here,' she began, and then stopped short as she saw the three Canadian airmen sitting at the end. 'Oh!' She turned accusingly on Maxine. 'You didn't tell me!'

'I didn't know, did I!' Maxine pushed her forwards. 'Go on, Kate, sit down. It's only a cup of coffee.'

'Yes, come on, Kate.' Janice, grinning wickedly, slid along the bench to make room. 'Come and sit down next to Brad. He's come all the way over from Pompey specially to see you. You can't disappoint him, can you!'

'I could,' Kate said grimly, but she did as she was told and found herself sitting close to the tall, dark-haired Canadian. 'I suppose this was all arranged between you, wasn't it? And what if I hadn't come down town this morning? What would you have done then?'

'Tried again next week,' he said, smiling at her. 'But I'm glad you did come. We don't know how long we'll be around, you see, and I don't want to waste a minute when I could be spending it with you.'

Kate stared at him. Her heart thumped and she felt a bit sick. 'What d'you mean?'

'Listen,' he said, leaning closer. She glanced around nervously but the others had drawn away and were in a huddle at the far end of the bench. Janice was sitting close to Erwin, far too close for a girl who was engaged to be married, Kate thought wildly, and there were two other Canadians there as well. She felt Brad's hand on her arm and jerked her head to look at him, beginning to get up at the same moment. 'I can't – I've got to go—'

'No,' he said. 'Listen to me. Drink your coffee and listen.' Kate looked down in surprise, having no recollection of having bought or asked for coffee. 'I've been wanting to see you, real bad,' he murmured in a low, urgent voice. 'Ever since that dance I've been thinking about you. I can't get you out of my mind. I can't get your face out of my mind, or your voice, or the way you looked at me when we were dancing – none of it. No, *don't* go away – please. I'm not going to hurt you. I'm not even going to touch you, if you don't want me to.' Kate looked down at his hand and he took it away from her arm. 'But please, Kate, please come out with me. Just once. Just so that we can talk a little – get to know each other before I go away.'

'That's just it!' Kate's panic was throbbing in her throat and chest and stomach. She could scarcely breathe. She put her hand to her mouth and shook her head, then managed to draw a deep, quavering breath and went on, rushing to get the words out. 'You're going away. It's no good, Brad, can't you see that? We all know what's going to happen,' she glanced around again, looking at the posters on the wall, faded now through having been there for so long, stained by cigarette smoke: *Walls Have Ears, Be Like Dad – Keep Mum*. She bit back the word *Invasion* but knew by his eyes that he understood. 'You don't know where you'll go or what will happen.'

'But that's just why I can't wait. Don't *you* see? I want to know you before I go – I want to know if what I think about us is true. I want to be *sure*.'

'Sure of what? *What* do you think about us?' She was beginning to feel angry, and the anger was pushing down her panic. 'Brad, all we did was dance together. You can't think anything. And just going out together once isn't going to tell you much more. You can't know me in just a few minutes. There's more to me than that!' Her eyes snapped but to her surprise Brad laughed and took her hand.

'Sure there is! And I'll enjoy learning it – even if it takes a lifetime.' His smile faded and they stared at each other. Kate felt a sudden surge of panic again and she could see her fear mirrored in his eyes. She tried to speak but no words would come. To her astonishment and fury, she felt tears form in her eyes.

'Let's get out of here,' Brad said quietly. 'Let's get away from this racket.'

Keeping Kate's hand firmly in his, he stood up, and she found herself standing with him. Silently, without even a goodbye to their friends, they pushed their way out of the basement, up the steps to the pavement. Out in the cold March air, they stood and looked at each other.

'Wh-where do you want to go?' Kate asked shakily.

Brad shrugged. 'Anywhere. Anywhere quiet where we can talk. Anywhere we can just be together.'

She hesitated for a moment, then said, 'We'll go out to Haslar. We can walk there, over Pneumonia Bridge.'

'Over *what* bridge?'

She grinned and felt herself relax suddenly. 'Pneumonia Bridge. It's called that because it's so high there's always a wind up on the top. They had to make it like that to get boats up and down Haslar Creek.' She led the way past Trinity Church, with its redbrick tower that was such a landmark from the Portsmouth side of the harbour, and along to the narrow bridge which crossed the neck of the broad creek, a harbour in itself filled with small boats. 'Some of these were at Dunkirk,' she said as they paused on the top and looked down into the grey waters. 'One of the ferry-boats went as well – the *Ferry King*. One of the women at Priddy's knows the man who took it over.'

'The *Ferry King*!' he said. 'Gee, that's the boat I came over on. You mean to say that little tub went to Dunkirk?'

He shook his head in wonder. 'There ought to be something on it – a notice or something, to tell people.'

Kate shrugged and they hurried down the slope of the bridge towards the sea-wall that ran along outside the Naval hospital. Some of the survivors of Dunkirk had come here, and there were always sick and wounded sailors arriving. If there were to be an invasion, there'd be more, she thought, and wondered what it was like for the nurses, many of them volunteers, to have to cope with some of the terrible injuries such men suffered.

The thought that Brad might be one of those men struck her like a knife in the chest and she staggered and clutched his arm to save herself.

'Hey, you OK?' He slipped his arm round her waist to steady her. 'Want to go back?'

Kate shook her head. 'No, I'm fine. Just turned my ankle, that's all.' She bit her lips hard and turned her face away so that he wouldn't see the tears that had sprung to her eyes. I ought to say yes, she thought. I ought to go back, get rid of him, stop this before it goes too far . . . But already it seemed as if it had gone too far, and she couldn't summon up the strength to stop it. I will, though, she promised herself. I'll tell him this is the only time. I won't see him again. I'll tell him I can't, because – oh, because there's someone else. I'm engaged like Janice, I only went to the dance for a bit of fun, it didn't mean a thing. He's imagining it all . . .

I'll tell him all that. I *will* . . .

'This is some place,' he remarked as they walked along the sea wall. On their left lay the narrow neck of Portsmouth Harbour, flanked by the bastions of Sallyport and Fort Blockhouse, with the city itself stretching away behind it. The pale tower of the Cathedral, miraculously untouched by the Blitz, stood foursquare and sturdy in the midst of the narrow, ancient streets of Old Portsmouth and further along the Southsea beach were the ruins of Clarence Pier and the funfair where Kate had often gone as a child, and then the white dome of the Pier where she and Brad had met.

Across the Solent lay the green bulk of the Isle of Wight, with its beaches and woods and fields. Kate had been there too sometimes, crossing over by one of the paddle ferries like the *Whippingham*, and walked from Ryde along the beach and the cliffs to Sandown and Shanklin. But the Isle of Wight had been closed to visitors for some time now, and nobody had been allowed to cross that strip of water unless they lived or had important business there. It's funny, she thought, we're supposed to be fighting this war for freedom and yet we seem to have lost all the freedom we ever had.

'There's a place called Portsmouth near where I live,' Brad said, 'in Ontario. It's on the shore of the lake – a port, but not as big as this place. I go sailing there.'

It was fine but there was still a bite to the March wind, and Kate pulled her collar up around her face. Brad took her hand and drew it through the crook of his arm, and she let it stay there, grateful for the warmth and savouring the feeling of being close to him again. Just remember it's the last time, she warned herself. Just don't let him get any ideas.

'What's it like where you live? Is it like here?'

He laughed and shook his head. 'I'll say not! The lake's as big as this stretch of water here – the Solent. Bigger, because you can't see the far shore.' He gazed across towards the Isle of Wight. The seaway was busy with ships, British, Canadian, American, some steaming into the narrow harbour entrance, some on their way to other, secret destinations. They all, Kate knew, bore armaments from Priddy's Hard – torpedoes and shells and bullets that she herself might have handled, and which would deal death in the coming weeks.

Brad was still talking about his homeland. 'And away from the shore it's nearly all forest, and more lakes. Canada's as much water as it is land, at least around that part. It's a great place for sport – sailing, swimming, camping, canoeing. You'd like it, Kate.'

She looked at him. 'How do you know that? You don't know anything about me. I might not like it at all. I might prefer our Portsmouth, with its shops and dance halls and everything.' She sighed. 'Well, the Portsmouth we had before the war, before everything was smashed to bits.'

Brad stopped and turned to face her. He took both her hands in his and looked down gravely into her eyes. 'I know more than you think, Kate,' he said quietly. 'I know you'd like it.'

Kate stared at him and then let her gaze fall. She could feel the scarlet colour run up her neck and all over her face. She snatched her hands away and walked on, thrusting her hands deep into her coat pockets. Brad fell into step beside her.

'Don't be mad at me, Kate. I know I'm rushing you, but that's because we don't have much time. Look,' he waved his hand at the stretch of water between them and the Island, 'look at all the ships. They're not on pleasure cruises. They're here to get ready for—'

'Stop! You mustn't say it!' She glanced swiftly around, as if expecting to see a German spy creeping up on them, as in the cartoon posters. 'You mustn't talk like that, Brad.'

'Well, OK. But we know what they're doing, all the same. We all know what's going on. And we both know that I'm going to be a part of it. I'll be gone from here soon, Kate, maybe not for a week, maybe not for two or three weeks, but soon. I don't want us to waste that time.'

'Waste it?' she said faintly.

'You know what I mean. I want us to use it properly. Get to know each other. I want to see as much as I can of you, while I've got the chance.'

'And then you'll be gone.' Kate's voice was flat. 'You'll be gone and you'll never come back.'

'Don't say that! Sure I'll come back. Just as soon as all this is over, as soon as I'm free to go where I want, I'll be back for you.'

'Oh yes,' she said, 'they all say that.' She mimicked an American accent. '*Sure, I'll marry you, honey, and you'll come and live with me on my ra-a-anch. We'll have a big house and big car and as many bathrooms as you want – so why not let's make a little hay now, while the sun shines, huh?* And then off he goes and she never hears from him again, and all she's got left to remind her of him is a little baby . . . No thanks!'

Brad stared at her. 'Is that what you really think of me?'

'I don't *know*!' she cried. 'How can I know? I know it's happened to a lot of girls, and why should I be any different? How do I know *you're* any different? We can't know all about each other, Brad, not just from having been to one dance. It's crazy!'

'Crazy,' he agreed, 'but that's the way I feel, Kate. It really is. And I'm not going to try to persuade you to do anything you don't want to. Believe me, I'm not.'

'I've heard that before too,' she said. 'The trouble is, you all know how to make a girl want to do things she shouldn't.'

At this, Brad flung back his head and roared with laughter. Kate watched him and thought, If I could only tell him the real reason why I can't see him again. But he'd think that was *really* crazy. It's better that he thinks I just don't trust him.

'Look,' he said, 'let's start again. We won't talk about

any of it. We'll just go for a walk together and enjoy ourselves. D'you have to go home for your – what d'you call it? Lunch?'

'Dinner,' Kate said. 'Lunch is what we have at about eleven in the morning – a sandwich or a bun, if we're lucky. Yes, I do have to go home, Mum'll be expecting me.' She hesitated. 'I'm sorry I can't ask you back . . .'

'That's OK,' he said easily. 'I know all about your rationing. Look, can you come out again afterwards, or maybe tomorrow? Go for another walk, say? Or we could go to the movies one evening. How about that?'

It can't do any harm, Kate thought, watching a group of nurses emerge from the hospital gate. Just seeing him once or twice, for a walk, or the pictures. It can't really do any harm.

'All right,' she said, and smiled at him. 'I'll have to help Mum this afternoon, but I'll come out for a walk to-morrow afternoon. So long as you don't expect anything more.'

'It's a promise,' he said, smiling back. His teeth were very white and his eyes very blue against the darkness of his hair. 'It's a promise, Kate.'

Chapter Ten

Pete came home the following Saturday, full of plans for what he was going to do now that he was back in Portsmouth. 'I want to see Pompey play at Fratton Park,' he declared, referring to the local football team. 'They've still got the FA Cup, you know, that they won just before the war started, and my mate Jimmy told me Monty's going to be their first President. He's been to Fratton loads of times, never seen them lose.'

'I would have thought Field-Marshal Montgomery would have better things to do than go to see football matches,' Win said. 'There's still a war on, in case you haven't noticed.'

'The poor bloke's got to have some time off,' George argued. He would have liked to go to Fratton more often himself, but there never seemed to be time these days, what with overtime and then the allotment to look after. He was busy over there now at weekends, digging and getting new vegetables in. Perhaps when the evenings grew lighter he'd be able to slip down with Pete one Saturday afternoon . . . He was so wrapped up in these thoughts that he missed what Sally was saying and came to himself to find the rest of the family staring at her in astonishment.

'What's up?' he said. 'Why're you all looking like Hitler's just walked in the door?'

'Haven't you heard a word we've been saying?' Win demanded. 'It's our Sally. Says she's give in her notice at Woolworths, got herself another job.'

George didn't wait to be told where the new job was. He turned on his younger daughter. 'What? You've left Woolworths? Without so much as a word to your mother and me? What are you talking about, girl?'

Pete, who was sitting in front of an enormous helping of shepherd's pie, bent his head and went on eating. He'd lived quite well in his foster home in the country – probably better than those left at home – but liked to give the impression that he'd been starved, and Win had been heaping his plate.

Win and George, however, laid down their knives and forks and gave Sally their full attention, while Kate hunched her shoulders as if in an effort to become invisible. You didn't have to do this right in the middle of supper, she thought, spoiling Pete's first evening at home.

Sally met her father's gaze defiantly. 'I've told you. I'm going to work at Priddy's Hard. With Kate.'

Their eyes turned to Kate and she shot her sister a wrathful glance. 'Did you know about this, Kate?'

'Not till last Saturday,' she said reluctantly.

'But you knew then. And you never said a word.' George glared at her. 'Don't you think you ought to have told us what your sister was up to?'

'It wouldn't have made any difference—' Kate began, but he thumped his fist down on the table, making the crockery rattle, and they all jumped.

'*Wouldn't have made any difference*? Her own father, and it wouldn't have made any difference, telling *me* what my own daughter was doing behind my back – is that what you're saying? That I've got no influence over my own family? No authority no more? That girl's not sixteen yet. She's under my jurisdiction till she's twenty-one – and so are you, for that matter. I give you a lot of freedom, you can't say I don't – some'd say I give you too much – but big things, things like jobs, you come to me about, me and your mother, you don't go off making your own arrangements, and don't you forget it.' His moustache bristled as he glowered around the table at them all. 'And that goes for all of you.'

The family sat in uncomfortable silence. Pete was still eating, but more slowly now. Kate looked at the table-cloth, noting a gravy stain close to her own plate. I wish Sally had never told me, she thought. What was I supposed to do? It *wouldn't* have made any difference. He knows what she's like, just as much as I do.

'It's not Kate's fault,' Sally said, speaking up with barely a quiver in her voice. 'I didn't tell her until the day I gave in my notice. I already had the job at Priddy's by then.'

'And that's another thing.' He transferred his attention back to his younger daughter. 'How did you manage to do that? You've got to be sixteen to work there, I know that.'

'You didn't tell them lies, Sally?' Win said. 'You know what we've always said about telling lies.'

'Yes,' Pete said, grinning, 'you'll get a spot on your tongue!' He pulled the shepherd's-pie dish towards him and began to scrape off the crispy bits round the edges.

'And you needn't stick your oar in,' his father told him sharply. 'Well, Sally? Did you lie to them?'

'What if I did? Boys lie about their age to get into the Army and people say how brave they are. What's the difference?'

'The difference—' George began loudly, but then faltered into silence. Sally gave him a triumphant look and his face reddened. 'Now look here, my girl. You needn't think you can get your way by being cheeky.'

'I wasn't being cheeky. I just asked a question.'

George floundered for a moment. He had lost control of the argument and was struggling to recover it. He took a breath and then said more quietly, 'And so did I. Did you, or did you not, lie to Priddy's Hard about your age: yes or no?'

'No,' Sally said instantly. 'They never asked me.'

'Never asked you? They must have asked you. Didn't you have to fill in a form? Didn't that ask your age?'

'Oh yes,' she said carelessly, 'but I didn't think that counted.'

'*Didn't count*? You signed it, didn't you? You put your name to it! Don't you realise that's a legal document? You could be had up in a court of law for putting lies on a legal document.' He shook his head. 'You could go to *prison*.'

'George, no!' Win exclaimed, her face white. 'They'd never put a girl like our Sally in prison. Not for just making a mistake on a form.'

'It wasn't a mistake,' George began, but Sally butted in.

'Course they wouldn't, Mum,' she assured her mother, her tone only slightly doubtful. 'Anyway, I never put lies. It asked when I was born, that's all. If they can't add up, that's not my fault.'

'And nobody ever mentioned the word *sixteen*?' her father asked sceptically.

'Well, the man might have said something like "you're sixteen then" – I can't really remember.' Sally's voice was so off hand that they all knew instantly that she remembered very well. 'Anyway, I've got the job and I've left Woolworths, so that's all there is to it. I'm going in on Monday morning with Kate. I can't see what all the fuss is about,' she added in an injured tone. 'I'd go in a few months anyway. What's the difference?'

'The difference is that you might *not* have gone in a few months,' her father told her. 'What we'd have done, if you'd not been so set on having your own way, would have been to sit down and talk about it, your mother and me, and then tell you whether you could throw up a decent, clean job and go and work in munitions. Sixteen isn't twenty-one. You don't go making up your own mind. What you do and where you work is for me and your mother to decide, and will be for another five years yet.'

'Kate works there.'

'Kate's got to do war work, you know that. It was that or the Services and we didn't want her leaving home. Anyway, she's older than you are – she can look after herself a bit better.'

'Look after herself? You mean she can stop bombs exploding?'

'No, I *don't* mean that. You know very well what I mean, and I won't tell you again about being cheeky.' George looked at his plate and his face set into grumpy lines, his mouth pushed out and a frown almost concealing his eyes. The frown ran right up over his forehead and creased his balding head. He looked like an angry baby. 'Well, I suppose there's nothing we can do about it now, not without causing even more trouble. You'd better go in on Monday morning and see what happens. But if anyone asks you the truth, you've got to tell them, see? I'll have no daughter of mine telling lies.'

Sally nodded demurely, but as Kate glanced at her she glimpsed a flash of triumph in her sister's eyes. She's got her own way again, she thought resignedly, and now I'll be expected to look after her in the Hard. And if she does get into trouble, it'll be my fault!

Just as if I didn't have enough to worry about.

Once supper was over, Kate started to get ready to go out. Sally followed her upstairs and sat on her bed, watching as Kate shook out her navy-blue skirt and took a pink blouse from her a drawer.

'Perhaps they'll let me come to dances, now I'm going to be working at Priddy's,' the younger girl observed. 'After all, if I'm old enough to do munitions . . .'

'Yes, but that's just it, isn't it. You're *not* old enough.'
Kate sat down on the end of her bed, in front of the
dressing-table. She leaned forward, peering into the
spotted mirror, and opened her tub of vanishing cream.
'And I don't know why you had to come out with it all
tonight, spoiling Pete's first evening at home.'

'I didn't spoil it. He got a second helping of shepherd's
pie and all the crusty bits, and no one even noticed.
Anyway, he doesn't care what I do; all he thinks about is
his music. Dad's going down the Marine recruiting office
with him next week, did you know that? He won't be
bothered about what I do now Pete's home again.'

'Sally! That's an awful thing to say. It's as if Dad
doesn't care about us.'

'No, it isn't. It's just that we're girls so it doesn't matter
what we do. We'll be getting married and having babies
and staying home to look after them. That's what Dad
thinks, anyway.'

'Not if the war doesn't stop,' Kate said sadly. 'There'll
be nobody to marry and we'll have to go on working as
long as it lasts. We might be too old to have babies by
then.'

'Like Mum, you mean. When do women get too old
to have babies, anyway?' Sally lay back on her bed and
stretched her arms. 'My friend Pam says they can have
them until they're fifty. I don't believe her. I don't know
anyone who's had a baby when they were fifty – that's
really old, isn't it?'

'Your friend Pam,' Kate said a little sternly, 'has too
much to say about babies. I'm not surprised Mum doesn't
like you going round with her. I think perhaps it's a good
job you are leaving Woolworths, if that's all you can find
to talk about.'

'Go on,' Sally said, rolling over onto her stomach and
reaching out to take the tub of vanishing cream. She

dipped her finger in and smeared some over her face. 'Don't tell me you never talk about that sort of thing at Priddy's. Anyway, where are you going tonight? Over to the Pier again?'

'No. We're going to Grange, there's a dance there tonight.' Kate fluffed powder over her face and retrieved the tub of cream. She took the cap off her lipstick and stretched her lips.

'Wish I could come too. I will, soon. They can't keep me in for ever.' Sally watched as her sister applied the lipstick. 'Dad goes mad if he sees me wearing make-up. When did he first let you, Kate?'

'When I was sixteen. I used it before that, though. I used to put it on at the corner of the street in the mornings and wipe it off again there in the evenings. I had to – they were calling me Death Warmed Up at work. He'll come round soon, Sal. You know you can always twist him round your little finger. He might rant and rave for a while, but he always gives in eventually.'

Sally shrugged. 'I don't care anyway. I do what I want to do, most of the time. Who's going to be at the dance tonight? Any of those Canadians you met at the Pier? What about that one who liked you – will he be there? What was his name?'

'Brad,' Kate said quietly. 'No, he won't be there. At least, I don't think so.' She picked up her hairbrush and stared into the mirror. Brad hadn't said definitely he wouldn't be coming, but she'd made it pretty plain that she didn't want to see him again. She could still remember the look on his face as he'd turned away. It hurt her to think of it, hurt her as much as it had hurt him. But I was right, she told herself fiercely, I was *right*. I had to do it – for his sake.

Sally was watching her face. She put out a hand and touched Kate's arm. In a low voice, she said, 'You ought to let him come, Katy. It's daft, when you both like each other. You do like him, don't you?'

'Yes,' Kate said softly, 'I do. I like him a lot. But that's just why . . . Oh!' She threw the brush down again and covered her face with both hands. 'Oh, I wish we'd never met each other! I wish I'd never gone to that wretched dance. I wish – I wish – I wish this horrible war was over, that's what I wish. I wish we could all go back to living a proper, ordinary life again and not have all this fighting and killing and bombing. I hate it – *all* of it – and I've had enough. I've had just about enough!'

Kate had seen Brad three times during the past week – once last Saturday, when they'd gone along the sea wall, then on Sunday, and finally on Wednesday when he'd taken her to the pictures at the Forum, in Stoke Road.

Each time, she'd sworn to herself that she'd tell him she didn't want to see him again. Each time it had been more difficult.

Brad had called round on Sunday afternoon. Hilda and Albert had come for dinner and were now settled in the front room where Albert would read the *Sunday Express* and Hilda would knit until they both fell asleep. Sally was upstairs experimenting with a new lipstick and Pete was stretched out on the floor reading *Hotspur* and playing tunes on his mouth-organ. George and Win had gone over to the allotment.

Kate had slipped out to join him and they'd walked out towards Stokes Bay, where Kate and her family had often gone to swim and picnic before the war. Now, there were big rolls of barbed wire all along the edge of the grassy common between the village of Alverstoke and the beach, and nobody knew what was going on there. Lorries and trucks had been trundling along the roads for months and it was clear that there was some kind of building work going on – Kate had heard rumours of huge concrete constructions on the beach, and there had been at least one accident when several men were killed – but nobody could imagine what it could be. It was best not to speculate, anyway. Walls had ears.

However, you could still walk out to the village with its stone church looking down Alver Lake towards Haslar, and you could wander in Foster Gardens with their round fishpond and the pergolas that would be covered in roses when summer came, or Anglesey Gardens with its smooth, level bowling green. You could walk along Green Lane, where the celandines were already opening like yellow stars and the great elm trees towered overhead. It was almost like being out in the country there, Kate said. And you could walk along Western Way, with the houses Kate dreamed of living in; each one different and set in its own gardens, and with proper bathrooms indoors.

'It's a funny little place, Gosport,' Brad remarked as they strolled along. 'Wherever you go, you come across water – all these creeks reaching up into the streets, and those old moats right in the middle of town. What were they for?'

'They're part of the old forts. They were built years ago, hundreds of years ago, in case the French invaded us. There are lots of them around here, all through Gosport and Portsmouth and up on the hill.' She waved a hand in the general direction of the northern reaches of the harbour, where Portsdown Hill rose like a great rampart in itself. 'A lot of them are still being used as Army barracks and things.'

'The *French*? You mean you English were afraid of being invaded by the French?'

'Well, they did it before,' Kate said with some dignity.

'In 1066.' She ignored his snort of laughter. 'We're not going to let them do *that* again.'

'But you're supposed to be on the same side.'

'We are now, yes – for what good that does us. It didn't take them long to give in when the Germans walked into Paris, did it? But we weren't when Napoleon was around.'

'I guess not.' They walked in silence for a few moments, then he said, 'Seems a bit odd to me, all the same, I guess it's because there are so many French in Canada. In a lot of places, they only speak French. Quebec – the next state to Ontario – is like that. You'd think you were in France.'

Kate found that equally hard to imagine. 'How big are the states?'

'Oh, pretty big. Bigger'n the whole of Great Britain, most of 'em. A lot of it's forest, or lakes, or prairie. You can go for hundreds of miles and never see a building or another human being. And a pal of mine lives on a road where, if you walked across to the forest on the other side – like crossing this street here – and just kept going, you wouldn't come out of the trees till you hit Hudson Bay. That's if the bears and the wolves didn't get you first,' he added.

'You'd have to go quite a way in before you met any of them though, wouldn't you?'

'Not at all. They come right down to the road – wolves in winter, bears in summer. Bears hibernate,' he added, seeing Kate's blank look. 'And then there's the cougars, of course.'

'Cougars?'

'Mountain lions. They can be pretty dangerous. And snakes, and – hey! I ought to be telling you all the good things about Canada, not scaring you. I don't want to put you off.' He gave her a comical look.

'Put me off?' Kate said, her heart thumping a little.

'Yeah. I want you to like the idea of going there.'

'Why – why should I go there? It's a long way. People like me don't go to places like Canada for a holiday.'

'Who said anything about holidays?' Brad asked with a sideways glance. Kate didn't answer and, after a moment, he said, 'We do have the big open spaces, though, more'n England. I guess that's why your towns seem so crowded. All those really tiny houses in rows, all jammed up against each other . . . What sort of a house do you live in, Kate?'

'Not one as nice as these,' Kate said, glancing at the large detached houses they were passing. 'Ours is what we call *semi*-detached – joined on to another house on one side but not the other. The ones in rows are called terraced, and lots of them have just two bedrooms upstairs and two rooms downstairs, with a little kitchen tacked on and no bathroom.'

'No bathroom?' He stared at her. 'How do people manage, then?'

Kate explained about the outside lavatory, sometimes at the bottom of the garden in older houses, and the tin bath brought in every Friday or Saturday night. He shook his head.

'I guess we've got poor folk too, back in Canada – and it's different in the outback, you don't expect modern comforts there, but I didn't expect to find them here, somehow. Not so many, anyway.'

'I don't think we're exactly poor,' Kate said, feeling affronted. 'It's just the way things are. We didn't start off with a brand new country and lots of space, we've had to make do with what we've had handed down to us. I dare say a lot more people would have had bathrooms by now if it hadn't been for the war.'

'Say, I didn't mean to be rude. Not that there's any shame in being poor. Not after the thirties – gee, I guess everyone had a taste of it back then.'

Kate said nothing. There were parts of Portsmouth, she knew, where children ran about with no shoes and ragged clothes, and scavenged for food amongst the market stalls of Charlotte Street. In Gosport, too, there were areas where the houses were ramshackle and tiny, with no more than a small backyard, and the people grey-faced and thin. But the war had changed a lot of that. Some of the streets no longer existed, having been almost wholly destroyed by bombs, and the people who had had no work during the 1930s were now either in the Services or working at places like Priddy's Hard. Even those who weren't engaged in war work had found other jobs, the women driving buses or milk floats or doing other work that was normally done by men. I suppose Mum would say it's an ill wind that blows no good, she thought, but it was a pity it took a war to make things better.

They came to the end of Ann's Hill Road, with the War Memorial Hospital on one side and the Wiltshire Lamb on the other. Kate pointed to a little row of cottages close to the pub. 'Those are the oldest houses in Gosport, so my mum says. They look like country cottages, don't they? She says she can remember when all this part was fields, so I suppose that's what they were.'

'Well, it's not too far to go to reach fields now,' he observed, glancing up Privett Road. Only half a mile or so further along was the gorse-covered area known as Browndown, where Kate and her brother and sister had often gone before the war to have picnics and pick blackberries. They'd gone home with huge baskets full and Win had made blackberry and apple pies, and pounds and pounds of jam. Now, it was War Department land, occupied by soldiers and surrounded by barbed wire and notices warning people not to go there. I wonder who'll get the blackberries this year, she thought, and what will have happened to Gosport by the time they're ripe? Somehow, she couldn't imagine soldiers making blackberry and apple jam.

'It's nicer at Rowner,' she said. 'We still go out there sometimes. There are lovely bluebell woods, and you can get primroses too. There's a little river – well, a stream really – and we used to fish for newts and sticklebacks and take them home in a jam jar. Dad used to make us take them back, though – he said it was cruel and they'd die if we kept them.' She laughed. 'We knew he'd say that but we did it all the same, because it meant we'd be able to go back next day and have another picnic!'

They had paused on the corner and she glanced at him. 'I ought to go now. I can catch a bus home from here, and you can get one down to the ferry.'

She was half-afraid, half-hoping that he would try to detain her, but he didn't. He just nodded and smiled, and then said, 'How about the movies one evening, then? I can get ashore most any night.'

Kate badly wanted to say yes. She could feel the attraction of him, drawing her like a magnet. But as soon as she acknowledged it, all her fears came rushing back, all her memories of boys she had known in the past who had gone away and never come back. Those other two Canadians who had gone to Dieppe. The twin brothers with whom she'd gone cycling and swimming. And Godfrey, the boy she'd loved and promised to marry.

'No!' she said, more sharply than she'd intended. 'No, I can't. I told you, Brad, I don't want to go out with anyone – not until after the war. I shouldn't have come out with you today. I knew I shouldn't.' She could feel tears sting her eyes, and she blinked angrily and turned away.

He caught at her wrist. 'Don't say that! Why the heck not? We've had a good time. We get on fine. Why shouldn't we go for a walk together? Why won't you come to the movies?' He turned her to face him and

138

looked down into her eyes, his face grave. 'Is there something you're not telling me? Is there another guy? Are you engaged – or married?' He looked down at her left hand.

'*No!* No, of course not – it's nothing like that.' She met his eyes briefly, then looked away. 'I can't explain. I just can't go out with you again.'

'I've told you, you can trust me,' he said quietly. 'I won't do anything you don't want.'

'It isn't that either,' she said wearily. 'I'm sorry, Brad, I just can't explain. It would sound stupid.'

'Try me,' he suggested, but she shook her head.

There was a moment's silence, then he said, still in the same level, quiet tone, 'Well, how about this for a pact, then? You come out with me once more – to the movies or a dance, or just another walk if you like – and I promise I won't ask you again. Unless you want me to. Well, I'll ask you once and if you say no, that'll be the end of it. I won't pester you, Kate. But just give me – give *us* – this chance, will you? That's not too much to ask, is it?' He paused. 'There's something you ought to know anyway. I'll be leaving Portsmouth pretty soon. We're being sent to an airfield somewhere. I'll be on flying duties then. If it's not too far away we might be able to come in on lorries, for a while anyway, so I'd still be able to see you sometimes – that's if you say yes.' He paused again. 'Will you say yes, Kate?'

She looked up into his eyes. They were almost black, with just a narrow rim of deep blue. Her heart gave a twinge. She wanted to tell him that it was too much, that the danger was not to her but to himself, but she couldn't speak the words. Instead, she nodded dumbly, and he grinned a wide, delighted grin.

'That's great! So what's it to be? The movies? Shall we say Wednesday, will that be OK for you? And maybe some supper afterwards – fish and chips, that's what you English like, isn't it?'

'All right,' she said in a whisper. They stood looking at each other for a moment, and then she turned and said in a husky voice, 'That's my bus coming. I'll have to go, Brad.'

'I'll see you on Wednesday,' he said. 'I'll wait for you at the gate to the Hard, OK?'

'OK,' she said and gave him a tremulous smile as she turned to climb aboard the bus. 'See you Wednesday, Brad.'

He gave her hand a final squeeze and let her go. Quickly, she scrambled aboard and ran up the stairs to the top deck. She found a seat and looked down.

Brad was standing at the bus stop. He stood there watching as the bus turned into Ann's Hill Road, and he stayed there as it trundled on its way.

Please let us just have these few days, Kate prayed. Please don't let them count. Please don't let the jinx work on him. I promise this is all it'll be. I *promise*.

The trouble with a jinx was that promises might not make any difference at all.

Kate had stuck to her vow. It hadn't been easy, and she almost lost her resolve as she sat in the Forum cinema beside Brad, watching the latest Bob Hope film. He didn't take her into the back row, he didn't put his arm around her, he just held her hand – but that was enough to set her blood racing. She could feel her heart quicken and a strange, melting feeling somewhere deep inside and although she'd been relieved when he led her to a middle row she began to wish they were at the back. I *want* him to put his arm round me, she thought longingly. I *want* him to kiss me and cuddle me. Oh, I *want* him . . .

And how will you feel when he goes away? a little voice asked. *How will you feel when you hear that he's been killed – like all those others? Like Godfrey?*

Just before the lights went up and the red velvet curtains drew across the screen, Brad turned to her. Kate opened her mouth to speak and he kissed her lips, so lightly that it could have been a butterfly's wing touching her. She gasped and only with an effort prevented herself from falling against him. And then he was drawing her to her feet, and she felt stunned and dizzy, swaying a little as she followed him along the row, thankful that he couldn't see.

'Fish and chips?' he asked when they were outside.

Kate hesitated. 'I – no, I'm sorry, Brad, I don't feel very hungry.'

He looked at her for a moment. 'Like to go for a drink, then? Is there a good pub here? I passed one or two on my way – the India Arms, d'you know that? Or the Isle of Wight Hoy, down by the ferry.'

She shook her head, thinking, If I don't tell him now I'll never do it. 'No thanks, Brad. Look, I'm sorry. I'd rather just go home, if you don't mind.'

He looked at her more closely. 'Or even if I do, huh?' he said quietly. 'So this is it then, is it, Kate? The brush-off. And I was hoping we were getting somewhere. I was hoping we were friends.'

'We are,' she said miserably. People were walking past them on their way home after the film. The street wasn't quite dark – there was half a moon, shedding a dim light, and she could see his face as she looked up, pale beneath his dark curly hair. 'I'm sorry, Brad.'

'Well,' he said after a pause, 'I can't say you didn't warn me. But it would help if you'd explain why.'

'It sounds so stupid.'

'Please,' he said. 'Please, Kate. It *would* help – to know just what it is you don't like about me.'

'Brad, there's nothing. It isn't you at all – it's me.' She shrugged helplessly. 'I *can't* see you again. I shouldn't

141

even have seen you now, or last Sunday, or even Saturday. It's because of what happens to the boys – men – I go out with. They – they get killed.' The words were blurted out and she stopped abruptly, biting her lips and staring up at him. 'There, I've said it. And it does sound stupid, doesn't it? But it's *true*.'

'I wouldn't say it sounds stupid,' he said after a small pause. 'I'd say it sounds crazy. Kate, you can't really believe that.'

'You see? I said you wouldn't believe me. Look, every boy I've been out with has gone off and got killed. The last one was my fiancé, Godfrey. He was on the beach at Dunkirk and he never came back. That ferry-boat I told you about – the *Ferry King* – the skipper saw him on the beach; he knew him, but he couldn't do anything to help him. *He saw him killed, Brad.*' Her voice shook and she rubbed her arm across her eyes. 'That's why I can't see you again. I can't let it happen to you too.'

'Oh, honey.' Regardless of the people swirling past them, he folded his arms around her and pulled her close. 'Oh, you poor kid. Carrying a burden like that. But listen, it doesn't make any sense. You can't really believe that it was your fault that those things happened. How could it be?'

Kate stood still. She knew she should push him away. The longer she let him hold her, the worse it would be for both of them. But I can't, she thought, not right away. I just want to feel him close like this, just for a few minutes. To feel the warmth and security and the *rightness* of being here in his arms . . .

'I don't know,' she whispered. 'I don't understand it either. But I've heard of it before. There *are* girls like me – I'm not the only one. I don't know why, I don't *want* it to be me, it's horrible – but until the war's over I just can't go out with anyone, not properly. It's not fair.' She stopped, then said more quietly, 'I shouldn't even have come out with you this week. I just hope – I hope it won't mean . . .'

'Of course it won't,' he said almost violently. 'It won't make a scrap of difference. Look, Kate, I've been in this war three years now and I'm not going to get killed at this stage. I'm too good a pilot, for one thing.' He grinned at her, then went on, 'The tide's turning, don't you know that? We're going to win, and the winning starts right here, in Gosport and Portsmouth and all along the south coast. And you're one of the people who are going to help win it, Kate, you and your pals out at Priddy's Hard. And there's to be no more talk of getting killed, see? Not me, not you, not anyone. We're going to *win*.'

She gazed up at him. The street was empty now, the cinema doors closed. A bus rattled past, its blinds drawn so that not even the dim blue lights inside would show, and then there was silence. She said in a small voice, 'But *some* people will still get killed. Even if – when – we win, there'll be men getting killed right up to the last minute.'

'Yeah, I guess that's right,' he admitted. 'But I don't plan to be one of them. And even if I am, it won't be your fault. Whatever we do, *it won't be your fault*. Understand me?'

'I understand you,' she whispered, 'but I still can't believe you. I wish I could, Brad – I really wish I could.' She was silent for a moment and then she said, very quietly, 'Take me home now, Brad. Please.'

For a moment he said nothing. Then he sighed and bent his head. His kiss jolted her heart. She heard herself give a tiny whimper and then pulled away. '*Please*, Brad.'

'Yeah,' he said, equally quietly. 'Sure.'

They walked from the Forum all the way to Elson. It was a long, slow walk through the dark streets and they held hands tightly all the way and talked softly together.

In that hour, Kate found herself telling him things she had never told even Maxine – things about her childhood, her family, her grief over Godfrey, her fear of the jinx she believed had settled over her. Brad, in turn, told her about himself and his own family – his mother and father, his two brothers, both also at war, his sister and her baby girl. She heard about his childhood on the farm, about trips he had made deep into the forest and on the lakes; the sailing, the canoeing, the skating and sledging in winter. 'The canal and lakes freeze over completely,' he said. 'You've never seen anything so beautiful, Kate. But you *will* see it, I know you will. And you'll love it just as I do. I know that too.'

They'd come at last to her door and he stood there with her. In the last five minutes or so, they'd fallen silent. Now, he took both her hands in his and brought them to his lips, looking down at her face. She lifted her eyes to his and felt her mouth quiver.

'I promised I wouldn't try to persuade you, Kate,' he said quietly, 'and I always keep my promises. But is it OK if I make another one?'

'What is it?'

Kissing each finger separately, he said, 'I, Brad Mackintosh,' she realised with a shock that this was the first time she'd heard his surname, 'hereby promise you, Kate Fisher, that I'll come back to see you the very first minute I can after this war finishes. And *then* I'll persuade you. By every star there is in heaven, I swear I'll tear the world apart to persuade you!'

Kate could not speak. She let him finish kissing her fingers and then, as he slid his arms around her, she moved into them and gave him her lips. They stayed together for a long minute and then broke apart.

'Go in,' he said huskily. 'Go indoors, Kate, or I won't be responsible for what I do next . . .'

Chapter Eleven

The dance was one of the regular ones held at Fort Grange, one of the old forts that were scattered all over Gosport. Grange was now an aerodrome and an empty hangar made a good dance hall, with bunting and streamers hung around the high walls. Back in 1940, when the Blitz was just reaching its height, one of the hangars had been bombed and set ablaze the very day after a dance, but that was almost forgotten now. With so many devastated buildings in ruins around the town, you couldn't spend your time worrying about the past.

Almost all the girls from Priddy's Hard were there. Kate had arranged to call for Maxine, but when she arrived at her friend's house she found Maxine's mother in tears, her father red with anger and Maxine herself white and tight-lipped.

'Um – shall I wait outside?' she asked, uncomfortably aware that she had walked into the middle of a row.

'No, come in, Kate.' Clarrie sniffed and pulled a hanky from the sleeve of her grey cardigan. It was sodden, as if she'd used it several times already. 'You can't stand out there in the cold.'

'I don't want to be in the way.'

'You're not. It's just a silly tiff, that's all. Families have them all the time, don't they?' She tried to smile, but the smile slipped and wobbled as if it wouldn't properly stick to her face. 'I dare say you have the odd spat round at number twelve, don't you?'

'Oh, we're always having them,' Kate said uneasily, trying to sound cheerful. 'It'll be even worse now our Pete's home. He and Sally always used to be at each other's throats and I don't suppose they'll be any better now.'

Maxine had gone upstairs when Kate came in. She clattered down again, her coat on and a defiant blaze of scarlet lipstick brightening her face. She stalked through the room without looking at either parent and said over her shoulder, 'Come on, Kate. There won't be anyone to dance with if we don't get there on time.'

Kate glanced at Maxine, waiting for her to say goodbye, but she was already opening the front door. She looked helplessly at Mr and Mrs Fowler. Clarrie tried another smile, but Bert was glowering at the fire and after a moment she said, 'Well, cheerio then,' and escaped into the street after Maxine.

'Gosh, whatever's been going on?' she asked, scurrying to catch up with her friend, who was marching along the narrow road as if setting out to war. 'You must have been having an awful row.'

'We always are having an awful row,' Maxine said grimly. 'And we always will, until I can get away.' She stopped and faced Kate. 'I tell you what, I wish I'd gone into the Wrens like I wanted to. I'd have been sent away then and never had to live with them again. Or I could have been in the ATS, or the WAAFs or even a nurse. Anything, it wouldn't have mattered. I wouldn't care what I had to do so long as I could get away. And what did I do? I signed on at Priddy's Hard so that I could stop at home with Mum because I thought she needed me. And now I'm bloody stuck!'

'But what's it all about? I always thought you got on OK with your mum and dad. What's happened?'

Maxine hesitated, and for a moment Kate thought she

was about to tell her. Then she shrugged and said, 'Oh, it's a long story. You don't want to hear it. Anyway, I didn't come out to moan, I want to enjoy myself. Here, d'you reckon your boyfriend'll be there tonight?'

'He's not my boyfriend.'

'Of course he is. You've seen him twice this week, haven't you? I bet he'll be there.'

'No, he won't,' Kate said shortly. 'At least, I hope not. I'm not seeing him again.'

Maxine raised her eyebrows. 'Not seeing him again? You never said anything about that!'

'I didn't want to talk about it.' Kate had barely slept since Wednesday night, when she'd finally said goodbye to Brad at the front door. She couldn't forget the sharpness of the pain she'd felt as she'd turned away from him and opened the front door, thanking heaven that she'd borrowed her mother's key that night and didn't have to ring the bell. She'd gone straight upstairs to bed, pulling the blankets over her head and ignoring her sister's questions, and it wasn't until Sally had fallen asleep that she allowed herself to cry.

'But you were getting on so well! And he looked a really nice bloke.' Maxine looked at her closely. 'You're not still worrying about that jinx business, are you?'

'What if I am? Look, I'm not the only one – I've heard of other girls like me whose boyfriends have all been killed. There *is* such a thing as a jinx, Maxie, and I've got it. I don't know why, but I have and I can't get rid of it. And I *can't* just forget it and go out with any boy who asks me, when I know he'll get killed. Especially when it's someone I really like,' she added in a low voice.

Maxine stared at her. 'Oh, Kate. That's awful. But I still don't see . . . look, men are getting killed all the time, thousands of them. There's a war on. It's just coincidence. You can't let it ruin your life.'

147

'It's not ruining my life. I just don't go out with anyone who might get killed. That's not ruining my life – not like putting the jinx on them is going to ruin theirs.'

Maxine sighed. 'Well, if you won't see sense . . . But at least enjoy the dance, Kate. You can dance with a boy without putting a jinx on him, can't you?'

'I hope so.' But she wasn't sure. The fear had become an obsession with her, and she was beginning to think she ought to stay at home and never come out at all. That way, nobody could get hurt.

'And if Brad comes, you'll dance with him?'

'He won't come,' Kate said, hoping fervently that this was true, even though she longed with all her heart to see him again. 'He won't come . . .'

Brad did not come to the dance. Kate found herself watching the door all evening, her heart leaping whenever it opened, and she didn't know if she was glad or sorry when the band played the last waltz and he still hadn't arrived. She danced it with a sailor from the Naval airfield and let him kiss her goodnight when he walked her to the gate. Then she joined the others to walk back together to Elson.

'You and Erwin are getting pretty matey,' Val said disapprovingly to Janice. 'And you're not wearing your ring. Does he know you're engaged?'

'Well, if he doesn't it won't be your fault,' Janice retorted. She hadn't been at all pleased by Val's continual pointed references to her fiancé. 'Anyway, it's none of your business. Keep your snout out of my affairs.'

'Well, I like that!' Val began indignantly, but Hazel intervened.

'Don't start bickering, you two. We've had a nice evening and Janice isn't doing anything wrong. We've got to have *some* fun.'

'And how d'you know what she was doing when she and Erwin nipped outside?' Val demanded. 'Go out with them, did you?'

'Well, if we were doing anything wrong, then we did it pretty quickly,' Janice said sharply. 'We were only out there ten minutes. And what about you anyway, Val Drayton? You were a good half-hour with that matelot with the sweaty hands. Maybe it was you that made them sweaty!'

'Now, you look here—'

'Oh, shut up, both of you.' Maxine was feeling dispirited and miserable. 'You're getting on my nerves. We came for a dance, that's all, not to criticise each other's behaviour. What does it matter if Janice goes around with other boys anyway? I dare say her Wally's making the most of his chances out in Egypt or wherever he is.'

'Maxie! That's an awful thing to say!'

'No, it's not. It's true. Look at all these Canadians and Americans – you can't tell me they're all single, but they all find themselves girls over here, don't they? *Some* of them must have wives and sweethearts at home but you wouldn't know it from the way they behave. Well, I bet our boys are the same. And so are a lot of the women. It's not just Janice.'

'I tell you, I haven't done anything wrong.' Janice sounded near to tears and Kate slipped her arm around her waist.

'Nobody's saying you have, Jan. It's just that we don't want you to get hurt.'

'Or hurt anyone else,' Val said waspishly, and Janice choked back a sob

Kate rounded on the tall girl. 'Leave her alone! Can't you see you're upsetting her? You're upsetting all of us – and you're not much better, Maxie, talking about our boys like that. Hazel's right, we've had a nice evening and it's being spoiled. Let it rest.'

Actually, she wasn't sure that they had had a nice evening. Janice and Erwin did seem to be getting too friendly, and Hazel herself, for all her staunch defence of her friend, had looked worried when they slipped outside. Val, whose lanky figure towered over some of the men, hadn't had many dances, which was probably why she was in a bad mood now, and Maxine had obviously not got over the row she'd had with her parents. Kate herself, torn between longing for Brad to appear and being terrified that he would, was now suffering an uncomfortable mixture of relief and bitter disappointment. The disappointment seemed to be uppermost.

'Let's just forget it,' she said again. 'We're tired out. We've all been working hard this week, there was that overtime we did today, and nobody knows what's going to happen next. It's getting us down.'

They walked the rest of the way in silence. The jollity of the dance had seemed forced tonight, as if everyone was on edge. As Kate had said, the pressure at Priddy's Hard was increasing; more and more armaments were being called for and more and more ships loading up with ammunition. The harbour itself seemed to be busier than ever, with ships steaming in and out all the time, and there were more soldiers about than had ever been seen during the whole of the war. There were rumours of a ban on travelling anywhere near the south coast, and while the word 'invasion' might not be on everyone's lips, it was certainly in their minds. The war seemed to be on the brink of a new phase.

Perhaps it really will be the last one, Kate thought as she turned her mother's key in the door and slipped inside. Perhaps Brad was right and it's all going to be over at last. Perhaps we really are winning.

And what would happen then? She remembered his

promise to come back for her. A promise she had never asked for, and wasn't even sure she wanted kept.

Maxine too was glad to have a key when she reached home that night. After the row before she'd gone out, she didn't fancy an interrogation when she came in and hoped her parents were both in bed. But when she came through to the living room, she found her father waiting up, and not even in his dressing-gown but still fully dressed as if expecting – or perhaps even intending – that there would be more trouble.

'So you've deigned to come home, my lady,' he began as soon as Maxine appeared.

Maxine dropped her key on the table and glowered at him. 'Don't start again. I've had a bellyful of it today. Anyway, I'm not late.'

'Not late? What time d'you call this, then?' He looked at the clock ticking on the mantelpiece. 'Gone eleven, and I know for a fact the dances at Grange stop at ten. So where've you been till now, eh?'

'Walking home, where d'you think? It's nearly two miles, you know that.'

'Two miles! I can walk two miles in half an hour.'

'Well, I can't. Not in these shoes anyway, and not after an evening's dancing *and* six days standing at a bench twelve hours a day filling shells. Anyway, what's the hurry? I thought you'd be in bed. You didn't have to stop up.'

'I wanted to see what time you'd come strolling home, my girl.' He glared at her from his armchair by the fire, which had obviously gone out an hour ago. 'I wanted to talk to you.'

Maxine heaved an exaggerated sigh. 'Well, now you have, so if you don't mind I'll go to bed—'

Bert Fowler thumped his fist on the arm of his chair.

'Oh no, you don't! You'll stop down here, in this room and listen to what I've got to say, and we'll have less of your cheek, if you don't mind. It's time we had this out.'

'Oh, you think so, do you?' Maxine's temper flared. 'I thought we'd already done that. Don't tell me there's more! If there is, I don't want to hear it. It's bad enough knowing what I know now. For God's sake, don't make it even worse.'

'There's no call for blasphemy,' he said. 'Your mother's brought you up to know better than that.'

'My mother!' Maxine sneered. 'As if *she* was fit to sit in judgement. She's nothing but a dirty slut!'

'*That's enough!*' Bert leaped to his feet and swung his hand at Maxine's head. She cried out and ducked, but he caught her a glancing blow on the temple and she staggered and fell against the table. One of the chairs toppled over and a plate and cup and saucer, placed there by her mother for Maxine to make herself a snack, fell to the floor with a crash. Snowy, the kitten, who had been curled up asleep on the chair, tumbled off in a blur of white fur and scurried under the other armchair.

'Now look what you've done!' Bert Fowler stood over her as she tried to pull herself up. Maxine threw him a furious look and opened her mouth to shout back, but at that moment they both heard the sound of footsteps hurrying down the stairs. Bert breathed heavily through his nose and stepped back. 'Now you've woken your mother, and she was upset enough already.'

Clarrie appeared at the door, wrapped in the old grey coat she used as a dressing-gown, her hair in paper curlers. She blinked at them both and Maxine saw that her eyes were red and swollen from weeping. She must have been crying almost all evening. She felt a pang of guilt, followed swiftly by resentment. Why should *she* feel guilty?

'Whatever's happening now? What are you doing?' She looked at Bert. 'You haven't hit her? You promised you wouldn't.'

'I said I'd do my best not to,' he growled. 'But if you'd heard what she said . . .'

'What? What did she say?' Clarrie looked from one to the other, but neither would answer. Maxine turned away.

'Never mind what she said,' Bert muttered. 'It don't matter.' He bent and began to pick up the broken crockery. 'Look at that. That's a good cup and saucer smashed to bits, a cup and saucer we've had ever since we got married. That was a wedding present, that was, from my Auntie Alice.' He shook his head. 'You go back to bed, Clarrie, love, I'll see everything's put right.'

'How can I go back to bed, wondering what you'll be doing down here, the pair of you? Let me put things straight, it won't take a minute.' She looked at Maxine. 'You go upstairs, love.'

'I haven't had any supper—' Maxine began, setting off a fresh roar of rage from her father.

'Supper! After all that's happened, all you've been saying about your mother, you're worrying about *supper*!' He stood up and flung out a hand. Clarrie screamed and Maxine ducked again but this time he was only indicating the smashed crockery. 'Don't you think you've done enough damage?'

'That wasn't my fault!' Maxine yelled at him. 'If you hadn't hit me—'

'Stop it!' Clarrie screamed. 'Stop it, stop it, stop it!' She covered her ears with her hands and glared at them both, tears springing to her eyes. 'I can't bear it any more, all this arguing and nastiness. I can't *bear* it! We used to be such a happy family. I thought we always would be. I don't know why it all had to go wrong. I don't know why it's got to be like this.' She sank into her armchair and began to cry, her thin shoulders shaking and heaving with sobs. Maxine and her father looked at her and then at each other. Maxine saw the blame appear on her father's face, and spoke quickly and angrily.

'You don't know?' she said, biting the words out. 'You really don't know? Well, you ought to. You ought to know how I'd feel – finding out that I was a *bastard*.' She raised her voice over her mother's cry of distress. 'Well, I am, aren't I? A *bastard*. Illegitimate, Born the wrong side of the blanket. And not even *his* baby.' She jerked her head at Bert Fowler, who stood breathing heavily, his hands clenched into enormous fists at his sides. ' "Father unknown", that's what it says on my birth certificate. *Father unknown*. He's not my father at all. He's Matthew's father, but not mine. You've been telling me lies all these years, lies about him and yourself and me. And you don't even know who my father was, do you? *Do you?*' she screamed. '*You don't even know who he was!*'

Clarrie was crying too much to reply. Bert looked down at her and moved across the room to lay his hands on her shoulders. He bent and spoke to her quietly.

'Come on, Clarrie, love. Don't cry like that, you'll make yourself ill. Come on, now. She's not worth it. She's just not worth it.'

Clarrie lifted her face. It was red and swollen, her eyes no more than slits between the puffy eyelids. She clutched at her husband's body and laid her face against him.

'She *is* worth it,' she wept. 'She's my daughter, isn't she? She *is* worth it, Bert.'

'But I'm my father's daughter too,' Maxine said cruelly. 'So maybe I take after him.' She looked at her mother with disgust and then added in a bitter voice, 'Only you wouldn't know, would you – because you don't know who he is. That's why I called you what I did when *he* hit me. I called you a slut. And that's just what you are.'

She turned and walked out of the room. Holding herself very taut and rigid, she walked up the stairs and into her bedroom, where she closed the door with exaggerated care. She stood for a moment, very still, and then gradually let her muscles relax.

It was only then that she fell on to her bed and began her own uncontrollable weeping.

Chapter Twelve

Sally started work at Priddy's Hard the following Monday morning. At seven o'clock, just as the sun was rising behind the tower of Portsmouth Cathedral, she was at the gate with Kate, being inspected by the duty policeman.

'New girl?' he said. 'You'll need to see the matron first. Medical check.'

'Why? There's nothing wrong with me,' Sally began indignantly, but Kate dug her in the ribs.

'Don't start answering back. It won't do you any good here. Matron's office is over there – she's very nice, we always go to her if we don't feel too good. She only wants to check that you're up to doing the work.'

'Well, of course I am.'

'Yes, but they don't know that until Matron's said so. Go on, and stop arguing.' Kate watched her sister go, and sighed. Sally's rebellious spirit had got her into trouble all through school and frequently at Woolworths, and now it looked as though it would get her into trouble at Priddy's Hard. She'll soon find out how strict the rules are here, Kate thought. You just can't take any chances when there are explosives about.

'Hello, Kate. Is your Sally working here now?'

Kate turned and found Ned standing close behind her. He was carrying the broom he used to sweep the magazine floors. The tiniest speck of gunpowder was swept up immediately and the floors kept immaculately clean so that dust couldn't gather and create a fire hazard. Soon, Ned would be working on the grassy hillocks between the buildings, keeping them closely mown, again to reduce the risk of fire. Nobody had ever forgotten the explosions of 1883 and 1902, and such an accident could be even worse now, with so many more munitions on the site. Every rule was designed to prevent such tragedies.

'I saw your Sally going over to the office,' Ned said, repeating his question. 'Is she going to work here now?'

'It seems like it.' Kate hoped he wouldn't say anything about Sally's age. The family had discussed it all weekend and come to the conclusion that it was better to let sleeping dogs lie. Sally had been accepted and she would be sixteen in a few months anyway. If she lost this place at Priddy's Hard she would have to look for another job, for it was unlikely they'd take her back at Woolworths, and she had threatened to go and work in Flux's Laundry if she had to. Win had put her foot down at that. Some of the women there were the roughest in Gosport and she wasn't having any daughter of hers mixing with them.

'That's nice,' Ned said with satisfaction. 'I like Sally.' He wandered off, swinging his broom, and Kate hurried to join the rest of the girls. They were waiting for her by the footbridge which crossed the road into the furze area.

'Come on,' Janice urged her. 'The whistle's going any minute, we'll be late clocking on.'

'The trouble with our Sally,' Kate said breathlessly, 'is that she *will* argue the point. She'll have to change her ways if she's going to work here.'

'The chargehands and foremen will soon knock her into shape – *you* don't have to worry about it.' Val pushed her along the narrow walkway above the paths running between the various huts and ramparts. One of the little trains was passing beneath them, towing a long line of small trucks filled with shells and explosives, and the woman driving it gave them a cheery wave. The narrow-gauge railway ran from Bedenham and Frater, the stores and mine depots a little further round the harbour shore, and all over the yards, transporting explosives from magazines to the Camber Dock where they would be loaded on to barges and taken across the harbour. At first, they'd been driven by men but, as more and more men were called up into the Services, women had taken over that job as well as many others. Now, there were few men under forty working at the Hard.

The girls clocked on and hurried through to the shifting room to change into their working clothes. Kate glanced at Maxine, who was hanging her coat on the hook beside her.

'You're quiet this morning. Everything OK?'

Maxine shrugged. 'As OK as it ever is, I suppose.'

'Hey, that doesn't sound like you.' Kate looked at her more closely. She looked paler than usual and there were dark circles under her eyes. 'You look really rough. Not getting a cold, are you?'

'Don't think so. Don't go on at me, Kate.' Maxine sounded unusually brusque and Kate looked at her in surprise, but before she could say any more the bell was ringing and they hurriedly stripped off the rest of their clothes, down to their underwear, and stepped over the red line. There would be no more chance of private conversation until lunchtime.

Kate sighed. We all seem to have problems, she thought. There's Sally starting work here when she's underage, Elsie looking miserable because she's still grieving over Graham, Janice messing about with a Canadian soldier when she's engaged to one of ours, and now Maxine's looking like death warmed up and obviously having some awful trouble at home that she won't even talk about.

As for me, her thoughts continued, I've done what I

swore I wouldn't do again. I've gone and fallen for a chap who'll probably be in France before the month's out, and if he gets killed I know I'll blame myself, whatever anybody else says . . .

Sally stood rather sullenly in Matron's office, stripped down to almost nothing and enduring a close inspection of her body. 'I don't know what you're looking for. I haven't got anything wrong with me.'

'No, I don't think you have,' Matron said cheerfully. She was a small, round woman built like a cottage loaf, with a rosy, smiling face. 'But I have to make sure, just the same. Some of the girls who come in here do have something wrong, you see, and it gives us a chance to put it right.'

'What sort of things?' Sally asked, but Matron shook her head.

'All sorts of things, and most of them you needn't worry about – as long as you behave yourself. And I dare say you've been brought up to be a good girl, haven't you?'

Sally nodded, mystified. Matron completed her examination and nodded with satisfaction. 'That's fine. You can get dressed again now. I'll just sign this form to say that you're A1, and you can pop across to the photographer's studio.'

'The photographer?' Sally stared at her. 'Am I going to have my picture taken?'

'You are indeed. And there's no need to worry about your hair – it won't be going into a fashion magazine!' Matron signed the form with a flourish and then handed her another sheet of paper. 'Take that with you, she'll need to see it.'

'She? Is the photographer a woman?'

'Most of us are, on Priddy's Hard,' Matron said drily.

'The men have gone away to fight the war, in case you hadn't noticed. Now off you go. The sooner you get through all the formalities the sooner you can start work.'

Sally hurried off in the direction she had indicated and found herself at the door of the studio. She had been inside a photographic studio before, when her father had taken the whole family down to Lawrence's in Elmhurst Road to have their portrait taken. He and Win had wanted a record of them all together before they were separated by the war and the portrait stood on the sideboard at home now, with George and Win sitting on a settee in front of velvet curtains and the family clustered around them – Ian in his new uniform, straight and proud at the back, the two girls on either side and Barney, just a few weeks old, in his long white christening robe on his mother's knee.

The studio at Priddy's Hard wasn't like that at all. There was no settee, no velvet curtains and no smart photographer. Instead, there was a hatchet-faced woman in overalls who motioned her brusquely inside and told her to stand in front of what looked very like a blackout curtain. She closed the door and Sally realised that there were blackout curtains on all the windows, undrawn despite the fact that it was now daylight outside. Two large spotlights shone on her face, almost dazzling her.

Sally stood where she had been told and smiled self-consciously. The woman, who had ducked under the big black cloth covering the camera, emerged and glowered at her. 'You don't have to grin like that! This isn't a holiday snap.'

'I'm sorry,' Sally said. 'I thought you always had to smile for photographs.'

'Not for this one. This is for when you're dead.' The photographer ducked underneath again. 'That's better. You look scared stiff now – much more the way you'll be.'

'Dead?' Sally squeaked. 'What do you mean? I'm not going to get killed, am I?'

'Well, we hope not. You won't be much good to us here if you are. Hold still, now. Don't blink.' There was a long moment of silence while Sally tried hard not to blink, and then there was a click. 'All right. That should do.' She emerged again. 'You can stop looking like a waxwork dummy, unless that's how you normally look.'

'Why d'you want a photo of me looking dead?'

'In case you do get killed, of course. There's a war on, or hadn't you noticed? If Priddy's gets bombed, there'll be any amount of dead bodies lying about. Of course, most of them'll be in bits and won't be recognisable, but those that are will have to be identified. So we take photos of everyone here. And you won't die laughing, I can tell you that.' The woman was removing the plate from the camera as she spoke, and inspecting it critically. 'I've seen dead bodies – had to take pictures of 'em, too – and I know.'

She spoke in a brisk, matter-of-fact tone as if photographing dead bodies was all in a day's work. Probably it was, Sally thought, leaving the studio to make for her next port of call. No wonder she looked as if her face had been hacked out of a lump of stone. Anyone would, if they had to do that.

Sally's next stop was the clothing store. Here, she was issued with her new working uniform – a white jacket made of flannel which she just knew was going to drive her mad with itching; navy serge trousers; a turban to keep her hair out of sight, and black shoes. She looked at these in surprise.

'What funny shoes. Have I got to wear them?'

'You've got to wear all of it.' The storewoman pushed the bundle into her arms. 'It's all made so there's no danger from sparks, see. Only takes a little one to set off an explosion. See, the shoes haven't got no nails in them, it's all little wooden pegs, like matchsticks. We don't take no chances round here.'

Sally nodded. Kate had never mentioned any of this – probably she was so used to it she just assumed everyone knew. Or maybe it was because people working in munitions, like those in the Services, just never did talk about their work. Everything was secret these days, and it was best to say nothing, just in case you let out something you shouldn't.

'You'll be working in the Laboratory,' Mr Milner told her later, leading her along the road between the hummocks of grass. The narrow railway ran along the middle and they kept to one side as the little engines passed, towing their rows of trucks. 'You'll be filling shells with gunpowder. I hope you're not nervous?'

Sally shook her head. She thought it sounded exciting, even though Kate had warned her that working with some of the explosives could turn your skin yellow and that the girls who did that were called Canaries. She followed Mr Milner to the building where she was to work, where she was handed over to the woman chargehand. 'This is Mrs Sheppard. She'll look after you from now on.'

Mrs Sheppard was a burly woman of about forty, with frizzy brown hair clustered round her face and the sallow skin of someone who had worked with cordite. She gave Sally a searching look.

'So you're the girl what used to work in Woolworths, aren't you? I've seen you on the hardware counter. Well, you'll find it a bit different here. No standing about gossiping – there's vital war work to do, and we don't allow slackers.'

'I'm not a slacker,' Sally began indignantly, but the chargehand cut across her.

'And I don't take no answering back, neither, so don't think you can cheek me just because I'm a woman.' She folded her arms over her sturdy bosom and glowered. Sally met her eyes and felt a twinge of dislike.

'I wasn't going to cheek you.'

'Just as well. But you're still a bit too quick to answer, so watch your tongue. Now come on, we haven't got all day. I'm late getting started as it is, what with having to come out and fetch you.' She turned and led Sally into a long shed. 'This is the shifting room. It's where we changes our clothes. You gets a hook and a locker – this is yours here, see? Got your name on it already. Take off all your clothes, down to your vest and knickers.'

'But I've already had an examination—'

'I told you, no cheek and no argufying. This isn't for an examination, it's for work.' She stared at Sally. 'Did Mr Milner say your name was Fisher? Ain't you got a sister here?'

'Yes, Kate Fisher.' Sally was beginning to unbutton her coat.

'Well, didn't she tell you nothing about it? Didn't she even tell you about magazine clothes? Or maybe you thought they were some posh fashion out of *Woman's Own*,' she suggested with heavy sarcasm.

'Yes, she did tell me, as a matter of fact. I just forgot – there's been so much to do this morning.' Sally wasn't far from tears and her voice rose a little. Mrs Sheppard scowled at her again.

'And there's no call to raise your voice to me, young lady. Come on, get a move on – we're not playing a game of Statues. You'll have to be quicker than this of a morning. Just imagine it's some nice Yankee soldier you're getting undressed for.' She ignored Sally's fiery blush and indicated the line painted on the floor. 'Now step over this red line and then put on your working clothes, and don't dare cross the line again until you undress ready to go home. That's the most important thing you'll learn here – never to put a foot off the clean areas. You'll see platforms in the Laboratory, all linked together, and that bridge you come over, that's all clean, and you mustn't ever go off that while you're in your uniform. And don't ever go into a clean area in your ordinary things. It's a serious offence. You understand that?'

Sally nodded. Kate had told her how careful they were over keeping the work areas clean. The tiniest speck of dust could be ignited by gunpowder and set off an explosion. So could the friction of certain kinds of cloth rubbing together. That was why you had to wear the special uniform.

'Got any curlers in your hair?' the chargehand demanded. 'Any rings, bracelets, necklaces, brooches? Put them in this bag, see. They'll be safe enough till you come out again. Money too, you won't be needing that while you're working.'

Sally did as she was told. She didn't really believe it could be that dangerous, but there was no point in arguing, not on her first day. She stepped across the barrier to put on the uniform. Mrs Sheppard did the same and then led her through to the clean area where Sally was to spend her days from now on.

Sally stared at it in dismay. It was a long, brick-lined tunnel, rather like the Dive café in the High Street, but nobody was sitting down drinking coffee, and nobody was smoking cigarettes. In fact, nobody was sitting down at all. The women and girls, all looking alike in their overalls and caps, were standing in long rows on either side of the benches that stretched from one end of the tunnel to the other. They each had a shell case in front of them – to Sally's eye, a bomb – and they were weighing out gunpowder and pouring it into the empty cases.

Sally took her place between two older women. She knew one of them slightly – it was Elsie Philpotts, who

164

had had one of the kittens Kate had rescued – and she felt better when Elsie gave her a quick grin of welcome. She listened carefully as Elsie explained what she had to do, and then joined in with the work, slowly at first but with increasing confidence, until Elsie laughed and told her not to be in such a hurry.

'We don't rush too much here. Could be dangerous, see. Better a bit late in this world than a bit early in the next, eh?'

'It's different here from what I expected,' Sally said. 'It seems funny, not having customers come in.'

'Oh, we has customers all right,' Elsie said darkly, 'only they don't exactly want to buy the goods. They get them all the same, though.' She tamped the gunpowder down into the shell. 'That's one for you, Ribbentrop. The next one'll have Goebbels's name on it. And every third bomb goes straight to Hitler, for his little collection. One of 'em's got to hit the mark, sometime!'

'That's right, Elsie,' said the woman on the other side of Sally. She had thick black eyebrows and a mole on her cheek. 'You give 'em their orders. Pity we can't just send 'em straight off on target, blast the lot of 'em to bits. Save killing all those poor perishers who don't have nothing to do with it.'

'Never mind about them,' joined in another girl on the opposite side of the bench. Her voice was rough and husky, as if she smoked a lot when she wasn't at work. 'They're Germans, aren't they? My dad says the only good German's a dead German. The more we kill, the better. It's our boys you want to think about saving.'

'Well, it'd save them too, wouldn't it?' the woman with the mole argued. 'I don't know why they don't just bomb wherever it is Hitler and them others are skulking – some castle or other, I dare say – and then we could just march in and take over. The soldiers wouldn't lift a finger to stop us, not if he was out of the way.'

'They would. They'd fight to the death.'

'Oh yeah? Like they did in Russia? I tell you, they don't want to be in this war no more'n we do. Rather be at home with the missus and kids, same as our blokes.'

The argument was becoming heated and Mrs Sheppard looked down the row and bellowed at them to be quiet. The husky-voiced girl scowled and stopped what she was doing for a moment. She felt in the little cloth bag hung round her neck and pulled out something that seemed to be pinched between her fingers. As Sally watched, she sprinkled some fine black powder on the back of her hand and bent her head to sniff it.

'Surely that's not gunpowder?' Sally whispered to Elsie. 'Why's she sniffing it like that? Is it to see if it's gone off?'

Elsie roared with laughter and everyone looked round. ''Course it's not gunpowder! It's snuff – ain't you never seen anyone take snuff before? All the rage in here, it is, on account of us not being allowed to smoke.' She indicated a brown stain on the front of the girl's overall. 'That's the fall-out, see. And you wait till you hear the row in the washroom later on when everyone unpacks their trunks.'

'Unpacks their trunks?' Sally repeated, bewildered, and Elsie chortled again.

'Cleans their noses, out, girl! They does it by breathing water up their noses, see, and then blowing it out – you'd think it was a school of bloody whales. Never been able to take to it meself, I'd rather hang on and have a fag on the way home, but those that gets a liking for it says it beats ciggies any day. You can get all sorts of different flavours, too – menthol, that's supposed to be good for colds, and even flower scents. Maggie over there uses Wallflower.'

'Well, I think it's disgusting,' Sally said, making up her mind not to look at the girl with the brown stain on her overalls again. 'It makes me feel sick to think of it. D'you mean to say a lot of people here do that?'

Elsie nodded. 'Old Mr Harvey, in the tobacconist's shop, he says there's more snuff sold in Gosport than anywhere else in the country. It's because of the armaments, see. There's always a good trade where there's a depot because of not being able to smoke and, this being the biggest one, it stands to reason.'

They worked on until lunchtime and then made their way out through the shifting room and back to the 'dirty' area. Taking sandwiches from their lockers, they wandered out into the early April sunshine and down to the shore. Sally, feeling a bit alone as she followed the rest, looked round in relief as she heard her sister's voice coming up behind her.

'How've you got on?' Kate asked, falling into step. 'Better than Woolworths, is it?'

Sally grinned ruefully. 'I hope it will be when I get my pay-packet! It seems so queer, working in a tunnel and not having customers coming and going. I never thought I'd miss the customers, but I do. And I don't like all the girls I work with. The one who works opposite me takes snuff!'

Kate laughed. 'A lot do. You'll just have to get used to it.'

At least I feel as if I'm doing something for the war.' They found a place to sit, overlooking the long inlet of Forton Lake. The tide was in and the water sparkled blue in the sunlight. On the far side they could see the buildings of Ratsey & Lapthorn, the sailmakers, and Camper & Nicholson, who built yachts. They were both engaged on war work now, but there were still plenty of yachts and dinghies moored in the creek. Some of them had been to Dunkirk.

'Mrs Sheppard says we've got to work overtime this week,' Sally said, unwrapping the greaseproof paper bag containing her sandwiches. 'I don't like her, and I don't think she likes me. You should have seen the way she glared at me just because I didn't work fast enough to start with.'

'Well, don't play her up,' Kate advised. 'Nobody likes her much but we have to put up with her. She could get you the sack, you know.'

'I do know. And I wanted to go shopping on Saturday. Now I won't be able to.'

'We'll probably finish a bit early. You'll be able to pop in and see the girls in Woolworths just before they shut. You ought to be used to working on Saturdays, anyway.'

'I am, but I'm not used to starting at seven in the morning and working till seven at night before we even start the overtime!' Sally moved her shoulders uncomfortably. 'My back's aching already, and I'm sure the smell's going to give me an awful headache. Honestly, Kate, you could have warned me.'

'I did. You didn't take any notice. You never do. Sorry, Sally, but you did this off your own bat and it's no good moaning about it now.' Kate lay back on the grass and closed her eyes. She wondered what Brad was doing now. If she walked round to the Camber Dock or Shell Pier, she would be able to look across the harbour and see the ship that had brought him from Canada. He would be at the airfield now, somewhere miles away. She sighed. He'd told her again that they might still be able to come into Portsmouth for the evening on lorries, but she had shaken her head and refused to agree to meet him again.

She still didn't know if she had done the right thing.

Chapter Thirteen

On 1 April, the coastline from the Wash right round to Land's End was closed. It wasn't only the coastline either – the ban extended inland for ten miles. If you lived in the ten-mile strip you couldn't go outside it and if you lived outside it you couldn't come in – unless you had a permit. You had to carry your identity card all the time, and the police could stop you and ask for it just because they felt like it. If you didn't have it, you could be sent to prison.

'Even babies?' Sally asked. She had lost hers twice already and Win had threatened to sew it on to her. 'Even kiddies like our Barney?'

'Even tiny newborn babies,' Win said firmly. 'It's serious, Sally. You've got to have it with you, especially when you're working at a place like Priddy's Hard.'

Sally made a face. The glamour of working with armaments and being part of the war effort had very quickly worn off when she discovered just how hard and tedious the work could be. For the first week she had had a permanent headache, she spent hours looking in the mirror for signs of yellowness, and she was sure she was already developing varicose veins in her legs from standing for so long. But there was nothing to be done about it. She'd signed on and now she'd have to stay there for the duration of the war. 'Serves her right, too,' her father said unsympathetically. 'She's made her bed and now she'll have to lie in it.'

'I wouldn't mind if I *could* lie in once in a while,' Sally said. 'Working at Woolworths and not having to get in till nine o'clock seems like luxury now.'

'Well, you knew you'd have to be in by seven,' Kate said. It had become her thankless task to haul Sally out of bed at six every morning. 'You can't say it's come as a surprise.'

Pete too had his concerns about the coastline ban. 'What about Pompey? How will they be able to play their matches if other teams can't come in? It'll mess everything up.'

'It's all right,' Kate said. 'They're classed as "vital to the war effort". So are entertainers and dance bands and people like that. You'll still be able to go and watch the matches.'

Pete nodded, mollified. He had been to the Marine recruitment office and been told that no more boy musicians were being taken on at the moment. He'd have to wait. He was still below call-up age and wasn't at risk of being conscripted, so George found him a job as errand boy at Lipton's. Sweeping floors, delivering groceries and helping in the stockroom wasn't what Pete had had in mind when he came home, but he liked the bike he'd been given, with its huge basket on the front, and was soon racing around Gosport whistling all the latest tunes, just like all the other errand boys.

'Something big's going to happen,' Win said as they listened to the news at nine o'clock that evening. 'It must be the Invasion.' She met her husband's eye. 'Well, we all know it, everyone knows it, I can't see why we shouldn't say so.'

'So long as it's just between ourselves,' he agreed, glancing at the walls of the room as if expecting them to sprout ears at any moment. 'But not outside, remember,' he ordered, fixing his children with a forbidding stare.

'You don't know who might be listening, especially with all these foreign Servicemen around.'

There had certainly been plenty of foreign uniforms in the streets during the past few weeks. As well as the Americans and Canadians, there were Poles, Czechoslovakians, French, Norwegians, Dutch, Greeks, South Africans, New Zealanders, Australians and Belgians. Most had arrived by ship, many of them recalled from North Africa, Sicily and Italy, but almost as soon as they appeared in Portsmouth and Gosport they vanished again. Some had come in long troop trains, getting off at tiny stations out in the countryside. Gladys Shaw told Elsie that they were all in huge camps or billets somewhere over the Hill, or in the New Forest, or even further west in Devon and Cornwall. The next time she came, she didn't say anything about them and Elsie guessed she'd been told not to talk about it any more.

Elsie had other things on her mind as well. Jackie Prentice had been round several times and they'd talked for a long time about Jackie's situation without coming to any real conclusion. The girl had seen the doctor, who confirmed that she was pregnant – Elsie suspected that until then she'd been hoping against all hope that it might be a mistake – and thought the baby was due in July. He said she might have missed a period the first month as she'd often done before, and conceived after that. He also said that Jackie might have some problems with the birth because she was so small, and she must see the midwife as soon as possible.

'But what about your dad? Did he say he'd break the news himself?'

Jackie nodded. 'I asked him not to do it just yet, though. Dad hasn't noticed anything – he said the other day I was getting a bit fat and ought to stop eating sweets, but that's all. And he's really not well; I don't want to upset him.'

'You're going to have to do it sometime,' Elsie said, thinking that Herbert Prentice was making a hobby of not being well. 'Look, would you like me to go round and see him?'

Jackie gazed at her. '*Would* you? Oh, Mrs Philpotts, he's always thought a lot of you.' This was a surprise to Elsie, who had never done much more than nod hello to Mr Prentice when she ran into him in the street, although she'd been quite friendly with Jackie's mother. 'I'm sure it would be better coming from you than the doctor. I mean, he was ever so nice to me but it's not like a woman doing it, is it? I'd be ever so grateful, I would, really.'

'All right then,' Elsie said, already half-regretting her offer. 'When shall I do it? Next week sometime?'

'Oh, not yet!' Jackie said immediately, and Elsie knew she was still dreading it. 'I mean, let's wait till after Easter, shall we? I don't want to spoil Easter for him.'

'All right. But you're getting bigger all the time, Jackie, he's bound to notice soon. And even if he doesn't, someone else will tell him. There's always some old gossip with sharp eyes and a sharper tongue looking out for girls like you.'

'Mrs Suggs from number six gave me a funny look yesterday,' Jackie admitted. 'I've been wearing Mum's old loose coat and she stopped me the other day and asked me if I wasn't feeling a bit warm. She was doing her best to see my stomach, I know.'

'Then it's high time something was decided,' Elsie said firmly. 'If you don't want people to know, you've got to go away – and that means your dad has got to know about it. You can't go off to a mother and baby home without telling him!'

'But I don't know if that's what I want to do.'

'Well, what else can you do?' Elsie demanded, beginning to lose patience. 'Honestly, Jackie, you don't have all that much choice, do you? You either ask your dad to let you stop at home, so that everyone knows and nobody will speak to you in the street – nobody except me, I mean, and a few others who aren't so mean-minded – or you go to a home and have it there, and if you're going to do that you ought to go soon or everyone will know anyway. And whichever you decide to do, *you've got to tell your dad*. There's no getting round that.'

Jackie gazed at her. There was obviously something else on her mind, and Elsie waited. As the moments passed, she began to suspect what Jackie was going to ask, and she felt her heart lurch with dismay.

'Well, I wondered,' Jackie said at last, hesitantly, and Elsie knew that she was right, 'I wondered if – perhaps – well, if I could come here. To you.'

'To – me?' Elsie said, for once rendered almost speechless. 'You mean, come *here*? Have your baby *here*?'

'Well, if I could. I wouldn't be any trouble . . .'

'No *trouble*?' Elsie repeated with a squawk. 'You want to come here and have your baby and you say you'd be no *trouble*? How d'you think we'd be able to keep it secret, eh? And what are you going to tell your dad? Just say "Sorry, Dad, can't come to see you for a couple of months because I'm going to live with Elsie Philpotts"? Don't you think he's going to want to know why? And who's going to look after him while you're away?' She gazed helplessly at the girl. 'Look, it's not that I don't want to help you, you know that, but it's a daft idea. I'm sorry, but it *is*.'

'I didn't mean that. Not for all that time. Just to – to *have* the baby. So that I don't have to go into a home. I can't have it at home, can I, not with Dad the way he is. He can't stand any disturbance. If I could just come here to have it and then go home again, that's all. Please, Mrs Philpotts.'

Elsie scratched her head. 'But what are you going to do

then? You can't get a baby adopted until it's six weeks old. I'm sure I've heard that.'

'I don't want to get it adopted,' Jackie said in a small voice. 'I want to keep it.'

There was a long silence. Elsie didn't know what to say. She took off the tea cosy and felt the pot. 'This is stewed. I'll have to make some more.' She filled the kettle, then emptied the pot and measured out two teaspoonsful of tea. 'Bugger Lord Woolton,' she muttered under her breath and added another heaped spoonful. Then she fished about in the back of the cupboard and brought out a small tin of biscuits she had been saving for Easter.

'Here you are,' she said, carrying it all in on a battered tin tray that Graham had once used for tobogganing down Portsdown Hill. 'Drink that. I've put sugar in, it's good for you.'

'You shouldn't be giving me your sugar ration,' Jackie murmured, but she drank the tea gratefully. 'I'm ever so sorry, Mrs Philpotts, for bringing all this trouble on you.'

'Don't talk daft, duck, you're not bringing any trouble on me at all,' Elsie said, hoping this was true. 'Now let's get this straight: you want to keep your baby, and you want to have it here, is that right?'

Jackie nodded, her eyes fixed on Elsie's face.

'And what do you want to do then? Go back to your dad? Or are you asking if you can stop here with me and Charlie?'

'Well, I'd go home, I suppose. I mean, Dad needs me, doesn't he?'

'And suppose he won't have you?' Elsie asked. 'Suppose he'll have you and not the baby? Have you thought about that?'

'Yes, but someone told me once that babies bring their love with them, and I thought – well, I hoped once he saw it he'd come round.' Jackie sounded uncertain, as if she were grasping at straws. And so she is, Elsie thought grimly. 'I'm sure it'll be all right, Mrs Philpotts.'

'But you haven't even told him you're expecting, yet! You're frightened to do that – how can you be sure he'll come round?' Elsie shook her head. 'You've got to tell him, Jackie, and see what he says about it all. I've told you, either me or the doctor will do it for you. Now, why don't you let me go round one day next week and have a word? It's got to be done. Then we can talk about where you have the baby and whether you keep it or not. It won't be easy to keep it,' she added gently. 'You know what people are like about kiddies that haven't got a dad. Apart from what it costs, and having it looked after while you're at work. Have you thought about that?'

'Yes, I've thought about it a lot. But I can't give it away, can I?' Jackie's blue eyes were huge in her small, pale face. 'I've got to keep it, for when Wilbur gets back.'

'Wilbur?' Elsie had almost forgotten the name of the baby's father. 'Why, you haven't heard from him, have you? He hasn't written to you?'

'No.' The girl looked away and bit her lip. 'But I'm sure he's coming back after the invasion, Mrs Philpotts. He promised he would – and what's he going to say when he finds out I've had his baby and given it away. What's he going to say then?'

Invasion. The word was in everyone's mind even if they didn't mention it. Once, it had been a word to fill them with dread – the fear that the Germans would be landing on their beaches and marching in to seize their towns and villages as they had taken France. Now, however, it was a word that brought hope and inspiration, for the invasion was to be the other way around. For the first time since Dunkirk, British and Allied soldiers would storm the shores of France, breach the Atlantic Wall and march in, not to take but to liberate villages and towns that had been under German Occupation for the past four years.

'It's not over yet, not by a long chalk,' George warned the family. 'Don't forget Dieppe. That was supposed to put a stop to it all, and what happened? It was an utter fiasco. This could be the same.'

'You shouldn't talk like that,' Kate said, although the mention of Dieppe brought painful memories. 'It's unpatriotic. Anyway, they've spent years getting ready for it. Look at all that building they've been doing out in the Bay. And all these troops coming back to get ready. They're not going to make a mess of it this time.' I hope, she added to herself.

'I've heard there's a big fleet of ships down in Cornwall,' Sally said. 'I don't know whose they are, though.'

'They're not anybody's. They're made of plywood.' Pete returned his father's exasperated glare. 'That's what I've heard, anyway.'

'You shouldn't be repeating daft talk like that. Plywood ships! What'd be the use of them? That's the trouble with all this chattering out of turn, people just get silly.' George reached up for his tobacco pouch and filled his pipe, ramming the tobacco in as if it had done him an injury. 'Plywood ships indeed! You'll be telling me next they're making rubber aeroplanes.'

Kate bit her lip. Someone at work had told her just that, but she dared not say so to her father. It did sound pretty silly, anyway. What use would such things be?

'Maybe they're going to use them as decoys,' she said. 'Let the Germans know about them and think we're going to attack from Cornwall, when really we're going from Pompey. That'd make sense, wouldn't it?'

George shrugged. He drew on his pipe and the smoke filled the little room. 'I still say we didn't ought to talk

about it,' he stated. 'Least said, soonest mended. Whatever they're going to do, Mr Churchill will make sure it's
done right, and I for one reckon we ought to let him get
on with it. That's his job, and we've got ours, and what
we've got to do is get on with them and keep quiet. What
about a game of cards before you lot go to bed?'

They drew their chairs up to the table and Win got the
cards out. They often played a hand or two before bed – it
took their minds off work and the war for half an hour,
and Win always said she slept better for a laugh or two.
George shuffled and dealt, and they fanned them out in
their hands.

I wonder what Brad's doing tonight, Kate thought. I
wonder if he's flying a bomber somewhere over Germany.
I wonder if he knows what's supposed to happen next . . .

Kate was worried about Maxine. Her friend had lost a lot
of her sparkle in the last few weeks, and now she was
looking really miserable, her face white and her eyes
ringed with dark shadows. Kate had already asked her
once or twice if there was anything wrong, but Maxine
had merely shrugged and muttered that she was all right
and not to keep on. But yesterday she'd gone off on her
own at lunchtime and when she came back it was obvious
she'd been crying. Kate decided that she couldn't let
things go on like this any longer.

'Let's take our dinner down on the shore today,' she
suggested as they entered the shifting room. 'Just you and
me. Have a good old chinwag.'

Maxine looked uncertain. 'I don't know that I feel
much like going down the shore.'

'Oh, come on.' Kate glanced out at the sky, with just a
few puffy white clouds drifting across the blue. 'It's a
lovely morning, real spring. It'll do us good.'

Maxine hesitated. 'Oh, all right, then. But don't get

huffy if I don't talk much. I'm not feeling all that grand, to tell you the truth.'

'Then you definitely ought to come,' Kate declared. 'Get some fresh air.' She hurried into her magazine clothes. At least I'll get her to myself for half an hour, she thought. I'll *make* her tell me what's wrong.

Maxine, however, didn't want to be made to do anything. Still rather reluctantly, she followed Kate down to the shore and they sat on the shingle beach, gazing out across Forton Lake. Most of the other girls had gone down to the Camber, where you could look across towards the jetties of the Dockyard and see the warships tied up, waiting for armaments to be brought across the harbour. You could exchange banter with the sailors loading the barges too, and some of the women had struck up romances with them. One girl had been dismissed after being caught in the hold with one, but she'd been seen around Gosport still hanging on his arm and looking decidedly plump and the gossip was that they'd had to get married.

Kate and Maxine sat in silence, eating their sandwiches, until at last Kate could bear it no longer. She looked at her friend's abstracted face and said gently, 'What's the matter, Maxie? Don't tell me there isn't anything – you've been miserable about something for ages. And I could see you'd had a row with your mum and dad before that dance. What's happened? Is it your Matthew?'

For a moment, she thought Maxine wasn't going to reply or, worse still, was going to tell her to mind her own business. Then the blonde girl heaved a deep, ragged sigh.

'Oh, all right. I might as well tell you. But you're not to pass it around, all right? I don't want the others knowing.'

'I don't go talking about my friends' private business,' Kate said, a shade indignantly. 'I won't tell anyone, Maxine.'

'All right, then.' Maxine sat with her knees drawn up to her chin and stared at the water, trying to find the right words. Once they'd been said, nothing could take them back. Kate would *know*. She wondered if it would make any difference to their friendship. 'It's funny, isn't it? We must be almost the only people who can sit and look at the water like this, now that there's all that barbed wire everywhere. But sitting here you wouldn't think there was a war on at all, would you?'

Kate waited. Either Maxine would tell her or she wouldn't. She couldn't force the words out of her. Her original curiosity and natural wish to know what was upsetting her friend was now subdued by the realisation that there was something seriously wrong. It wasn't something you could go on and on asking about.

'It's my mum,' Maxine said suddenly. 'It's what she did – years ago. Before I was born.' She ducked her head and rested her forehead on her knees. 'It's *why* I was born. She – she wasn't married, Kate. Well, she was by the time I was born, but not when – when . . .' She gave up on the difficult words and added in a choking voice, 'She *had* to get married.'

There was a small silence. Kate looked at the water and tried to take in this information. She could understand Maxine feeling upset that her mother had 'anticipated marriage' as people called it. But it wasn't that unusual, not enough to cause the sort of rows and misery it was obviously creating in the Fowler household.

'It's not that bad, Maxie,' she said gently. 'It happens to lots of girls. I expect it was a bit of a scandal at the time, but I dare say people forgot about it pretty quickly. One of my cousins—'

'You don't understand,' Maxine broke in. Her voice was dreary. 'I saw my birth certificate. They'd been married five months when I was born. Five months! They couldn't even have pretended I was a seven months' baby. But the worst of it is – the *worst* of it . . .' Her voice was choking again. 'It's what it says about my father. It says – it says . . .' She took a deep breath, a breath that seemed to hurt her chest. 'It says *Father Unknown*. She didn't even know who he was, Kate. *She didn't know who my father was.*'

Kate stared at her. 'But – but how couldn't she know, Maxie? I mean, she must have—'

'Because he wasn't the only one, of course!' Maxine's voice was harsh. 'She must have been going with two or three men all at the same time – well, within a few days of each other – or maybe even more than that. She was a *slut*, Kate!' She was crying in earnest now, the sobs wrenching themselves from her chest.

Kate moved closer and laid her arm across her shoulders. 'Oh, Maxie.'

'*Father Unknown*,' Maxine wept, her voice bitter. 'That's what it says. *Father Unknown*,' She dissolved again into heartbroken sobs and Kate held her close, not knowing what else to do.

'But – she did get married,' she ventured at last. 'Your – your dad . . .'

'Oh yes, she got *married*. Goodness knows why he took her on. He must have known – she was four months gone.' Maxine raised her head and stared at Kate with reddened, swollen eyes. 'He married her, he gave her his name and made her *respectable* – but he didn't let her put him down as my father, did he? He could have done, then it would have been just as if they'd been a bit hasty before they got married. I could've understood that. But he made them put *Father Unknown*. It's as if he didn't want *me* at all. It was just *her* he wanted, even though she was a slut and carrying some other man's baby.'

Kate shook her head. She could find no words of

comfort. She tried to think what it must have been like for Maxine, coming across the birth certificate that had been hidden from her for so long and trying to take in all this sudden information. 'It must have been an awful shock,' she said at last, thinking how lame the words sounded.

'You can say that again,' Maxine said wryly, echoing the slang that had come across with the Canadians and Americans.

'It couldn't have been because he didn't want you, though,' Kate said diffidently. 'He didn't *have* to take you as well when they got married. He could have made her get you adopted.'

'I wish he had! Then I wouldn't have to live with *her*, knowing the sort of person she is, knowing what she did.'

'But they *wanted* you. They must have done – both of them. Isn't that what really matters? You've always got on well, haven't you, up to now?'

'Yes, but it was lies, wasn't it? It was all lies. All pretending – pretending we were an ordinary, happy family, pretending he was my dad and Matthew was my brother.'

'But he is! He *is* your brother.'

'My *half*-brother,' Maxine corrected her. 'You see? I haven't got a father, I've only got half a brother and my mother's a slut. Would *you* want to live in a family like that, Kate? Well, would you?'

Kate felt helpless. She could understand her friend's pain, and yet . . . 'Yes, but can't you try to forget that and just remember that you've been happy until now? I've always thought what a nice house yours was, someone was always laughing, your dad made jokes, your mum was always smiling . . . It's all so different now. Everyone looks so miserable, and you're breaking your heart.'

'*They've* broken my heart,' Maxine said stonily. 'And it's not my fault they're miserable. It serves them right.'

'But they've done their best—'

'No, they haven't. They'd have done their best if they'd put his name on the certificate instead of *Father Unknown*. They could have done – nobody would have known. They could have said he was my father.'

'But that would have been another lie,' Kate pointed out. 'You were saying that it was all lies and pretending, but if they'd done that—'

'Well, it would have been a *better* lie, wouldn't it!' Maxine cried, jumping to her feet. 'It would have been a lie nobody would ever have found out. I wouldn't be having to lie awake at night wondering who my father was, and how many men she went with, and why *he* married her. Things I'll wonder about for the rest of my life. Things I'm never, ever going to know.' She bent and snatched up her sandwich bag. 'I shouldn't have told you – I might have known you wouldn't understand. *Nobody* can understand.'

'Maxie!' But the girl was already stalking away, her back like an iron rod. Kate stared after her for a moment, then scrambled to her feet and ran after her. She caught her by the shoulders and forced her to turn round. 'Maxie, don't. I *want* to understand – I want to help you. But it's a lot to take in all at once. You've had weeks thinking about it.' She looked at her friend's tragic face. 'You can't go back to work looking like that. I'm taking you to Matron.'

'What's the use of that? I'm not ill.'

'You're not fit to work,' Kate said firmly. 'You ought to go home.' She bit her lip, realising what she had said. 'Maybe Matron'll let you lie down on the bed here. But you can't come into the magazine in that state – you'll make the gunpowder all soggy!'

Maxine laughed a little, as Kate had hoped she would. 'All right, then. I do feel a bit rough. Perhaps she'll think

I've got flu or something. But I'm not going home. Going home's the worst part of the day now.'

They walked across to Matron's office and Maxine was given an aspirin and a cup of tea and taken to lie on the bed. Kate returned to work, trying to get to grips with all that Maxine had told her and wondering what it must be like, not to know who your father was. And – worse – to know that your mother had been so different from what you had always believed.

Chapter Fourteen

By Easter, it was as if Britain had been completely sealed off from the rest of the world. Nobody was allowed to leave or to enter the country, unless on official business. All military leave had been stopped. The countryside was filled with soldiers, camping in fields and even along roadsides. Military and civilian police checked everybody at railway and bus stations and searched cinemas, theatres and even hotels and guest houses. Anyone not carrying their identity card was arrested at once.

You couldn't pretend it wasn't happening. Sometimes, Kate thought it was a bit like Germany had been before the war started, when the Jews had to wear yellow stars and live in ghettoes, walled away from the rest of the country. But that had been a policy of hate and was what had started the war in the first place. This was different because the whole populace believed it was right. This was in order to win the war and ensure that nobody, ever again, should have to live behind walls, afraid to go out, afraid even to stay in. This was for freedom for everyone.

Yet even then, people still lived behind walls – the walls of their own fears and disappointments. Herself, afraid to go out with a boy in case she jinxed him. Elsie, still grieving bitterly over her son. And poor Maxine, trapped in the knowledge that her parents were not what she had thought.

I don't know how you get over those kinds of walls, Kate thought.

The Easter holiday was the quietest on record. Nobody could go away, even to visit relatives, and nobody from outside the ten-mile strip could come to visit. It was early for the beach but people in Gosport would have gone for picnics, if not to swim, or they might have gone for walks over Browndown or to the Warren, or gathering primroses in the woods at Rowner. George and Win had always taken the family up to Fareham on the bus on Easter Monday, and either walked out to Wallington, beside the little river, or up on to Portsdown Hill. Nobody did these things this Easter. They were either working overtime or reluctant to go too far from home in case something big happened. It wasn't like a holiday weekend at all.

On Good Friday Win, Kate and Sally walked round to the local church. It was a long service, lasting three hours, but you didn't have to stay the whole time. People came and went, staying to join in the quiet prayers for peace and remembering the day of the Crucifixion. There were no flowers on the altar and only a purple cloth to add a sombre glow. It was like Sunday in the streets, with all the shops and cinemas closed, so that even if you weren't a churchgoer you couldn't help but be aware of what Good Friday meant. It made the brightness and celebration of Easter Sunday all the more joyful – even though, as Sally grumbled at breakfast, there were no chocolate Easter eggs.

'You're too old for Easter eggs now,' Win told her. 'They're for children.'

'I don't see why. Anyway, I wasn't too old when the war started and now I'll never be young enough again, so I've missed five years. And Barney's never even seen a proper Easter egg.' Sally gazed mournfully at the boiled egg her mother had set before her.

'Well, enjoy a proper egg. It's supposed to be a treat, and I've done my best with them. It's all we used to have when I was a girl.' Win had boiled them in onion skins so that they were coloured orange and gold. 'And it's not often we can all have an egg for breakfast.'

'Your mother's right,' George told her. 'We've all got to be thankful for what we can get. You should know that by now.'

He spoke mildly, however. He and Win were feeling happy today because a letter had come from their son Ian who was at sea somewhere in the Far East. His letters didn't come very often and told them very little, but the fact that he was still able to write to them was all they needed. They would have known soon enough if anything happened to him, of course, but they still needed the comfort of reading words he had written, on paper he had touched and held. Win kept all his letters in a shoebox and got them out every now and then, reading them right through from the beginning. He had been away now for three years and she sometimes wondered if she would even recognise him again when he finally came home.

She and the girls had been to church again that morning, their hearts lifted by the white cloth and flowers that adorned the altar after the sobriety of Friday. There were no bells at their local church, but they'd heard that those at Alverstoke had been rung, and would be rung again for the eleven o'clock service. The two girls decided to take Barney out to hear them. For five years bells had been silent, to be used only in the event of an invasion, and now at last they were to sound their joyful notes again.

'I'd like to ring bells,' Barney said, listening to the clamour. 'How do you do it?'

'You just pull ropes, I think,' Sally said vaguely. 'I don't think it's very easy, though, Barney. I've heard that people can get pulled up on the ropes if they're not careful.'

'I'd like to be pulled up on a rope. I could climb it.'

'I think you have to be a lot bigger before you can ring bells,' Kate told him, taking his hand as the bells fell silent. 'Let's go home now. We'll catch a bus some of the way.'

'I want to go to the beach.' The church was only a quarter of a mile from the shore at Stokes Bay, and although it was a year or more since they'd been allowed out there, Barney could remember picnics on the shore and paddling in the cool water.

'We can't. We're not allowed to.'

'I *want* to.' His mouth set mutinously and he stood still, planting his feet apart. Kate tugged at his hand but he was like a rock.

'Barney, we can't. The soldiers are there.'

'I *like* soldiers. I talk to them.'

'Not these soldiers. They won't let you go on the beach, Barney, honestly.'

'I *want* to.'

'Well, you can't,' Sally said impatiently. 'We're not allowed. Nobody's allowed. Come on, Barney, or we'll miss the bus.'

Barney took a deep breath. He opened his mouth and let out a roar. 'I want to go to the beach and talk to *soldiers!*'

'*No*, Barney. You can't. Come on, or we'll have to walk all the way home.' They took a hand each, trying to tug him along.

'I'm not going home,' he bellowed. 'I'm going to the *beach*.' He twisted his hands out of theirs and ran away. Kate and Sally looked at each other and raced after him. They caught him, but he was like an eel, twisting and slithering from their grasp until eventually he tripped and fell, bringing Sally down with him. Furiously, she got up, brushing down her dress, and Kate grabbed Barney and held him tightly. He immediately set up a howl.

'Now look what you've done!' Sally stared down at her skirt. 'This is my new frock, clean on this morning, and it took me hours to make it. It's all covered in dust now and – *look* – there's a tear! I'm never taking you out anywhere again, Barney, never!'

'I've hurt my knee,' he sobbed, bending over to examine his leg. 'Katy, look, I've hurt my knee, there's all blood coming out.'

'It's only a graze.' Kate was almost as cross as Sally. 'Now, come on and stop that yelling. The people in the church must wonder what on earth's going on. *Stop it*, Barney. Walk quietly now, holding my hand. We're going to catch the bus along Ann's Hill Road and go home for dinner.'

'I'll tell Mummy you were nasty to me,' he hiccuped, dragging his feet so that they had to haul him along like a sack of coal. 'I'll tell her you wouldn't let me go to the beach. I'll tell her you pushed me over.'

'Walk properly, Barney. And it won't make any difference telling Mummy. She knows we're not allowed to go to the beach, and she knows we wouldn't push you over. (Not that I'm not tempted, sometimes)' Kate muttered to Sally as they marched along with Barney snivelling and dragging his feet beside them. 'He can be such a little monkey, yet at other times he is so sweet. He was lovely on the way out here.'

'That was because he thought we were going to the beach,' Sally told her. 'He's always the same. Always wants his own way, and nice as pie as long as he thinks he's getting it.'

Kate glanced at her and grinned. 'Takes after you, then,' she remarked casually, and laughed when Sally gave her an indignant look.

'What d'you mean by that?'

'Well, there's the way you gave in your notice at Wool-

188

worths and got yourself a job at Priddy's Hard. If that's not being determined to get your own way, I don't know what is.'

Sally stared at her. She opened her mouth to say something wrathful, and then laughed.

'All right. But at least I don't stamp my foot and scream the place down to get it.'

Kate grinned again, forbearing to remind her of the times when she'd done just that when she was younger. Barney was quietening down now and Sally took his other hand. They walked along the Avenue and let him scramble about in the roots of the huge trees that lined the pavement.

By the time they climbed upon the bus at the stop by the War Memorial Hospital, the tears were forgotten and Kate looked at her little brother with some envy.

If only she and Maxine could forget their own problems so quickly.

Maxine had also gone for a walk. She had been to the Roman Catholic church in the High Street and then caught a bus to Lee-on-the-Solent. She felt restless, wanting to be somewhere different from her usual haunts.

Clarrie had asked if she would be back for Sunday dinner. 'I've managed to get a nice piece of lamb. You've always liked lamb.'

Maxine would have been more likely to come home if she'd been told there was nothing but scrag end. The way her mother crept about the house, making such obvious, painful efforts to ingratiate herself, made her flesh creep. There's no point in trying to make up to me now, she wanted to scream. You've done all the damage you could possibly do, and there's nothing you can do to make up for it. Nothing. *Nothing.*

'I don't know if I'll be back,' she'd said ungraciously. 'I

might be going out.' She didn't say where and her mother didn't ask. She just turned away, her face already crumpling, and Maxine felt a surge of disgust, mixed uncomfortably with guilt. In her heart of hearts, she didn't want to be unkind yet she didn't seem able to help it. She didn't seem able to help the way she felt or the way she spoke to either her mother or her father. Just looking at them reminded her of what she had found out, and brought back all the pain and bewilderment she'd felt as she'd stared at the birth certificate in her hands. *Father unknown*, she thought, the words burning into her brain. *Father unknown* . . .

'Hello, Maxie.' The voice startled her out of her thoughts. Turning, she saw a face she recognised – a square, sunburned face, topped by a thatch of ginger hair only half-concealed by the peaked cap of a Naval Petty Officer while the badge on the sleeve showed him to be a member of the Fleet Air Arm. A wide mouth grinned at her and small blue eyes winked.

'Joey Hutton!' she said in surprise. 'I thought you were in the Far East somewhere. You were on the *Illustrious*, weren't you?'

'That's right. I came home.' He brandished an arm rather stiffly. 'Picked up an injury and got sent back. Infection set in, see, and they reckoned I was a bit of a liability on board ship – better off at home.' He winked, 'Bit of luck, eh?'

Maxine regarded him dubiously. She'd known Joey Hutton since she was a five-year-old in the infants' class at Elson School. His sister Susie had sat next to her for a while and it had been eight-year-old Joey's job to meet Susie from school and take her home. He was one of those boys who'd always been in trouble, and Maxine had been half-fascinated and half-repelled by him. Her mother, who didn't like the family, had warned her not to play with him, and there had been something in his face that gave her a feeling of excitement, deep in her stomach, which had scared her a little.

The memory of her mother's warning was enough now to make her smile at him with more warmth than she would otherwise have done. 'So what are you doing out here at Lee?' she asked, tilting her head to one side.

'Stationed here, what d'you think?' He gestured with a thumb over one shoulder, towards the Naval air station at the far end of the village. 'Up at *Daedalus*, What are *you* doing?'

Maxine shrugged. 'Just out for a walk. You know – get a bit of fresh air. Don't get much of it during the week.'

He looked at her appraisingly. Even before he had joined the Navy as an apprentice, he'd begun to acquire a reputation with the girls, and his years away had given him an air of jaunty confidence. Maxine felt the familiar twinge of excitement in her stomach and smiled back at him, glad that she was in her best clothes after going to church.

'So where's the boyfriend?' he enquired. 'You're not going to tell me you're out for a walk on your own. Not on Easter Day.'

'Why not?' she challenged him. 'My boyfriend might be away. Or I could have a dozen, for all you know. I might even be engaged – or married. I might just *want* to go for a walk on my own.'

'Oh no,' he said, grinning. 'I'd have heard about that. My mum keeps me up with all the local gossip.' He gave her a strange look, as if he knew more about Maxine than she did herself. 'Anyway, since you aren't with your boyfriend today, why not come and have a drink with me? I was just going to stroll down to the Inn by the Sea. We might get a sandwich as well – walk a bit further afterwards, unless you're in a hurry to get home.'

Maxine hesitated, then nodded. 'All right. I'm not in a hurry. Nobody'll worry about me,' she added with a touch of bitterness.

Again, he gave her that curious look, and she felt uncomfortable, reminding herself that she'd never really liked Joey Hutton all that much. Still, that was years ago and they were both different now. And he was certainly good-looking – his hair more auburn than ginger and although his eyes were a bit small they were a very bright blue. His fair skin was reddened by the sun rather than brown, but there was a tough, determined look about his square face. Maxine liked a man to look tough.

He held out his good arm, crooked at the elbow, and she slipped her hand through it. It felt good, to be walking arm-in-arm with a man, especially one as tall and handsome as Joey. She noticed several girls glancing enviously at her as they strolled along, and her depression began to lift. Maybe this was all she needed, just to feel special to someone for a while. Maybe Joey was nicer than she remembered. All boys were horrible when they were young, anyway. They all dipped girls' pigtails in the inkwells on their school desks, or shut them in cupboards, or put dead – or even live – spiders in their lunch bags, or did dirty things in the boys' lavatories, like seeing how high up the walls they could pee. It didn't mean they wouldn't grow up to be nice men.

'What are you doing now?' he asked as they walked along. 'I'd have thought you'd be in one of the women's Services.'

'I thought you said your mum kept you up to date with all the gossip?' she retorted. 'I'm at Priddy's Hard. Been there for three years. I heard Susie joined the ATS.'

He nodded. 'Having a smashing time, by all accounts. I'm surprised she's lasted so long without finding herself in the family way!' He laughed at Maxine's expression.

'Don't tell me you're still an innocent young miss. Not these days.'

'I don't see why not,' Maxine said stiffly. 'Some of us are still respectable girls.'

'Crikey, you sound like someone in a Victorian story.' He squeezed her arm against his side. 'Don't worry, Maxie. It's nice to meet a girl who's not too free and easy. Some of the ones I've met – whew!' He whistled and rolled his eyes. 'They've got 'em off before you've even found out their names. Not that I'm complaining!'

Maxine didn't answer. She was used to flirting, and enjoyed a bit of kissing and cuddling in the back row at the pictures or in one of the shelters along the beach, but it had never gone any further than that. With Joey, she had a feeling it would be expected – and not just a bit further either, but the whole way. Her heart thumped uncomfortably and she wondered whether she ought to say she had to go home after all, yet that worm of excitement was still uncurling in her stomach, and there was a tingle in her blood and a strange ache somewhere near the tops of her legs. I don't want to go home, she thought. I want to go with him. It can't do any harm. Not in broad daylight.

They walked along to the Inn by the Sea and Joey bought her a shandy and himself a pint of beer. The pub was serving sandwiches as well – beef sandwiches, they were called, but you'd have to look hard to find much meat amongst the marge and brown sauce. Still, they were filling and quite tasty. Maxine and Joey took them outside and sat on a low wall, looking at the barbed wire that ran along the head of the beach and wondering what was really going on.

'It's something pretty big,' Joey said, giving the impression that he knew all about it. 'They're using the Tower as the HQ. I've seen some Yankee bigwigs going in there. Could've been Eisenhower himself.'

'No!' Maxine glanced along the front to the Tower, which had been built in the 1930s as a pleasure attraction. Beneath it were the Winter Gardens, ballroom and cinema, and she'd often been to dances there. Now, the white tower was covered in green and khaki camouflage paint and the ballroom and cinema were closed. It would be an ideal place to run an invasion programme, she thought. Perhaps Joey was right. But – General Eisenhower? Here, in little Lee-on-the-Solent? It didn't seem possible.

'We're not important enough here,' she said doubtfully. 'He'd be in Pompey.'

'Yes, but they don't go to places like that, you see,' he told her officiously 'That's just where they'd be expected to go, and then the enemy would be able to bomb them. They use little places that no one's ever heard of. Anyway, we all know the invasion's going to start from round here. It stands to reason – look at all those things they've been building at Stokes Bay and Southsea. They're not doing that for fun.'

Maxine glanced round nervously. 'You shouldn't be talking like that.'

'Come on, Maxie, everyone knows! A spy would only have to be here five minutes to realise that.' He lifted his empty glass. 'Want another drink?'

Maxine shook her head. 'No, thanks. I ought to be getting back.'

'Why? It's Sunday afternoon – what've you got to get back for?' He stared at her, then smiled slowly and reached for her hand. 'I thought we were going to spend the afternoon together. Walk round to Stubbington and then catch a bus home. You could ask me to tea.'

'No! I couldn't!' Maxine's voice was sharp. She bit her lip and let him hold her hand. 'Sorry, but – well, I don't want to take anyone home. Things – things aren't too good there at the moment.'

'I see.' He was silent for a moment, then said, 'Well, you can't be in too much of a hurry to get back then, can you? So how about that walk? Maybe we could go into Fareham, go to the flicks. I'll see you home, you needn't worry. No strings. How about it?'

Maxine looked at him. His square face was open and cheerful, his blue eyes twinkling, his grin engaging. The little worm of excitement was quieter now, but still there, ready to uncurl. She realised that she wanted it to uncurl. She wanted to feel that tingle again.

'All right,' she said. 'Let's do that.'

Chapter Fifteen

They walked to the end of the road that ran along the top of the cliffs and turned right for the village of Stubbington. It was only a mile through a country lane, with one or two cottages, a smallholding or two and farmland. The village was no more than a cluster of cottages gathered round a village green with a small wooden gazebo in the middle. Maxine and Joey stopped and went over to it.

'I've never properly looked inside this,' Maxine said, peering into the dim interior. 'Why, it's the War Memorial!'

They gazed at the obelisk inside, inscribed with the names of the men of the village who had fallen during the 1914–18 war. It looked as if it had been meant to have a fountain as well, but no water was running now. 'I suppose they'll put names from this war there too, when it's all over,' Maxine said in a quiet voice, and turned away abruptly. 'Let's go outside again, Joey. It's making me feel shivery.'

They went out into the sunshine again and sat on a seat, looking at the peaceful scene before them, and gradually Maxine began to recapture her mood. Joey took her hand and she turned and smiled at him.

'You wouldn't think we were so near town. It's real country here. I used to come out on my bike, sometimes – ride up to Brockhurst and then out through Rowner and back through Lee, down to Stokes Bay and along the

Military Road. You can't go down there any more, it's all closed off now.'

'Too many forts and Naval establishments,' he nodded. 'Gosport's riddled with them – always has been.'

'D'you like the Fleet Air Arm?' Maxine asked. She knew that he had gone to Cornwall for part of his apprenticeship and then to Scotland, but she hadn't seen him since he'd first gone away, apart from the occasional glimpse in the street, and she and Susie Hutton hadn't really been friends since they left Elson School, Maxine to go on to the Central School and Susie to Privett.

Joey nodded. 'It's OK. Better to be a Regular than called up and just shoved anywhere. At least I've got a trade. When I come out of the Navy, I'll be able to get a job with one of the big aeroplane manufacturers – de Havilland or someone like that. I might even train to be a pilot.'

'But it'll be years before you can leave, won't it?' Maxine asked doubtfully. 'The war'll be over and done with. Will they need so many planes then? How much longer have you got?'

'Another six or seven years, if I come out at thirty. I might stay longer. But I reckon there'll be big opportunities outside. Air travel won't stop just because the war's over, Maxine. They'll be building big passenger planes to take people all over the world. France, Italy – even America and Australia. People will be going everywhere by plane. There'll be millions of jobs for blokes like me, who've done a good apprenticeship and got experience.'

He spoke confidently, again as if he had inside information, and Maxine couldn't help being impressed. She stole a glance at him, noting the determination of his square jaw, the firm set of his lips and brows. I believe he could be right, she thought. And, whatever happens, I believe he'll do well. He wouldn't settle for anything else.

Joey caught her glance and held it. Maxine felt a leap of excitement. She licked her lips and smiled. 'How about this idea of going to the pictures, then?' she asked, trying to keep her voice light and casual. 'We could catch a bus to Fareham or go down to Gosport. I don't really mind which.'

'Nor do I.' He lifted her hand and looked at it. 'Nice hands you've got, Maxie, No one would think you worked in munitions.'

'We wear gloves.' Her heart was beating fast. 'Some of the girls go yellow but I've been lucky. I think it depends on whether you sweat a lot.' She stopped, aware that she was talking too quickly and that her voice was trembling. Joey grinned and she felt her colour rise. He knows I'm feeling nervous, she through a little crossly, and he knows why. She pulled her hand away and lifted her chin. '*I* don't sweat at all,' she said. 'Only common girls sweat.'

He laughed. 'You know what they say – pigs sweat, men perspire, ladies glow. I bet you're a lady, Maxie, aren't you?' He glanced at her pink cheeks and winked. 'You're glowing now, anyway – and very pretty you look too.'

'I don't know what you think you're doing,' she said coldly. 'Flattery will get you—'

'Everywhere!' he finished wickedly, and she couldn't help laughing. 'Well, you can't blame a bloke for trying.'

'You'd better not try any harder, that's all,' she warned him. 'I meant what I said before. I'm not like some of those other girls you were talking about.'

'I know that.' He gave her a reassuring smile and reached for her hand again, pulling her to her feet. 'Come on – let's see what's on at the pictures. And I promise I won't try any funny stuff once the lights go down.'

Maxine stood up. She looked up into his square, freckled face with its twinkling blue eyes, and hoped that he wouldn't be *too* true to his word. A little bit of 'funny stuff' – an arm around her shoulders, a kiss or two – were what a girl enjoyed in the back row at the pictures. She didn't want it to go any further than that – at least, she didn't think she did – but she'd be disappointed if he didn't even try.

'All right,' she said, and smiled at him as, hand in hand, they walked across the green towards the Fareham road.

It was gone ten when Maxine finally reached home and this time both her parents were waiting for her. Clarrie was white with anxiety and Bert was furious. He jumped up from his chair as she came into the room and began to shout at her.

'Where d'you think you've been? Your mother's been out of her mind with worry. She was expecting you in for dinner. We were just thinking about going down the police station.'

'In case I was in a cell?' Maxine stared at him defiantly. 'I suppose you thought I'd been had up for being drunk and disorderly?'

'No, *not* in case you were in a cell, and don't you dare take that tone with me, my girl.'

'And don't *you* call me *your girl*! I'm not, and never was, and you know it! You've always known it!' To her fury, tears sprang to her eyes and she rubbed her hand angrily across her face. Clarrie was weeping in her chair, her hands over her face, and Maxine threw her a glance of contempt. 'You've told me lies since the day I was born,' she said in a trembling voice. 'And now you're trying to tell me what I should do. *You* – telling *me* what to do! As if you had any *right*!'

'I've got every right, and so has your mother. You're living under our roof.'

'Call me a lodger, then!' she spat. 'You wouldn't tell a

lodger what to do. You wouldn't wait up for a *lodger*. I'll pay you rent – I pay for my keep anyway. How much more d'you want? Ten shillings? A pound? I'd have to do overtime to manage any more.'

'Maxine!' Clarrie's hands fell away from her ashen face. 'Don't talk like that, please. We don't want you to pay rent. We don't *want* you to be a lodger. You're our daughter!'

'Not *his* daughter,' Maxine snapped. 'Yours, worse luck.'

'*That's enough!*' Bert lunged at her, and his open palm caught her across the cheek. Maxine cried out and staggered back, and Clarrie screamed. Bert stopped himself and planted both hands on the table, glaring across it. His face was a deep, angry red and his eyes bulged. Maxine, staring at him with one hand to her face, thought for a moment he was about to have a stroke, and felt suddenly frightened.

'I can't stand any more of this!' she cried, feeling behind her for the door handle. 'It's awful living here, just awful. I can't take any more – I'm going to find somewhere else to go. Elsie Philpotts'll take me in – she's got a spare room. I'll ask her first thing tomorrow morning. Then it won't matter where I go, or what I do, or how late I come in at night. It won't be any more of your business. You won't ever have to worry about me again!'

She wrenched the door open and almost fell through it into the passageway. Behind her, as she slammed it shut again, she could hear her mother bursting into tears yet again. The sound tore at her heart, but she could not go back. Racked with anger and misery, she ran up the stairs and shut herself into her bedroom.

Someone'll take me in, she thought, sinking on to her bed and covering her face with both hands. Someone's got to. I can't go on living here any more. I just can't.

It might have been a Bank Holiday Monday, but the work at Priddy's Hard continued as if it were an ordinary day. Everyone was aware that the country was preparing for an enormous push against the enemy, and the gathering of thousands of troops all along the south coast made it clear to all those who lived there that once again they were in the front line. The Invasion would take place from somewhere nearby, and the excitement was mounting.

'*We'll* teach 'em,' Pete crowed, clenching his fists and punching them into the air. '*We'll* show 'em who's boss! Ha! We'll get 'em all – Hitler, Ribbentrop, Rommel – the lot. They'll wish they'd never been born. Wish *I* could help torture 'em. *I'd* give 'em what for, I would.'

'Pete!' Win remonstrated, bringing in the cornflake packet. 'You know we don't torture people in England.'

'We'll do it in France then. Why shouldn't we?' he demanded, forestalling her next objection. 'They've been torturing people all through the war. They've been torturing people in concentration camps – they've been torturing our *own* people, in POW camps. Why shouldn't they have a taste of their own medicine?'

Win couldn't answer. Try as she might to be Christian, she couldn't find any defence for Hitler and his henchmen, yet she knew that torture must be wrong. It must do something bad to the torturers as well as those they tortured, she thought. They couldn't be quite the same human beings once they'd done some of the terrible things that were beginning to be reported in the newspapers.

'I don't know, Pete,' she said honestly. 'Of course they ought to be punished, and I hope they will be. Once the war's over I expect they'll all be put on trial somewhere or other. But it's not for people like us to decide, and whatever happens they won't be tortured. That would make us just as bad as them.'

'I wish I could help decide,' he said. 'I wish I could be a judge. It doesn't sound to me as if they'll get what they deserve at all.'

'They will,' Win said. 'They'll go to Hell. They'll burn forever. Then they'll know what torture's like.'

Pete stared at her in surprise. Win attended church every Sunday but she seldom talked about God or religion. She might say that someone would go to Heaven, but he'd never heard her talk about Hell like that. He caught a sudden glimpse of that place through his mother's eyes and shuddered at the thought of the men who had brought about this war, burning forever in fires that would never go out.

'D'you really believe that, Mum?' he asked, awed, and his mother nodded.

'I do. They're evil, you see,' she told him, her voice urgent. 'They're really evil. It doesn't matter how much we pray for their souls, people like that don't have any chance. Not unless they repent, and I can't see Hitler and all those others doing that.'

There was a short silence and then Sally's footsteps sounded on the stairs. Win, who had been standing rooted to the spot as she considered the fate of Hitler, turned abruptly and returned to the kitchen while Sally came into the room, still brushing her hair.

'What's up with Mum? She looks upset.'

'Nothing. We were just talking about Hitler.' Pete pulled a chair up to the table and poured cornflakes into his bowl. He put out his hand for the sugar and Sally moved it smartly out of his reach.

'One level teaspoonful, that's all. Not half a pound. That sugar belongs to all of us.'

'I was only going to take one spoonful,' he protested. 'D'you know you've got nail varnish on?'

'No! I haven't, have I?' Sally stared at her nails in mock astonishment. 'However did that get there?'

'I didn't think you were allowed to wear it at Priddy's Hard,' he said righteously. 'You'll have to take it off.'

'I only put it on on Saturday.' Sally had been allowed to go to the local 'hop'. 'I'm not taking it off again yet, it's hardly chipped.'

'Bet they'll make you.'

'They won't even see. I'll keep my hands out of sight.'

'I thought they inspected you.'

'Not always.' In fact, Sally knew that the girls were always inspected, but she had saved up for her nail varnish and felt sure she could slip through without its being noticed. 'I don't see what harm it can do anyway. If you ask me, they make too much fuss, just because they had that big explosion Grandad goes on about. My fingers aren't going to explode because I've got a bit of nail varnish on.'

Pete snorted with laughter. 'I'd like to see that! Exploding fingers! I wonder if they'd all go off together, or one at a time, like a row of fireworks. Wish I could come and watch.'

'There's going to be nothing *to* watch,' Sally told him tartly. 'Are you going to keep all those cornflakes to yourself or could you pass them over to me? Some of us have got work to go to.'

'*I've* got work to go to,' Pete said with dignity. 'I promised to go and help stocktake while the shop's closed. It's a very important job.'

'Oh yes? What d'you have to do, then?'

'I don't know, exactly,' Pete confessed, 'but it's very important, so there. Bet you've never done it at Priddy's Hard.'

'We don't need to,' Sally said loftily. She had no more idea than Pete what stocktaking was. 'We don't have stock.' She started on her cornflakes.

Kate came into the room, ready for work. She had had her breakfast and fed the kittens and was now ready to go. She glanced briefly at her sister as she shrugged into her jacket. 'Come on, Sally, or we'll be late. They don't make allowances just because it's a Bank Holiday.'

Sally swallowed the last spoonful of cornflakes and gulped down some tea. She put her bowl down on the floor for the kittens to lick up the last of the milk – something her mother strictly forbade – and got up, keeping her hands out of sight and winking at Pete as she followed Kate out of the room. He waited until the door closed and then helped himself to another bowl of cornflakes.

Neither girl spoke as they hurried through the streets of Elson. Sally was only half-awake, and Kate was thinking about Brad, wondering where he was now. She'd been half-hoping to get a letter from him, but nothing had come so far. He took me seriously, she thought. He thought I really didn't want to hear from him again.

It was what she had wanted him to think, to keep him safe. Yet now she felt a deep regret that she had turned away the only man to have caught at her heart since Godfrey had been killed.

But I had to do it, she told herself. I had to make him go. I couldn't take the risk.

She didn't really believe that Brad would come back for her after the war. A lot of girls had gone out with GIs and Canadians, and some of them had found themselves 'in trouble' afterwards, with a baby on the way, but once the men had gone away, few remained in touch, whatever their promises had been. It was wartime, they were far away from home and they took advantage of what was on offer. You couldn't really blame them. They knew that some of them were bound to be killed, and they wanted to enjoy as much as possible while they could.

The sisters arrived at the gates and scurried in under the police guard's eye, then separated to go to their own shifting rooms. Sally caught up with Elsie Philpotts, who was talking to Maxine. As Maxine turned away, she thought it looked as if the older girl had been crying, but Elsie ignored her questioning glance. They thronged into the long shed and began to take off their clothes.

'What's this?' Mrs Sheppard was beside her. She grabbed one of Sally's hands and held it up, staring at the fingernails. 'You've got bloody nail varnish on!'

'So what?' Sally asked. 'It's not doing any harm.'

'Not doing any harm? You know you're not allowed to wear nail varnish in the magazine. Get it off!'

'Can't,' Sally said rudely. 'Didn't bring any nail varnish remover.'

'Well, then, you'll just have to go home and do it, won't you? That'll be half a day's pay docked. Double time, too, for Bank Holiday.'

'That's not fair,' Sally began, but the chargehand was already walking away. 'You're just a bully,' she muttered. 'A big fat bully. I'm *blowed* if I'll go home!'

Mrs Sheppard's hearing was better than Sally had thought. She turned quickly and marched back. 'What was that? What did you say?'

'Nothing.' Sally faced her defiantly. The other girls had stopped undressing and were watching. Elsie stepped forward, looking anxious.

'She didn't mean nothing, Mrs Sheppard. She's new here, she didn't realise—'

'And *you* can keep out of it, Elsie Philpotts. Everybody's told the rules the minute they walk through the gates, you know that. And I heard what she said – she called me a big fat bully.' The chargehand's eyes glittered with anger. 'That's insolence, that is – rank insolence. And deliberate flouting of rules. She'll have to go.'

'Oh no, you can't do that.' Elsie's face flushed. 'Give her a chance – she's just a kiddy. She'll take it off, won't you, Sal?'

'I already told her, I haven't got any remover. What am I supposed to do, go to the paint shop for some stripper?'

Elsie looked exasperated. 'Don't be silly! Look, I'm trying to help you!'

'Well, you needn't bother,' Mrs Sheppard said brusquely. 'She's dismissed. Hear that?' she said to Sally. 'You can go home, right away, and keep your nail varnish on, if that's what you want. I'm not wasting valuable time arguing the toss. There's a war on, in case you hadn't noticed it, and we've got important work to do.'

Sally stared at her. 'Dismissed? What d'you mean?'

'What d'you think I mean? You're to go home. Nail varnish!' she muttered as she turned away. 'These girls! Barely out of nappies and think they know it all.'

Sally looked after her. She looked down at her red fingernails, then up at Elsie. 'I don't see what's wrong with them. Why can't we wear it?'

'Because it's inflammable, see? If there was a spark it could catch fire, and you know what that means. We can't take any risks, not with gunpowder and cordite and stuff.'

'But that's daft,' Sally said. 'It never catches fire at home. I've never heard of *anyone's* fingers catching fire. Why should it happen here? There's never any sparks anyway.'

'No, because we're all so careful.' Elsie began to undress rapidly. 'Look, I don't have time to talk about it. I'm sorry, Sal, but you heard what she said. You'd better go home and take it off.' Dressed only in her vest and knickers, she stepped over the red barrier and started to put on her magazine clothes.

Slowly, Sally pulled her jacket around her and walked out of the shed. She felt angry and bewildered. It didn't seem fair that she should be turned away just for wearing nail varnish. It was a stupid rule anyway. How could a little drop of nail varnish start an explosion? She just didn't believe it.

And what did 'dismissed' mean? It couldn't be the sack, or Mrs Sheppard would have said so. It probably just meant she was being sent home for the day, thus losing a day's pay at double-time. That was over thirty shillings – as much as she'd earned in a whole week at Woolworths. It wasn't fair.

Sally walked out of the gate. The policeman called her over. 'What are you doing, going out already?'

'I've got to go home,' Sally said. 'It's all right, I'm not taking anything out that I shouldn't.'

He looked at her suspiciously. 'Let's see in your bag.'

'It's only my lunch,' she said, annoyed.

He looked inside and peered at her sandwiches, wrapped in their greaseproof paper. Sally folded her arms and waited with exaggerated patience. 'All right. Go on, then,' he said.

'Thanks for nothing,' she retorted ungraciously, and snatched back her bag. She walked through the gate with her head held high, determined not to let him see how humiliated and miserable she felt. That horrible Ma Sheppard, she thought. I'll get back at her, just see if I don't.

She didn't go home. She had no intention of letting her mother know what had happened. She hung about, wandering the streets of Gosport and eating her sandwiches until it was time at last for the workers at Priddy's Hard to knock off, and then she joined the throng as they streamed out through the gates.

'Where have you been all day?' Kate demanded, catching up with her at the corner of Cider Lane. 'Elsie told me you'd been sent home.'

'It's that stupid Ma Sheppard,' Sally said in an aggrieved tone. 'Getting on to me just because I had nail varnish on. Don't you tell our Mum, Kate. She'll only go on at me.'

'But haven't you been sacked? Mum'll have to know that.'

'Sacked?' Sally shook her head. 'No, it was just for today. I'm going in tomorrow, same as usual. She just wanted me to lose a day's pay, that's all. But I'll get my own back, one way or another!'

Kate looked at her doubtfully. Maybe Elsie had got it wrong, she thought. Maybe Sally hadn't actually been dismissed. She decided it was probably best to do as Sally asked and not mention it at home. They'd find out soon enough, when she went in next day.

Sally kept her nail varnish on for the rest of the evening. At bedtime, she took it off and the next morning she got up as usual and sauntered into Priddy's Hard with Kate, as if nothing had happened.

Mrs Sheppard wasn't there. She'd tripped on an uneven paving slab on the way home, they heard, and broken a bone in her foot. She'd be laid up for a fortnight at least.

Sally passed the usual daily inspection without a hitch. Nobody said a word about her dismissal.

Chapter Sixteen

Elsie walked home that Monday deep in thought. Maxine had come to her during the eleven o'clock lunch break, when she'd been making a cup of tea at the steam outlet pipe – a procedure that was forbidden but done whenever the chargehands turned a blind eye – and asked if she could talk to her privately. Elsie had taken one look at the girl's pale, miserable face and made a second cup of tea.

'We'll go over by the blackberry bushes,' she said, handing Maxine the enamel mug. 'Mind that, it's hot . . . Are you all right, love? You look a bit rough. Not getting flu, are you?'

'No, I'm all right.' They walked across the grass and sat down beside the moat, looking down into the green water. It was massed with frogsspawn. 'Looks like the sago pudding we used to get at school,' Maxine observed. 'It was horrible – used to make me feel sick to eat it, but we had to.'

Elsie nodded. She'd been a school dinner-lady for a while at Leesland School, and enjoyed it, but there had always been trouble with the children when sago pudding was served. Semolina was nearly as bad, although macaroni and rice had proved acceptable. She had often wondered why those who decided on the menus didn't just give the kiddies what they liked instead of forcing them to eat things they hated. 'The pigs did well on those days,' she said. 'We used to send buckets and buckets of the stuff round to the pig farm.'

Maxine didn't answer, and Elsie realised she wasn't listening. She had unwrapped her sandwiches but didn't seem inclined to eat them; instead, she was staring at the moat as if she were seeing something quite different.

'What is it, Max?' Elsie asked quietly. 'What's up?'

For a moment, she thought Maxine wasn't going to answer. Then the blonde girl dropped her sandwiches on her lap and put both hands to her face. Her shoulders shook, and tears dripped through her fingers as she broke into huge, hiccuping sobs. Elsie stared at her in dismay and put her arm around Maxine's heaving shoulders. 'Here, you mustn't cry like that. You'll make yourself ill. Whatever is it? Whatever's happened? Has someone died, or something? Is it your mum? Is she poorly? I saw her round at Aylings the other day when I was in there for some hot-cross buns, and I thought then she didn't look well. What's the matter?'

'There's nothing the matter with *her*,' Maxine hiccuped. She took her hands from her face and looked at Elsie tragically. '*She's* all right. It's just – it's just – oh, Elsie, I can't go on living at home. I've got to find somewhere else. I wondered – I wondered if I could come and stop with you for a bit. You've got a spare room, haven't you? I mean, it wouldn't be forever. I'd try to find somewhere else, only it's not easy with the war and everything – but I can't stop at home with *them* any more, I just *can't*.'

Elsie stared at her, astonished. 'Whyever not? What are they doing to you? Don't they *want* you no more? Whatever's wrong, Maxie? I thought you were a happy family.'

'Family!' Maxine said bitterly. 'That's a joke.' She bit her lip and heaved in a huge, ragged breath. 'I can't tell you about it, Else – not now. Maybe one day . . . But I just need somewhere to live. Please. I'd pay you proper rent and everything, and I'd help you round the house, and do my own washing, and all that. I wouldn't be any trouble.'

'Oh Maxie . . .' Elsie began sorrowfully, but Maxine rushed on.

'I haven't *done* anything, Elsie, nothing bad. And I'm not in trouble, don't think that. It's just that me and Mum and – and Dad – well, we just can't get along any more and it'd be best for everyone if I was out of it. Please, Elsie. *Please*.' She caught the older woman's hands in hers and gazed imploringly into her eyes.

Elsie gazed back helplessly and struggled to find the right words. 'Maxie, you know I'd help if I could. I've thought for the last few weeks there was something the matter, you've looked so pale at times, but you've always had a smile and a joke. I don't know what the matter is, but you can tell me. It won't go no further.'

'I just need somewhere to live,' Maxine repeated hopelessly. 'Nobody can do anything about it, Elsie, but I can't stop at home any more. I can't.' Her sobs had eased now and her voice was flat and lifeless. She let go of Elsie's hands and turned away, staring forlornly into the stagnant waters of the moat.

Elsie stared at her and struggled to find the right words. 'But what about your parents? What do they think about this? They can't want to lose you.'

'They'll be better off without me. It's just rows, rows, rows all the time, Else. Honestly, they'll be glad to see the back of me – especially *him*.' She spoke the word with such a depth of bitterness that Elsie was shocked. 'As for *her* – well, I can't even *look* at her now without feeling sick. You don't know what it's like. It's awful.'

'But all families have rows.'

'Not like this. All families aren't like ours, I know they're not.'

'All the same – they've got a lot to put up with, you

know. This war – it's got on everyone's nerves. And what with all the troops coming in, and whatever's going on out in the Bay – it's making us all on edge. You don't want to put too much importance—'

'It's nothing to do with that!' Maxine cried. 'It's nothing to do with the war! You don't understand, Elsie.'

'Well, I can't, can I, not if you won't tell me,' Elsie pointed out. 'Not that I want to pry . . . But don't you think your poor mum needs you at home, Maxie? I mean, she must be worried half out of her mind about your brother – out in the Far East somewhere, isn't he? And she really doesn't look well. It doesn't seem right for you to just up and leave her now.' She paused and then said quietly, 'I know what it's like to lose a child, Max. It's the worst thing that can happen. You never, ever get over it.'

Maxine flushed and scowled. She wiped away some of the tears and said sullenly, 'She wouldn't be losing me. I'm not going to die.'

'But your brother might. And if she didn't have you at home . . .' Elsie sighed. 'I don't know what to say, Maxine, and that's the truth. I can see you're upset, I don't know what it's all about, and I'm not sure I want to, it's none of my business – but I don't see how leaving home and going off to live with someone else is going to put things right. It seems to me families ought to stay together, especially in times like this.'

'So you won't help me?' Maxine said flatly.

'It's not that I won't help you. I'd *like* to, I really would. But I'm not sure it wouldn't make things worse. It'd break your mum's heart if you left home. Is that what you want?'

'Why not?' Maxine sounded bitter. 'She's broken mine.' The whistle blew for the end of the lunch-break and she stood up, screwing the paper back around her uneaten sandwiches. 'Sorry, Elsie, you haven't had time to eat your lunch.'

'It doesn't matter.' Elsie got up too and faced the younger girl awkwardly. 'Look, if you want to have a talk, you know where I live. Come round any time.'

'It's not a talk I want. I told you what I want, and if you won't help me I'll just have to find someone else.' She started to walk back towards the magazine.

'Maxine! Don't take it like that. Look, you did sort of spring it on me. Let me think about it a bit. Let's have another talk.'

'It won't do any good,' Maxine said tonelessly. 'You're on her side – I can see that. Even though you don't know anything about it. Even though you don't know what she's really like.' She marched away, and Elsie stared after her, then followed more slowly.

She couldn't leave it there, she knew. Maxine was in real trouble – although what it could be, Elsie couldn't begin to imagine. But she obviously needed help and Elsie wasn't the sort who could stand by and do nothing.

I'll have to talk to her again, she decided, before she does something daft. But how can I take her in, when I've already got Jackie Prentice begging for a bed?

Jackie had agreed at last to let Elsie go round and talk to her father. She had refused to be present, however, and when Elsie knocked on the door that evening, she wished she was anywhere else but there. I don't know why I agreed to this, she thought, and if it hadn't been for the fact that our Graham was sweet on the girl I wouldn't have done. But she knew that wasn't true. Her soft heart made her an easy touch for anyone in trouble, even when it was of their own making.

It took a long time for Herbert Prentice to come to the door but eventually he opened it and peered out, his pale, rheumy eyes suspicious. He didn't recognise Elsie at first.

'It's no use,' he began in a whining voice, 'I don't buy nothing at the door, and I don't give to charity neither, only the Red Cross and they already been round once this week.'

'I'm not selling anything, Mr Prentice,' Elsie said loudly, knowing that the blast of the bomb that had injured him and killed his wife had also damaged his hearing, 'and I'm not collecting, neither. I'm Elsie Philpotts – I was a friend of your wife's – and I've come to talk about your girl Jackie.'

'Philpotts? Charlie Philpotts's missus?' He peered closer. 'Oh yer, I reckernise you now. What's this about my Jackie, then? What's she bin up to? Not bin causing no trouble, I hope.'

'Can I come in, Mr Prentice? I don't want to talk on the doorstep.' Elsie glanced around. The Prentices lived in an ordinary street of terraced houses but the net curtains on the windows across the road were already beginning to twitch. There would be no secrets if she had to stand here for long, she thought. The people peeping through those curtains could probably lip-read, and what they couldn't hear they'd make up.

'Come in? Well, I dunno about that. I wasn't expecting visitors.' He chewed his upper lip for a minute. He had a straggling moustache, with stained ends, and his head was bald except for a wispy grey tonsure. He appeared to be about sixty and Elsie remembered that he and Jackie's mother had married late. He stared at her as if expecting her to give up the idea of coming in, but she remained silent and after a moment or two he said grudgingly, 'Oh, all right, then, only don't expect a cup of tea or nothing. There's a war on.'

Elsie refrained from saying that she'd noticed this and

followed him along a dark, narrow corridor, bumping into the handlebars of a bicycle as she did so. 'Whoops! Mind my bike!' she said, copying the Jack Warner catchphrase. 'I never knew your Jackie rode a bike, Mr Prentice.'

'She don't. It's mine and I don't ride it no more. Doctor says I can't take the exercise. I'm going to sell it but I ain't got round to it yet.' He led her into the back room, a small, cluttered space about twelve feet square, and indicated one of the armchairs by the fireplace. 'You'd better sit down. And you don't have to shout, I ain't deaf.'

'Thanks.' Elsie lowered herself into the chair and tried to imagine this room with a baby in it. The Prentices couldn't be well off, what with Herbert not being able to work and Jackie on a low wage, and their furniture was mostly what had been saved from the bombing together with a few bits and pieces given them by the WVS. The house hadn't been badly damaged and they'd got it patched up, but the walls were stained with smoke and water and the floor was covered with torn linoleum. You could see Jackie did her best to keep it clean, but it wasn't the sort of place you'd like to bring up a baby.

'So whass this about my Jackie?' He was searching for something on the mantelpiece and mumbling so that Elsie had to strain to hear the words. 'Don't tell me she's bin and got the sack . . . I dunno whass the matter with that girl lately, she's gorn all to pieces. Eats like a horse one day, says she feels sick the next. I tells her, it's her own fault, she's too particular. Says she can't abide the taste of tea no more, all she wants is water . . . no goodness in water, no wonder she keeps feeling faint. I told her, go and see Dr Berry, and she did but would she tell me what he said? Never a word. Ah, here they are.' He waved a set of dentures in the air before poking them into his mouth. 'Thass better.' He bared the teeth at Elsie and plonked himself in the other chair. 'Now then, whass this all about?'

He wasn't much easier to understand with the teeth in than he'd been without them, but Elsie said, 'You'll have to prepare yourself for a bit of a shock, I'm afraid, Mr Prentice. It's not very good news.'

He stared at her. 'There ain't bin another raid, has there? I never heard no siren. My Florrie was killed in an air-raid, back in the Blitz, when I copped my packet and all. My Jackie ain't bin bombed as well, has she?'

'No, nothing like that. I shouldn't have put it that way. She's all right – it's just that . . .' Elsie searched for the right words and finally decided it was best to come straight out with it. 'Jackie's in the family way, Mr Prentice, that's what.'

He stared at her. His mouth worked, the moustache wobbling over the ill-fitting teeth. The rheumy eyes reddened and for a moment she was afraid he was going to cry. Then she realised he was angry.

'My Jackie? Expecting? Is that what you're telling me?'

Elsie nodded. 'I want to try to help her.'

'And how d'*you* know about it?' he demanded belligerently. 'Your boy, was it? I seen him around – ginger feller, like you. He and my girl used to knock about a bit together, before the war. Him, was it?'

Elsie caught her breath. 'My Graham's dead, Mr Prentice,' she said sharply. 'He was killed back in 1941 and he never got no girl into trouble.' As far as I know, she added silently. 'This was a GI your Jackie was going with, before last Christmas.'

'A GI?' He made no apology for accusing Graham. 'A Yank? What was my girl doing, going round with a Yank?'

Elsie made no reply. It was all too clear what Jackie had been doing. Herbert Prentice stared at her again. 'So what's it got to do with you, then? Why are you here, and where's my girl? Tell me that. Ain't she got the neck to face me herself? Got to get someone else to do her dirty work, has she?'

And if she had, who could blame her, Elsie thought with distaste, wondering how Jackie put up with living here in this near-slum with this unpleasant old man. But you had to remember he'd been bombed and lost his wife, and make allowances.

'Jackie often pops in to see me,' she said. 'And when she found out what had happened, she needed a woman to talk to. It's only natural. She was afraid of upsetting you so I said I'd come round for a word, sort of smooth the way.'

'Afraid of upsetting me!' he said. 'Pity she didn't think about that before.'

There was a short silence. Elsie cast about for what to say next. At last, she said, 'Only, time's getting on, Mr Prentice, and we've got to think what to do about it.'

'Oh, we have, have we?' he said. 'And who's *we*, then? You, me and the gatepost? I don't see the girl anywhere in the room and it's none of your business from what I can make out, so it looks like it's me who's got to do any thinking there is. And I dunno what she expects *me* to do, not in my state of health.'

'Well, that's why I've come,' Elsie said. 'I'm ready to help, any way I can. Only, like I say, we haven't got too much time.'

'It might be a help,' he broke in, 'if someone was to have the common courtesy to tell me how much time we *have* got. When's this,' he balked at the word *baby*, 'when's it due?'

Elsie took a breath. I've got to remember he's had a shock, she thought. Shock takes people in all sorts of different ways, and he's not a well man. 'July, as far as the doctor can tell.'

'The doctor? You mean she's bin to the doctor and he never told me? He's bin here and sat in that chair and never said a word?' This seemed to anger the old man even more than his daughter's situation. 'I'm only her *father*! Don't I have a right to know?'

'I expect she asked him not to say. She thought it would come better from me. Anyway, you know now, and what we've got to do is think what's best for her and the kiddy. It's your grandchild, Mr Prentice.'

'Yer, and its other grandfather's in America somewhere, living in some big house. What's *he* going to do about it, eh? Tell me that. And the bloody GI what got her into this mess, what's *he* got to say for himself? Seems to me it ain't just for me to decide what to do, but it all falls on my shoulders as usual. As if I hadn't got enough to put up with.' His voice descended into a self-pitying whine and Elsie gazed at him with disgust.

'So what d'you reckon we ought to do, then?' she asked, determined to make him face up to what was happening. 'You're the one that's here. You're Jackie's dad. You got to take some responsibility.'

'Oh, I have, have I?' he said again. 'And how's it my responsibility, eh? Tell me that. It was her mother what brought her up. I was out at work all the time, slaving me guts out to get the money to buy her frocks and toys and stuff. I hardly ever saw her when she was a nipper. I thought she was being brought up respectable, but I never had no say in it meself, that was her mother's job. And then when we was bombed and my Florrie copped it, it was like living with a stranger. She was my girl but she never had nothing to say to me, just cooked me food and put it on the table, and did the jobs around the place, the washing and cleaning and all, and that was it. She wasn't never no company. And when she started going out with that bloke that you say was a Yank, well, I hardly saw her at all, not to talk to. So what responsibility did I have in it, eh? Tell me that.'

Elsie gazed at him and thought of Jackie, working hard at the dairy and coming home tired at night to cook her father's supper, do his washing and ironing as well as her own and clean the house. The sweeping and brushing and scrubbing. The standing in queues early in the morning or during her brief dinner-hour, trying to get their rations. Why, the poor girl must have been worn out. No wonder she'd had no energy for conversation.

'Still, I expect you helped her a bit,' she said with a touch of sarcasm. 'Dusted around a bit, did the vegetables and that. I expect you talked to her, didn't you?'

'Dusting?' he said. 'Vegetables? Women's work, that is. And what have I got to talk about, stuck here at home on me jack all day, eh? Tell me that.'

I could tell you a lot, Elsie thought, but it wouldn't help us now. Aloud, she said, 'Well, what d'you want her to do? Go into a home for unmarried mothers? Only she'll have to be quick because there might not be any places.'

'Go into a home? My Jackie?' He stared at her, his moustache quivering, and Elsie thought for a moment that he was about to show some real fatherly feeling. Then he said, 'And what about me? Who'd cook me supper and do me washing? Course she can't go into no home.'

'So she can stop here, then? Have the baby here? You don't mind what people say?'

'None of their bloody business,' he muttered. 'Lot of nosy old baggages anyway. Mind, I won't have her showing me up. She'll have to stop work, and she can't go out till it's all over. I won't have them poking their noses in and chewing the rag over my business.'

'And how are you going to manage?' Elsie asked in exasperation. 'Who's going to do your shopping for you? Is there anyone else who'll do it?'

'Well, you said you'd help out.' He peered slyly at her. 'Got to do your own bits and bobs, haven't you? Wouldn't be much trouble to do ours as well. We don't want much. And she can do all the housework and washing and that, while she's indoors.'

Elsie thought of the girl, trapped inside the small house with this horrible old man, and shuddered. 'And what about when the baby comes? She'll have to take it out sometime. You can't keep a kiddy locked up indoors for ever.'

He looked at her. 'Well, she'll get it took away, won't she? Thass what these others girls do, ain't it? Get it adopted by some rich family. There won't be no need for it to go out before that, it ain't going to want to go to the pictures or nothing.'

Elsie took a very deep breath. Count to ten, she told herself. Count to *twenty*. He doesn't know what he's saying. He hasn't had time to think about it. He'll take a different view when he's got used to the idea. He'll come round.

But when she looked into the rheumy eyes and caught the hardness that lurked in their depths, and saw the selfish pout of the lips beneath his stained moustache, she knew that he wouldn't come round. He would never think of Jackie or of the grandchild to come, because there was only room in his small, mean mind to think of himself.

She stood up. 'I'll go now, Mr Prentice. Jackie asked me to come and tell you and I've done that. She knows where I am. And she knows I'll do all I can to help her. But if you'll take my advice, you'll think about how you can look after her in this bit of trouble, because if you don't, you might find she doesn't stop here and go on looking after *you*. And you might think about how you'll manage without her, because that's what I'd like to know. Tell me *that*!' And she turned and marched out of the house, slamming the door behind her.

Outside, she stalked up the road, her head high and her back straight. But once round the corner, she slowed and then stopped and leant against the wall for a minute.

I don't think I managed that at all well, she thought dismally. I don't think I was any help to young Jackie at all.

'I don't know what to do about it,' she told Charlie later on as they finished their supper. They'd had a few slices of lamb, left over from the tiny joint Elsie had queued for an hour to buy on Saturday morning, together with some pickles made from last year's onions and the late tomatoes that had never got ripe. Together with a good heap of mashed potato covered with OK brown sauce, it had made a tasty meal, but Elsie had hardly noticed the flavour. 'That poor girl, having to live with him. It's no wonder she looked for someone to give her a bit of loving. I really think we'll have to have her here, Charlie. I don't see where else she can go. At least she can still pop in and keep an eye on him – he can't be left to himself, anyone can see that.' She shook her head. 'And then there's Maxine. She worried me, she really did. She looked so upset, and the way she talked about her mum and dad – well, I don't mind telling you, it made my blood run quite cold. It was as if she really hated them. It's not natural, a girl going on like that about her parents. I mean, I don't really know them, I only know her mum by sight and I've seen her out with her hubby once or twice, but they seem a decent couple. Ordinary sort of people, you know, like us. I wouldn't have thought they'd be unkind to the girl.'

'Did she say they was?' Charlie put down his knife and fork and wiped his moustache with the back of his hand.

Elsie thought for a minute, then shook her head. 'No, I don't think she did, as a matter of fact. She didn't really say anything – except that she couldn't go on living there. She never went into details and I couldn't really ask.'

'Well, I don't see as you can interfere without knowing a bit more,' Charlie advised her. 'It never does no good, sticking your oar into other people's business. You could get into trouble if you let her come here and the Fowlers turned nasty about it. They could get the police on to you – enticement, it's called. I've heard about it.'

Elsie stared at him. 'I never thought of that! Surely not – it's not as if she was a kiddy. She's old enough to know her own mind. All the same – you're right, I ought to be careful.' She bit her lip and looked down at her empty plate. She'd managed to eat her sandwiches during the tea-break but still felt hungry when she got home. 'You know, Charlie, I fancy a bit of bread and jam. How about you?'

She got up and fetched the bread from the kitchen, and took a pot of blackberry and apple out of the cupboard. The blackberries had been picked at Priddy's Hard last autumn, not far from where she and Maxine had been sitting today. There was always a good crop by the moat.

'Maybe I could have a chat with Kate Fisher. Her and Maxine are friends, she might know a bit. I wouldn't be asking her to tell tales. I just want to help.' She scraped margarine on to the bread and then spread a teaspoonful of jam on top, shaking her head sadly. 'I don't like to see youngsters at loggerheads with their mums and dads, I really don't. I keep thinking – suppose it had been us and our Graham. Suppose we'd been all at cross purposes just before he'd been killed. We'd never have been able to get over that. But these youngsters, they don't look at it that way.'

'Nobody thinks it's going to happen to them, that's why,' Charlie said. 'I dunno why, when there's been a war on for the past five years and God knows how many killed . . . But the young ones all think they're charmed, somehow.'

The ginger and white kitten, which had been curled up on Elsie's chair, woke up and came over to her. Elsie's face softened and she picked the animal up and cuddled her. 'You're a little sweetheart, aren't you? You won't go away and leave home, will you? I tell you what, Charlie, I'm glad young Kate saved these kittens. She's made a real difference to the place, Fluffy has. It's given me heart, having her to come home to of an evening.'

'Oh, so I don't count, then,' he said, pretending to be offended, and Elsie laughed.

'Course you count, you old silly! But a kitten's different. She's so helpless – she *depends* on us. It's like a baby, in a way. Having someone depend on you – it's what I've missed.' She sighed, and the lines of her face saddened. 'I thought after Graham grew up that we'd have some more little ones around us, to look after and love. We never will now. But at least we've got Fluffy.' She held the kitten against her face, hiding the sudden tears. 'Silly old fool,' she said huskily.

Charlie looked at her. He wasn't deceived. He knew just what Elsie was thinking, and just how she felt, and he knew that at this moment it wasn't sympathy that she wanted but a little bit of jollying.

'That's right,' he said, but his voice came out gruff rather than jolly. 'Silly old fools, the pair of us.'

Chapter Seventeen

Maxine went home after work because she had nowhere else to go, and ate the meal her mother had prepared because she was hungry and there was nothing else to eat. She didn't speak to Clarrie at all, and afterwards she climbed slowly and heavily up to her room, taking her kitten with her, and sat on her bed stroking the white fur and staring at nothing. She felt drained with misery, too exhausted to think clearly about anything. She had pinned such hopes on being able to live with Elsie, and now that this didn't seem possible, her mind seemed to have gone blank. She didn't know what to do next.

She heard the back door open and close and the sound of her father's voice in the kitchen. The tap ran and she knew he was washing his hands. Now he'd be drying them on the roller towel behind the kitchen door. The tap ran again; her mother was making a pot of tea. They were talking in low voices and she knew they were talking about her. Clarrie would be telling him that Maxine had come in and eaten her tea without a word. She'd be crying again – she was *always* crying, Maxine thought in disgust – and he'd be patting her shoulder and wiping her eyes and telling her it was all *that girl's* fault. Ugh!

Footsteps sounded on the stairs. He was coming up to change out of his working clothes. But to Maxine's surprise, the sound stopped outside her door and someone knocked. Snowy lifted her head and Maxine froze.

'You in there, Maxine?' He sounded gruff and a bit

uncertain. She couldn't quite make out if he was angry or wanted her to come down and make things up. She didn't answer. 'Come on, girl, open the door. I want to talk to you.'

'Well, *I* don't want to talk to *you*,' she retorted, and heard him sigh noisily.

'Look, we can't go on like this. We've got to have it out. There's things I want to say to you. Things you've got to know.'

Clarrie's voice sounded from the bottom of the stairs. 'Bert, don't. I don't want her—'

'It's for the best, Clarrie. I've told you that.' He spoke through the door to Maxine again. 'Come on, let me in.' She heard him turn the knob. 'I'm not going to do anything to you.'

Maxine jumped up, dropping the kitten on the bed. She ran over to the door and leaned against it. It wasn't locked, none of the bedroom doors had locks, but there was a small bolt and she slid it across. 'I don't want you in here. Go away.'

'Maxine, don't be daft. We've got to talk about this.'

'There's nothing to talk about. Anyway, it's nothing to do with you, and you can't order me about – you're not my father!'

There was a short silence. Then he said, in a voice that sounded painful, as if it came through a throat that was suddenly swollen, 'That's not a nice thing to say, Maxine. Don't all the years I've brought you up as my own daughter count? Don't you think I've always treated you as my own girl? Don't you think I've loved you like my own?'

Maxine felt a surge of emotion so powerful that she couldn't even identify it. Rage – pity – guilt – sorrow and regret – they were all there, gathering into a hard knot of pain that grew within her breast, so hard and tight that she was afraid she might burst. Her father, the man she'd always believed to be her father, who had treated her as his own, who had loved her and played with her and told her off when she was naughty, who had even once put her across his knee and spanked her, and then cuddled her afterwards and dried her tears with his own hanky, the man she had looked up to and loved, he was out there now, begging her to let him in, and she knew that he was begging for more than simply to enter her room. He wanted to come back into her heart.

For a moment, she stood still, unable to cope with the turmoil of emotion. And then the truth rushed back into her mind, and rage overcame all those other emotions and she remembered that he was also the man who had lied to her.

'It was *lies*!' she screamed at him. 'All those things you did – they were lies! I don't care *what* you've done – or why you did it – it was all lies, and when people really love each other – really, *really* love each other – *they don't tell lies*!'

The silence was like a wall between them. For a moment, Maxine thought he had gone downstairs again, so quietly that she hadn't heard him. Then she heard a muffled sound, halfway between a groan and a sigh, and she felt a savage satisfaction in knowing that she had hurt him.

The thick, solid silence was split by the ringing of the doorbell. There was a moment of hesitation and then she heard her mother go to open the front door. She heard voices and then Clarrie called up the stairs.

'It's for you, Maxine. It's Joey Hutton, Susie Hutton's brother.'

Joey! Maxine's heart leaped. She snatched up her coat from where she'd thrown it over the end of the bed, and pulled open the door. Her father was still on the landing and she brushed past him, shaking off his hand when he laid it on her arm.

'Let go! I'm going out.'

226

'Maxine, we've got to talk about this. You've got to know what happened.'

'I don't want to know. I'm not interested. *I'm going out.*' She was halfway down the stairs. 'And you needn't wait up for me either. Leave the door unlocked.'

'Maxine—' her mother began.

'If you don't, I won't come home at all.' She gave them both a defiant stare. 'I'll find somewhere else to go, and you'll never see me again. Hear that? If I find you waiting up for me tonight, I'll turn right round and go away and you'll never see me again!'

She pushed past her mother and made for the front door. Joey was standing there, tall and good-looking in his Naval uniform, and she pinned a bright smile on her face and took his arm.

'Hello, sailor. Where are we going tonight, then?'

Joey grinned at her. He didn't seem to notice that anything was wrong. Perhaps he wasn't the noticing sort, or perhaps he just didn't care. It didn't matter, anyway. For a few hours, Maxine was determined to forget the unhappiness of home.

Maxine came in late that night, to find her father alone in the back room, sitting at the table and reading the newspaper. He looked up as she came in, but Maxine avoided his eyes and marched through to the kitchen.

'If you're making a cup of tea, I'll have one too,' he said as she began to fill the kettle.

Maxine shrugged. She waited in the kitchen until the water boiled and made a pot of tea. '*One for each person and* none *for the pot*,' she recited under her breath. She took the milk bottle out of the dresser and poured a little into two cups, then added one saccharin tablet for herself and two for her father. She took his cup into the living room and put it on the table by his elbow.

'Thanks, love. Where's yours?'

'I'll take it upstairs.'

'Bring it in here,' he said. 'I want to talk to you.'

'Oh, not another row,' she said wearily. 'I'm fed up with it all. And I'm tired.'

'I don't want to have a row. There's things you ought to be told, Maxine. Things your mother never wanted you to know.'

'Well, that's all right, then, because I don't want to know them!' She turned away and he put out his hand and took hold of her sleeve. 'Let go!'

'Sit down,' he said quietly. 'Fetch your cup of tea in here and sit down. We've got have a serious talk about all this.'

'I'm *tired*—'

'So am I. We all are. We've been tired ever since this war started and we'll go on being tired till it's over. But that don't mean we can let things slide. Not important things.' He waited a moment. 'If it's not tonight, Maxine, it'll be tomorrow. Or the next day, or even the day after that. You've got to know what happened. It'll help you to understand.'

'Understand what?' she demanded bitterly.

'Understand why you were born,' Bert said, in an exhausted voice. He rubbed his hand over his face. 'Look, just listen to me tonight and I won't ever ask you to do anything again. Once you know, you can do what you like. I'll have done all I can then – it'll be up to you. But all this talk of moving out . . .'

'Nothing you say's going to make any difference to that. I'm going as soon as I find somewhere to go.'

'Well, maybe and maybe not. But it's upsetting your mother, it's upsetting her a lot, and I don't like to see it. I've always tried to look after her – look after all of you – but all this is getting beyond me. What with our Matthew being away as well, maybe getting shot or sunk at any moment, and now you – we've got to sort it out, Maxine, we've got to sort it out one way or another.'

He paused and she looked properly at him for the first time, noticing how grey his face was, how sore and tired his eyes looked. Once upon a time she would have tried to comfort him, but now her heart felt like a stone. Yet there was something stirring there – some shred of love and pity still trying to make itself felt. Abruptly, she turned away, meaning to go upstairs, but once again Bert caught her sleeve.

'Please, love. Just sit down for five minutes and listen to me. That's all I'm asking.'

'Oh, all right,' she said ungraciously. 'I can see you won't rest till I do.' She fetched her cup of tea and then sat down opposite him at the table. 'Go on, get it over with.'

'You've got to listen properly. Try to think what it was like for her.' He stopped and sighed. 'It's not easy, talking about this after all this time. It's not easy at all.'

'Don't suppose it is,' Maxine said bluntly. 'It means you've got to admit she was a tart—'

'*No!*' His fist thumped the table and she jumped as their tea slopped into the saucers. She saw him draw in a deep breath and struggle to control himself. 'No,' he said more quietly, 'she wasn't. She was a lady, your mum, a real little lady. Pretty as a picture, with her yellow hair – just like yours, it was – and her big blue eyes. All the boys were chasing her but she wouldn't look at any of them. That was half the trouble.'

He took a sip of tea and Maxine waited. She was still half-inclined to go upstairs. She didn't want to think about her mother at eighteen or nineteen, pretty and popular and – worst of all – looking just like Maxine herself. She tightened her jaw and stared into her cup.

'She was choosy about who she'd go out with,' Bert continued. 'She didn't like being "pawed about". She didn't even want to be kissed, not the first time she went out with a boy. She thought you ought to get to know each other first. She took it all very serious – too serious, perhaps, but that ain't a bad fault.'

'Well, *someone* pawed her about,' Maxine said caustically, and saw his face flush with anger. She waited for him to erupt again but Bert was evidently determined not to lose his temper. He took a deep breath and waited a moment before speaking again.

'Don't try to antagonise me, Maxine. This is a serious talk, not a shouting match, and I'm not going to let you push me into one. I'm telling you something important, so just listen, will you?' He gave her a straight look and Maxine shrugged, trying not to show that she was feeling uncomfortable.

'All right,' she said offhandedly. 'Get on with it, then.'

'I went out with your mother a few times that year,' he said. 'I'd always liked her – she was so pretty. And she was good company, too – always had a smile and a laugh. Everyone liked Clarrie. Just because she was choosy about boys didn't mean she was stuck-up or anything like that. Anyway, I took her to the pictures and church dances and things like that, and I started to think maybe there was a chance for me, though I couldn't really believe it, there were so many other boys after her. I mean, why pick me?'

Maxine yawned and glanced at the clock.

'All right,' he said a little sharply, 'I won't take much longer. I just wanted to tell you what your mother was like, so you could see how she's changed.'

'And I suppose that's all my fault?' Maxine sneered. 'Having me changed her for the worse. Well, I can't help that, can I? I couldn't help being born. Nobody asked *my* opinion.'

'No,' he said, 'you couldn't help being born. And your mother couldn't help it either. It wasn't her fault things turned out the way they did, and it wasn't mine either. That's what you've got to try and understand.'

'So whose fault was it, then?' she asked disbelievingly. 'My father's, I suppose. *Father Unknown.* His fault.'

'Yes,' he said simply, 'that's whose fault it was. Your father. And the reason she never knew who he was is because she never saw him.'

'*Never saw him?*' Maxine echoed incredulously, but he raised one hand and silenced her, going on as if she had not spoken.

'She never saw him, Maxine. She never saw his face, nor – nor nothing. She didn't know who he was, because he jumped out at her from the bushes one night as she was walking home and attacked her.'

There was a tiny silence. The ticking of the clock sounded suddenly very loud. Maxine felt the blood pound in her ears and heard it roar, like heavy waves breaking on Stokes Bay beach. For a second or two she felt as if she were out there, in the darkness of midnight, hearing the thunder of the sea and feeling the fear of some terrible threat.

'Attacked her?' she said at last in a small, dry voice. 'You mean he – he *raped* her?'

Bert nodded. His face was tight and crumpled, as if someone had screwed it up like a paper bag. He looked almost as if he were about to cry.

'That's right,' he said. 'Your mother was raped.'

Maxine felt the shock like a blow to her whole body. For a few moments she couldn't catch her breath, but when Bert tried to help her by patting her back, she shoved him away, shaking her head violently. The silence stretched on, winding itself about them like a shroud. He nudged the tea closer to her elbow and Maxine stared at it

231

as if she didn't know what it was. She had no idea how much time had passed.

'Well, if you want to know what I think,' she said at last, 'I think she asked for it.'

Bert stared at her. '*Asked* for it?' he repeated in astonishment. 'How d'you make that out, girl?'

'Well, it stands to reason, doesn't it? She was leading boys on. She'd go out with them, let them take her to the pictures and spend money on her, and then she wouldn't even give them a goodnight kiss. No wonder they got fed up with it. I'm just surprised it didn't happen sooner.'

His face reddened. 'Haven't you got no sympathy at all? Can't you even think for a minute, *just one minute*, what it was like for her? She was a decent, respectable girl from a decent, respectable family and she didn't want to let them down. This is 1918 we're talking about – we'd just been through a flipping World War, there was all sorts of people about in Gosport – soldiers, sailors, Marines, half of them shell-shocked, just waiting to get back home. They didn't even come from round here, most of 'em. It could've been *anyone*. It didn't have to be someone she knew. Anyway, the lads Clarrie went out with – and there weren't all that many of 'em, just me and Bill Bassett and Ernie Morris, and maybe one or two others – we all had respect for the girls we took out. There's not one of us chaps would have done a thing like that, not one.'

'So one of them could be my father?' Maxine said, fastening on to the names. 'Mr Bassett that lives round Priory Road, you mean him? Or Jean Morris's dad? You mean me and Jean Morris could be *sisters*?'

'No, I *don't* mean that!' he bellowed, losing his temper at last. 'Haven't you been listening to a bloody word I've been saying? What I'm telling you is that it wasn't *none* of them – *none* of us chaps that lived round Elson. We were all decent blokes and we wouldn't ever have done nothing like that, not in a million years.'

'Well, someone did,' Maxine said, noting with some satisfaction that she'd caught him on the raw. She was still feeling shocked by his revelation, and somewhere deep inside flickered pity for her mother, but the greater part of her shock came from the realisation that her father – *her father* – had been a man who leaped out of bushes and attacked a young girl on her way home . . . She shook her head angrily, determined not to believe it. 'It must have been someone she knew. Who else would know she was walking home on her own? What time was it, anyway? Where were these bushes?'

'It was in Daisy Lane,' he said wearily. 'It was a Friday night and she'd been down Stoke Road to see her grandma – she lived round the back of where the Forum is now. Your mother lived in Richmond Road then, and it was the quickest way home. Nobody would have known she was going to be there just then. He was just lurking about, waiting for the first girl to walk by, and it happened to be her. He dragged her into the bushes and put his hand over her mouth and – and done it. There was no lights and she never saw him, and she didn't even know she was expecting for three months.'

Maxine was silent for a moment. Then she said, 'Did she go to the police? You can be put into prison for rape.'

'Yes, if they can find out who done it. What chance was there of that? They couldn't go round questioning every bloke in Gosport, could they? They couldn't go in St George's Barracks and out Browndown and all them places, asking all the Servicemen where they were that night. Most of them wouldn't even have been there by then. Anyway, she was too upset about it all. Too ashamed.'

'Too ashamed? I thought you said it wasn't her fault.'

'It wasn't, was it! But she said she felt as if it was. She

233

said she felt dirty. And besides that, she knew another girl it happened to – never mind who – and she did go to the police, and what happened? First off, they wouldn't believe her. Then they treated her like dirt and made out it was her fault. And they got a doctor in to examine her, a police doctor, and she said that was worse than what the bloke did in the first place. Clarrie couldn't face all that and I didn't want her to.'

'You? How did you come into it?'

'Well, I was going out with her then, wasn't I? I was supposed to be meeting her that night, so she wouldn't have to walk home on her own, and I got a flipping puncture in me bike and had to walk down. I was just at the end of Daisy Lane when she come running out, crying and sobbing and her frock all torn. I tell you, if that bloke had been there then I'd have killed him with me bare hands, I would straight.' His big, solid face looked as hard as rock, the jaw clenched as he remembered that night. 'I wanted to go after him, but she begged me not to – said he'd be miles away by now, and all she wanted was to get home. So I took her back. I never saw anyone in such a state, never.'

'And is that why you got married?'

'In the end, yes,' he said. 'Mind you, I wanted her to marry me right from the start, only I knew she could have any bloke she wanted and she wasn't likely to look at me. Even when we started going out – well, I knew there was another bloke she fancied more. I never knew who he was but I reckon he got killed or maybe caught that 'flu that was going round then, because it never come to nothing and she never said. Anyway, she was too upset about what happened to want to go out with anyone, but I used to go round to see her just the same and we'd sit in her front room and just talk, and then – well, then she found out she was in the family way. And, of course, I said we'd better get wed, and her mum and dad thought it'd be the best thing too, and Clarrie said yes and we fixed it up.'

'And then I was born,' Maxine said. 'And you put *Father Unknown* on the birth certificate. You didn't want anyone thinking I was yours.'

'That wasn't by my wish!' he cried. 'I'd have taken responsibility for you, no two ways about it. It was Clarrie's father – your grandad – insisted on that. He took her down the registrar's himself and let the cat out of the bag. He told the registrar what had happened and that you weren't my kiddy, and that's what he said had to be put. I found out after that you could be what they called "a child of the marriage", being as you were born after the wedding, but it was too late then. You can't alter what's on a birth certificate, see. It's there for good.'

'But you could have told me!' Maxine shouted back. 'You could have told me you wanted me to be yours.'

'How could we tell you all this when you were a kiddy? We talked about it sometimes, your mother and me, but we always decided it was best to let sleeping dogs lie. We'd have told you when you needed your certificate, but until then it seemed best to say nothing.'

'That's why you wanted me to go to Priddy's Hard and not into the Services, wasn't it,' Maxine said. 'So that I wouldn't need it. You didn't want to tell me.'

'We didn't want to upset you,' he said. 'Can't you understand that, Maxine?'

'But it *did* upset me, didn't it!' she cried. 'It's just about broken my heart, knowing I wasn't your daughter and not knowing why. It's made me think all sorts of things – and even now I don't know what to think! I'm never going to know who he was, am I? I'm never going to know who my real father was, for the whole of my life – never!'

'And d'you *want* to know?' he demanded. 'Realising what sort of a man he was, d'you really want to know?'

Maxine stared at him. 'But his blood runs in my veins, doesn't it.' She stretched out her arm so that the thin blue lines were visible under the pale skin. 'That's *his* blood running there, not yours. *His*. Because he's my father and you're not. And how am I ever going to be sure I'm not as bad as he was?'

They looked at each other. At last, Bert took hold of her hand and held it awkwardly. Maxine made one half-hearted effort to pull it away, then gave up and let it rest. Nothing seemed to matter any more.

He looked down at the palm and then up into her face.

'And don't it make no difference,' he asked heavily, 'that it's been me what's looked after you all these years? Me that's been a *dad* to you all this time?'

Maxine felt hot tears come to her eyes. She wanted to say yes, of course it made a difference, it made all the difference in the world. But deep inside there was still that hard, bitter voice, reminding her of the lie that she had believed ever since she was a little girl.

She snatched her hand away and got up.

'I don't want to talk about this any more,' she said, feeling as if she had a stone in her throat. 'I'm going to bed.'

This time, he made no attempt to stop her and she walked stiffly from the room and climbed the stairs. At her parents' door she paused. Inside, she could hear muffled sobbing. Her mother was still awake.

Maxine hesitated for a moment and then went into her own room, closing the door firmly behind her.

Chapter Eighteen

A few days after Easter, Sally persuaded Kate to go to another dance at the drill hall. 'You know they're the only ones Dad'll let me go to, and then only if you come too. Come on, Kate, you'll enjoy it. You know you love dancing.'

Kate pursed her lips reluctantly. Dancing had lost its attraction for her since she'd met Brad. Nobody had ever danced as he did, not even Godfrey, and she knew there wouldn't be anyone at the drill hall even half as good. But then she didn't really want to dance with anyone else anyway. She just wanted to be with Brad, twisting and twirling in the jitterbug or – better still – held in his arms for the intimate tango or the dreamy waltz.

'Please, Kate,' Sally urged her, and she sighed and gave in.

'All right, then. But we're coming straight home afterwards, all right?'

Sally shrugged. 'That's OK. I don't suppose there'll be anyone interesting there, anyway.'

Kate gave her a sceptical glance. Sally was obviously hoping to meet 'someone interesting' at the dance. She was desperate for a boyfriend now, and had been disappointed to find so few young men at Priddy's Hard. Being a Naval Armament Depot, she'd expected to find a number working there in 'reserved occupations' but instead it was staffed mostly by women and older men. The only men Sally could find to be interested in were the sailors who came over from their ships on the lighters, to load up ammunition, but so far she hadn't been assigned to working in that department.

They took some trouble in dressing for the dance. Kate wore the black checked skirt and red blouse she'd worn the night she'd met Brad, and Sally produced a gypsy-style blouse, with a low, frilly neckline, and a swirling orange and brown skirt she'd made from some material she'd got in the haberdashery shop in Stoke Road. 'They found it at the back of a cupboard. You'd think they'd have found everything there was to find by now, wouldn't you? It was under a bolt of blackout cotton.'

'It's curtain material!' Kate said, staring at it.

'So what?' Sally twisted round and the skirt flared out around her, showing off her slim legs. 'I think it's lovely.'

So did Kate. She looked enviously at her sister in her flamboyant outfit and wished she'd got something new to wear. The check skirt suddenly seemed very ordinary and the red blouse was beginning to go under the armpits. I haven't had a new frock in two years, she thought, staring dispiritedly at herself in the mirror. Even if Brad did come tonight, he wouldn't be interested in me.

They called for Maxine on the way. She came out of her door, looking flushed and defiant. Kate gave her a half-questioning, half-cautious glance. She never knew quite where she was with Maxine these days. Sometimes the other girl needed to talk, sometimes she shut up like a clam. Kate knew she'd been going about with Joey Hutton in the last week or so, but Maxine had told her nothing about him and she didn't think it was serious. Joey would be going away soon anyway, like all the other young Servicemen. Even if he stayed at *Daedalus* he wouldn't be able to get out much, not once the invasion started.

'Well, here we go for another evening of glamour,' Maxine said cynically as they walked along the street. 'I suppose you feel really grown up now, Sally, going to dances with the rest of us.'

'Do me a favour,' Sally said. 'The local hop? I'm waiting to go over to Southsea and hear some really good bands. My friend Pam goes – she's seen Joe Loss, and Ambrose, and the Squadronaires and *everyone*. I think it's really mean of our dad not to let me. He'd stop me doing everything that might be fun, if he could.'

'Well, he can't stop you growing older,' Maxine said. 'Your turn'll come, Sal.'

She sounded subdued, however, and Kate looked at her again and touched her arm. 'Things much the same?' she asked quietly.

'How could they be any different?' Maxine returned in a tight voice. '*She's* still her, and *he's* still him. And I'm still me. None of that's going to change.'

'I know, but – well, I thought perhaps you might have had a talk – sorted things out a bit.'

'There's nothing to sort out – only where I'm going to go and live. I thought Elsie might give me a room,' she said resentfully, 'but she's on *their* side. I should've known she would be. She's the same age – they all stick together, old people like that.'

Sally was staring at them both, her eyes bright. 'What's all this about? You're not going away, are you, Maxine?'

'No, she's not, and it's none of your business,' Kate began sharply, but Maxine shook her head.

'It doesn't matter, Kate. Sally doesn't go spreading gossip. I'm just not getting on too well at home, that's all, Sal. I'm trying to find somewhere else to live.'

'Leave home, you mean?' Sally's eyes widened. 'But can you do that? Can't they *make* you stay at home?'

Maxine shook her head. 'I don't see how. You don't have to live with your parents if you don't want to, not when you're my age. The stupid thing is, I could have left to go into the Services and I wouldn't even have had to worry about finding a room, but because I stayed at Priddy's Hard I'm stuck. But I still don't have to stay with *them*.'

'I'm not sure you'll find it easy to leave, though,' Kate said doubtfully. 'I don't suppose all that many people in Gosport let rooms. And there's all the other things you'd have to pay for – food, and all that. And a gas fire, if you had one in your room. You'd have to do your own washing, too. D'you think you'd be able to manage it all, Maxie?'

'Well, I shan't know until I try, shall I?' Maxine said crossly. She was aware that she hadn't thought of any of these things and had no idea what it might all cost. 'Seems to me you're no better than Elsie, Kate. You're just trying to make difficulties.'

'No, I'm not. I'm just trying to think about it sensibly. I know when my cousin Dottie got married and moved into two rooms she found it hard to manage at first. She said she didn't have any idea how much things cost, and she spent her spare time cooking, washing and ironing, and hardly ever poked her nose out of doors in the evenings.'

'Well, she was married, wasn't she. She got her entertainment at home.'

'Her hubby was sent off three weeks after the wedding,' Kate said stiffly. 'She was just having to do all the things Auntie Jane did for her when she was living at home.'

Maxine shrugged. 'Don't see why she had to move out then, if he was going away so soon.'

'They didn't know he was going to. Anyway, that's nothing to do with it. I'm just saying there's a lot to think about.'

'And *I'm* just saying you don't know anything about it!' Maxine burst out. 'You don't know what it's like, Kate, living with people you – you *hate*. Nobody knows what it's like! It's horrible.'

The other two girls were silent. Sally glanced at her sister and knew that Kate was feeling hurt and angry but wasn't going to say so. She had a closed-in look on her face that Sally knew well. With unaccustomed diffidence, she said to Maxine, 'Isn't there anyone else, apart from Mrs Philpotts? There must be someone with a spare room. Someone older, living on their own – a widow, perhaps. You might find someone who'd really like to have a girl to go and live with her. Someone who'd cook you a meal – even do your washing.'

'Oh, don't encourage her,' Kate said. 'People don't let rooms to single girls, Sally. They don't mind a married couple, but girls stay home with their parents till they get married, and that's all there is to it.'

They walked on in silence. Neither of the two older girls felt much like dancing now. They'd never quarrelled seriously before but now both felt miserably aware of a gulf between them. Maxine was deeply hurt by Kate's reaction and felt betrayed. She'd told Kate the most intimate secret of her life and felt that it hadn't been treated properly. Now there had been another revelation – an even worse one – and she wanted desperately to share it with her friend, but felt as if she had lost trust in her. She had nobody else to talk to and felt alone and lost.

Kate herself felt guilty and bewildered. She knew she'd let Maxine down but didn't know how to cope with the situation, and she couldn't think of a way to say so. Unconsciously they drew apart as they walked along the pavement, so that there was no risk of their arms touching accidentally.

Sally, who didn't know what Maxine's problem was, thought about it for a few minutes then shrugged it off. This was her first night out in her new skirt, and who knew what might happen? I might meet someone really handsome, she thought. Someone who'll see me the minute I walk in and fall in love at first sight. Her body tingled with anticipation and she almost skipped.

Kate sensed her sister's excitement and felt old and jaded. I wish I could feel like that again, she thought. I wonder if I ever will . . .

It turned out that Sally was the only one who really enjoyed the dance. Neither Maxine nor Kate were in the mood, and there was a lack of young men of their own age. Joey was on duty that night, and although Maxine had hoped that he might slip out, he didn't arrive. Kate, who was subconsciously looking for Brad all the time, even though she knew he couldn't possibly be there, felt a cloud of vague disappointment hanging over the whole evening. The few men who were there seemed to be no more than boys and she was reduced to dancing with Maxine, the two of them holding each other stiffly and not looking at each other's eyes. They'd danced together often enough before – girls often did – but tonight they could both feel their friendship slipping away, like a boat slipping its moorings, and neither knew how to draw it back.

The dance ended at ten o'clock and they walked home together, the silence of the two older girls masked by Sally's excited chatter.

'Did you see me dancing with that dark-haired boy? Wasn't he good-looking! He's asked me to go to the pictures with him next Wednesday. He lives at Camdentown and he works at Bedenham. He's called Neville – isn't that a smashing name? I've never met anyone called Neville before. I think it's ever so smart.' She waited for a moment and then said in a hurt voice, 'You might say something, Kate. This is my first date. Neville might be my first real boyfriend. I might even *marry* him.'

Kate opened her mouth to say something crushing and then closed it again. Sally was right, this was an exciting moment for her and there was no reason to spoil it just because Kate herself felt miserable.

'He looked all right,' she said, aware that her voice was lukewarm. 'But you'll have to ask Dad before you can go to the pictures with him.'

Sally tossed her head. 'I don't see why.'

'Because you will, that's why,' Kate said snappily. 'And you needn't look at me like that, it's not my fault. You know what our dad's like. He'll probably want Neville to call for you so that he can have a look at him.'

'Have a look at him? He's not a monkey in a zoo!' Sally said indignantly. 'I shan't tell him then, and you're not to either. Pretend you don't know anything about it. How am I ever going to get a boy if I've got to bring them home to be inspected by Dad? It's stupid!'

'He just doesn't want anything to happen to you.'

'What could happen to me, just going to the pictures with a boy? There aren't any raids now and we know the Germans can't invade us. I don't know what you're talking about, Kate.'

Kate said no more. She felt too weary and too jaded to argue with Sally, certainly to discuss the risks of going out with young men. Maxine spoke instead.

'She means you could be *taken advantage of*. You know – he could do things you don't want him to do.'

'We're only going to the pictures!'

'Yes, but it's what could happen on the way home afterwards. He might want to kiss you.'

'Ooh, I hope so!' Sally said with a delicious shiver.

'And he might want to do more than that,' Kate said, feeling that if her sister were to be given instruction, she ought to be the one giving it. 'Just don't let him, Sal. A kiss is all right, but don't let him go any further.'

They arrived at Maxine's front door and paused. Kate wanted to say something to close the distance between them, but she didn't know how. Miserably, she felt that she had failed her friend, yet she didn't see what else she could have done. Girls just didn't go and live by themselves before they were married.

' 'Night, then,' Maxine said stiffly, and turned towards her door.

'See you tomorrow,' Kate said, trying to sound as if there were nothing wrong, and Maxine shrugged.

'S'pose so.' She unlocked the door and disappeared inside, shutting it abruptly behind her.

Kate looked at it for a moment and then turned away. Sally was still chattering about the dance.

'. . . and did you see us doing the foxtrot? He's ever such a good dancer, Kate. He's been over to Southsea, to Kimball's and the Pier and *everywhere*. If we start going out together regularly he'll take me. Dad wouldn't stop me then, would he? Not if I'd got a steady boyfriend to go with. And you could go too, only of course you'd have to stay on the other side of the room. You wouldn't want to play gooseberry.'

'Oh Sally, for heaven's sake stop jabbering!' Kate said, losing her patience. 'Anyone'd think you were the only girl in the world to go out with a boy! There are other things to think about as well, you know. It's not the most important thing there is. I wouldn't trust him anyway. I'm sure I've seen him with a red-haired girl and he looked pretty keen on her, from the way they were going on.'

There was a brief silence. Then Sally said, 'I don't know what's the matter with you, Kate. You've been like a bear with a sore head all evening. If you want my opinion, you're just jealous because you can't keep a boy yourself. They go out with you once or twice and then don't want you any more. If you want *my* opinion—'

'I don't!' Kate cried, putting her hands over her ears. 'I *don't* want your opinion, Sally! Keep it to yourself!'

But Sally continued remorselessly, and the words penetrated between Kate's fingers. 'If you want my opinion, you're turning into a bitter old woman, and you'll never get married! Nobody's *ever* going to want you and you'll stop at home with Mum and Dad all the rest of your life!'

Kate felt the tears spring to her eyes. She bit them back and turned her face away from her sister. They walked the rest of the way home in silence, and when they arrived Kate went straight to bed while Sally regaled her parents with the delights of the evening. Neville's name cropped up several times, but the subject of the pictures on Wednesday evening was carefully avoided. Kate, lying in bed upstairs and staring at the ceiling, could hear her excited voice and felt a sense of guilt settle over her like a heavy black cloud.

What's the matter with me? she wondered. I'm quarrelling with everyone. I seem to have lost my way completely and I don't know where to go next.

She rolled over and buried her face in her pillow. As she drifted uneasily into sleep, the faces of Godfrey and Brad crept into her mind, merging together in her dreams. When Sally came in, her pillow was soaked with tears.

Chapter Nineteen

On Wednesday evening, Kate and Sally left the house together to go to the pictures at the Criterion cinema. It was small, and a bit of a fleapit, and didn't get the big films that the Forum showed, but it was cheaper and you could see all the cowboy films, and older ones that were coming to Gosport for a second time. It stood on the crossroads where Forton Road turned into Brockhurst Road. Kate and Sally walked down Crossways to reach it, passing the hall where they had been taken to collect their gas masks when the war started.

Neville was waiting at the door of the cinema beside a tall, gangling young man who was studying the pictures of Roy Rogers and Trigger.

'Ned!' Kate said and turned accusingly to Sally. 'You never told me you'd invited him along.'

'It's a surprise,' Sally said innocently. 'I thought you'd be pleased to have someone to sit with.' She smiled at Neville, who looked every bit as handsome as she remembered. 'Hello, Neville.'

'Hello, Sally.' He took her arm and winked at Ned. 'See you later.' The two of them walked into the tiny foyer and paid at the window. Kate and Ned looked at each other.

'You don't mind, do you, Katy?' he said anxiously. 'Only you said ages ago you'd come to the pictures with me, and you've always been too busy. So when Sally said you were coming tonight and she didn't want you sitting on your own, I thought . . .' His voice trailed off and he looked at her with his puppydog eyes. Kate sighed.

'I suppose it's all right. Only I'm meant to be keeping an eye on Sally, and now I shan't even know where she's sitting. Well, we'd better go in. I'll pay for myself.'

'No, I want to pay for you. I know you're not my girlfriend, Katy, but I want to pay for you just the same. And I'm going to buy you some chips on the way home, too.' He was getting his money out as he spoke and handed two florins through the window of the little box-office. 'Two one-and-ninepennies, please.'

'You don't have to spend that much,' Kate began, but the girl had already passed him the tickets. There wasn't much difference between the one-and-ninepenny seats and the one-and-threepennies, especially if you were sitting in the middle, but it was a measure of how much a boy thought of you. As they walked into the darkened cinema, behind the usherette with her torch, Kate glanced round to see if she could spot Sally and Neville. She was pretty sure they'd be in the back row.

The Pathé Pictorial News was showing, with all the usual pictures of troops being inspected or grinning broadly as they clambered into lorries, and of politicians meeting in London. The King and Queen were shown visiting 'a town in the north-east', and there was some dramatic film of Mount Vesuvius erupting.

'Gosh, look at that big cloud of smoke,' Ned said, enraptured. 'It's like the biggest bomb in the world. Coo, that'd kill all the Germans, wouldn't it, a bomb that big. The Japanese, too. I wonder why we don't make bombs that big at Priddy's Hard.'

'Don't be silly, Ned,' Kate said sharply. 'Nobody could ever make a bomb that big, and if they could they wouldn't be able to get it into an aeroplane.' She didn't like watching the news. It was bad enough hearing about all the fighting on the wireless, but seeing pictures of it made her feel sick. They were showing some film of a German ship being sunk now and she couldn't help thinking of all the men and boys who were drowning, almost before her eyes. British men like Godfrey, with wives and sweethearts and children at home; German men who hadn't asked to be in the war but had been conscripted to fight on Hitler's side, even if they didn't believe in what he was doing.

Elsie, who never forgot her bitter grief over Graham, said that the only good German was a dead German. But Kate couldn't believe that. They were people just like us, she'd said once, and they couldn't all be as evil as Hitler. Why, our own Royal Family had German relatives.

'Well, they're Germans too,' Elsie had retorted. 'And they're ashamed of it – you can tell that by the way they changed their name. They used to be Battenberg, didn't they? And then they changed to Windsor so they didn't sound German. They're just hoping we'll forget.'

'That's an awful thing to say. The King and Queen are wonderful – look at the way they go all over the country, cheering people up.'

'I'd rather have Arthur Askey any day,' Elsie said. 'And I haven't noticed them coming round giving concerts or going over to entertain the troops like he does, along with George Formby and Gracie Fields and all them people. All they have to do is put on their best clothes and smile, and then go back home to eat a good dinner off gold plates.'

The news also reported massive air attacks taking place on Germany. Hundreds of Allied planes were shown taking off from RAF stations and surging across the Channel like mighty flocks of birds to bombard the German coastal defences, their huge black bombs falling on land that had already been destroyed by battles and occupation. People had been happy there once, Kate thought, staring at the grim black and white pictures; they farmed the fields and grew flowers in their gardens and played on the beach. Now there were army camps stretching across the devastated fields, and walls like fortresses built along the tops of the beaches. She couldn't see how it could ever be the same again.

'Gosh, that was smashing,' Ned said when the News finished and the famous cockerel stretched its neck and crowed in apparent triumph. 'We're bashing them to bits, Kate. The war'll soon be over and we'll have helped win it. I bet those bombs we saw blowing up those German planes were ones you made.'

'Yes, I suppose they might have been.' The thought didn't give her any comfort, however, nor pride. All she could think of was the people her bombs had killed and maimed. People like Godfrey and the Tompkins twins. People like Brad.

Fear gripped her heart like a clenched fist as she thought of Brad.

'Here,' Ned said, pulling a paper bag out of his pocket. 'I brought you these.'

The bag contained sweets – two ounces each of toffee crunch and pear drops, already sticky from having been in his pocket. 'These are your sweet ration, Ned,' Kate said, trying to hand them back. 'You can't give them all to me.'

'Yes, I can if I want to. I wanted to get you a box of chocolates but they didn't have any. You hardly ever see chocolates now. They're for you.'

'We'll share them.' She offered him the bag and he took a pear drop and began to crunch it noisily. The 'little' picture – the second feature – was starting now. It was the story of an American boy who had a raccoon for a pet. They stared at it, not completely sure what a raccoon was or why his parents objected to his keeping it in the house, but the scenery was nice and there was nothing about war in it. Kate began to relax.

The big film was the usual Roy Rogers and kept Ned transfixed all the way through. He didn't try to put his arm around Kate, nor even hold her hand, and she didn't expect him to. It was quite nice to be out with him really, she thought, watching the big white horse gallop up a flight of stairs in the saloon. You didn't have to worry about fending off unwelcome attentions, and you knew he wouldn't be affected by the jinx. You were both quite safe.

She almost forgot about Sally, sitting at the back with Neville, and only looked for them as the lights went up at the end of the evening. When she finally caught sight of them, they were in the far corner of the back row, entwined in each other's arms. Kate jumped up and scrambled along the rows to reach them, arriving just as Sally surfaced, her cheeks flushed, her hair tousled and a dreamy smile on her face.

'Hello, Kate,' she said, half-dazed and half-defiant. 'Did you enjoy the film?'

'Well, at least I saw it!' Kate snapped. 'Come on, Sally. You're coming home with me – now. What on earth d'you think Mum and Dad would say if they saw you like this?'

'Well, they haven't and they're not going to,' her sister retorted, straightening her skirt. 'And you're not to tell them, Kate. If you do, I'll tell them about the time I caught you and Jacky Benson on the settee in our front room . . . Nev and me're in love, and it's none of their business.'

'None of their business? You're not even sixteen yet!'

'It's all right,' Neville broke in. He had an attractive, rather deep voice and he gave Kate a reassuring smile. 'I'll look after her – you don't need to worry. And we'll walk home with you and Ned, only if you don't mind we'll walk a little way behind.'

He winked, and Kate struggled with mixed feelings of annoyance and amusement. She remembered rather more clearly than she wanted to the night Sally referred to – when Jacky had come round to show off his new uniform and they'd almost got a bit too carried away as they said goodnight. She shook her head at them both. 'All right. I won't say anything. And you can walk home with us, Neville – only you'll walk in front, all right? She's my sister and I'm responsible for her.' She turned to Ned. 'Come on. Let's go and buy those chips.'

They bought a pennyworth of chips each and sauntered through the twilit streets, eating them out of yesterday's *Daily Mirror*. The print had come off on the chips so that they had bits of news printed on them, the words showing backwards like mirror-writing. It didn't seem to affect their taste, though, not once they'd been liberally showered with salt and doused with strong black vinegar.

Ned turned off at the corner of Cider Lane and Kate walked slowly behind Sally and Neville, who had their arms around each other's waists. She felt sad and lonely as she watched them pause to kiss goodnight at the door. She could remember her own first boyfriend, when she'd been much the same age as Sally was now, and the soaring revelation of what being in love could mean. I don't suppose it'll last more than a month, she thought, any more than it did with me and Micky Drew, who had quarrelled with her only a week or so later and was now in Africa or somewhere. But it's lovely while it does last, and she doesn't get all that much fun out of life. I can't spoil it for her.

Sally broke away from Neville's arms and turned to knock on the front door. Neville gave Kate a wave and she caught up with her sister, reaching her just as the door opened and their mother let them both in.

'Well,' Win said, pulling the blackout curtain closed

behind them, 'you look as if you've had a good time. Good picture, was it?'

Sally caught her sister's eye and her lips trembled with laughter, but when she spoke, her voice was demure.

'It was smashing,' she said. 'Wasn't it, Kate?'

Neville was waiting for Sally when she came out of work the next evening. Kate, who was walking with her, caught sight of him first and felt a pang of anxiety. This was Sally's first boyfriend, she was only fifteen and things seemed to be moving too quickly. Before she could say anything, Sally nudged her sharply in the ribs.

'There's Neville! He said he'd come and meet me. He must have come down on the train from Bedenham. Oh Kate, isn't he good-looking! He looks just like Clark Gable with that smashing pencil-thin moustache and those dark eyebrows.'

'Oh, it's a moustache, is it?' Kate said disagreeably. 'I thought he'd been eating liquorice bootlaces.'

'That's a horrible thing to say!' Sally gave her an angry look. 'You know what I think? I think you're jealous, because the only bloke you can find to go out with is Ned.'

'I'm *not* jealous.' Kate began furiously, and then stopped. Perhaps I am, she thought. Perhaps I'm miserable and upset because I'm worried about Brad and still unhappy over Godfrey, and scared about the jinx, and I'm taking it out on Sally. It *was* a horrible thing to say. She gave Sally a remorseful glance. 'Sorry, Sal. I didn't mean it. He does look a bit like Clark Gable.'

Neville had spotted them amongst the crowd of women streaming towards the gates, and was walking swiftly in their direction. He gave Kate a friendly grin, and then drew Sally's arm through his. 'Hello, sweetheart. Missed me?'

'You bet,' she said, gazing up at him with shining eyes, and Kate dropped back, letting them walk off together in front of her. Sweetheart! she thought. They've barely known each other a week. What on earth is Dad going to say when he finds out?

Sally had no intention of telling her father anything about Neville. They walked home slowly, taking a longer way round than Kate, who just wanted to get home and flop into a chair with a cup of tea. After a bit, Neville slipped his arm around her waist and she leaned her head on his shoulder. She felt a warm, blissful excitement, and the touch of secrecy added to the romance.

'Are you going to meet me every day?' she asked.

'Want me to?' He smiled down at her, and her heart skipped a little.

'Mmm, please. It was lovely to come out and see you there.' She touched her hair, newly released from the turban she wore at work. 'Mind you, I don't look very glamorous. You can't keep yourself nice, working with munitions.'

He nodded. 'You look glamorous enough to me, Sally. I'm not exactly in my Sunday best myself.' He indicated his working clothes ruefully. 'I wondered if you'd recognise me in these duds.'

'I think you look smashing.' They smiled at each other.

He said, 'D'you have to go straight home? I thought we might have a bite to eat in the Dive and go for a walk, or something.'

She hesitated. 'I'd better. I had another row with old Mother Sheppard this morning and I don't want Kate spilling the beans to Mum and Dad before I get home. Honestly, she's really got it in for me and you know what fathers are, they always think the boss must be right. *He* doesn't have to work with old Ma Sheppard!'

Neville grinned. 'What was the row about? Wish I could have been there.'

'Oh, it was just stupid.' Mrs Sheppard had been furious to find Sally working at the Hard when she returned from her sick leave. Still limping with her broken toe, and only able to wear an old slipper on that foot, she had been in no mood for back-answers, and had been watching Sally every minute, obviously hoping to pick her up on sloppy work. But Sally had learned her job well during the time the chargehand had been absent and worked quickly, her nimble fingers taking the shell-cases apart and her keen eyes examining the fuzes as efficiently as any of the older hands. To add to the chargehand's irritation, she was also well aware of her scrutiny and couldn't resist the odd wink or grin of triumph at the other girls. Mrs Sheppard saw her and her dark face set in a scowl.

'You want to be careful,' Elsie had muttered. 'It's not a good idea to get on the wrong side of that old cow.'

Sally shrugged. 'Don't care. As long as I do my work right and don't wear nail varnish, she can't do a thing about it.'

The row today, she told Neville, had been over a cup of tea that Sally had made at the steam outlet pipe. Although this was really against the rules, the chargehands usually turned a blind eye provided it was done when no one was watching. Sally had slipped out at dinnertime, bold as brass, with her enamel mug and half a spoonful of tea, and waltzed back in right under Mrs Sheppard's eye. Realising she was caught, she tried to brazen it out. 'Cuppa, Mrs Sheppard? I made it specially for you!'

The chargehand glowered. 'Like hell you did! You know it's against the rules, doing that.'

'You mean you don't want it after all?' Sally enquired, wide-eyed, and looked past her. 'Would you like it then, Mr Milner?'

Mrs Sheppard whirled round but there was no one there. Furious, she whipped back, but Sally had already slipped away to her bench and the mug of tea was nowhere to be seen. Elsie and the others gazed back innocently.

'Was there something you wanted?' the girl who took snuff asked sweetly. 'Only, we're on our dinner-hour now, and there's a concert on in the canteen. You wouldn't want us to miss it, would you?'

Mrs Sheppard turned a deep red and looked for a moment as if she would burst. Then she turned and stamped away, and the girls jostled out of the room, giggling, and made for the shifting room to change their clothes ready for the concert.

'Was it a good concert?' Neville asked when Sally finished telling him her story and they had laughed over it.

'Not bad. One of those ENSA things – a couple of singers, a comedian and a bloke who did impressions. None of them were as good-looking as you, though.'

Neville grinned and preened a little. 'And I bet none of the girls were as pretty as you.'

'Well, of course, not!' Sally said, and they both laughed again.

'Sure you won't come down the Dive?' he asked, looking into her eyes. 'We might get that table at the far end, where no one can see you.'

Sally felt a little thrill run through her. 'We-ell . . . Oh, all right! It doesn't really matter if Kate tells them about old Ma Sheppard. She'll probably tell them I'm with you anyway. Dad'll hit the roof, but I don't care. I don't care about anything now I've got you.'

Neville smiled and slid his arm round her waist. 'Let's not bother about the Dive,' he whispered. 'Let's find somewhere quiet where I can tell you just how pretty I think you are . . .'

Chapter Twenty

Nobody along the south coast of England could be in any doubt that the war was increasing in intensity. Hurricanes, Lancasters and Flying Fortresses flew over day and night, heading for the railways of France and the cities of Germany; the Solent and the Channel were crowded with ships; the great Naval harbours were equally thronged and the ten-mile Coastal Ban was being strictly enforced. You were likely to be picked up at any time by the police or the Army and asked for your identity card, and if you didn't have it you would be arrested at once and risk at least one night in the cells, possibly more.

'It's getting worse,' Elsie said to Charlie as she laid down the *Evening News* after tea. 'I heard today that the RAF bombed somewhere in France and killed over a thousand people – *French* people. That's not right. We're supposed to be protecting them.'

'It's the sort of thing that happens in wars,' Charlie said sombrely. 'The wrong people suffer. Mind you, if the French had held out against the Jerries, things might've been different. Seems to me they caved in too quick and left us to carry the can. Look at all them French soldiers and sailors, no bloody use to us at all now. And all them French ships we scuttled that could've been on our side. Bloody waste, that's what it was, a bloody waste.'

Elsie stared at him in astonishment. Charlie rarely spoke out like this, preferring to let her do all the ranting and raving. She cast about for something to lighten his mood.

'Well, we've still got that French ship out near Hard-way – the *Corbière*. That's been firing off its guns all right whenever a Jerry plane's come over.'

'Not got French sailors on board, though, has it,' Charlie said. 'It's our boys on that ship. And look at it this way, Else: if the French had stuck to it there'd have been a damn sight more than a thousand killed by now. They got off light, if you ask me. Got off *light*.'

His last words were interrupted by the shrill of the doorbell. Elsie answered it and found Jackie Prentice standing outside, her arms full of shopping bags.

'Jackie! Come in, love.' Elsie ushered her inside. 'What-ever have you got there? Been doing some shopping for the baby?'

Jackie shook her head. Her face was swollen with crying and her eyes filled with fresh tears. Quickly, Elsie took the bags from her and dumped them on the table, while Charlie grabbed his newspaper and shuffled out. 'I'll go down the shed, Else.'

'Yes, all right, love.' She spoke absently, giving Jackie an anxious look. 'Sit down there, in his chair, he's been keeping it warm special. I'll just boil the kettle for a cuppa . . . Now, you just take your time and then tell me what's the matter. What's happened now? It's not the baby, is it? You're all right?'

Jackie sniffed, gulped and nodded. 'I think so. I saw the midwife today . . . Oh, Mrs Philpotts!' She broke into a storm of tears and Elsie, already out in the kitchen turning up the gas, came hurrying back in. 'Oh, I don't know what I'm going to do, I really don't! Oh, Mrs *Philpotts*!'

'There, my duck, there.' Elsie sat down beside her, folding her arms about the thin shoulders and drawing her against her own broad cushion of a bosom. 'That's all right, now, you have a good cry . . . Let it all out. It's good for you. Don't you worry now, we all gets a bit weepy when we're expecting . . . Just let it go and you'll feel better. A good cry's what we all wants from time to time . . . Why, if I had a pound for every time I've come home of an afternoon and sat down in this very chair and just cried my eyes out, I'd be a rich woman. Never told my Charlie, of course, he don't have the slightest idea. Got a hanky? Here, have mine . . . That's right, have a good blow. There goes the kettle, whistling its head off. All right, I'm coming, I'm coming!' She hurried back to the kitchen and began to clatter cups and saucers. 'A cup of tea, that's what you need, and then you can tell me all about it. We'll soon sort it out, whatever it is.'

Jackie blew her nose and wiped her eyes. The first storm was over but her words were punctuated with hiccups and jerky sighs. She took the cup of tea Elsie handed her and sipped it gratefully. 'Oh, that's nice. You make a lovely cup of tea, Mrs Philpotts.'

'It's because I don't take no notice of Lord Woolton,' Elsie said ruefully, thinking of the tea ration. 'Not when it's needed for medical purposes, anyway. Now, tell me what all this is about. What's in them bags?' She had a fair idea of what was in them but it was as good a way as any of getting Jackie to start talking.

'It's me things,' Jackie confessed. 'All me bits and pieces. Oh, Mrs Philpotts, I can't stop at home any more. It's so awful there. He just keeps on and on at me all the time, and I can't do a thing right. He won't eat my cooking, he says I don't wash the clothes properly and the place is a mess, and – oh, he just goes on and on. And he says Mum would have been ashamed of me. He says I'd have broken her heart like I've broken his.' The tears began again. 'He said tonight he was *glad she was dead*, so she didn't have to see me like this!'

Elsie sat down beside her and laid her arm over the shaking shoulders. She felt deeply sorry for Jackie, yet she could understand Herbert's reaction. An illegitimate baby was a scandal and a shame, even in wartime, and the fact that the father wasn't a local boy meant that they couldn't even put it right by getting married. An American soldier . . . She wondered how many other girls had been taken in by their promises. There was young Kate Fisher too, hankering after another one, though Kate probably hadn't got this sort of worry hanging over her.

Still, Herbert Prentice was being a bit stupid, driving his daughter away like this. He depended on her to look after him. You'd have thought he could have shown a bit more sense, and a bit of common humanity too. It wasn't just the shame of an illegitimate baby that Jackie was suffering. She'd lost someone she'd loved and who she'd believed loved her, as well. She'd given her whole self and been betrayed.

'Did he actually turn you out?' she asked when Jackie's sobs had diminished again. 'Won't he come round?'

Jackie looked at her. 'He never turned me out, no. He just kept on and on shouting at me and in the end I thought I couldn't stop there any more. So I packed up my bags and come away.' She nodded towards the clutter of shopping bags on the table. 'Once I got out I didn't know what to do, so I – I come here. I thought perhaps . . .'

'You thought you might be able to stop here,' Elsie nodded. 'Well, I did say I'd take you in if it come to it, and it looks as if it has. But I'm a bit worried about your dad, all the same. How's he going to manage, on his own?'

'Oh, I'll go in every day and get his dinner and see to his washing and that. But I reckon he can do more than he lets on. He'll manage.'

Elsie nodded. She'd suspected as much herself, when she walked round to see Herbert. She'd seen it before, men who'd been injured at work and took the chance of being able to knock off and stop at home, letting their wives and families keep them. But she didn't think Herbert Prentice would give in now without a fight. He'd make Jackie feel as guilty as he could, even if it meant living in a pigsty and half-starving himself.

'Well, you can stop here and welcome, Jackie. There's our Graham's bed upstairs – he's not going to need it again, more's the pity, and I know he'd want me to look after you. Now, have you had your tea? I can make you some beans on toast if you like. I always think beans on toast is a nice thing to have when you're feeling a bit down.'

Jackie shook her head. 'No thanks, Mrs Philpotts. We had a bit of fish tonight.' She started to cry again. 'I know it wasn't very nice – it was that *snoek* stuff, I dunno what sort of fish that is but it was all I could get – but there was plenty of mashed potato to go with it, and a bit of beet-root. He likes mashed potato and beetroot, usually. But just lately he doesn't seem to like *anything* I do.'

'All right,' Elsie said quickly, anxious to stop another outbreak of tears. 'You can have something later on. Let's take your stuff upstairs now, there's a cupboard and a chest of drawers – they've been needing a bit of clearing out. I'll do it now.' It was Graham's things that were still there, old clothes and a few toys from when he was a kiddy and before he joined the Navy, things Elsie had never had the heart to throw out even though she knew they could be used for the war effort. Now was the time to do it, she thought, setting her jaw as she led Jackie up to the small back bedroom. I'll put them all in an old pillow-case and take them round the WVS place first thing in the morning. Not the toys, though. They'll come in handy for the baby.

I'm sorry, Graham, she thought, pulling things out of the drawers and pushing them into the pillowcase without even looking at them. I'm sorry, but it's time to say goodbye. And she brushed a hand fiercely across her eyes, angry at the tears that burned and ached in her throat.

Another Allied raid that week killed over five hundred people in Paris. People were beginning to echo Elsie's words that there seemed to be no sense in it: what was the point of attacking France when it was Germany that was the cause of all the trouble? But others argued that this was all to get the place ready for Allies to invade, and it was known that 'Bomber' Harris believed in saturation bombing – the destruction of large areas – which would strike terror into the hearts of the enemy as well as ruin their communications and deprive them of large numbers of troops. It was just unfortunate that the French had to have losses as well, but there again you'd got to remember they'd had it light so far. *They* hadn't been blitzed, like Britain, they hadn't lost half their capital city and seen God knows how many others laid waste like Coventry and Liverpool and Pompey itself. They didn't have all that much to complain about, really, when you came to look at it.

'I dunno,' George said as he read the pages of the *Daily Express*. 'I don't reckon it's any picnic, being occupied by the Germans and having them rule the roost over you. They say in some places you've only got to speak out of turn and you can get shot dead there and then. And they gets all the best of everything, you know – the ordinary working folk like you and me are half-starved.'

'They still never had to go down the air-raid shelter night after night, scared out of their wits, and then come up of a morning to find their homes smashed to smithereens,' Win retorted. 'But the long and short of it is that war's no picnic for anyone, George, and it'll be a good thing when it's all finished with, and that's what I reckon

Mr Churchill and General Eisenhower are set on doing now. Get it over and done with.'

The same thought seemed to be in everyone's minds. At Priddy's Hard each magazine was in competition to see who could turn out the most bombs, shells or torpedoes a week, and the results were chalked up on a blackboard in the canteen. The narrow-gauge trains running from Bedenham and Frater were loaded as heavily as they could be, and their timetables doubled. Ned was taken off sweeping and cleaning and put to riding on the last truck.

'It's a smashing job,' he told Kate, his wide grin almost splitting his face in half. 'It's as good as riding shotgun for Wells Fargo!'

'Well, don't forget you've got explosives on board,' she warned him, 'and not gold! There'll be a mighty big bang if that lot goes up.'

He shook his head. 'It won't. It's safe as houses.'

Kate watched the little train trundle away and rolled her eyes. 'He lives in a world of his own, Ned does,' she said to Maxine, who was standing beside her. 'If he can go to a couple of cowboy pictures a week he's happy, and now he's got a job on the train he's in heaven.'

Maxine grunted. 'He's only ninepence in the shilling, if you ask me. I'm surprised you go around with him.'

'Oh, Ned's all right. Not the sharpest knife in the box, but he's good-hearted and he doesn't have many friends. We've known each other since we were babies – our mums were friends at school.'

Maxine shrugged. She was still behaving coolly towards her friend, although Kate suspected that she really wanted to be friends again. But she seemed happier now that she was going out with Joey Hutton, and Kate hoped that things were better for her at home. 'Aren't you afraid this jinx of yours'll get him?' Maxine said pointedly.

Kate bit her lip. There was a sarcastic bite to Maxine's

voice but she decided to take no notice of it. 'Not really,' she said quietly. 'I'm not going out with him in that way. He's not my boyfriend, and he's not in the Services. Anyway, never mind that, Maxie – tell me how *you're* getting on. You've been seeing a lot of Joey Hutton, haven't you? Is it getting serious?'

'For goodness sake! We've only been going out together a couple of weeks.' But that was long enough for some people to get serious in wartime, as they both knew. Some people got engaged, or even married, in less time than that. Maxine hesitated, then grinned suddenly, 'Mind you, he is a smasher! I wouldn't mind getting serious with him.'

Kate met her eyes and saw the warmth return to them. They smiled at each other and linked arms, knowing that no more need be said about their quarrel. Kate felt a rush of relief and hugged Maxine's arm against her side.

'How about things at home? I've been thinking about you a lot, Maxie. How's it all going?'

Maxine shrugged. 'No better. No reason why it should be, is there? *He* tried to make excuses for her – said she'd been attacked one night down Daisy Lane and never knew who it was, but I reckon it must have been one of the boys she'd been going round with. Seems to me she led 'em on. I reckon she asked for it.'

'Maxie!' Kate stared at her in horror. 'You never told me that!'

'No – well, it was only a few days ago that he told me. I haven't felt like talking about it much.'

'No . . .' Kate frowned, trying to understand. 'So, when they put *Father Unknown* on the birth certificate . . .'

'Well, that's it, isn't it!' Maxine burst out. 'They didn't have to put that, did they? They could have *said* it was his. At least I'd have *thought* I had a proper dad. Now I'll never know who he was! I'll always know he – he – oh, it's horrible, Kate, it's really horrible, thinking about it, knowing what sort of a man my father was! And it's always going to be the same. It's never going to go away, never!'

Kate hardly knew how to reply. After a few moments, picking her words as carefully as if she were tiptoeing through a minefield, she said, 'But you've got to try to *make* it go away, Maxie. You can't let it ruin your whole life.'

'I'm not! I'm having a good time. I'm going out with a smashing bloke, and once I can find somewhere else to live I'll be able to forget all about *them*. They can go to hell for all I care!'

Her bitter tone appalled Kate. 'But don't you see, Maxie, you do care, or you wouldn't be so upset. Moving out isn't going to make any difference to that. Anyway, where are you going to go? Have you found anywhere yet?'

Maxine shook her head, looking deflated. 'I asked Elsie but she wouldn't give me a straight answer – said I ought to try and make it up with them. I could ask her again, I suppose. You'd think she'd be glad to have a lodger. I know she's got a spare room and that dried-up old hubby of hers can't be much company.'

They returned to the magazine. Lunch-breaks were shorter than ever now and it was hardly worth getting changed to come outside, but the whole yard was gripped by a fever of urgency to produce more and more munitions, and nobody grumbled. For the rest of the day, the women laboured at their benches, and a seemingly endless stream of torpedoes and shells was loaded on to the barges to be transported across the harbour. By seven o'clock, when they knocked off for the night shift to begin, everyone was exhausted.

Maxine caught up with Elsie just as they crowded out through the gates. 'Hiya.'

'Oh hello, Maxie,' Elsie said, a little awkwardly. 'Haven't seen much of you lately. How are you getting on?'

Maxine pulled a face. 'As well as anyone can get on when they're living with people they hate.'

Elsie shook her head. 'You mustn't talk like that. They're your mum and dad.'

'*She* is. *He's* not. And she's nothing to write home about, anyway.' Maxine gave a little bark of laughter. 'Hear that? Write home! I tell you, Elsie, if I could get away I'd never even send a postcard!'

Elsie looked at her sadly. 'I don't like hearing you talk like this, Maxine, I really don't. What have they done to upset you so badly? I just don't understand it.'

'No, you don't, do you?' Maxine took a deep breath. They were walking along the road together, surrounded by other people on their way home but everyone was chattering and nobody was taking any notice. 'All right, I'll tell you. They were only married five months when I was born, Else.'

'Oh,' Elsie said. 'Oh, I see . . . But that's not so awful, is it? I mean, I know it's not very nice to find out, but they did get married, didn't they? I can't see why you should hate them just because of that. It happens to quite a lot of people, if truth be told, and you're no angel yourself.'

Maxine flushed. 'I've never got into trouble, though, have I! Anyway, that's not all there is to it. It's worse. You see, he's not my real dad. It says on my birth certificate *Father Unknown*. And that's the truth of it – she doesn't know who he was. *She doesn't even know who he was.*'

Elsie stopped and stared at her, and two women walking immediately behind bumped into her and swore. She ignored them. 'Maxine! Whatever do you mean? She wasn't a—'

'I don't know, do I! Oh, he *says* not – he says she was a real goody-goody, butter wouldn't melt in her mouth, all the boys were after her but she wouldn't let anyone have more than a kiss. That's what he *says*.'

'So . . .' Elsie looked at her helplessly. 'I don't understand.'

'He says she was attacked,' Maxine said flatly. 'One night, walking through Daisy Lane. *He* was supposed to meet her but his bike had a puncture. Someone dragged her into the bushes and she never saw his face.'

Elsie gazed at her, shocked. 'Oh, Maxie. That's awful. Your poor mother!'

Maxine shrugged. 'And poor me too. Have you got any idea what it's like not to know who your father is, Elsie? To know he was *that* sort of man? That's if it's true.'

'Oh, but surely—'

Maxine began to walk on very quickly. 'Look, Elsie, I don't really want to talk about it, all right? We're never going to know, are we? All I know is, I can't go on living with them, and if you'd let me have your spare room I'd be your friend for life. I would, really.' She stopped and caught Elsie's arm, looking urgently into her face. 'I'd pay a proper rent, and I'd help you round the place. I'd do housework and washing, and help cook and – and everything. I just want to get away, Elsie. I've *got* to get away.'

'But – look, I can see this has been a shock to you, but – well, can't you think again? Never mind what happened years ago, they've done their best by you since, haven't they? Brought you up, given you a good home? He's been a good dad to you, even if you weren't his. It's not every chap'd do that, you know. Can't you look at it from their side?'

'No,' Maxine said shortly. 'I can't.' She began to walk on.

Elsie hurried after her. 'Look, love, I'd help you if I

could. You may be right, it may be a good idea to get away for a bit, give you all time to think things over. Only . . .'

Maxine stopped and said eagerly, 'You'll let me come, then? You'll let me have your spare room?'

'I can't.' Elsie shook her head. 'Maxie, I'm ever so sorry, I can't. You see, I've already taken in someone else.'

'Someone else?' Maxine echoed. 'Who?'

'Jackie Prentice. I don't know if you know her. She used to go out with my Graham and I've always had a soft spot for her. Then they were bombed out and her mum was killed and her dad's been an invalid ever since, and she often pops in to say hello. And now—'

'I don't understand,' Maxine broke in. 'Why does *she* need to come and live with you?'

'Well, because she's got into trouble, you see,' Elsie said unhappily. 'She was going out with a GI and he promised to marry her, only now he's gone away and she's expecting, and her father won't have her at home any more. She came round to me a couple of days ago with all her stuff in carrier bags, and just begged me to take her in. She wants to have her baby with me. I'm sorry, Maxine.'

'You're taking in a girl who's *expecting*?' Maxine said incredulously. 'You're letting some – some *slut* come and live with you, when you knew I needed somewhere to go? Without even giving me a thought?' She began to walk on again, her steps so fast she was almost running. Elsie panted after her.

'Maxie, don't take it like that! I'm sorry. It's just – if you could see her . . .'

'I don't want to see her!' Maxine said savagely. 'I can see my mum any day, I don't need to see another slut. It's all right, Elsie, you don't need to apologise, and you needn't bother to talk to me again. I can see just what sort of a friend you are!' They came to an alleyway and she wheeled sharply to her left. 'I'm going this way tonight,

and you needn't bother to come after me. I'll find someone else to give me a room. I'm not stopping there a
minute longer than I have to, but *you* needn't worry about
me. You go home to your slut and her baby, and good luck
to you!'

Chapter Twenty-One

Kate sat on the shore alone, reading a letter from Brad. Although she'd believed him when he said he wouldn't forget her, she hadn't really expected to hear from him again. Remembering someone and actually keeping in touch were two different things. Sometimes – as in the case of the Canadians who had been killed at Dieppe, and many others like them – it wasn't the men's fault. But all too often it was a case of girls being taken advantage of, and the girls lucky if all they were left with was a broken heart.

Like Jackie Prentice, she thought. Elsie had told her about the frightened, desperate girl who had come to her front door a few weeks ago, begging for help, and how Elsie had taken her in for Graham's sake as well as her own. 'I've got to say, it could as easy have been my Graham's kiddy as anyone else's,' Elsie had said frankly. 'He was no saint, my son, and I dare say if he'd lived longer he'd have ended up getting some young woman in the family way and having to marry her. So I might as well help young Jackie, because if it wasn't her it would've been someone else!'

Not everyone would have taken that point of view, Kate thought. Maxine didn't, for a start. It was common knowledge now that Maxine had asked Elsie to take her in but Elsie couldn't because she'd already got Jackie in her spare bedroom. Maxine was furious and called Jackie every name under the sun, until some of the other women at

Priddy's Hard had rounded on her and told her they were fed up with hearing about it, and there were plenty worse off than her. She'd shut up then and had gone about ever since with a face as long as a wet weekend, refusing to talk to anyone, even Kate. Everyone was against her, she said when Kate tried to cheer her up with a joke, but she didn't care because she had Joey. Joey was the only one who understood.

Kate sighed and looked at her letter again. Brad had enclosed a photograph with it, a small square that showed him in uniform, his cap pushed back on his head, straight, white teeth showing in a broad grin. *So that you won't forget what I look like*, he'd written. So she made up her mind to send him one of herself and scrabbled through her box of photos and letters until she found a snap taken in the garden one day not long after the war had started, with the last film her father had been able to get for his box Brownie camera. She'd been four years younger then, of course, but she still had that summer frock and, with her face partly shaded by a big straw hat, you could hardly see any difference. She'd been laughing at something Pete was doing as her father snapped. It was a happy picture and she thought Brad would like it.

The letter itself didn't tell her much about where Brad was or what he was doing now – the censor would have crossed out any information like that – but at least she knew he was safe and somewhere in the area. He must be, since there was no mail allowed in or out of the ten-mile strip now. But what it did tell her was that he missed her and loved her and wanted to be back with her. *As soon as we finish this little job*, he wrote, *I'll be back for you, just like I promised. And you'll wait for me, won't you, so that we can go dancing again. Oh, little lady, little lady, I love you . . .*

Kate folded the letter and pressed it against her breast. The words echoed in her mind – *I love you, I love you, I love you* – I love you too, Brad, she thought, but even as her heart soared she felt the dread weight of the jinx press down on her mind. What have I done? she thought in sudden panic. I never meant this to happen. I never meant him to love me – I never meant to fall in love with him. How did I let it happen? Oh Brad! If anything happens to you, if you get killed, like all the others, I shall never forgive myself, never.

She drew her knees up to her chin and wrapped her arms about them, staring across the harbour. It was early May now and the colour of the sky was deepening from the paleness of winter through the tender, robin's-egg blue of spring towards the deeper hues of summer. There was real warmth to the sunlight, and it was a pleasure to be on the shore, listening to the soft rippling of the waves on the shingle beach. A few years ago we'd have gone swimming on a day like this, she thought. In a week or two, on Whit Bank Holiday, we'd have had our first picnic out at Stokes Bay. Not this year, though, not with it all barricaded off with barbed wire and soldiers and heaven knows what going on there. Perhaps next year – but who knows what will have happened by then?

From here, she could see the Semaphore Tower with the masts of HMS *Victory* behind it. You could hardly tell that Portsmouth was so badly bombed, behind those undamaged landmarks. The jetties of the dockyard were thronged with ships, jostling each other as if impatient to be off, and more ships could be seen, both far into the upper reaches of the harbour and out through the narrow neck between Sallyport and Blockhouse which led to the Solent. From the little Camber Dock at Priddy's Hard, barges and lighters were crossing all the time, loaded with more munitions. War, war, war, she thought. It's all we've had for the past five years. Five years! I'm sick of it . . .

'Katy! I've been looking for you.' She turned quickly at

the sound of Ned's voice. Looking more like a scarecrow than ever with his shambling gait and loosely swinging arms, he was loping down the shore towards her, a beaming grin on his face. 'I've got something to tell you. Something really good.' He flopped down beside her, gazing at her expectantly like a spaniel expecting praise for retrieving a stick.

Kate put her letter away in her pocket. 'What is it? What's happened?' A tremor of excitement rippled over her skin. 'Is Hitler dead? Is it all over?'

He stared at her as if the possibility of Hitler dying or the war ending had never occurred to him. 'No, it's not that. It's me, Kate. You'll never guess.' His beaming grin widened. 'I'm going to be allowed to drive the train! *Me* – a train-driver! Just like at the pictures.' He made the *whoo-whoo* sound of a train's whistle. 'I'm going to drive it all day between here and Bedenham and Frater. *Me*!'

Kate looked at him. 'You? Drive the train? Are you sure, Ned?'

'Course I'm sure. Mr Milner said so himself. One of the women what drives it has been took sick, got an appendix or something, and the others are all too busy doing key jobs, so as I've been riding shotgun – I mean, helping with the loads and that – he said why not let me have a go. And I did!' The grin almost touched his ears. 'I drove it all the way to Frater! And he said I did very well and I could do it regular. What d'you think of that?'

'Well, it's lovely, Ned,' Kate said rather dubiously. 'Only I thought it was quite a skilled job . . .'

'Women do it,' he said with a touch of indignation. 'There's lots of women do it. I can do it just as well as them. Mr Milner said so.'

'Well, if Mr Milner says so . . .' Kate still didn't feel sure. It seemed a huge responsibility for someone like Ned – driving a train, even a small one, loaded with explosives.

But I suppose it's not that difficult really, she thought. Not like driving a car or a bus, for instance. It's on tracks and it doesn't go very fast. 'We'll all have to look out for you when we hear it coming,' she said, making a joke of it. 'You won't forget to whistle, will you?'

'Not likely!' Ned made the *whoo-whoo* sound again. 'Just like Wells Fargo, Kate, but it'll be me driving!'

'Well, I don't suppose there'll be many Indians,' she said, smiling at him. 'And nobody like Billy the Kid holding you up. You ought to be quite safe.'

He guffawed and jumped to his feet. 'Come to the pictures tonight?' he asked, holding out his hands to pull her up. 'There's a new Hopalong Cassidy on at the Cri. We can go after tea.'

She hesitated, thinking of the letter in her pocket. But going out with Ned wasn't like going with anyone else. Nobody could accuse her of two-timing Brad, just by going to the pictures with Ned. 'All right. I don't mind. But don't you use your sweet ration. I've got some toffees, I'll bring them.'

He nodded cheerfully and swung her hand in his, still elated by his promotion to train-driver. They walked back to the magazines together and then Kate turned away to go to the shifting room.

Poor old Ned, she thought, stripping off her outdoor clothes and stepping over the red line. It doesn't take much to make him happy. Maybe the world would be a better place if we were all more like him. Maybe it would be better if we didn't all *want* so much – if we were content with cowboy films and little trains and a bag of toffees. Maybe it would be better if we were content just to *like* each other, and not think so much about *love*.

That's all I meant to do with Brad, she thought, pulling on her magazine overalls. *Like* him. But somehow along the way I've ended up loving him.

Sally too was preoccupied with romance. By now her parents had found out about Neville – it would have been impossible to hide from them the fact that she had acquired a boyfriend, since she was out with him almost every evening – and, although they weren't pleased about it, they'd met him when he called for Sally one Sunday afternoon and given their grudging approval. He was well set-up, George admitted, his hair was neat and not slicked back with too much Brylcreem, and he was polite and well-mannered. Win was less impressed. 'To my mind, he's still a bit flashy,' she told her husband after the two had gone off up the street together for their walk. 'Too pleased with himself. I wouldn't be surprised if he's not a bit of a spiv. And why hasn't he been called up?'

'Didn't she say he's not eighteen yet? I dare say he'll get his papers soon enough.' George was putting on his boots, ready to go over to the allotment. 'At least he's a local boy, and not some fly-by-night GI. We can be thankful for that, Win.'

'I suppose so.' Win had looked at Kate. 'D'you know anything about him, love? Have you seen him around much?'

Kate shrugged. 'I've seen him around, but I couldn't say I ever actually knew him. As a matter of fact, I did think I'd seen him about with a red-haired girl – I saw them on the ferry one Saturday night when we were going over to the Savoy but I don't know who she was.'

'Does Sally know that?' Win asked, raising her eyebrows, and Kate shrugged again.

'I told her but she just ignored me. Said whoever it was, it must be all over now anyway. She can't see any wrong in him at all, Mum. Not that I'm saying there *is* anything wrong,' she added hastily, wishing she could rid herself of the faint distrust she felt whenever she thought of Neville.

Sally had told her she was just jealous, and she had a nasty feeling that her sister might be right. 'He's never said anything out of place to me.'

'Well,' Win observed practically, 'I don't suppose it'll last. It's just a boy-and-girl thing. It'll all fizzle out in a week or so.'

Sally would have been furious to hear her mother say that. To her, this was the biggest romance since *Romeo and Juliet*. She knew, without any doubt at all, that she and Neville were meant for each other. They would be together for the rest of their lives, living in eternal bliss, with never a cross word.

'Nobody's ever loved anybody like I love you, Neville,' she said dreamily as they sat entwined on a secluded seat in Foster Gardens. They'd walked all the way down there from Elson and had peered into the round pond, looking for tadpoles, before settling on the seat by the rockery. 'I'm ever so glad you came to that dance.'

'So'm I.' His arm was round her shoulders and he turned her towards him and kissed her lingeringly on the lips. Sally sighed blissfully and pressed herself against him. She felt his arms tighten and his mouth grow harder. The kiss grew more passionate and her dreamy, drifting bliss turned to dizziness. 'Oh, *Neville* . . .'

He slid both arms around her and held her tightly for another kiss. Sally felt the floating sensation again and this time let herself drift higher, her mind whirling as Neville's lips moved on hers. It was exciting and still a little frightening but she could enjoy the sense of danger, knowing that she still had control and could stop him the minute she wanted to. 'Oh Neville,' she whispered when his lips left hers for a moment. 'Oh Neville, I love you so much . . .'

At the other end of Gosport, Maxine and Joey lay in a sheltered hollow in the bluebell woods at Rowner. They had gone a good deal further in their love-making than Sally and Neville, but Maxine was still holding back from going 'all the way'. She too was aware of the danger, and even more so since hearing her mother's story and that of Jackie Prentice. What she wanted most from Joey now was comfort, and after they'd kissed and caressed for a while she drew herself away a little and sighed.

'What's the matter?' He was slightly aggrieved. 'Have I done something you don't like?'

'You know I like everything you do! It's not that, Joey. I just can't forget what it's like at home.' She had told Joey about the rows, though not about their cause. She was afraid that he would turn away from her in disgust once he knew the truth about her birth. It's all very well for Kate to say I mustn't let it ruin my life, she thought, but it will. As soon as people know, they won't want to have any more to do with me.

'Not even when you're with me?' he asked teasingly, and trailed his fingers over her breast. Maxine squeaked, and he grinned and kissed her hard.

'I forget everything when you do that,' she murmured, winding her arms round his neck. 'But then it all comes rushing back again. It's so awful, Joey. I've just got to find somewhere else to live.' She hesitated. 'I suppose your mum wouldn't let me come and live at your house? I mean, there's your room, isn't there? You're not using it now you're at *Daedalus*.'

'And I'm not going to be stationed there much longer,' he said, rolling away a little and speaking gloomily. 'When this balloon goes up we'll all be sent away. I could be over in France in a few weeks, Maxie, d'you realise that?'

'Oh no!' She stared at him in dismay. 'I thought you were supposed to be staying here. Surely they've got to have someone at *Daedalus* to repair planes and things when they come back.'

'Yes, but I don't know for sure I'll be one of them.' He slanted her a look. 'I could go away and not come back for years, Maxie, like your Matthew.'

'I couldn't bear it! You're the only good thing that's happened to me, ever. I can't let you go.' She pulled him back towards her. 'Oh Joey, what are we going to do?'

'You know what I'd like to do,' he murmured, stroking her with lingering hands.

'I don't mean that! I mean if you go away, and I'm still stuck at home and can't find anywhere else to live. At least if I was at your house I'd feel closer to you.' She gazed at him. 'Couldn't you ask her?'

'We-ell.' He pursed his lips. 'She *might* agree – if we were engaged.'

'Engaged!' Maxine's heart leaped. 'You mean – are you asking me to marry you. Are you *proposing* to me?' None of Maxine's friends had had a proposal yet, except Janice. A sudden hot excitement flowed through her veins.

'Well . . .' Joey looked almost as startled as she was. 'I suppose I am, really. I mean, why not? If I'm going away soon, we ought to get something decided. And if we were engaged and you were living with my mum, well, there's no reason why we shouldn't . . .' He moved closer again and rubbed his body sensuously against hers. Maxine gasped a little and tried to keep her mind on the discussion.

'Joey, don't. I can't think properly when you do that. Are we going to get engaged properly? With a ring and everything?'

'I suppose so. We could go down to Hug's and see what they've got. I can't afford anything too flashy though. No big diamonds or anything.'

Hug's was the little jeweller's shop at the bottom of Gosport High Street. Everyone went there for their engagement and wedding rings, as well as silver bracelets and sparkly brooches. Maxine had never been given anything from Hug's but, like all the other girls, she often stopped and gazed in the window, dreaming of the day when she would own one of the lovely things she saw there.

'I don't want a big diamond. Just a little one will do, to show you love me.' She gazed at him.

He moved his hand down her body. 'So if we're going to get engaged, and if I'm going away . . .'

She looked anxious. 'Joey, I don't know. I want to, but . . .'

'But what? There's nothing to be scared of, Maxie. I won't hurt you.'

'It's just . . .' She whispered, 'I'm scared. I've never – I mean, you're my first—'

'I should think so too!' he said teasingly. 'You've never been engaged before, have you?'

'No, but Joey, I don't want to rush. It's been so nice, these past few weeks, just going out together and getting to know each other.'

'We could get to know each other a lot better,' he coaxed her.

'Yes, but not tonight.' She felt her cheeks colour. 'I can't tonight. I'm – well, you know.'

'Oh, I see.' He rolled away from her. 'You never mentioned that.' He sounded a little sulky, like a child who has been offered a sweet and then had it taken away again.

'Well, I wouldn't, would I! You didn't need to know, not if we were only kissing and – and that. Look, I can't help it, Joey. I didn't know you were going to propose to me, did I? And even if we're engaged, it doesn't mean that I'd want to go all the way – not straight off.'

'But I'll be going away soon.' Half an hour earlier, this had been only a vague possibility, but Maxine was too upset to notice the change. 'And if you want to come and live at our house . . .'

'I know.' The joy of the past few moments was dimmed and she felt a wave of misery. Surely they couldn't be quarrelling already, only minutes after his proposal. 'Joey, I'm sorry. I just never thought – it's not the sort of thing a girl tells a boy anyway. Look, it only lasts a few days. I'll be all right by the weekend.'

'I suppose so.' He turned towards her and slid his arms around her once more, laying his mouth against her ear. 'So you will, then?' he whispered. 'You'll let me love you properly on Saturday? Or Friday night? And then we'll go down to Hug's and get a ring on Saturday morning.'

Maxine felt as if she were being swept along on a tide she couldn't control. 'Yes. All right.' Her heart beat fast at the thought. 'And you'll ask your mum if I can come and stay at your house?'

'We'll go back to tea after we've got the ring,' he said. 'We'll tell her we're engaged and she's bound to say yes. It'll be all right, Maxine. Everything's going to be all right.' He kissed her again, a wild kiss of passion and exultation. 'Friday night, eh! Friday night!'

'And Saturday,' Maxine said, letting her mind skid away from the promise she had somehow made and thinking only of the ring she would be able to wear, and the move she could make at last. 'On Saturday we'll be engaged. Oh, Joey.'

He pulled her hard against him and she let him slide his hand into her blouse and unfasten her brassiere. The feel of his hands on her breasts excited her so much that she was almost ready to let him have his way there and then. In fact, she was not menstruating at all – the excuse had come to her in her panic, but although she longed to let him make love to her she dared not tell him she'd lied. And in truth, there was still a part of her that was relieved not to have to make that final commitment.

There was still a part of her that was afraid.

Chapter Twenty-Two

As May drew on, soldiers poured into the town. British, American, Canadian, they filled the streets with their tanks, lorries, DUKWs and 'Funnies' – tanks that had been adapted specially for this great thrust. There was the 'Crab' with its chain-flail that could clear a ten-foot swathe through a minefield; the 'Bobbin' which would lay a broad canvas mat over soft sand to provide a firm track for other vehicles; a Churchill tank with a swivelling jib that could bridge a thirty-foot gap in thirty seconds; and, most fearsome of all, the 'Crocodile' with its flame-gun that could flash terrible death at a range of over 100 yards.

It was only later that the citizens of Gosport, and the other seaside towns which found themselves hosts to the masses of troops, discovered what these strange contraptions were that had suddenly arrived on their doorstep. For now, they were just tanks, and the men aboard them 'our boys', ready to go to war and bring long-awaited salvation to the world.

Kate came home one evening to find lorries parked all along Cider Lane. Soldiers grinned and hailed her as she walked down the street, and she waved back, slightly disconcerted at the thought of all these men camping outside the house. As she arrived at her own door, it opened and a red-haired corporal emerged, looking over his shoulder and saying something to Win, who had followed him along the passage. Kate waited for him to come out and then went in, wondering what he had been doing inside the house.

'He just came in for a cold bath,' Win explained. 'There's been a stream of 'em in and out all afternoon. They're not supposed to talk to us really, but they've been living in their lorries for weeks, poor perishers, and we've all been letting 'em in to clean up a bit. You can't wash properly in half a pint of water in the back of a lorry. They cleared up after themselves,' she added as Kate went through to the kitchen.

The bath had been taken back outside and hung on its nail, and you would never have known that Win had been entertaining soldiers all afternoon. Kate gave her mother a comical look. 'So this is what goes on when the rest of us are out of the house! How long have you been asking soldiers in for a bath? What will our dad say when he finds out?'

'Now, there's no need for that kind of talk.' Win bustled out to fill the kettle. 'It's all part of the war effort – and you needn't laugh like that neither, Kate. Barney's had the time of his life, haven't you, love? They've been showing him their uniforms, and their guns, and everything.' Kate began to laugh again. 'Stop that giggling – you've got a dirty mind since you went down Priddy's Hard to work.'

It was the same all over Gosport. The narrow streets were crowded with huge vehicles, their tracks denting the kerbstones, and the air was filled with the deep rumble of men's voices as they talked, and with their songs and laughter as they entertained themselves to pass the time. Some had mouth-organs or penny-whistles and their music floated through the air. It was like a vast party, yet the tension never evaporated, for when the guests left this party some would be going to their death.

Many residents who found soldiers outside their homes made them cups of tea and asked them in for baths or scratch meals. Most of them knew someone whose son was in the Services, and they did it for these boys in the hope and trust that someone, somewhere, would be doing it for their own. Because some of these boys – the Americans and the Canadians – were so far from home. You just had to ask them in, even though it wasn't really allowed. Some of the sergeants made sure the rules of not talking to the residents were followed; others turned a blind eye.

The men sat at tables in little back rooms, drinking tea and bringing small packets of photographs out of their pockets to show their hosts. 'This is my wife, Mary-Jane . . .' 'These are my kids. That's Benny, the one with no front teeth, he's the biggest, that's the baby, Polly-Ann, she's a real little princess . . .' It was heartbreaking, Win said, when you knew some of these children wouldn't see their fathers again, and when babies like little Polly-Ann wouldn't even remember them.

Kate wondered where Brad was. Was he camping out-side a house somewhere, being invited in for a bath, drinking tea or Camp coffee and showing the same photo-graphs he had shown her? Perhaps even showing his hosts the snap she had given him of herself, laughing in the garden, telling them she was his sweetheart?

The rest of the family arrived home for supper. Sally had walked home with Neville, lingering through the streets, and George had gone straight over to the allot-ment for half an hour. There was so much to do at this time of year, and not much time in the day to do it in, so he walked home as fast as he could, snatched up his fork and spade and hurried up the alley to do a bit of digging and planting.

Win had made a cottage pie with the meat left over from Sunday's small joint. One advantage about having a family was that you could put all the coupons together to get a bigger piece of meat – when the butcher had any, and with care it could see you through two or even three days. Today it was minced, moistened with some Bisto gravy, thickened up with carrots and onions and covered with mashed potato. It was tasty, even if there was more potato than meat, and they sat down to it with anticipation. Just as Win began to serve it, the doorbell rang.

'If it's one of them soldiers, tell 'em the baths are closed for the day,' George said. 'They must be cleaner than we are by now.'

Kate went to the door. It was not a soldier who stood there but an airman, and she was already opening her mouth to ask what he wanted when she saw his grin and let out a yell of surprise. He held out his arms and she flew into them.

'*Brad!* Brad, where have you come from? How did you get here? Are you with all these others in the streets? Where have you been? Are you all right? Oh, I've missed you so much!'

There was a loud cheer from the soldiers outside, and Kate laughed shakily and dragged him indoors. She slammed the door and went into his arms again. They were still kissing when George came through to see what was going on and he coughed loudly and said, 'Who's this bloke then, Kate? I take it you know him!'

'It's Brad!' Kate said, emerging from the kiss and lifting a flushed, laughing face to her father, 'It's Brad, that I met back in March over on South Parade Pier. He's a Canadian pilot.'

'Well, I can see that,' George said, looking at the uniform. 'You'd better ask him in. I must say, it's the first I've heard of any Brad. D'you know anything about this, Win?' he asked as he went through to the back room. 'Our Kate's got a Canadian bloke with her, been carrying on like nobody's business out there in the passage, says they've known each other for the past two months or more. Nobody told *me* about this.'

'Nobody told me, neither.' Win looked at the tall young man, standing there with his cap off, his curly hair even darker than Kate's. 'So this is why she's been mooning about like a lost soul all these weeks. Well, you'd better sit down and have a bite to eat and introduce yourself.'

Brad shook his head. 'I won't have anything to eat, thanks, Mrs Fisher. We've got plenty of rations. I wouldn't say no to a cup of coffee, mind.'

'It's Camp,' Kate warned him and he grinned.

'I've got used to that!' Sally lifted Topsy and Turvey off a spare dining chair, where they lay entwined in sleep, and Brad squeezed up at the table between her and Kate. 'I wondered if you'd be able to come out for a while,' he said to Kate. 'That's if your ma and pa don't mind.' He paused. 'Don't know how much longer I'll be around. Things are starting to hot up.'

'Of course I'll come out. But it'll be dark soon.'

'You can go in the front room,' Win called from the kitchen. 'Have a talk there – nobody'll disturb you.' She came back, carrying a cup of coffee. 'There, I know it's not what you Canadians are used to, but we don't get much real coffee here.'

'That's OK, Mrs Fisher.' He smiled at her, showing straight white teeth, and she smiled back. Kate and Sally glanced at each other and widened their eyes a little; Win didn't always take readily to strangers. George cleared his throat.

'So what d'you do when you're at home, Mr—'

'Call me Brad,' the Canadian said easily. 'Why, I help my father run his business. We have a general store, in a small town not too far from Ottawa. Nothing grand, not like your big stores in Portsmouth, but we aim to sell most things and we know just about everyone in town – they all come in for their bits and pieces. Everything from horse-feed and tools to saucepans and balls of string, that's us!'

'Sounds an interesting sort of place,' said George, who loved foraging about in toolshops. 'D'you sell seeds and gardening tools as well, or is it mostly household stuff?'

'Oh sure, we sell anything and everything. It used to be a trading post, you know, dealing with Indians as well as settlers – it was way out in the country then. I guess you'd call my ancestors pioneers. Now the town's grown up around us and we're just about the oldest family there.'

'Where did your family come from, then?' Sally asked. She leaned her chin on her hand and gazed at him. 'Were they English?'

'Scots, I believe. My name's Scottish, you see – Mackintosh. Came over from the Highlands, I guess. I'd like to go to Scotland someday – see where they came from.' He turned away from Sally and smiled at Kate. 'I'll take you with me!'

Kate glanced nervously at her father. This was going too fast! But George was still looking interested, and Win was already making another cup of coffee. Kate swallowed the last of her cottage pie and stood up.

'Let's go in the front room. You can bring your coffee with you. I don't suppose you've got all that long, have you?'

'Not long enough,' he agreed, following her and turning at the door to give Sally a wink. 'Not long enough, by a long chalk.'

Kate closed the door behind them. She was just in time to catch Sally's whisper. 'Isn't he smashing, Mum!'

Brad was already slipping his arms around her waist. She leaned against him and buried her face in the roughness of his uniform jacket. 'Oh Brad,' she said. 'It's so lovely to see you again.'

'You too, little lady,' he murmured, and lifted her face

286

with one hand. 'Now let me see, where were we, when we were interrupted?'

The kissing went on for longer this time. Kate felt herself melting in his arms, losing all sense of time and place, aware only of the man who held her so warmly and the kisses they shared. This is right for me, she thought. This is the man I've been waiting for, the man I'll love all my life . . . The thought of Godfrey drifted into her mind yet although she knew she had loved him as well, there was no sense of betrayal. I gave you all I could, she thought, addressing his ghost, and then we were parted. I've grieved for long enough. Now I can live my own life again. And then Godfrey's picture faded, although she knew she would never forget him, and she gave herself up entirely to Brad.

'Kate,' he murmured in her ear. 'Kate, my sweetheart, my love, my little dancing lady . . . I wish I could stay longer. I don't want to leave you now.'

'I don't want you to go,' she whispered, already feeling the anguish of yet another parting. 'I want us to be together for ever.' She had forgotten the jinx, forgotten everything but her deep, stretching love, her need for the man who had stolen her heart in the dance they had shared.

But they both knew that he must. War took precedence over everything.

'Will you be able to come to see me again?' she asked, when they were sitting quietly, their arms around each other. And then, laughing a little: 'D'you realise, you haven't even told me how you got here! It's as if you just dropped out of the sky.'

He gave her an odd look and then grinned. 'Well, maybe I did just that. As it happens, a few of us were sent down to one of the 'dromes near here for a bit of extra training. You can guess I got away the first minute I could to come and see you!' He kissed her again, nuzzling her hair. 'Mm, that's good – you smell sweet as cherry pie. But as for managing to come again – well, little lady, I just don't know. We're heading for an airfield somewhere near a place called Cirencester – can't tell you any more'n that.' He grinned ruefully. 'Probably shouldn't even have told you that much. I guess it's too far to come on a lorry.'

'Yes, it is.' Kate had never been as far as Cirencester, although she'd heard of it. She hesitated. 'Brad, I know you can't tell me much – but I need to know *something*. I don't even know what kind of aircraft you fly. Is it fighters or bombers? Don't tell me if you can't,' she added hastily.

He chuckled. 'I don't think you're a spy, Katy, but as it happens I shan't be flying either of those. My job's different.' He paused, then shook his head. 'No, I can't say. You'll just have to wait until it's all over.' He drew her close again. 'I'll tell you everything then. There'll be all the time in the world, when this is finished, and we're going to spend it together.'

Together. The word had never sounded so lovely. It's all I want, Kate thought, letting herself drift away again on a cloud of kisses. Just to be with Brad, for the rest of my life. Together . . .

Jackie Prentice was now almost seven months pregnant – as far as anyone could tell. She was quite big, despite her small frame, and Elsie looked at her anxiously a few times, wondering if the girl could have got her dates wrong. She spoke to the midwife one day, after the woman had been to check Jackie over.

'Think it could be a bit earlier? She's gone up like a balloon this last fortnight.'

Mrs Porrit shrugged. 'Can't really tell. The head's not engaged yet so she's still got a while to go. I'd say she's just having a big baby.'

Elsie felt even more worried. 'But she's such a little thing! Will she be able to manage?'

'Don't you worry about that, Mrs Philpotts.' The midwife was middle-aged and had years of experience. 'It all depends on the size of the pelvis, you see. Most women are built the right size. I've never known a baby so big it couldn't squeeze through somehow. Mind you, she might not have an easy time, but it'll pop out in the end. They always do.' She checked that everything was back in her shabby leather bag and snapped it shut. 'In the last resort, the doctor can operate, of course, but we don't want that. Dangerous for both of 'em.'

'Oh dear.' Elsie gazed at her in consternation. 'You don't think it'll come to that, do you? She's a nice kiddy and she's been through a lot, what with losing her mum and then her dad being so awkward over it all.'

'Don't you worry, Mrs Philpotts. I've brought hundreds of babies into the world and they've all grown up big and healthy. Well, most of 'em, anyway. You're bound to lose a few, but young Jackie's won't be one of them. It's a lusty little fellow she's got in there, mark my words. He's not going to give in easy.'

'You reckon it'll be a boy, then?' Elsie said eagerly. In the few weeks since Jackie had moved in, she'd almost forgotten that the baby wasn't her own grandchild, and was looking forward to the birth almost as much as if it really had been Graham's. Whatever it was, it would be welcome, but a boy would be – well, almost like another Graham. She'd already made up her mind that he and Jackie would have a home with her and Charlie for as long as they liked. For always, she hoped.

'Oh, it's a boy all right,' the midwife stated definitely. 'I can tell by the way he's laying, see. And them strong arms and legs he's kicking out – a footballer or a boxer, he'll be, no doubt about that.'

She wobbled off on her bicycle and Elsie climbed the stairs to the back room, where Jackie was still lying on her bed, Fluffy stretched out beside her, deeply asleep. The girl looked pale and wan, she thought, feeling anxious again, and she'd complained about feeling tired. She hoped that Mrs Porrit was right and that everything was going to be OK.

'How're you feeling now, my duck?' she asked. 'Not very nice, being poked and prodded like that, is it, but it'll all be worth it in the end.'

Jackie looked at her. 'What's it *really* like, having a baby, Mrs Philpotts? Does it hurt as much as people say it does.'

Elsie hesitated. She didn't believe in beating about the bush, yet there was no sense in scaring the girl more than she had to. Whatever it was going to be like for Jackie, nothing could be done about it. 'It's a bit different for everyone,' she said slowly. 'For some people yes, it is bad – but for others it's not much worse than going to the lavatory. Honestly, that's really what it's like – when you've got a bad stomach ache and you're a bit bunged-up.' She paused, thinking of ways to take that frightened look off the girl's face. 'But I've always reckoned it helps to think happy thoughts,' she said gently. 'It's not good for the baby to let yourself get down. You want to try to take things easy – not get worried or upset. I know it's been hard for you, what with your dad and all, but you've got to try to put all that behind you and think about your baby.'

'I wish I could,' Jackie said. 'But Dad starts going on at me again every time I go round there. I can't leave him to look after himself, Mrs Philpotts – he can do quite a lot, but he'd never manage to cook himself a decent dinner, and he'd never do any washing. I've got to go round every day.'

'No, you haven't,' Elsie said with decision. 'You don't have to go round at all, if you don't want to. I'll do it. I'll cook a bit extra every day and pop it round to him between two plates – it's only a few streets, or Charlie can take it on his bike. And I'll bring his bits of washing back here. There can't be all that much to do, it's not as if he's going out doing a dirty job. And I'll dust and sweep round a bit a couple of times a week. It won't take long.'

'But you're working twelve hours a day as it is!'

'Well, you're helping out here, aren't you,' Elsie pointed out. 'A real treasure you've been, getting some of the housework done during the day and doing the veg for dinner and all that. It won't make no difference to me to go round and do a hand's turn at your dad's. That's settled.' She nodded decisively and then sat down on the edge of the bed. 'And there's something else we ought to get settled too, while we're in a mood to talk things over. What are you going to do with this baby once it's born, eh?'

Jackie's hands immediately moved to cover her swollen stomach. 'What d'you mean?'

'You know what I mean,' Elsie said kindly. 'Have you thought any more about getting it adopted?'

Jackie's eyes filled with tears. 'Well, I'm going to have to, aren't I? I haven't heard a word from Wilbur. I think – I think he's forgotten all about me.' The tears slid down her cheeks and her mouth crumpled. 'I *can't* keep it, can I. I don't have any choice.'

Elsie knew this was true. Girls in Jackie's position didn't have any choice. Apart from the shame and stigma of having an illegitimate baby, how could they afford to keep it? Girls weren't paid anything like as much as men, and once the war was over there wouldn't be the jobs anyway. And it was almost impossible to go out to work when you had a kiddy at home. The only possibility was going into service – if you could find someone who didn't mind you having a child – and the war had changed all that too. Hardly anybody had servants these days.

'Well, I think you could have a choice,' she said. 'Me and Charlie have talked this over. You know our position. Now we've lost Graham we've got no one. We'd always wanted a big family, see, half a dozen kiddies running in and out, but it wasn't to be and now he's gone – well, we won't even have any grandchildren to play round our feet and keep us green. Seems to us you've come along like an answer to a prayer – so if you'd like to stop along with us, like a sort of daughter in a way, and keep your baby – well, we'd like to have you here. You can stop at home here as long as you like – we're both earning good money, there won't be no problem about that. And once this flipping war's over and I can leave the Hard, you can get some sort of a job and I'll look after the little 'un. How does that sound?'

Jackie stared at her. 'Oh, Mrs Philpotts . . .' she whispered, and her eyes filled with tears again. 'Could I? Could I really stop here? And keep my baby? Oh . . .' Her hands moved again on her stomach.

Elsie looked away, feeling her own eyes sting. 'That's settled as well, then,' she said brusquely, and heaved herself off the bed. 'I'll go and make a nice cup of tea. You come down when you're ready, love. Oh,' she stopped at the door, 'and by the way, if you're going to be here permanent we'd better get something else settled as well. You'll have to stop calling us Mr and Mrs Philpotts. We're Charlie and Elsie, see?' She surveyed the girl on the bed and shook her head in mock exasperation. 'Oh, for crying out loud, my duck – don't start piping your eye *again*. You'll flood us out of house and home, that's what you'll do!'

*

Elsie had been quite open about Jackie's arrival, telling the other women in the laboratory and ignoring the barbed comments and disapproval displayed by some of them. 'It's an old story,' she declared. 'There's been plenty of girls caught like this before and there'll be plenty more. There's not many saints in Priddy's Hard, if the truth be known.'

'She was daft, though, wasn't she,' the snuff-taker said. 'Going with a GI in the first place, and then letting him leave her with a bun in the oven. Silly little fool!'

'She's not the first and she won't be the last,' Elsie repeated, and then glanced at Sally. 'Not that that means she won't suffer for it. Having a baby out of wedlock's no picnic, and if she's going to keep it she's got a lifetime of it ahead of her.'

'Make your bed and you've got to lay on it,' the snuff-taker said, and let out a coarse guffaw. 'Mind you, she's done the laying bit already!'

'She's a nice kiddy,' Elsie said angrily, 'and she's decent too. She's not a hussy like some of them in here what I could name.' She stared pointedly across the table. 'All she's done wrong is let herself be taken in by a lot of sweet promises. Told her he loved her, told her he'd marry her and take her back to America – and the silly girl believed him, but that don't make her a tart.'

Most of the women agreed with her, although they didn't say so at once. It wasn't done to show too much sympathy for a girl who'd got into trouble. But as the weeks went on, they'd started to bring a few bits and pieces in for the baby, passing them to Elsie in an offhand sort of manner. 'Found this old bonnet of our Susie's in a drawer, thought it might do for that girl you've got stopping with you' . . . 'Knitted up these bootees last night, hadn't got anything else to do and this bit of baby wool was just lying around' . . . 'This little blue matinée jacket was our Freddy's, only he was twelve pounds born and went straight into second size, so it never got worn . . .' Elsie took all the small gifts home to Jackie as proof that she would be accepted again, even though she'd been a silly girl.

Sally listened to the comments and thought of Neville. He wasn't a GI and he hadn't promised to marry her, although she was quite sure he would, eventually, but she knew quite well that if she allowed him, he would persuade her to do just what Jackie had done with her American. He wouldn't deliberately get her into trouble, of course, and he wouldn't leave her in the lurch, but she shivered at the thought that he might make a mistake. Her father had already pointed out to her that she wasn't sixteen yet and, although he'd been vague about exactly what that meant, she had been left with the impression that it was against the law to expect a baby before you were sixteen and you could go to prison for it.

Elsie was telling them now about how Jackie's father had made the girl so miserable she didn't want to go round to him any more. 'I've told her I'll take him his dinner,' she said, examining a fuse before fitting it to the shell. 'And I'll bring his bits of washing home to do with ours. She's being a real help to me round the house, I'll say that for her.'

'So she should,' said a woman further down the line whose mouth was always so screwed up with disapproval that she had permanent splayed lines all round her lips, like a drawstring purse. 'Ought to think herself lucky she's found a soft billet. I'd soon show her the door if she come whining to me.'

'Well, it's not likely she ever would,' Elsie retorted. She and Jean Sproggs had never got on. 'You've never lifted a finger to help anyone but yourself. You wouldn't even give someone a smile in case it cost you something. You're a nasty, selfish bitch, that's what you are, and everybody knows it.'

'Say that again, you old cow!' Jean Sproggs took a step towards Elsie but the women in between them grabbed her arms and held her back. 'Wait till we get outside then – I'll sort you out all right!'

'Oh yeah?' Elsie retorted. 'You and whose army?' She pulled a face at the other woman, and Sally laughed. That seemed to enrage Jean Sproggs even more and she grabbed Sally's turban and yanked it off her head. Sally's dark curls tumbled round her cheeks and at that moment Mrs Sheppard walked by. She stopped dead and stared at Sally.

'What are you doing with your hair uncovered?'

'She snatched my turban off.' Sally pointed indignantly at Jean Sproggs, who was now back in her position, industriously fitting a fuze. The turban lay on the floor, close to Sally's feet where Jean had kicked it. Mrs Sheppard looked at it cynically.

'Oh yeah, and three pigs just flew past the window. Now you listen to me, my girl, I've had just about enough of you. If it was up to me, you wouldn't be working here, as you know very well, and then there wouldn't be half the trouble there is in this shop. I could hear the yelling and shouting right down the other end. I dunno what the row was about, but I do know you was in the thick of it.'

'I wasn't!' Sally exclaimed, and several of the others chimed in as well. 'She really wasn't, Mrs Sheppard. It wasn't nothing to do with her. Anyway, it wasn't a row, it was just some of us having a laugh, that's all. You got to do something to pass the time.'

The chargehand gave them a dubious look, but she knew by the bland innocence on their faces that they weren't going to tell the truth. She glowered. 'You lot, you're all the same. Stick up for each other through thick and thin.

All right.' She turned her attention back to Sally. 'But you just go careful, Sally Fisher. I've got my eye on you. One more step out of place and you'll be out of those gates so fast your feet won't touch the ground.'

Sally gazed back with limpid eyes, and Mrs Sheppard turned away, still scowling. The women watched her go and then the snuff-taker muttered, 'She means it too, Sal. You'd better watch it.'

'Well, I don't think it's fair,' Sally said in an injured tone. 'It was nothing to do with me. She wants taking down a peg or two, she does.'

They went back to their work. Nothing more was said about Jackie Prentice, and Jean Sproggs and Elsie maintained an icy silence with each other. But Sally's mind was as busy as her nimble fingers. Mrs Sheppard had been unfair to her before, and she was sick of it. She made up her mind to get her own back.

Within a week, Ned was driving the narrow-gauge railway engine regularly between the three yards of Bedenham, Frater and Priddy's Hard. You could almost see his beaming grin before you saw the train, Kate remarked to Sally as it chuffed towards them, Ned pulling on the whistle. 'He's just like a kid with a new toy. You wouldn't think it was all loaded up with explosives.'

'He's too dim to think about that,' Sally said dismissively. She was feeling uneasy about Neville. He hadn't waited for her for two days now and she was afraid she'd lose him if she didn't let him go further with his kisses and caresses. I *could* let him go a bit further, she thought anxiously. We don't have to go all the way. Not till I'm sixteen, anyway. Maybe not even then . . . She felt nervous at the idea. Suppose something went wrong. Suppose she got into trouble, and then Neville was called up and sent away and killed before they had a chance to get married. She didn't want to be left like Jackie Prentice, literally holding the baby.

Sally was also still busy planning to take Mrs Sheppard down a peg or two. She'd watched what the chargehand did each day and seen her pull down the blackout blinds as dusk fell and the lights were switched on, and an idea had come to her. The next morning, she slipped in early and by the time the others arrived she was standing at her bench, the picture of innocence.

'What have you been up to?' Elsie demanded suspiciously. 'Look as if butter wouldn't melt in your mouth, you do.'

'Nothing,' Sally said, but the grin on her face belied the word. Elsie looked at her narrowly and then turned back to her work. She was worried about Jackie, who hadn't looked at all well that morning, and to make matters worse she'd had another dust-up with Maxine on the way in.

Elsie hadn't meant to argue with the blonde girl. She felt sorry for Maxine and wanted to help – it was just that she couldn't do the one thing Maxine wanted. She knew too that Maxine deeply resented the fact that it was Jackie Prentice she was helping instead – a girl who was 'in trouble', as Maxine's own mother had once been. To Elsie's mind, this ought to have made her more sympathetic, but it hadn't, and perhaps this had shown in her voice when she caught up with Maxine at the gate and spoke to her.

'Hello, how're you getting on, then?'

'How do you think?' Maxine's voice was sullen. 'Not that you'd care.'

'Don't be daft, girl, of course I care.' She made to take Maxine's arm but the latter shook her off. 'Come on, don't be like that. We're friends, aren't we?'

'Friends! Funny idea you've got of friendship, that's all I can say. Friends help each other, at least that's what I was always brought up to think.' She broke off abruptly and bit her lip.

Elsie nodded. 'So your mum and dad did bring you up to have the right ideas then, didn't they? Not so bad after all, then.'

'You'd think so, of course – you're on their side, always have been.' Maxine quickened her steps. 'Go away, Elsie, I don't want to talk to you no more. You've shown me plain enough what sort of a friend you are.'

'You know it's not like that,' Elsie began, but the other stopped and whirled round to face her.

'Oh? What *is* it like, then? You knew I needed somewhere to live, I asked you ages before that Jackie Prentice came along with her sob-story about how she'd been let down. But did you say yes to me? No, you didn't. You were on their side even then – couldn't I think again, couldn't I try a bit harder – it was always *me* that had to do it all, wasn't it? None of it was my fault. I didn't ask to be born, I didn't ask him to marry her and then not be put down as my dad. I didn't ask for any of this.' She rubbed her eyes angrily. 'I tell you what I wish, I wish she'd given me away, had me adopted, so at least I'd have known that I had two parents who *chose* to have me. And now look what you're doing – you've taken in some little trollop and you're treating her like a queen, and you say you're *my friend*!' The scorn in her voice was like a knife scraping down Elsie's spine. 'Well, I can do without friends like you. I don't need friends at all, if you want to know. I've got someone now who really does love me, and I shan't need any of you soon, because we're getting engaged at the weekend, and then we'll get married and nobody'll be able to tell me what to do any more. And I'll have my own place. People don't mind letting rooms to married couples. So there!' She stalked off, leaving Elsie open-mouthed.

Kate came up beside her. 'Whatever's the matter with Maxine? She looked as if she was giving you a real mouthful.'

'She was.' Elsie turned and looked at her, still dazed. 'She said she was getting engaged at the weekend, and then getting married. I didn't even know she was going out with anyone special. Did you know about it, Kate? Who is it?'

'Engaged!' Kate echoed in astonishment. 'Married! Well, I suppose she must mean Joey Hutton, but they've only been going out together for a few weeks. I never realised it was that serious.' There was no reason why it shouldn't be, though, she thought. She'd known Brad only a few weeks and she was deeply, hopelessly in love with him.

Elsie shook her head. 'I hope she's not going to do anything silly. It's not worth getting married to the wrong bloke, just to leave home. I dunno, Kate, everything seems to be falling to bits just lately. This war's getting us all down, that's what it is, and with this invasion hanging over our heads we're all starting to feel the strain.'

'We've got to carry on though,' Kate said. 'We can't crack up now, not if it's getting as close as they say.' She thought of Brad again and shivered. 'If our boys are going over to France, they're going to need all the munitions they can get.'

Chapter Twenty-Three

As if embarrassed by her outburst, Maxine avoided the rest of her workmates at dinnertime and slipped out through the gates, saying that she had some shopping to do. She came back just in time for the afternoon shift, with no bags of shopping, and shrugged when Kate enquired if she'd managed to get what she wanted.

'They didn't have any in.' She didn't explain what she'd been expecting to buy and Kate knew that she hadn't been shopping at all. She just didn't want to talk about the announcement she'd made to Elsie.

Elsie was thoughtful all afternoon. She would have liked to get home at dinnertime herself, to see how Jackie was, but their break was only half an hour and she would never have been able to make it in time. She was also reluctant to get into conversation with Jean Sproggs, who kept looking at her with a nasty glint in her eye, as if she was waiting for a chance to start the argument again.

'I dunno,' she said to Sally, 'the time seems to be going slower than ever today. And what's the matter with you? You've been like a cat on hot bricks all day. Going out with Neville tonight, are you?'

Sally frowned. 'I don't know. I haven't seen him for the past two days. I hope he's not going off me.'

'Going off you? 'Course he's not, you silly girl! All the same, it won't do either of you no harm not to see each other for a bit. You've not been able to put your mind to anything else the past couple of weeks. You've got to remember, young love doesn't last long and it's not that important. It might seem the end of the world if it all fizzles out, but there's plenty more fish in the sea.'

'It won't fizzle out! Me and Neville love each other. We're only waiting till I'm sixteen—' She stopped and blushed. Elsie gave her a keen glance.

'Only waiting for what? I hope you're not going to do anything silly.'

'We're waiting to get engaged,' Sally muttered, concentrating on the fuse she was fitting. 'That's all. I don't know what else you thought I might mean.'

'Nor do I, I hope,' Elsie said. 'We don't want any more young girls getting into trouble. You make sure that young man don't try any funny stuff. They're all the same, these fellers. I know – I've been young, and kicked over the traces a bit too, but I was lucky. My Charlie came along in the nick of time and saved my bacon.'

Sally, who had met Charlie several times, gave her a sceptical look. Elsie always talked about Charlie as if he were a knight in shining armour, but as far as Sally could see he'd always been a dried-up stick of a man, half his wife's size, with a voice like sandpaper. I'm going to do better for myself than that, Sally thought derisively.

The afternoon drew to a close. They were all doing overtime now and wouldn't knock off until eight o'clock. By then, it would be getting dark and the blinds would have to be drawn. Sally fidgeted at her desk, glancing at the chargehand who always did this job. She was feeling suddenly nervous, and wondered if she could pretend to have a headache and get sent to the Matron's office.

Before she could do so, however, Mrs Sheppard glanced at the big clock on the wall and marched across to the windows. She jerked at the first cord and the blind slid down, cutting out all the light. The second followed suit. Then she came to the blind opposite Sally.

Sally put down her tools. Her hands were trembling. Elsie glanced at her and opened her mouth to ask if she was feeling ill. Then she followed Sally's glance and she too laid down her tools.

One by one, the women realised that something was about to happen. The room was suddenly silent.

Mrs Sheppard felt the stillness. She turned to look at them, her hand on the wooden acorn that held the blind cord. 'What's the matter with you lot?' she asked belligerently, and gave the cord a pull.

There was a brief pause. The chargehand stared at the blind, and then the whole magazine erupted into laughter and a babble of voices.

'Coo, look at that!' 'Did you ever see anything like it? It's her to a T!' 'Who d'you think done it?' 'I dunno, but whoever it is, she's wasted in here, oughter be doing cartoons in the *Daily Mirror*.' 'Nice picture, ain't it, Mrs S? Remind you of anyone, does it?'

On the black surface, someone had chalked a caricature. It was of a heavy, muscular face with a sullen mouth and thick black eyebrows drawn together in a murderous scowl. The small, piggy eyes stared out as if marking each person there down for instant dismissal. One of them had a distinct shadow around it, as if it were meant to be a black eye. The nose was swollen. And in the middle of the double chin was a huge, yellow spot.

Mrs Sheppard turned round and glared up and down the long room.

'Who done this?' she demanded in a voice that shook with fury. 'Who done it? I'll have their guts for garters. I'll have 'em chucked off the Hard and I'll make sure they don't get no reference. I'll have 'em up for libel.' She turned and stared at the caricature again. 'Libel! That's what it is. *Libel!* You can go to prison for that.' She took a step forwards. 'Who did it? *Who the bloody hell did it?*

302

There was complete silence. Everyone there knew that Sally had been in the magazine first that morning. Everyone knew that there had been no chance since then for the blind to have been tampered with. Nobody said a word.

'Well?' the chargehand persisted, and Sally trembled, but to everyone's surprise it was Jean Sproggs who spoke up.

'Take it easy, Mrs S,' she said brusquely. 'It's just a bit of a joke, innit? Can't you take a joke no more? We got to do something to get a giggle these days, and if we can't laugh at the chargehands, what is there left?'

The others burst into a loud guffaw, as much of relief as of amusement. Mrs Sheppard took a deep breath and turned redder than ever. Then, evidently realising that nobody was going either to own up or tell who had done it, she turned and stalked out of the room. The women laughed again and Sally sagged thankfully.

'Phew! I thought she was going to pick on me for a minute.'

'She would have, too,' Elsie said, looking again at the drawing and grinning. 'And I tell you what, your life wouldn't have been worth living if she had. Not that it's likely to be anyway,' she added thoughtfully. 'She'll have it in for you even more now.'

'Oh no, she won't,' Jean Sproggs said. She had come to stand beside them and was admiring the surly face looking out of the blind. 'She's no fool, Marcie Sheppard. I known her since she was at school – we used to sit together. She's had this coming for a long time but she knows when she's beat. She'll remember that every time she draws down a blind. I reckon she'll leave you alone now, Sal.'

'Thanks,' Sally said, surprised to find the woman standing up for her, and Elsie nodded and added, 'Yeah, you're right, Jean. Bullies like Mrs S always cave in if someone stands up to them.' The two women looked at each other cautiously and nodded before returning to their places for the last hour's work.

They would never be friends, Elsie thought, but it was good to know they'd all stand together when they had to.

On Friday night, Maxine went home and told her mother she wanted to have a bath. Clarrie stared at her in surprise.

'On a Friday, love? You usually have your bath Saturday teatime, ready to go out for the evening.'

'Well, this week I want to have it on Friday,' Maxine snapped. 'Nothing wrong with that, is there? You ought to be pleased I like to keep myself clean.'

'Well, of course I am, love, but . . . I suppose it'll be all right. I'll light the geyser. You can leave the water afterwards. I might as well use it too, save wasting it.' She went upstairs and Maxine heard her struggling with the Monster. She put the kettle on for some tea, hoping it would steady her nerves.

She'd been like a cat on hot bricks all day, thinking of her promise to Joey that tonight she would let him love her 'properly'. This meant 'going all the way' – something that she'd been brought up to believe no respectable girl did before marriage. And look what a lie that was, she thought bitterly, getting a bottle of milk out of the meatsafe by the back door.

By the time she had poured a cup of tea, the Monster had been defeated and hot water was gushing into the bath. Maxine went up to the steamy little room and crumbled a scented bath cube into the water, then turned off the tap the moment it reached the blue line her father had painted on the side of the bath to show the five inches which were all you were supposed to have. I'd just love to have it right up to my neck for once, she thought wistfully, but she dared not let it go on running. Clarrie would hear and there would be another argument, and Maxine would be in the wrong – something she wasn't prepared to allow to happen.

Climbing in, she felt thankful that they had a proper bathroom, not like Kate whose family only had a tin bath that had to be brought in from the yard. You couldn't suddenly decide to have a bath on a different night when the whole family was involved. It was just too much trouble to organise.

She thought of the evening ahead and her heart began to thump again. For all her bold talk, Maxine had had very little sexual experience. She'd been out with plenty of boys, most of them as inexperienced as she, and had enjoyed plenty of kissing and some fumbling, but she had never allowed anyone to go 'too far' – which was generally understood to be anywhere below the waist. Now, she had promised that Joey could go not only 'too far' but 'all the way' and she was excited and scared, both at once.

I hope he's got one of those rubber things, she thought anxiously. I'd die if he got me into trouble. I'd never be able to face Mum and Dad, not after everything I've said. I wouldn't even have the excuse that Mum's got – not that I believe that, I still reckon it was someone she knew that she'd led on. And anyway, tomorrow, me and Joey will be engaged and I'll have a ring on my finger, so even if things do go wrong we'll be getting married and it won't really matter . . . And the main thing is, once we're engaged I can go and live at his house. I'll get away from here – away from *them*.

The water was cooling. She got out and dried herself, then crossed the landing to her bedroom, yelling down the stairs to her mother, 'I've finished!' She was in her room with the door closed before Clarrie came up with a kettle of boiling water to heat up the bath, and she sat on the bed for a minute or two to try to calm her thumping heart and decide what to wear.

I'll put on my black skirt, she thought, and my green blouse. Joey likes me in green. And I'll put on my new brassière and knickers, the ones I got with last month's clothing coupons. Her heart skipped again. *She* would put them on, but it might be *Joey* who took them off. Her nervousness grew.

Where would they go? Unless Joey had managed to persuade his parents to go out for the evening, which wasn't very likely, they couldn't go to his house. With soldiers everywhere, there was hardly any privacy to be found, and it was light until after nine o'clock. They'd probably go for a walk. Maybe to Foster or Anglesey Gardens, where there were shrubs and bushes. Or perhaps Joey knew somewhere else. She hoped it would be somewhere nice, somewhere romantic. She wanted tonight to be something she'd remember all her life.

After a while she put on the new underclothes, glancing quickly at herself in the mirror, and then the black skirt and green blouse. She went downstairs to eat the supper her mother had prepared, then back to her bedroom to put on Pond's Vanishing Cream, powder and bright red lipstick. Ready at last, she took one more look in the mirror, drew in a deep breath and then went downstairs again.

'You look nice, love,' Clarrie said. 'Going anywhere special?'

'Just for a walk,' Maxine said shortly. 'I might be late back, you don't have to wait up.'

'Why will you be late if you're just going for a walk?' Clarrie began, but Maxine was already on her way out. She shut the door behind her and stalked up the street, holding her head high to hide the nervousness that was rapidly turning into something very like fear. I wish I'd never agreed to this, she thought, I wish he'd never asked me. Yet at the same time, she was excited. She thought of his kisses and her heart seemed to melt, and when she thought of what more was to happen her legs trembled.

Joey was waiting at the corner. He looked tall and handsome in his Naval uniform, and excitement flooded Maxine's body. She smiled at him, trying to look bold and confident, and he grinned back and tucked her hand into the crook of his arm.

'You look gorgeous, Maxie.'

'Thanks.' She could think of nothing else to say for a moment, then asked, 'Where are we going?'

'I thought we'd catch a bus out to Titchfield. We'll go in one of the pubs and have a drink and then walk along the river. You can get all the way down to Hillhead. It's pretty.'

Catching a bus to Titchfield meant walking to Brockhurst and then going to Fareham. When they finally arrived in the village, with its pretty cottages and houses, Maxine was glad to go into a pub and have a drink. She asked for a shandy and Joey had a pint of brown ale.

'It's nice here,' she said, looking around at the interior of the pub. It was different from the pubs in Gosport, with their floors covered in sawdust and their smell of beer. It was older, with sturdy beams across the ceiling and wooden benches around the walls, and it had a big inglenook fireplace. It was a real country pub, she thought.

Joey winked. 'It's nice anywhere!' He gave her a suggestive look and Maxine blushed. Joey lowered his voice. 'I don't want to stop here too long, though. We've got better things to do, eh, Maxie?' His fingers stroked her thigh under the table and Maxine's heart jumped. She gave him an imploring look.

'Don't do that, Joey. Someone will see.'

'So what? Nobody here knows us.' His fingers stroked higher and Maxine closed her eyes.

'Please don't.'

'Don't panic, I'm not going to do any more – not here.' He still kept stroking. 'This is just to warm you up. Bit nervous, aren't you?' She felt him move the fabric of her skirt against the skin of her inner thigh. 'There's nothing to worry about,' he murmured. 'You're going to enjoy it. I'll make sure you enjoy it.' He stopped stroking suddenly and pulled her to her feet. 'Come on, let's go. I don't know as I can wait much longer!'

Maxine could barely stand up. Her legs trembled and her whole body felt weak. Shakily, she followed him to the door and out into the village street. Joey grinned and took her hand, leading her through the square and past the houses to the little bridge where the River Meon ran the last lap of its journey to the sea. They climbed a stile and began to walk slowly along the path.

'It's not a very big river, is it?' Maxine chattered brightly, trying to keep her mind off what was going to happen somewhere along this path. 'Not much more than a stream, really. It's pretty, though. I went on the train once, all the way along it up to Meonstoke. It was really pretty. We got off at Soberton for a picnic on the way back, it's ever so pretty there. Have you ever been along the Meon Valley line, Joey? It's really—'

'Pretty,' he said, and stopped to draw her into his arms. 'Shut up, Maxie. I'm not interested in the Meon Valley line or the river, or anything except you. *You're* the prettiest thing I know.' He kissed her.

'Oh, Joey,' she whispered, laying her head against his chest. 'Joey, I do love you.'

'Good. I love you too.' He kissed her again. 'Come on, let's find somewhere quiet. I know just the place, but it's a bit further along – near Titchfield Haven.'

Titchfield Haven was the spot where the Meon flowed into the Solent. There was no wide dramatic estuary, just a peaceful trickling through the reeds and then the tiny harbour where a few people kept dinghies and small fishing boats. Maxine had been there occasionally before the war, but for family picnics or outings Clarrie and Bert had tended to concentrate on Stokes Bay or Lee, with occasional expeditions to Hillhead to collect cockles, and had seldom travelled as far as this.

Hand in hand, Maxine and Joey wandered along the river path. There were a few young couples like themselves, but once they had left the village behind they had it to themselves. They stopped at a small bridge and leaned over it, Joey's arm around Maxine's waist and his lips nuzzling her ear and neck. She shivered and wished suddenly that they could keep their lovemaking at this stage. I'm scared, she thought. I do love him and I want us to be together, but I still feel scared, and I don't know why.

'Come on,' Joey said gruffly. 'It's not far now, the place I've got in mind.'

He led her further along the path. There were small trees growing alongside it, and thick bushes. On the other side of the bushes was a field, green with soft new grass. Gripping Maxine's hand tightly, Joey ducked under the low branches of a spreading tree and pulled her into a small hollow, encircled by bushes and out of sight of the path. He drew her down on to the grass and pressed her shoulders so that she lay on her back, looking up at him.

'How about this?' he whispered. 'Nice, isn't it?'

'How did you know it was here?' Maxine asked, and he shrugged.

'Used to come round here when I was a nipper.' He leaned on one elbow and looked down at her, one hand moving lightly and lazily on her neck. 'Anyway, that doesn't matter. What's important is that we're here – together.' His face grew serious. 'I'll be going away, Maxie. I'm joining one of the big carriers soon. Everyone knows the big push won't be long now.' He paused. 'I don't know how long it'll be before I see you again.'

'Oh Joey.' Her eyes filled with tears. 'But we can still get engaged, can't we? You can still ask your mum if I can go and stay with her?'

'Oh sure,' he said easily. 'That'll be all right. She'll be glad of the company.' He bent and kissed her lips. His hand had slipped down from her neck and was lightly caressing her breasts. Maxine felt a wild shiver race through her body; her skin tingled and her blood roared in her ears. She clung to him, feeling the kicking of her heart against his chest, her mind in a turmoil.

'So now we're going to make love properly,' he whispered, sliding his hand still further down her body. Maxine felt him pull her skirt up over her knees, then higher still. His hand felt beneath it and touched her leg. Very lightly, his thumb stroked the thin, tender skin on the inner side of her thigh, and moved gently into the warm creases of her body.

Maxine stiffened. 'Joey . . .'

'Ssh. It's all right.' His touch became even more intimate and she gave a little cry. 'Just lie still, Maxie. There's nothing to worry about. Here.' He drew away slightly and removed his hand. Maxine felt a sudden wash of relief and then gasped as he guided her hand down his body. He had unfastened the buttons of his trousers and she felt the warmth of his flesh. He closed her hand around himself and she felt the rigid hardness and gave another cry, of real alarm this time, jerking herself away.

'*Joey!*'

'Don't be daft, Maxie!' His voice was sharp. 'Don't do that! Come on.' He was speaking more roughly now, thrusting himself against her. She felt the hard rod press between her legs and squirmed in recoil. Joey laughed. 'That's it, that's better! You like it really, don't you? All the girls do. And they like this as well.' He kissed her again, pushing his tongue into her mouth. 'And this.' His hand was between her legs again, the fingers moving busily, the thumb working itself against her.

'Joey, no! You're hurting me.' She squirmed again in an effort to escape the probing fingers, the pressing thing that was trying to invade her. 'Please, Joey – stop.'

'Stop? Don't be daft.' He was breathing heavily now, pinning her to the ground. There was a small stone digging painfully into the middle of her back. She felt a wild surge of panic.

'Joey, Please! I can't – I don't want to! I've changed my mind. *Please* stop, Joey, please.'

He paused and stared at her. His eyes were reddened, his face suffused. She noticed how small his eyes were, how loose his mouth. He was suddenly ugly.

'I can't do it,' she said urgently. 'I really can't – it's too soon. I'm scared.'

'I thought you loved me,' he said angrily. 'You said you'd do anything – you wanted to get engaged—'

'I do! I do want to get engaged. I just don't want to – to do this. Not yet. Maybe in a little while.'

'I won't be here in a little while. And I want it *now*.' He thrust himself against her again.

'If we were actually engaged,' she began miserably.

'Oh, I see! You want a ring on your finger first. And when you've got that, you'll say you want to move in with my mum first. And by that time, I'll probably be going away and it'll be too late. Hang on!' He stared at her, his eyes redder than ever. 'That's what this is all about, isn't it? You just want to get away from your mum and dad. You want a comfy billet with my mum, sleeping in my room, with my ring on your finger – and then when it's all over, you'll just bugger off with some other bloke and it'll be bye-bye Joey. That's if I'm still around to say goodbye to.' He clenched his hand hard against her body, where only a few moments before he had been caressing so tenderly. 'You know what you are? You're a cock-teaser! You've been leading me on all this time and all you wanted was my mum and my room. I bet you were thrilled to bits when I said I'd be going away soon, weren't you? Played right into your hands.' He pushed his face against hers. 'You never meant to let me do this, did you? You never meant a word of it.'

'No! Yes, I did mean it! I did love you – I do! I just feel so scared. I can't help it, Joey! I'm frightened.'

'And I've told you there's nothing to be frightened of!' he almost shouted. Then, more quietly, obviously trying to recapture his tender mood, 'Come on, Maxie. This is Joey – your own Joey, remember? You can't be frightened of your Joey, now can you? We love each other. We're going to get engaged. We *are* engaged. We'll get the ring first thing in the morning. You can choose it yourself – whatever you want. And we'll go and see Mum straight away.' He kissed her more gently, the kind of kiss that Maxie enjoyed, that had her soft and melting in his arms. He slid his hand down her body again, pressed it between her legs, pushing them apart. 'Come on, Maxie. Come on.'

There was a breathless pause. Maxine felt him push one of his legs between hers. He thrust hard in an effort to prise her legs apart and she screamed and wrenched her whole body away from him, taking him so much by surprise that he fell sideways and rolled away from her. Maxine scrambled to her feet but even as she got up he grabbed her ankle and brought her crashing down again. For a few moments they rolled together and she felt his heavy, hot breathing against her face and his hard, angry hands on her body. 'Joey! No! Don't do that! No! *No!*'

'Don't think you're going to get away with this, Maxine

Fowler,' he panted. 'Leading me on, when all the time you – hadn't got any – any *intention* of – *hold still*, you little bitch!' He had her flat on her back again, his hands gripping both her shoulders as he reared above her. She felt the hard rod against the taut fabric of her knickers and he grunted with frustration and reached down to rip them away from her body. Then he was pushing into her, pushing hard against the barrier of her skin. Maxine cried out again and he slapped one hand savagely over her mouth. 'Shut up, you bitch. Shut up – shut *up*, shut *up*, shut *up*!'

With each word he thrust harder and more painfully. She was crying now, trying to beat him off with her fists, but without any apparent effect. It was as if he had gone mad, as if he were in another world, as if he could not stop now but had to go *on* – and *on* – and *on* – until it was all over. Again and again he thrust, and then a sharp pain seemed to rip her flesh and she felt him push his way into her body, an alien sensation she had never experienced before, never even dreamed of, and he was straining above her, his eyes bulging, the veins standing out on his forehead and neck, his face scarlet. She stared at him, terrified. Suppose he was having a heart attack, suppose he died like this. What would happen to her? Her body shook with sobs.

Suddenly, it was over. Just as she thought he was about to burst, he gave a final groaning shout and then collapsed on top of her. It's happened, she thought in horror. He's died, or had a stroke or something, and we'll be here for ever. She tried to push him off but he was a dead weight and she couldn't even shift him. *I shall die too . . .*

After a moment she realised that he was still breathing heavily, and relief flooded through her. She pushed him again. 'Joey. Get off me. I can't breathe.'

He rolled away and gave her a narrow look. Maxine scrambled up, trying to straighten her clothes. Her knickers, the brand new ones she had bought with her last coupons, were ruined, her skirt and blouse torn and dirty. She pulled them around her and found her shoes, which had been kicked off in the struggle. She was crying again, tears pouring down her cheeks.

Still breathing hard, Joey said, 'You're not going to tell anyone about this. They won't believe you. They'll say you asked for it – and you did.'

Maxine flung him a desperate glance. 'Leave me alone. I don't want to see you again.'

'Not even to go and buy the ring?' he taunted her. 'Not even to go and see my mum and ask if you can go and live with her?' Maxine was already turning away, climbing out of the hollow. 'Nobody will believe you!' he shouted after her. 'Everyone knows what you're like – a cock-teaser. Leading men on! You asked for it! You asked for it, and you got it – *and I bloody well hope you enjoyed it, you stupid little bitch!*'

His voice followed her along the path. It was growing dark now and Maxine barely knew in which direction she was running, but after a few minutes she found herself at Titchfield Haven. She could hear the water slapping gently against the harbour walls and the boats jingling softly at anchor. She began to run towards Hillhead and Lee-on-the-Solent. Don't let him follow me, she prayed. Please don't let him follow me.

Joey didn't follow her. She half-ran, half-walked all the way to Lee. There, dishevelled and exhausted, she managed to catch a bus down to the War Memorial Hospital and then another one out to Elson.

It was late when she finally put her key into the front door. For once, she would have been thankful to find her mother waiting up for her. But for once, both Clarrie and Bert had gone to bed.

Chapter Twenty-Four

'There's someone special coming to the canteen today!'

The whisper ran round Priddy's Hard like a flame licking at a twist of newspaper. Nobody knew where it started or who the 'someone special' was. But there were often ENSA concerts in the canteen at dinnertime, some of them with famous people performing – Charlie Chester, Arthur Askey, Gracie Fields – so everyone assumed it would be someone like that. Elsie guessed Vera Lynn, Sally hoped it would be Anne Shelton, who had started to sing with Ambrose's band when she was only fifteen. Jean Sproggs said she knew already and worked all morning with her drawstring mouth pursed smugly. 'She don't know no more than the rest of us,' Elsie sneered. 'Just likes to make out she does, that's all.'

In the other magazine, Kate was too concerned about Maxine to bother with who would be in the canteen. She looked as pale as death, her eyes shadowed, and although she'd plastered her face with make-up there was a livid bruise on her cheek. When Kate asked if she was all right, she snapped at her and turned away, but not before Kate had seen the tears in her eyes.

'Well, you don't look it,' Kate persisted. 'And you never came in at all on Saturday. Were you poorly?'

'Yes, that's it. I had a tummy upset. I'm all right now.' She picked up the next shell and started to examine the fuze. 'Don't keep on at me, Kate.'

Kate shrugged. 'Well, if you're sure. You'll come over

to the canteen though, won't you? Everyone's buzzing about this "special visitor", whoever it is.'

'Suppose so.' But Maxine's voice was dreary and Kate suspected she was on the verge of tears again. Something had happened to her over the weekend, she was sure, something bad. Perhaps her father had been knocking her about. After all the rows that had been going on in that house, Kate wouldn't be at all surprised, but she wished Maxine would tell her.

'You know you can tell me anything you want to, don't you,' she ventured. 'I'm your friend, Maxie. I want to help you.'

'Nobody can help me.' The voice was low and tremulous, and Kate felt even more disturbed. She looked uncertainly at her friend, but Maxine's back was turned and she knew it would be no use probing further. With a sigh, she continued with her own work, but she was determined to make Maxine go to the canteen with her all the same. A few patriotic songs or a good laugh would cheer her up a bit.

The dinner-break came at last and the women left their benches and made their way over to the canteen. Rather than make a fuss about persuading Maxine to join them, Kate had quietly taken it for granted and had been pleased when her friend came along, making no comment. Together, they walked past the grassy hillocks that protected the magazines and huts from blast damage in the event of an explosion, joining up with groups of women from all the other buildings until a great throng was making for the canteen. It really must be someone special, Kate thought, her heart quickening with excitement. Perhaps it was a big film star – Clark Gable or James Stewart, both now American Air Force pilots flying in England. Or one of the singers – Frank Sinatra or Bing Crosby. Or a glamorous woman star like Mae West or Vivien Leigh. It might even be the King, she thought. He had already visited Priddy's Hard once, soon after the war had started. Perhaps he'd been so impressed he'd decided to come again.

'There's Ned waving at you,' Maxine said suddenly. 'He must have just come off the train.' They waved back at the tall, loose-limbed figure loping towards them, and he gave them his wide smile and fell into step beside Kate.

'You haven't been to the pictures with me for weeks,' he said accusingly, and Kate felt guilty. Since Brad had suddenly reappeared she had forgotten all about Ned. She was content to sit at home writing long letters, pouring out her love for him, and reading over and over again his letters to her.

'I'll come next week, if there's a good film on.'

'I expect there'll be a Western,' he said with satisfaction, and she nodded wryly. There usually was.

They squeezed into the canteen and found seats somewhere near the back. It was packed with workers, all restless and excited. There had never been such a large crowd in there before. The buzz had certainly gone round that this was someone really important. I just hope we're not going to be disappointed, Kate thought. She glanced around and saw Elsie with Sally and the other women from the laboratory, just a few seats away. Janice and Hazel were two rows in front. Mr Milner was standing on the platform with some of the other bigwigs, and Kate stared at them in surprise. The ENSA concerts were usually introduced by one of their own performers or an MC they brought with them.

'Who do you think it is?' she whispered to Maxine, but before Maxine could reply the Officer-in-Charge, resplendent in his best uniform, stepped forward and lifted his hands to request silence.

The chatter died instantly. Several hundred faces stared at him expectantly. He stood for a moment looking down at them and then said, 'Ladies and gentlemen, today I have had bestowed on me a very great honour; indeed, it is an honour bestowed upon every one of us at Priddy's Hard. We are being visited by one of the most important men in the country – in the entire world – who has taken time out from his busy life and the tasks that direct the course of the war we've been fighting for five long years, to come and speak to us. I need hardly tell you, ladies and gentlemen, how proud I am to introduce to you – *Field Marshal General Montgomery* himself!'

There was a moment of stunned silence as the stocky figure, wearing battledress, swaggered out on to the stage, and then the entire canteen erupted into cheers. With the others, Kate found herself cheering, clapping, stamping her feet. Like everyone there, she knew that Montgomery – 'Monty' – was Mr Churchill's right-hand man. The two of them, with the American General Eisenhower, were working together somewhere near Portsmouth – nobody was quite sure where, or if they were they didn't talk about it – but everyone knew that the three of them were going to make sure the war was won by the Allies. Hitler didn't have a chance against those three.

At last the cheering died down. Monty hadn't raised his hands for silence as the Officer-in-Charge had done. He had simply stood there, straight-backed, his hands behind his back, his khaki-clad chest thrust out arrogantly. He wasn't very tall, but he still managed to exude an air of self-assurance. You wouldn't want to cross him, Kate thought.

As silence fell, he began to speak. His voice was sharp and incisive. He didn't mince his words; he went straight to the point. The country was facing its greatest test so far, he said. In a little while – perhaps weeks, perhaps only days – the most massive effort ever would be made to subdue the enemy. The men and women of His Majesty's

Forces would be confronting the greatest peril they had yet faced, and they would be placing their entire trust in people like those he saw before him now – the women and men of Priddy's Hard, who worked to provide them with the munitions they needed to win their battles and bring peace to the world.

'You have achieved great things in this war,' he declared, his voice ringing in the rafters of the big canteen. 'You are tired and perhaps a little downhearted that the war has gone on for so long. But it is you, more than anyone else, who can bring it to a speedy end. Work a little longer, and a little harder – that's all I ask of you – and perhaps sooner than you think you will see the results of your labours. Your reward will be peace and freedom, the freedom once again to live your lives as you wish. Your greatest reward will be the knowledge that you have played your part – a most important part – in bringing that freedom to the rest of the world, in helping our brave boys – our soldiers, our airmen and our sailors – to win the war.'

He stopped speaking and there was another moment of silence before the canteen's roof was almost blown off by the cheers. Even those on stage – the Officer-in-Charge, the Directors and Assistant Directors, the Managers and the Naval Officers who had been invited for the occasion – were clapping hard, their faces wreathed in smiles. Kate felt the warmth of patriotism flood her veins and a great swelling of pride lift her heart. She turned to share her emotion with Maxine and was horrified to see the tears pouring down her friend's cheeks.

'Maxie! Whatever is it?'

The other girl shook her head. 'Nothing. I can't – I've got to get out of here. I can't bear it – I just can't *bear* it!' She turned and pushed her way out through the crowd while Kate watched helplessly, unable to follow. She caught Elsie's interrogative eye and shrugged. There was something very wrong with Maxine and they both knew it, but neither had any idea what it was or how to help her.

Monty and the others had left the stage and the workers began to file out of the canteen. All around her, Kate could hear the excited conversations. 'Isn't he smashing! He's like Mr Churchill – he can make you believe anything just by the way he says things. I feel I can work twice as hard now, just because he's asked me to. I feel I could work all *night*!'

Elsie caught up with Kate as they squeezed through the door. 'Whatever was the matter with Maxine?'

'I don't know. I'm really worried about her, Else. She's not well, and I think it's something to do with what's been happening at home. She never came in on Saturday, you know, said she had a tummy upset, but she looks to me as if she's been crying all weekend. But she won't tell me anything. I don't know what to do.'

Elsie was silent for a moment. 'I feel bad about her, Kate,' she said at last. 'She asked me if she could come to us, you know, and I had to say no because I'd just taken in young Jackie. I had to do it – I couldn't say no to her, not in her position – but I'm wondering if I shouldn't have said yes to Maxine as well. They could have shared the room, at a pinch. Perhaps I ought to have another talk with Charlie and then think about it.'

'I think she needs something like that,' Kate said soberly. 'And she needs it soon. I tell you, Elsie, I'm really worried about her. The way she's going on, I just don't know what she might do!'

Maxine had heard Monty's words without really taking them in. A week ago, she would have been as thrilled as the rest of them to see the great man strut out on to the stage and hear his voice exhorting them on but now, like everything else, it all seemed to be happening in a fog. She felt as if she were behind a sheet of Perspex, able to see out but with a mistiness between her and the rest of the world; able to hear but with everything slightly muffled. It was as if she had been set apart, like a ghost, able to move through the days and do what was expected of her, but not really a part of it all.

Always, in the front of her mind, was the memory of Friday night. The panic, the terror, the pain and the sheer horror of what Joey had done to her. And the black shadow of shame that hung over her like a stifling and filthy blanket she could not push away.

This is what Mum felt, she thought with a shiver. This is what happened to Mum . . .

She had come in on Friday night, trembling and tear-stained, expecting to find either her mother or father to be waiting up for her. It wasn't even very late – one or both of them were sure to be still around. But tonight they'd gone to bed early and the house was in darkness. She had unlocked the front door and stumbled in, groping for the light switch, and then dropped into a chair at the table and laid her head on her arms. The tears had come again then, and great, uncontrollable sobs that seemed to come from deep inside her, wrenching their way up painfully through her breast and almost tearing her shaken body apart with their force. I must stop this, she thought in panic, I'll wake everyone up. But she couldn't stop, and it was as if a part of her stood apart, watching in amazement as her body shook and trembled and cried, as if she were in a dream and hardly knew whether she were herself or somebody completely different, half-experiencing the terror, half-detached from it. She felt a little as she had done once when she had hurt her eye, her body reacting to the pain but her mind refusing to accept it.

'Maxine! Maxine, whatever's the matter?'

Clarrie stood at the door, her old grey coat wrapped around her thin body. Maxine lifted a swollen, tear-soaked face and stared at her before dropping her head on her arms again, and Clarrie came swiftly across the room, dragged a chair up and sat down beside her, enfolding Maxine in her arms. For the first time in months, Maxine didn't push her away.

'Oh, *Mum*.'

'What is it?' Clarrie whispered. 'What's happened?'

Maxine shook her head. She was unable to speak but in any case she knew she could never tell anyone what Joey had done. It was too shameful, too disgusting.

Clarrie held her more tightly. 'Has somebody hurt you? Who was it?' There was another pause while the girl continued with her wrenching, racking sobs. 'Come on, love, you've got to tell me. Were you out with Joey Hutton?' Maxine nodded. 'Did he hurt you? Tell me, love. You can tell me anything. I'll understand.'

There was a movement at the door. Maxine and her mother both glanced up. Bert was standing there in his pyjamas, his thinning grey hair sticking out around his head, blinking as if he'd only just woken up. 'What's going on here?'

'It's Maxine,' Clarrie said, as if he couldn't see the girl weeping at the table. 'Someone's hurt her. Look at the state she's in.'

He came further into the room. 'Who's hurt her?' He spoke to Maxine. 'What did they do to you, girl? Were you by yourself?' Maxine shook her head helplessly and he glanced at his wife. 'Who was she with tonight? Didn't you tell me she'd been knocking about with that Hutton boy lately?' He addressed Maxine again. 'Did he do this? Did he hurt you?'

'Oh Dad!' Maxine sobbed, and he reached out and laid his big hand on her arm.

'Put the kettle on, Bert,' Clarrie said in a low voice. 'She can't talk while she's like this, all upset. She's had a shock – she needs a hot cup of tea with plenty of sugar in. Not saccharin, sugar. Never mind the rationing.'

He went out to the kitchen and they heard him filling the kettle and turning on the gas. Clarrie gathered Maxine closer against her and rocked her gently, as she'd done when her daughter was a small child. 'There, there,' she murmured. 'It's all right, love. You're home now. You're safe. Nobody can hurt you now. Mum's got you. Mum's looking after you.' Her eyes filled with tears, which slipped down her cheeks and ran down her neck into the collar of her nightdress as she tried to wipe them away with the back of her hand.

Bert returned with three cups and saucers on a tray. He put it on the table and set one of the cups close to Maxine's elbow. 'Drink this, love. It'll do you good.'

'I can't,' Maxine hiccuped, but Clarrie held the cup for her. 'I can't drink anything.'

'Yes, you can. Just a sip, look.' She held it against her lips. 'A little sip, that's all. That's right, love. Now another one, eh? That'll make you feel better. Try and drink the rest, there's a good girl, and then you can tell us what's happened.'

Maxine shook her head violently. 'I can't. I can't.'

'Yes, you can,' Bert said quietly. 'We're your mum and dad. You can tell us anything.'

She raised her head and stared at him and, for a moment, both he and Clarrie feared an outburst against them, like so many there had been in the past few weeks. But Maxine's face simply twisted again with emotion, and as she let her head fall yet again a torrent of fresh tears burst from her. Clarrie and Bert looked at each other in dismay.

'She's been hurt bad,' Clarrie said. 'Someone's hurt her real bad.'

'I can see that, love. I'd just like to get me hands on the bloke that done it too.' His big hand stroked Maxine's hair and she gasped and flinched. 'It's all right, Maxie love. It's all right. It's only me. It's your dad. I'm not going to hurt you, love.' He talked to her softly, his deep voice murmuring in her ear, and gradually she relaxed. Clarrie too kept her arms about her, patting and stroking her shoulders as if she were a little girl who had fallen over and hurt herself, and slowly the tears grew less until at last she gave a long, shuddering sigh and lifted her face.

'Oh Mum,' she said again, brokenly. 'Oh Mum, I've been such a fool, such a stupid, *stupid* fool.'

'There, there,' Clarrie said, patting her again. 'It's all right. Whatever it is, it's all over now. Come on, love, finish your tea and then try and tell us what happened. You can't keep it to yourself, it's bad for you. Come on, now.' She waited a moment, then asked gently, 'Was it Joey?'

Maxine nodded miserably. 'He – we went for a walk. We went to Titchfield and walked down the river. He – he said he knew a place.' Her face was scarlet. 'Oh Mum, I'm so ashamed of myself.'

'There's no need to be, love. It wasn't your fault.' Clarrie waited a moment. 'Tell us all about it, there's a good girl. Nobody's going to be cross with you.'

Maxine gave her a doubtful look. 'You might be when you know . . . We were going to get engaged. He said we'd go to Hug's tomorrow and get a ring, and then – and then—' Another fierce paroxysm gripped her. 'I thought we'd get married,' she sobbed. 'I thought we'd get married before he went away.'

Clarrie looked over Maxine's head at Bert and shook her head. He was looking grim. He said quietly, 'Whatever he done to you, Maxie, it wasn't your fault. Just remember that and tell us the rest.'

'I was going to go and live with his mum,' Maxine said brokenly. 'He said she'd give me his room while he was away. I told him I wanted to get away from home.' She stared at them, her eyes filled with remorse. 'I'm sorry. I'm *so* sorry.'

Clarrie put her hand to her eyes and Bert reached over to touch her shoulder. 'It's all right, love,' he said huskily. 'She's not going to leave now – are you, Maxie? You'll stop with your old mum and dad now, won't you?'

'Oh Dad,' she wept. 'Oh Dad, I've been so horrible.'

'Never mind that. Tell us what happened when you walked down by the river with that Joey Hutton.' His mouth set again in sombre lines. 'Not but what we can't guess. Tried to take advantage of you, didn't he?'

She nodded. 'I – I'd said I would,' she whispered. 'I've been so miserable and he – he said he loved me, and – and I loved him too. I thought I did, anyway. But when – when he . . .' Her voice broke and she gulped and swallowed before going on in a whisper, 'when he wanted to – to – well, I just couldn't. I couldn't let him. And he was so angry. I tried to get away.' Her eyes widened as she relived her panic. 'I tried to get up and run off but he wouldn't let me. He grabbed my leg and pulled me down and I screamed and asked him not to do it, but he wouldn't take no notice, he was like a wild animal, he just went on and on, and I couldn't stop him and – and it hurt so much, oh Mum, it hurt so much. And then he sort of flopped down on top of me and then I thought he'd *died*. I thought *I'd* die too because he was so heavy and I couldn't breathe . . . And then I managed to push him off and I said I was going, and he told me I wasn't to tell anyone. Oh Mum, he said such awful things. He called me horrible names. He said – he said I'd asked for it, I'd led him on and it was all my fault. He said nobody would believe me.' She was crying hard again. 'I ran all the way to

Titchfield Haven and then down to Lee. It was dark and I was frightened he'd come after me and – and do it again. And then I got a bus and came home and – and you weren't here, you'd gone to bed. Oh *Mum*.'

There was a brief, horrified silence. Clarrie and Bert stared at each other. Clarrie's face was like ashes, Bert's scarlet with rage. They looked at each other and then at Maxine, who was shuddering and exhausted.

'You poor little love,' Clarrie said at last. 'You poor, poor little love.'

Bert started to get to his feet. 'I'm going round there. I'm going round their house now and give him a good thrashing. Then I'm going down the police station—'

'No!' Maxine caught at his sleeve. 'No, Dad, please don't do that. I couldn't bear it. They'll ask me all sorts of questions and he'll say I'm telling lies, and I can't *prove* he did it. I can't prove it was – what it was. And it'll be in the papers and everything, and everyone will know. Please, Dad, *don't* go to the police.'

He hesitated and looked at Clarrie. She shrugged. 'She's right, Bert. You know what they're like, you've got to be able to prove it, and how can she do that? It's her word against his.'

Hard and sharp in her mind was the memory of the night when this had happened to her – the shame she had felt, the mud and dirt that had rubbed into her clothes and skin beneath the bushes, dirt that seemed to cling to her for weeks afterwards no matter how much she washed, dirt that seemed to have smeared itself into her very soul. The misery of it all flooded back into her heart and mind – the certainty that she wouldn't be believed, would be tainted for the rest of her life by the suspicions of other people, the dread that she might be pregnant and then her shame apparent to all.

'And they'd get a doctor in,' she went on, shivering at

the memories, 'and make her go over it all again, and then she might have to go to court and tell a judge. It's not worth it, Bert. You know it's not. Best to try to forget it. Put it behind us.'

'Well, all right.' He remained standing. 'But I'm still going round to give him what for. I don't see as he ought to be allowed to get away with it.'

'But he's not there!' Maxine cried. 'He's stationed at *Daedalus* – he doesn't go home all that much, only for his Sunday dinner. And there's no point going to *Daedalus*. They won't let you in and they won't let you see him. They'll say the same as he did – that I asked for it.' She remembered using the very same words about her mother, and turned to her. 'Oh Mum, I'm sorry about all those things I said. I didn't know what it was like.'

'It's all right, love.' Clarrie didn't remind her that her own attacker had leaped upon her from some bushes and she hadn't even known for certain who he was. 'I know you didn't understand. How could you? Nobody could, unless it happened to them. I didn't want it to happen to you, though, just so that you could understand. I'd rather you'd gone on hating me than that.'

Maxine took her hand. 'I don't think I ever really hated you, Mum,' she said. 'I was just so muddled up about it all. I felt so hurt that we were all different from what I'd always thought. And that Dad wasn't really my proper dad.' She turned towards her father. 'I *wanted* you to be my dad,' she said piteously. 'You always had been – and when I found out, it was like having the biggest present I'd ever had, taken away from me. I just felt so upset about it all, and I didn't really know what to think or feel, or *anything*.'

Bert's eyes were moist. He cleared his throat and said gruffly, 'I don't see how it matters whether I was your "proper" dad or not. It was me that knew you when you were born and when you were a baby. It was me helped feed you and play with you and bring you up. I reckon that makes me your *proper* dad, more than that bloke what hid behind bushes. And look how many people've said you take after me! Why, you're more like me than our Matthew ever was or ever will be.'

Maxine's mouth wobbled into a faint smile. 'Mrs Jackson down the road always says I'm your spitting image.'

'There you are, then.' He patted her hand. 'Now look, I'm going to make another cup of tea, never mind blooming Lord Woolton, and then you can have a bath, Maxie – I'll go and light the Monster while the kettle's on – and then we'll all go to bed. And you're to have a lay-in in the morning. You can forget about work. I'll take a note in, say you're poorly.'

'But we're so busy!'

'The others can do it,' he said firmly. 'You're not in any fit state to work. The doctor'd say the same thing.' He glanced at Clarrie. 'Come to think of it, it might be a good idea for her to see the doctor, don't you reckon?'

'Why?' Maxine asked. 'What could he do about – oh!' Her hand flew to her mouth and she stared at them both with wide, terrified eyes. 'You don't think – you don't think – I *couldn't* be, not the first time surely! I don't even know if he – if he – oh Mum, say it can't be true. Please, Mum, *please* say it can't be true.'

Clarrie looked at her sorrowfully. 'Well, we'll hope not, love. We'll *pray* it's not true. But it can happen any time. It doesn't matter if it's the first or not, and from what you say . . .' She shook her head and said quietly, 'It was the first time for me too, when I had you.'

Maxine sat as if frozen. Her face was dead white, her

eyes like black holes in a sheet of paper. She put both hands slowly to her face and covered her mouth with her fingertips.

'A *baby*,' she breathed in tones of pure horror. 'I could be having a *baby* . . .'

Chapter Twenty-Five

The whole weekend had been taken up with the dreadful thing that had happened to Maxine. The three of them went over it all again and again – Maxine's infatuation with Joey Hutton, her desperation to get away from home, the solution he had offered and the payment he had demanded. Because that was what it was, Bert said angrily. He'd intended taking advantage of her all along. He'd pretended he wanted to marry her, and agreed that she could go and live with his mother. None of it would have happened, Bert said, even if she hadn't panicked and run away. He'd have had his way on Friday night and that would have been the end of it.

'But we were going to Hug's,' Maxine said. 'We were going this morning, to get an engagement ring.' Her eyes filled with tears again, and dripped all over Snowy, who was fast asleep in her lap. The kitten gave a tiny mew and dug her miniature paws into the girl's skirt.

Bert snorted. 'And the band played "Believe It If You Like"! I tell you, girl, you'd not have seen hide nor hair of him again. Up at *Daedalus*, ain't he? Well, it's easy enough to say he's on duty, can't come out, or being drafted away, ain't it? Specially these days. No, Joey Hutton wouldn't have showed his face round here again for months. He'd have been gone for the duration, and you'd have been left holding—' He bit the words off abruptly. 'Well, anyway, you wouldn't have got no ring,' he finished. 'I've still got a good mind to go round there, you know. Tell his mother what her precious son's been up to.'

'It won't do no good, Bert,' Clarrie said. 'She wouldn't believe you, and what's more she'd spread it round that our Maxie's a – well, you know. Anyway, it's Maxie we've got to be thinking about now. What we're going to do next.'

'I don't see as there's anything we can do,' Maxine said drearily. 'I'll just have to go back to work on Monday and hope for the best.' She looked at them with frightened eyes. 'What am I going to do if – if—'

'We'll cross that bridge when we come to it,' Clarrie said hastily. 'After all, it might not happen. You might be all right. We'll just have to wait and see. There's no sense in bothering the doctor just yet. When are you due to come on again?'

Maxine blushed. She had never discussed such things in front of her father. Still, she realised that he must know about them, because her mother was still having her own periods. She thought for a minute. 'In a couple of weeks, I think. I'd need to look at the calendar.' She marked the days with a tiny 'x' in one corner. Matthew had asked once what it was and she'd said she was getting up her courage to kiss him goodnight on those days. He'd never asked again but she'd noticed that he steered clear of her when there was an 'x' on the calendar, and she always had a little chuckle over this.

There was nothing to chuckle over now. She got up and looked at the calendar hanging on the wall. It was one she'd made herself, with a pretty Christmas card stuck onto a piece of cardboard and the months carefully drawn out below. She'd given it to her mother for Christmas, just before she'd found the birth certificate that had started all the trouble.

'Thirtieth of May,' she said. 'Isn't there any way of telling before that?'

Clarrie shook her head. 'There's not, love. And even if

you miss, it doesn't mean anything – you can miss once or twice just through being worried. I've known it happen lots of times.'

'So when will I know for sure?' Maxine asked desperately. 'I don't know that I can go through months of worrying.'

'You won't have no choice, I'm afraid.' Clarrie hesitated. 'The doctor can tell when you're about two months gone . . .'

'*Two months!* But suppose I'm *not* expecting. If I went and asked him to tell me, he'd know I'd been . . . I mean, he'd think I was a . . .'

'That doesn't matter,' Bert said firmly. 'Doctors aren't paid to think – not things like that, anyway. And they're not allowed to tell other people, so no one else would know. Anyway, you could tell him what happened. He'd believe you.'

'Would he?' Maxine said doubtfully. She sighed and stroked Snowy, who was still curled up on her lap. The tiny animal set up a loud purring. Maxine raised her head and looked at her parents. 'I want to say how sorry I am,' she said tremulously. 'For all the horrible things I said to you. I never knew what it was like – I didn't know how bad it was. Anyway, I'm sorry. Really sorry.'

'Oh love, don't fret,' Clarrie began, and Bert huffed a little and broke in, 'You don't want to go worrying about that now, Maxine. That's all in the past. And it was our fault anyway, for not telling you the truth. We didn't want to upset you, but I can see now we were wrong. You had a right to know about it.'

'Yes, but I can see it was hard to know when to tell me,' Maxine said thoughtfully. 'It's not the sort of thing you want to talk about it – especially to the person who was the baby.' She gazed at her mother. 'Didn't you ever feel you hated me, Mum? For bringing such trouble on you?

Didn't you just want to send me away as soon as I was born, and forget I even existed?'

'Of course I never thought that!' Clarrie's voice was filled with horror. 'You were *my* baby. I always loved you. I can't say I was pleased to find you were on the way,' she added honestly. 'Nobody would be, would they? But once I'd got used to the idea, I always wanted to keep you. That's why . . .' She glanced at her husband, who shook his head.

'That's not why we got married, Clarrie, and you know it. It was why we got married *then*, I admit – we had to bring things forward. But I always wanted to marry you, and when I knew what had happened . . .'

'You married Mum so that people wouldn't say nasty things about her,' Maxine said. 'But you can't have wanted me as well, not really. Not another man's baby.'

Bert looked at her. He was a big man, used to manual labour, and he didn't show his feelings easily, yet with all that had happened in the past day or two he seemed as vulnerable as a child. When he met Maxine's eyes she felt almost as if she were looking directly into his heart, and she caught her breath at the expression she saw there.

'To start with,' he said slowly, 'that was what it was. I wanted your mother, and I was willing to take on whatever she brought with her. I promised to be a proper father to her baby, no matter who the real father was and how it had come about. But when you were born and I looked at you for the first time,' he blinked rapidly and took a small, shivering breath, 'well, you were mine then, just as much as if your mother and I had been wed for years and she'd never knowed another man in her life. You were my little princess from the day you were born, and that's the honest truth.'

There was a long silence in the small room. The ticking of the mantelpiece clock sounded very loud. Then Snowy woke suddenly, sat up and gave a loud miaow, and they all laughed a little shakily.

'She wants her dinner,' Maxine said, stroking the small, hard head. She looked through a mist of tears at her father and nodded. 'I hope I'll always be your princess, Dad.'

Making things up with her mother and father didn't mean that Maxine was able to put her experience completely behind her. She had hardly slept all weekend, afraid that every time she closed her eyes she would see Joey's face above her, reddened and distorted, and feel the wrenching pain of his assault. And she was haunted by the dread that she might be pregnant. I deserve this, she thought, for the way I've been treating Mum – but what will I do if I'm expecting? There's nobody to come and marry me, the way Dad married Mum. And I can't bring this shame on them – I can't.

By Monday she was, as Kate and Elsie noticed, red-eyed and pale with exhaustion, but she was determined to go to work. 'I can't ask the doctor to sign me off,' she said to Clarrie. 'He'd want to know what was the matter, and what could I say? Anyway, we're too busy, I've got to go in.' It was harder than she'd expected, though, to go in and talk to the others as if nothing had changed, to smile and joke and even laugh, to go into the canteen and hear Monty talk to them about helping sailors to win the war.

Sailors . . . The sailors that 'every nice girl loved'. The sailors who had 'a wife in every port'. Sailors like Joey Hutton, who promised you heaven and gave you hell . . .

'I can't bear it,' she cried, and pushed her way out of the canteen, thrusting Kate and Elsie aside in her sudden panic. 'I just can't bear it!'

Elsie and Kate looked at each other. Kate said, 'I'll go after her,' but Elsie caught her arm.

334

'No. I'll go. I'll tell her she can come to me after all. She can share with Jackie. Jackie won't mind – it'll be good for her to have some young company. I wish I'd agreed to have her when she first asked me.' She hurried after Maxine, her broad bottom wobbling, and Kate hesitated, biting her lip. I ought to go too, she thought. Me and Maxine have been best friends ever since we were little. She ran after Elsie, hoping they could catch the blonde girl before the whistle went. There were only a few minutes left now before the afternoon shift began and Maxine really hadn't looked fit to be at work at all. I'll take her to Matron, she thought, and ask if she can lie down for a while.

By the time she caught up, Elsie and Maxine were standing together and Elsie was talking quickly. Maxine listened, her face pale and her eyes swollen, shaking her head from side to side. 'I don't need it now, Elsie,' she was saying as Kate caught up. 'It's all right, I tell you. I don't need anywhere to live.'

'But why not? You were desperate for somewhere last week. What's happened?' Elsie looked closely at her. 'Is it Joey Hutton? You said you were getting engaged. Has he—'

'Don't talk to me about *him*!' Maxine cried wildly. 'I never want to hear his name again. I'm not seeing him any more! I tell you, Elsie, I'm all *right*. I don't need anyone's help – not any more.' She broke off abruptly and turned away. 'Just leave me alone. Please.'

'But Maxie,' Kate said, scurrying along beside her, 'you look so upset. We can see there's something wrong. Please tell us – we're your friends. We want to help.'

'Nobody can help,' Maxine said in a small, piteous voice. 'Nobody can do anything to help. I'm stopping at home with Mum and Dad, and that's all there is to it. I don't want to go anywhere else.'

They gazed dubiously at her. 'Are you sure?' Kate

asked. 'Is everything all right, then? With your mum and dad, I mean?'

'Yes,' she said tersely, and walked a little faster. 'Yes, it is. Please, Kate, leave me alone. I can't tell you anything more – I just can't.' Her voice shook and she drew in a deep, shuddering breath. 'I'll be all right if only you'll *leave me alone*.'

They reached the shifting room just as the whistle blew for afternoon work. Kate and Elsie glanced at each other and shrugged. If Maxine didn't want to tell them, they couldn't force her, and if she didn't want to be helped there was no more they could do.

In silence, the three of them went into the long shed and began to take off their outdoor clothes.

When Sally came out through the gates that evening, she found Neville waiting for her. It was the first time she'd seen him since the previous Friday, and she looked at him uncertainly, not sure whether to be pleased or annoyed. He grinned at her and crooked his arm, for all the world as if nothing was wrong, and she decided to be annoyed. A little bit annoyed, anyway – not enough to start a row.

'Where've you been? I thought you'd gone off me.'

'Gone off a pretty girl like you? Don't be daft. I've been busy, that's all. The war effort, you know.' He squeezed her arm against his side and she felt a tingle of excitement. It was too soon to show it, however.

'You weren't working all weekend, surely.'

He winked and laid his finger against his nose. 'Can't tell you. Secret.'

Sally looked at him doubtfully. 'First I've heard of you doing secret work.'

'We're all doing secret work,' he said. 'Anyway, if it's secret you wouldn't hear about it, would you? That's what secret means, silly!'

She decided to change direction. 'Well, I don't see why you couldn't have let me know. I waited half an hour last Friday evening and you never came, and I stayed in all day Saturday.' It occurred to her a little belatedly that this wasn't the impression she'd intended to give. 'Only because I was helping Mum, mind. I could've gone out, I just didn't want to.'

'So that's all right then,' he said cheerfully, and Sally realised that she wasn't going to win this one. Neville smiled at her. 'Come on, Sal. Don't let's argue. Let's go and have a cuppa at the Dive. I thought we might go to the pictures tonight. There's a new film on at the Forum, it looks good.'

'I'd have to go home first and tell Mum. And I'd want to change – I can't go to the pictures like this.' She indicated her old skirt and blouse.

He frowned impatiently. 'It'll be too late then. You don't need to change, Sal. It'll be dark in there anyway, nobody's going to see you.'

'I've still got to let them know. Couldn't we go tomorrow instead?'

'No, we can't. I'm doing something else.'

'Oh.' Sally waited for him to tell her what he'd be doing, but he said nothing. 'Are you working overtime or something, then?'

'No, I'm not, and I don't want you asking me a lot of questions either! It's my own private business what I do when I'm not with you. You don't own me, Sally!'

Sally blinked at the sharpness of his voice. 'I'm sorry, Nev. I only asked if you were working overtime.'

'And I've told you I'm not.' There was a strained silence for a moment as they walked along, then he shrugged and gave her a lopsided grin. 'Sorry, Sal, it's just that things are a bit frantic at work. You know how it is. We've got this important job on – well, I can't say any more, shouldn't even have said that much. But if we don't go to the pictures tonight, we won't be able to go at all this week, that's all.' He slanted a comic, puppy-dog look at her. 'And I do want to take you out. It's been rotten, not seeing you all weekend.'

Sally smiled at him in relief. 'Oh Neville, I'm sorry too. I was just afraid – well, I thought you were fed up with me. I thought maybe you'd got someone else. Our Kate said she'd seen you with a redhead not long ago, going over on the ferry, and I thought, well . . .'

'Don't be daft!' he said, but he was looking angry. 'Someone else? I'd like to know who's spreading rumours like that. I don't know any redheads, so you needn't worry about that! Now – are we going to the pictures or not? Look, if we go straight to the Forum instead of going down the Dive first, we can catch the second picture halfway through and see the big one, and if you're worried about being late we needn't bother to sit round again.' He disengaged his arm and slid it round her waist. 'We'll go in the back row. I just want to be able to sit beside you and feel you close. Come on, Sal. They won't worry about you, surely. They'll know you're with me.'

She hesitated, longing to agree. 'Oh, all right, then. So long as I'm in by ten. Anyway, I don't really care if they tell me off. It won't be that bad – I can twist Dad round my little finger. Mum'll shout at me a bit and then it'll be all over. And it'll be worth it.' She smiled at him.

'That's my girl,' Neville said complacently. 'I knew you'd come round. Come on, let's hurry. We might as well see as much as we can.' He lengthened his stride.

Sally scurried to keep pace with him. She felt nervous and excited and grown-up at daring to go out without letting her parents know where she was going or when she'd be back. She knew that she would get into trouble for it but she'd been genuinely afraid that Neville had tired of her, and dared not take the risk of losing him. Nothing her parents might do to her could be as bad as that.

Unlike Kate and Maxine, Sally had been too young to have any freedom before the war began. For her, it was a way of life, something so normal that you didn't take too much notice of it. She was accustomed to restrictions, to rationing, to the blackout, to 'keeping mum', yet she knew that she was missing something to which she felt entitled, and she was determined to have it. I'm not letting *anyone* stop me having a boyfriend, nor going out with him just whenever I like, she thought, hurrying along beside Neville. Not Hitler, not Mr Churchill, not Monty, not Mum or Dad, not *anyone*. This is *my* life, and I'm going to live it the way *I* want.

She pushed aside the thought of her mother wondering where she was and perhaps worrying about her all evening, and breathed a sigh of pleasure and relief. Neville loved her after all, and that was all she cared about.

Chapter Twenty-Six

People became accustomed to having soldiers outside their front doors, cooking meals on primus stoves and sitting about cracking jokes, flirting with passing women and playing mouth organs. In the Fisher house, there was a constant troop of men in and out, using the lavatory at the back, washing at the kitchen sink or having baths. 'You've got to have cold baths though,' Win warned them. 'We can't afford to keep on heating up water.'

Brad came only once more before being moved to the airfield at Down Ampner, and as they said goodbye Kate was gripped by the fear that she might never see him again. She had tried yet again to persuade him not to visit her, but he still refused to believe in the jinx. 'I've never been superstitious and I'm not going to start now. People get killed in wars, Kate, and maybe I'll be one of them – though I'll do my darnedest not to be! – but if I am, *it won't be your fault*. Understand?' He held her shoulders and looked into her eyes. 'You've given me the best few weeks of my life,' he said quietly. 'I'm going to make it my business to stay alive for you. I don't mean I'll try to save my own skin – I'll fight, of course I will – but I'm coming back, and we're going to get married and go to Canada and make a good life for ourselves. That's a promise, little lady, and you've got to believe it.'

Seeing the determination in his face, hearing it in his voice and feeling his arms about her, Kate did believe it. But when he had gone and she lay alone in bed, hearing planes drone overhead to bomb Germany, her fears returned to haunt her. The jinx was like a monster lurking in the shadows, creeping closer and closer as the day of the Invasion drew near.

'They're calling it D-Day,' Win had said as she got supper ready, the day Monty had come to Priddy's Hard. 'D for Day and H for Hour. We're not going to know when it's going to be, but they'll announce it when it happens. Then all these soldiers will go to France some-where . . .' She stopped, glancing at Kate.

'And get killed,' Kate said quietly. 'Not all of them, we hope, like at Dieppe, but a lot of them.' She stared at the tablecloth and added with intensity, 'I hate this war. I *hate* it. What's it all about? Why did it start – can anyone remember? It's been going on so long, and so many people have got sucked in that I don't think anyone knows, any more.'

'Well, it was about Hitler taking over Europe, wasn't it,' George said. 'About him marching into Poland. We said we'd go to war if he did that and he did, so we didn't really have no choice.'

'And what good has it done them?' Kate's voice was bitter. 'They're no better off – in fact, they're *worse* off, and so are a lot of other people. I can't see that it's done any good at all.'

'That's enough of that sort of talk!' her mother said sharply. 'It's unpatriotic, that's what it is, and I'm sur-prised at you, Kate. You heard what Monty said in Priddy's Hard. We've all got to pull together and fight for freedom. What was it Mr Churchill said right back at the beginning? Something about having nothing to offer us but blood, sweat, toil and tears? He didn't tell us lies, we knew what it was going to be like, and maybe it's been worse than even he thought, but we've stuck it out this long and we're not going to give up now. And I'll have no more talk like that in this house. You ought to be ashamed, and you with a nice Canadian boy that thinks the world of you, too.'

Kate flushed and felt the tears come to her eyes. 'I know, Mum, I'm sorry. It's just that sometimes I feel so frightened. I've known so many boys that have got killed. And I can't help thinking about Godfrey and what happened to him. I'm just so scared it'll happen to Brad as well.'

Win's face softened. 'I know, love. It's hard. I went through the same during the First War, and I never stop thinking about our Ian, out there in the Far East. The things you hear about those Japanese just don't bear thinking about. But he's all right so far, and please God he'll stay safe. And we all hope your Brad will, as well.' She glanced at the clock. 'Where's our Sally? She ought to be home by now.'

'I expect she met Neville. He waits for her at the gates most evenings and they go for a cup of tea at the Dive.' In fact, Neville hadn't been at the gates so often in the past week or so and Sally had come out of work every evening with a hopeful face and then, as often as not, trudged home disappointed.

'Well, she ought to be here by now. She knows what time supper is.' Win went out to the kitchen and Kate could hear her clattering saucepans in an irritated fashion. She looked at her father.

'I still don't understand how they're going to get all these lorries and tanks and things across to France, Dad. Won't they bomb the ships on the way over? Or attack them when they try to land? I don't see how it's going to work.'

'Ours is not to reason why,' he said. 'Ours is but to do and – well, anyway, I reckon Mr Churchill and Monty and General Eisenhower know what they're doing. We've just got to leave it to them.'

One person who might have known a bit more about the Invasion and D–Day, as it was rapidly becoming called, was Gladys Shaw from April Grove in Portsmouth. She came over to see Elsie again that evening, after an absence of several weeks, and was surprised to find Jackie there. The two girls had never met before and regarded each other cautiously.

'Jackie's had a bit of bad luck,' Elsie said, referring to the bump that nobody could fail to notice. 'It's a bit awkward for her at home so she's come here for a while. She used to go out with Graham at one time.'

'Oh, I see.' Gladys didn't know what to say. Graham had never mentioned Jackie to her, but he must have known her pretty well if she had stayed friendly with Elsie. She wondered if Jackie knew that it was Gladys who had been with him the night he was killed, and felt the familiar guilt like a pit of misery in her stomach. It was never far away, and always came to the surface when Graham was talked about.

'Gladys knew Graham as well,' Elsie explained to Jackie as she handed Gladys a cup of tea. 'He used to give her a hand with the ambulance, didn't he, Glad? In fact, he was doing that when—' She stopped abruptly. 'Well we won't talk about that now. It's good of you to take the trouble to come all this way, love, when you must be so busy at Fort Southwick.'

'I'm not there any longer,' Gladys said. 'I've been moved to the village – to Southwick House. Can't tell you what we're doing there, of course, but it's why I came over now. I don't think we're going to be able to get any more leave for a while.'

'No more leave? Not even to go and see your dad?'

Gladys shook her head. 'Nobody's going to be allowed out of the village. It's being cordoned off.' She drank some tea, signifying that this was all she could say, and the talk turned to other things. Elsie asked after the people of April Grove and heard about Gladys's sister Diane who was friendly with an American airman, and Tim Budd's bit of trouble with the police, and Olive Harker who had been seen knocking about with a soldier who wasn't her husband Derek, and Betty who had married that conchie who'd been blinded by a bomb. They didn't mention Ethel Glaister because that would have meant bringing in her daughter Carol, who had had an illegitimate baby and had to give it up for adoption, and that seemed a bit tactless in the circumstances.

After about an hour, Gladys got up to go. 'I'll be off now. Thanks for the tea, Mrs Philpotts. Good luck, Jackie. I hope everything turns out all right.' She hesitated for a moment. 'I don't suppose I'll be able to get over for a while. We don't know when D-Day is, of course, but it can't be far off now.' There was a moment's silence as they all realised just how important this time was. 'It could be the end of the war,' Gladys said quietly. 'It'll take time, of course, but maybe in a few months . . .'

'It could be over by Christmas!' Elsie said with a wry laugh. 'That's what they say, isn't it? That's what they said when the First War started – all over by Christmas. Well, it's got to be true sometime, hasn't it? And maybe this year it will be.'

'Over by Christmas,' Gladys said, thinking of Graham who had been killed by a mine and her own mother who had been machine-gunned in the street. 'Let's hope so, Mrs Philpotts. Let's hope so.'

They looked at each other and then Elsie moved towards her and gave her a kiss on the cheek. 'Thanks for coming,' she said huskily, seeing Gladys out of the front door. When she came back, she was wiping her eyes.

'I must say,' she observed to Jackie, who was sitting in

Charlie's armchair, 'my Graham did have good taste in women. You, and Gladys, and young Betty Chapman – you were all girls I'd have been pleased to have as a daughter-in-law.' She stood still for a moment, gathering herself together, and then picked up the empty teacups and spoke briskly. 'Well, that's that. Let's have another cup of tea!'

The moon was shining as Sally and Neville walked slowly home from the cinema. They had kissed their way through most of the film, and Sally had very little idea as to what it had been about. She had spent the entire time in a haze of bliss.

She had had to let Neville slip his hand inside her blouse. He'd been so persuasive and his kisses had drained away all her resistance, so that eventually she didn't even want to stop him, not even when she remembered she was still wearing her winter vest. Neville didn't seem to mind anyway. He pushed his hand inside and found her breast, and she gasped and felt a blaze of excitement flare through her body. The sensation of his fingers stroking her skin made her melt deep inside, and when his lips touched hers again she felt like she was about to swim away on a cloud of delight.

The only fly in the ointment had been when they came out of the cinema, and a red-haired girl had jostled up against them in the crowd and given Neville a cheeky look. 'Who's this, then?' she'd chirped, jerking her head at Sally. 'Taking your little sister to the pictures, are you?'

Neville laughed, but his laugh sounded false. 'Just a friend,' he said easily, and Sally felt his arm slide away from her waist. 'Enjoy the film, Brenda?'

'I dare say I saw more of it than you did,' she retorted with a wink. 'Been getting in a bit of practice, have you?

Shouldn't think this little girl'd be able to teach you much, though.'

Sally felt the colour run up into her cheeks. The girl smirked at her and said, 'Your lipstick's smudged. Better wipe it off before you get home or Mummy and Daddy'll wonder what you've been up to!' She winked at Neville again. 'See you Friday, as usual?'

Neville looked embarrassed, but before he could reply they were coming out into the darkness and the girl had melted into the crowd. He looked down at Sally and slipped his arm around her waist again, but she moved away slightly. He grabbed her and pulled her back.

'Who's she?' Sally asked, her voice coming out in a squeak.

'Oh, just a friend,' he said, and she felt a quick spurt of anger.

'You said that about me too! What sort of *friend*? She seemed to know you pretty well – and what was that about Friday? D'you go out with her on Fridays, is that it? Have you got a girl for every night of the week?'

'Don't be daft!' Neville said abruptly. 'Anyway, you always have a bath and wash your hair on Friday nights. What am I supposed to do, sit indoors knitting?'

'You could do the same thing,' she said, but it was a weak reply and Neville snorted contemptuously. 'Well, you could go out with your mates, couldn't you? You don't have to go out with another girl.'

'Who said I *did* go out with a girl? *I* never said so.'

'No, but you do, don't you?' Sally said, removing his arm again. 'You go out with *her* – Brenda or whatever her name is. You said you loved me but you go out with another girl. Maybe more than one.' She felt the tears come to her eyes. 'You've been stringing me along all this time.'

'And what have you been doing to me?' he demanded.

They had walked several hundred yards by now and only a few people were passing. He snatched her wrist suddenly and pulled her into an alleyway. 'You say you love me, but all you'll let me do is kiss you! Isn't that stringing me along?'

'I do love you!' She was crying now. 'I thought you liked kissing me!'

'I do, but a bloke wants a bit more than that with his steady girlfriend.'

'You did do more,' she whispered. 'In the pictures – I was scared stiff the usherette was going to shine her torch at us.'

'And with you still wearing a winter vest?' he said scornfully. 'A proper passion-killer *that* is!'

'And I suppose *she* doesn't?' Sally flared, her anger returning. 'I suppose *she* lets you do whatever you like – on Friday nights! Well, maybe you'd better take her out on other nights as well. Maybe you'd better forget all about me.'

'Come on, Sal,' he said, moving closer against her. 'There's no need to be like that. I told you, she's just someone I know. I can't help knowing other girls, can I? *You* know other boys – you must do. It doesn't mean anything.'

'*She* seems to think it does.' She wriggled away from him. 'I thought you loved me. How can you, if you're going out with other girls? You've been two-timing me, Neville.'

'So what if I have?' he blustered. 'We're not engaged or anything. I can go out with who I like. You don't own me, Sally Fisher. You're only a kid anyway.'

There was a brief silence. She looked up at him, seeing the moonlight glimmer in his eyes. Suddenly, his face half in shadow, he looked harder. The love she had thought she'd seen before had gone and was replaced by a sneer.

She felt a surge of rage, mingled with the pain and misery of betrayal. With a swift movement, she twisted away and raised her hand to slap his face.

'All right, then! Go back to your ginger girlfriend – and you said you didn't know any girls with red hair! See if I care – there's plenty more fish on the beach!' Even more annoyed by her mistake, she turned to march out of the alleyway, but he caught her wrist again, tightening his fingers around it so cruelly that the skin burned and she cried out in pain. 'Let go! Let go of me!'

'Sally—'

She was never quite sure whether his voice had been pleading or angry. Furious and in tears, she pulled away again and ran out of the alleyway. There was no one about now and she raced along the street, thankful for the moonlight and thankful that she had been the fastest runner at school. She heard Neville's footsteps behind her, but after a few minutes the sound stopped and she knew he had given up. She ran a little further, then slowed to a walk.

At the corner of Cider Lane, she stopped and felt for her hanky. She scrubbed her face fiercely, determined to get rid of all signs of tears before she went indoors. There would be trouble enough when she faced her parents, over her staying out without letting them know. She didn't want them, or anyone else, knowing about tonight's humiliation as well.

'What in the name of all goodness were you *thinking* of?' Win demanded for the umpteenth time. 'You must have known we'd be worried about you. Not coming home for your supper, and with the streets full of soldiers! Anything could have happened.'

'I thought you'd realise I'd gone out with Neville,' Sally said sulkily. She looked at her sister. 'I thought you saw him waiting for me.'

'Well, I didn't.'

Sally suddenly burst into tears again. She had come in full of bravado, but she was unable to hide her misery any longer. 'Oh, the beast, the horrible, horrible beast! He's been lying to me all along. He's been two-timing me. I hate him! And to think I let him—' She stopped abruptly, turning scarlet, and her mother and father looked at her sharply.

'Let him what? What have you been doing, Sally?'

'Nothing,' Sally muttered through her tears. 'We haven't done anything – nothing wrong, anyway. Just kissing and – and that's all.'

Win gave her a searching look. 'Are you sure that's all?'

'More or less,' Sally mumbled. 'Honestly, Mum, it was just kissing. I wouldn't let him go any further.'

'So he did try to do more? Right, that's it!' George slapped his hand on the table. 'That's the last time you go out with him, or any other boy, until you're sixteen years old. Eighteen, if I have anything to do with it. You obviously can't be trusted so you'll have to stop at home or go out with your sister.' He ignored Kate's protest. 'It's no good arguing, neither of you. You're my responsibility until you're twenty-one years old. And that goes for you too, Kate, especially the way things are at the moment with all these soldiers around the town. You go out together or not at all.'

Sally sobbed and Kate glared at her. 'Now look what you've done. I've got to play nursemaid to you, and I'm not even allowed to go out with my own boyfriend.' She appealed to her father. 'You don't really mean I can't go out with Brad if he comes again, do you? You liked him when he came round here.'

'I don't say I didn't,' George stated. 'But he's a Canadian and he's an airman and we don't know anything about him. You don't even know where he is now, or what

349

he's doing. I know what young blokes like that are like. You're best staying at home. If he wants to see you, he can come here and welcome, but that's all.' He got up heavily. 'Now, your mother and me have worn ourselves out to-night, worrying about you, young Sally, and we're going to bed. You go up first.'

Sally opened her mouth, but both she and Kate knew there was no arguing with their father when he spoke in that tone of voice. They glanced at each other and then went out to the kitchen to wash before going upstairs. Sally realised suddenly that she'd had nothing to eat since lunchtime, and took a couple of biscuits out of the tin.

'I'm sorry, Kate,' she said when they reached their bedroom. 'I never meant all that to happen.'

Her older sister gave her a withering glance. 'You're a stupid little idiot. I don't see why I've got to suffer as well. If Brad comes now, we won't be able to go out anywhere together, and it's all your fault.' Her eyes filled with tears. 'Not that he's likely to come any more. He'll be flying over to France.' She bit her lip hard and stared at the little photograph he had sent her. 'And then I'll never see him again.'

Chapter Twenty-Seven

It was the last week of May. The weather was dismal, wet and chilly. It didn't feel like summer at all. Over the whole of the south coast hung a pall, not only of cloud and mist, but of tension and waiting. The soldiers in the streets hung about in groups, smoking and talking, glancing around them as if waiting for a bus that never came. Overhead, the sky was black with aircraft on their way to bomb Germany, and the air was filled with their drone.

Sally was sunk in misery. From walking on air, almost dancing along the streets, she had changed to a heavy trudge, as if every step were too much for her. Her parents, anxious about Ian whose ship had been reported caught up in battle in the Far East, barely spoke to her and although Kate had some sympathy for her, she was too annoyed over her own curfew to display it.

'It's your own silly fault. Anyone could've told you the sort of bloke he was. Those good-looking ones always think they're God's gift to women. I expect he had half a dozen of you on a string.'

'So why *didn't* anyone tell me?' Sally challenged her, and Kate shrugged.

'You wouldn't have taken any notice. You never do. Got to know best.' She turned away and picked up that week's copy of *Woman*. There was a picture of a woman factory worker on the cover, with her hair rolled back under a turban like the ones the women wore at Priddy's Hard. She was standing beside some sort of machine, smiling, and she looked smart and pretty with her bright lipstick and well-shaped eyebrows. Inside the magazine there were two short stories and a serial as well as a knitting pattern, recipes for making the most out of your rations and household hints. Kate considered it worth every penny of the threepence it cost, and once she and her mother and Sally had all read it they passed it over the fence to Mrs Bragg next door, who in return gave them her copy of *Woman's Own*. They also had *Picture Post* every week, and *Tiny Tots* for Barney.

'There's letters here all the time from girls who've been let down by their boyfriends,' she told Sally, turning to the Evelyn Home page. 'You ought to read them and see what she tells them.'

Sally was reading a book about Worralls of the WAAF. She shook her head scornfully. 'She always says the same thing. She'd be on Mum and Dad's side, anyway. They don't know what it's like to be in love, these old people.'

'They must have been once,' Kate pointed out. 'Or we wouldn't be here!'

'Yes, but it was donkey's years ago and they've forgotten now. Anyway, I don't believe anyone's *ever* felt like I did about Neville.' Sally sniffed and felt up her sleeve for her hanky. 'It was different, Kate. Like Romeo and Juliet. I can't believe he'd have someone else, not really. And the other night – well, maybe it was my fault after all.'

'You shouldn't have let him even kiss you, let alone anything else. Dad's right – you're too young for all that, Sally. And he *has* been going round with that ginger girl. Val Drayton told me she'd seen them coming out of the Forum. He's not worth wasting your time on, honestly.'

Sally scowled. She looked at her book again, at the cover picture of a laughing WAAF girl standing beside a Spitfire. 'I wish I was old enough to join up. That's what I'd like to do, fly aeroplanes. Girls do, you know. They take them from the factories to the airfields. I could do that. Or I could be a mechanic. I'm fed up with Priddy's Hard.'

'But you've only been there a few weeks!' Kate exclaimed. 'You can't be fed up already.'

'I can. I *am*. I thought it'd be more interesting. All I do is stand at a bench all day long looking at flipping fuzes! It's so boring.'

'Well, that's just too bad,' Kate told her sharply, 'because you're there now and you're stuck with it. You won't be able to leave until the war's over, and you won't be able to join the WAAF either. You should have stopped at Woolworths and then you could have registered as soon as you were sixteen.'

'I hated Woolworths!'

Kate shut the magazine and got up. 'You know your trouble, Sally? You think the whole world revolves around you. You think everything's got to be done for your benefit and you think you're entitled to enjoy everything. Well, it's time you realised that life isn't like that. We're *all* fed up. We're *all* bored. We'd *all* rather do nice interesting jobs and have lots of fun. But we can't, because all these other jobs have got to be done and someone's got to do them, and we're the someones. And we just have to make the best of it, and it's time you started to do the same. Anyway, we get paid good money at Priddy's. You won't get anything like as much anywhere else. She looked down at her younger sister. 'Shall I tell you something else? *I'm* fed up, too – fed up with hearing you whine and grumble and moan all the time about how horrible things are for you. Well, they're pretty horrible for me too, a lot of the time. I've lost a lot of people I liked. I lost my *fiancé*. And I'm scared to death I'll lose Brad as well. So don't come running to *me* expecting sympathy because you picked the wrong boy. You're lucky to have got off as lightly as you have.'

She threw the magazine down on the bed and stalked out of the room. Sally heard her going downstairs. The back door slammed and she knew Kate had gone out for a walk, or maybe to see Maxine. That much was allowed – George had agreed that Kate couldn't be kept indoors like a naughty child, when she'd done nothing wrong – but for Sally the rules were as tight as ever. She could go out at weekends, during the day, but she had to say where she was going and when she'd be back, and stick to it. She was only allowed out in the evening if Kate went too, and they had to be back by nine-thirty, even though with double summertime it was light until eleven.

There was no clue as to how long this rule would continue. For ever, I expect, Sally thought gloomily. Till I'm twenty-one. It's like being in prison.

She picked up the copy of *Woman* and leafed through it resentfully. Kate's getting old too, she thought. She's forgotten what it's like to be in love. Perhaps she never has been, not really. Nobody understands, nobody at all.

The thought of Neville pricked her mind, and she began to cry all over again.

Elsie had been anxious about Jackie for the past week. The girl didn't seem right at all; she was pale and kept being sick, and when Elsie came home on Tuesday evening she said the baby was kicking all the time. 'It feels like an octopus, there's arms and legs everywhere. You don't think it's twins, do you?'

'I'd have thought the midwife'd know if it was,' Elsie said, although she had heard that people did sometimes have twins without knowing that was what they were expecting. She looked closely at Jackie. 'Seems to me it's dropped. You were carrying nice and high before, and now it's gone a lot lower. I think we ought to get Mrs Porrit round, first thing in the morning, see what she says.

Why don't you go upstairs and lay down on the bed for a bit? You'd be more comfortable.'

'I don't feel comfortable, whatever I do,' Jackie said restlessly. 'I think I might go for a bit of a walk. Maybe that'll help it settle down.'

Elsie didn't like the idea of Jackie going out by herself. 'I'll come with you. We'll just go a little way – down Daisy Lane and through Elmhurst Road. I want to have a look in Bull's window. They've got some of those new utility tea-sets in. We've broken so many cups lately we're down to handles!'

They set off down Carnarvon Road, crossing the road by the Gipsy Queen to go down Daisy Lane. The Central School stood on their right and Leesland Infants' and Junior School on their left. There were big horse-chestnut trees in full flower at the edge of the playground, their white 'candles' ignoring the blackout and standing proud and bright above the sprawling leaves. When October came the boys would be shaking sticks in the branches to knock the conkers down, and the teachers would be hard put to it to stop them climbing up to collect them, and then there would be conker fights all over the playground.

Leesland had been evacuated at the beginning of the war, but since the bombing had more or less stopped the children had come back. The playground was empty now, of course, but at playtimes it was full of children skipping, playing with balls or fivestones, or just chasing each other about. They had all sorts of games, and while some, like tag and Grandmother's Footsteps and Farmer Wants a Wife, went on all year round, others – like conkers and fivestones – each had their own particular seasons. Before the kiddies had been evacuated and she'd gone to work at Priddy's Hard, Elsie had been a dinner-lady and she'd liked to watch them playing. Maybe I'll do that again once it's all over, she thought.

'D'you still feel happy about stopping with me and Charlie and keeping the baby?' she asked as they walked along the lane. 'You haven't said much about it lately. You don't want to worry about it, you know. We're not going back on what we said – we'll look after you. And the kiddy.'

Jackie was walking slowly. The baby was obviously a heavy burden now and she looked as if she were in constant pain. Mrs Porrit had said the baby was lying against a nerve and it was just like having sciatica. Jackie said it was like toothache all down her leg. Poor kid, Elsie thought, she's all by herself really, even though she's got me and Charlie. It's not the same as being married and having a husband. And that father of hers isn't any help; even though I have taken over from her completely, he starts going on at her the minute she walks in the door to visit him and doesn't stop till she's outside again. I wouldn't put it past him to persuade her to give the baby away. You couldn't deny it would be easier for her to do that.

Jackie sighed. 'I dunno, Elsie. I'm beginning to wonder if I'll be able to look after it properly. How will I know what to do, with you out at work all day? I don't know anything about feeding or changing it, or anything like that, and suppose I drop it? I've never even held a tiny baby.'

'You don't need to worry about that,' Elsie told her bracingly. 'It all comes natural, once you're a mother. Mrs Porrit'll show you how to bath it – you can do it in the kitchen sink to start with. And I'll be here in the evenings. You'll be all right.'

'But I feel so tired all the time. And what will I do when it cries? Someone told me they cry all night, and that means you and Charlie won't get no sleep neither.' Jackie's voice was beginning to rise in panic. 'Even if I get it adopted, I've got to keep it six weeks, and feed it and everything. I don't think I'm going to be able to manage.'

'Listen,' Elsie said, 'what you've got to remember is that once the baby's born you won't feel tired. Well, not like you do now, anyway. That big bump you're carrying round'll be gone for a start. You've still got to eat for two, because you've got to make your milk, but you'll have plenty of go. You'll feel a different person, you will, really.'

By the time they reached the end of Daisy Lane, it was clear that Jackie was tiring, and Elsie suggested they turn and walk back. 'I can look in Bull's any time,' she said. 'We don't want you going pop in the middle of Daisy Lane, do we!' Secretly, she was more anxious than she let on. Jackie had another month or more to go, as far as they'd been able to tell, yet she looked as if she were ready to give birth at any moment. She must have got her dates wrong, Elsie thought, yet both the doctor and Mrs Porrit thought she was due in July and they ought to know.

'You'll feel different when the baby's born,' she told the girl again. 'You won't want to part with it then. Nobody ever does. Most girls have to, but I bet they regret it all their lives, especially when they don't know where the baby's gone. I bet there's plenty of women around even now who gave kiddies away when they were tiny and always have a little cry on their birthdays, and look at everyone they see who's the right age, wondering if it could be their boy or girl. You won't have to do that.'

Jackie gave her a grateful smile. 'I know. I'm really lucky. I suppose I'm just a bit scared. It's all so different from anything else.'

'Are you worried about the birth itself?' Elsie asked, and Jackie nodded. 'Well, there's nothing to be ashamed of in that. It's no picnic, but most of us live to tell the tale, and once you've got your baby you forget. It's soon over.'

They reached home at last and Jackie went to lie down while Elsie made some tea. Charlie was in the shed, mending Elsie's shoes that had worn a hole in the heel, and Elsie took a cup down to him. She stood at the shed door, watching as he drank it.

'I done me best,' she said, 'but she seems proper down. There's something not right there, Charlie, whatever the midwife says. She didn't ought to look as white as she does, and the baby's gone right down this past couple of days. I don't mind telling you, I'm worried.'

Charlie wiped his moustache. 'You don't think she's going to have trouble with this kiddy, do you? I mean, you don't think she'll lose it – have a stillbirth or something? Not if it's as lively as she says.'

'No, I don't think that. But I'm still worried. What I'm wondering is if it's the wrong way round, and that's why she thinks it feels like twins. Breech birth, it's called, and it could be real bad if it is. Well, there's nothing we can do about it now, but I'm going to go round to Mrs Porrit's first thing in the morning, on the way to work. I'll pop home at dinnertime to see what she says.'

She went back up the garden path, past the Anderson shelter and the newly planted tomatoes. When she peeped into Jackie's room to see if she wanted another cup of tea, she was pleased to see the girl fast asleep, the lines of pain that had creased her forehead smoothed out. That'll do her good, Elsie thought, closing the door softly. Sleep's the best thing for them both, just now.

She went downstairs again and looked at the pile of washing she'd done yesterday morning before going to work. Jackie had made a start on the ironing, but the standing made her back ache and she'd given up. I suppose I might as well have a go at it now, Elsie thought, and went out to the kitchen to start heating up the irons. I can listen to the wireless at the same time. The Brains

Trust is on tonight, and then some nice orchestral music, with Rawicz and Landauer on their pianos. I'll call Charlie up too – he likes them.

Her anxiety about Jackie did not go away, however. It stayed with her all that evening, and kept her wakeful during the night. There's something wrong there, she thought as she tossed and turned. I just know there is.

Please God, don't let her lose this baby now.

Maxine's fear was not that she might lose a baby, but that she might actually be pregnant. Her period was due this week, and every morning she woke up praying that she would find blood on her sheets – but each morning they were as clean and white as when she had gone to bed. Every time she went to the lavatory she muttered the same little prayer but, as day after day it went unanswered, she began to lose hope. I'm going to have a baby, she thought despairingly. I'm going to have Joey Hutton's baby. Oh *God*, please help me!

She felt as if she were living in a nightmare. Every time she closed her eyes, she was back in that grassy hollow, with Joey's hot breath on her face and his hands roughly groping at her body. The same terror washed over her, and she lay awake with the light on, afraid of the darkness, afraid to go to sleep. When eventually she did, she found herself in a world of jumbled dreams and woke crying out and struggling, convinced that it was happening all over again.

Outwardly she forced herself to behave as if everything were normal. She got up in the morning, went to work, tried not very successfully to join in the chatter and jokes of the other women. She shrugged her shoulders when Kate asked if everything was all right, and when Elsie enquired after Joey she said merely that he'd been drafted to important work and couldn't get off the station.

She couldn't bring herself to tell them the truth. Elsie might understand – she'd taken in that young Jackie Prentice, after all – but Maxine couldn't face the shame of telling her and Kate and the others what Joey had done. They'll say I asked for it, she thought, and even if they don't say it, they'll think it. They'll be disgusted with me.

It seemed strange that, after so many months of hostility between herself and her parents, they were the only ones with whom she could be open.

'What am I going to do if there's a baby?' she wailed to her mother. 'Mum, whatever am I going to do?'

'You don't know it's happened yet,' Clarrie said, trying to comfort her. It was a strange situation for her too; for months, Maxine had treated her like dirt and now she had reverted overnight to her old loving self. Clarrie would have been overwhelmed with thankfulness had it not been for Maxine's humiliation and despair. Now, grateful though she was to have her daughter back again, she would almost have preferred Maxine to go on hating her rather than suffer like this. 'You've been late before,' she said. 'And it's only a day or two so far. Worrying like this can put it off, you know.'

'I can't help worrying, though! Isn't there anything I can do to bring it on? A girl at work said she took castor oil when she thought she'd got caught. Couldn't I try that?'

Clarrie was shocked. 'Of course you couldn't! That's killing the baby – if there *is* a baby! And that reminds me, you ought to go to Confession. You're not pure any more, you've got to have Absolution.'

'Go to Confession? Tell Father Murphy? Mum, I couldn't tell *him* about it!'

'I'm sure he's heard lots worse,' Clarrie said grimly. 'Anyway, you must. You can't go to Mass like you are now. He won't blame you, Maxie, not really. He'll give you some penances of course, he has to do that, but he knows how girls can get into that sort of situation without meaning to.'

Maxine bit her lip and said quietly, 'But I did mean to, Mum. I mean, I didn't want Joey to do what he did – but I *did* mean to go all the way with him. I wanted to.'

Clarrie was silent for a moment, then she said, 'Well, you'd better tell Father that as well. At least you thought better of it, even if you did leave it a bit late.'

I don't think even that's true, Maxine thought. I was just scared. I panicked. And then, when he got so angry and so rough, I just wanted to get away. I realised I didn't love him, after all – and I didn't want to do it any more. So maybe Mum is right, in a way.

'I'll go on Friday night,' she said. 'I haven't been for a while anyway.' She looked at her mother. 'I've been having such horrible thoughts lately – I couldn't go. Now I'll have to tell him all about those too, and he'll know just what an awful person I am.'

Clarrie shook her head. 'You don't have to tell him about those, love, not unless you want to. They're just between you and me and your dad. You tell him what's happened to you now, and then you'll feel better. And perhaps then you'll come on, and everything will be all right.'

'I hope so, Mum. I really do hope so.' But she couldn't really believe that everything would be all right, even if she did turn out not to be having a baby. She couldn't believe that anything would ever be right again.

Chapter Twenty-Eight

Sally's resentment extended to her work and grew worse as the week dragged on. It didn't help that Jean Sproggs had been wrong and Mrs Sheppard now had her knife planted firmly into her. The chargehand, who knew very well that Sally had drawn the caricature on the window blind but couldn't prove it, was determined to catch her out in some offence that could get her dismissed. And this time, she'd stay dismissed!

'You'd better watch your step, duck,' Elsie muttered to her as they glanced up from their work to find the woman's dark eyes fixed upon them. 'She's got it in for you, and she's not a good person to cross. She'll have you up in front of Mr Milner at the first excuse.'

'Don't care,' Sally said indifferently. 'Hope she does. At least I could register for the WAAFs then. I could be a pilot.'

'And you reckon they'll take you if you've been chucked out of Priddy's Hard? Don't be daft, girl – you won't stand a chance, with them or anyone else. You'd have to go where you were sent, and you'd get a worse job than you've got here and with no home comforts to go back to. You don't know when you're well off, that's your trouble.'

Elsie turned away, determined not to be involved in any fresh trouble Sally might get into. Kate had told her about the row at home and, while Elsie might previously have had some sympathy for an inexperienced girl who had got in a bit too deep with her first boyfriend, she was now too anxious about Jackie to concern herself with anyone else.

These girls, she thought, they think they know it all, and look what happens. She wasn't at all sure that something similar hadn't happened to Maxine. Her white face and hollow eyes told their own tale. There'll be another bellyful of arms and legs there soon, if I'm not much mistaken, she thought grimly.

Mrs Porrit had come to see Jackie and felt the bulging stomach all over. 'Well, I dunno what you've got in here,' she'd said at last. 'It's not twins, I'm sure of that, but I dunno which way it's laying. It seems a bit awkward, that's why you're feeling so rough. Daresay it'll sort itself out by the time it comes to be born, though. They usually do.'

'But what if it doesn't?' Jackie asked fearfully, and the midwife shrugged.

'Don't you worry about that, love. We'll know what to do when the time comes. You're not due till July, are you? Plenty of time, then.'

Elsie, hearing this when she arrived home that evening, shook her head dubiously. 'Didn't she say nothing about the way it's dropped?'

'She didn't think it had, not really. She said I was carrying too high anyway, that's why I had all that heartburn. It's got to settle a bit lower.'

'Well, I suppose she knows best.' But Elsie wasn't convinced. She'd asked her next-door neighbour to keep an eye on Jackie, and to pop in and out a few times during the day, and she had promised to send her boy down to Priddy's Hard gate on his bike to let her know if anything happened while she was at work. Her heart jumped whenever anyone came into the laboratory, thinking it might be a message that Jackie had started labour.

Sally worked sulkily, her resentment growing. They

were all the same, these old people; they'd forgotten what it was like to be young and didn't care. It didn't matter to them that girls like Sally were missing all the fun they ought to be having before they got married and had to settle down. It's not our fault there's a war on, she thought mutinously, but we're the ones who're having to pay for it. We're the ones who have to work twelve hours a day or more on flipping bombs, and can't go out in the evenings.

'You – Fisher!' Mrs Sheppard was bearing down on her. 'You're not paying attention. That fuze isn't properly attached! Don't you realise, if it goes out from here in that state, it could go off at any time and blow a whole ship to Kingdom Come? I should have thought we'd got enough enemies already, without you joining in!'

Sally flushed. 'That's a horrible thing to say. It's like saying I'm a traitor.'

'And so you are, if you don't do your work right.' The chargehand pushed her dark face close against Sally's. 'I'm giving you one warning, and that's it. If you don't pull up your socks, you're dismissed. And this time you *won't* slink back in, pretending you don't know what the word means. You're out on your ear, my girl, and then even Woolworth's won't want you back.'

Sally glowered at her. 'All right, all right. You needn't go on about it. I'm a bit tired, that's all. I'll do the fuze again.'

'You will, and I'll watch you do it. I'll have no sloppy work in here.' The woman stood beside her as she worked on the shell and then gave a grunt. 'That looks a bit better. Now make sure you do the others right, too – and remember, I've got my eye on you, Fisher.' She marched away.

Sally glanced round at the other women. They were working industriously, their heads bent, but once Mrs Sheppard was on the other side of the laboratory they glanced up at Sally and one or two of them winked. 'Old

364

cow,' the snuff-taker said contemptuously, and Sally grinned and felt better.

'I'll get my own back,' she said, and Elsie gave her a warning look.

'I hope you're not going to do another rude picture. She knows you did the last one – you won't get away with it again.'

'I shan't do that. I'll think of something else. She needs to be taken down a peg or two.'

For the rest of the day, Sally worked steadily, her eyes innocently wide whenever Mrs Sheppard glanced in her direction, but as she went through the careful, mechanical work of tamping powder into the shells and examining and fitting fuzes, her mind was busy thinking up ever more elaborate schemes for getting back at the charge hand. As the day went on, her bitter disappointment over Neville and her resentment against her parents and sister grew and merged together, until by the end of the afternoon she was seething with it. I'll show them, she thought, no longer quite sure precisely who she meant by 'them', but knowing that it was only by doing something drastic that she could burst the bubble of fury that was building like a volcano inside her. I'll *show* them, I will!

She walked out of the laboratory, still deep in thought. The others were chattering and laughing together, thankful to be released from twelve long hours of standing at a bench, and strode on without noticing that she was lagging behind. Kate, who normally looked out for her, was nowhere to be seen and she knew that Neville wouldn't be at the gates. She didn't even want him to be there.

Clattering feet close behind her made her turn quickly. 'Ned! What on earth are you doing, creeping up on me like that?'

'I didn't mean to creep. I thought Kate might be with you.'

'Oh, she doesn't bother to wait for me any more,' Sally said bitterly, ignoring the fact that she had so often wished Kate would go on without her. 'Anyway, it's no use you asking her to go to the pictures with you, we're only allowed out in twos now. You'd have to take me as well.'

'Oh.' Ned gazed at her. 'Why?'

'Because of all the soldiers. Dad thinks we'll be grabbed and shoved into a Churchill tank and wake up in France. And when we do go out, we've got to be in by half past nine. You can't go to the pictures if you've got to be home by half past nine, you'd never see the end of the big film.'

'Can't you tell your dad I'd look after you?'

Sally laughed scornfully. Then an idea struck her and she narrowed her eyes at him. 'Tell you what, though, there is something you could do for me. And then I'd ask Dad to let Kate go out with you, if you like.'

'All right.' He brightened. 'What is it?'

'You drive the train now, don't you? Well, you know our chargehand, old Ma Sheppard?'

He made a face. 'She used to shout at me when I was cutting the grass in between the magazines, said I didn't do it properly. It's nothing to do with her how I cut the grass,' he said, his voice rising. 'That's the groundkeeper's job, not hers.'

'That's her. Got to have her finger in all the pies, bossy old cow. Well, when she comes in of a morning she always walks along beside the track, you know, just where it goes round that curve. You must pass her every day.'

'I do.' He sniggered. 'I generally give a little whistle, just to make her jump.'

Sally smiled. 'That's even better. All I want you to do, then, is come round a bit faster tomorrow – put on as much speed as you can – and then whistle right in her ear. Really frighten her. Will you do that?'

'All right,' he said amiably. 'Is that all?'

'It'll do for a start,' Sally said, grinning. 'I've got a few other tricks up my sleeve as well, for the rest of the day. By the time she goes home tomorrow, she'll be a bag of nerves!'

'I'm getting the midwife again,' Elsie said. 'It's not right, you being like this. You haven't been well all the way through, I know that, but you shouldn't be this bad. I'll send Charlie round right away.' Going downstairs, she said to her husband, 'That girl's in labour or I'm a Dutchman. She's got a real bad backache and she's been sick twice since I came in, yet there's nothing for her to bring up. I reckon she's been sick all day, with nothing to eat. She'll bring it on just by retching. You'd better fetch Mrs Porrit.'

'In labour?' Charlie dropped his newspaper. 'Blimey! But I thought she wasn't due for another month?'

'That's what everyone thought, but I've always had me doubts about that. Anyway, it's not unknown for babies to come early, and I reckon this one's made up its mind to put in an appearance now, so get on your bike, Charlie and get round to the midwife's as quick as you can. I'm worried about the girl. The baby's not been laying right and if it hasn't turned she could be in trouble.'

Charlie grabbed his bicycle clips from the clutter on the sideboard and fumbled them round his ankles. His bike was in the passageway and he wheeled it out through the front door and rode off down the street. Elsie bit her lip for a moment, then hurried through to the kitchen and put on the kettle. Hot water, that's what would be needed, and if it wasn't the baby coming after all, then they'd all be ready for a cup of tea.

Almost before she'd got the gas lit, she heard Jackie cry out upstairs. She thrust the kettle on to the flame and ran up to the back bedroom. Jackie was lying half across the bed, her arms reaching up the wall, scrabbling at them in her pain. She stared at Elsie with wild eyes and screamed again.

'It hurts!' she yelled at the top of her voice. 'It hurts! Aaaah! Aaaah! *Aaaaaaah!*' She collapsed suddenly on the bed, panting hard, her hands feeling for the agony in the small of her back as if she wanted to rip it out. 'Oh, Elsie, it's awful. What's the matter with me? What's *happening*?'

'It's all right, duck. It's all right.' Elsie dropped to her knees beside the bed. 'Just you hold still now. It's the baby, that's all. You're having your baby.'

'But I can't be! It's not due yet. And it's not in the right place, she said so. It can't be born yet.' She stared at Elsie again. 'Do something to stop it. I can't have it now. I'm not ready, I'm scared. And it hurts so much. I can't have it now, I *can't*.'

'I don't think there's much you can do to prevent it, love. Look, I've sent Charlie round for Mrs Porrit, she'll be here in two shakes, and she'll make sure everything goes right. There's nothing for you to worry about. It'll soon be over and you'll have your baby in your arms.' She saw the beginning of the pain again in Jackie's eyes. 'That's it, love, let it come. It's your muscles, see, trying to push the baby out. There's nothing wrong, it's all natural. Now, just you hold my hand – hold it as tight as you like.'

She screwed up her own face in pain as Jackie clutched her fingers, squeezing them so tightly she was afraid the bones would break. Again the girl cried out, fighting the agony as she writhed on the bed, and it seemed an eternity before the spasm passed and she collapsed once more, her forehead streaming with sweat.

'I can't bear it,' she sobbed. 'I didn't know it would be like this.'

'It won't be long,' Elsie said, praying that the midwife

would arrive soon. 'Try and relax a bit, love – they say that helps. Try and think about something else. Have you picked out a name yet? You'd got a list the other day, hadn't you? Which one d'you like best? I like David, myself.'

'I don't care what it's called so long as it stops hurting me like this,' Jackie said resentfully.

'Now, you can't talk like that. It's not the baby's fault, is it? And you'll love it once it's here. What have you picked for a girl?'

'I dunno. I thought Veronica was nice but I'm not sure. Maybe Ann.'

'Veronica Ann, that would be lovely,' Elsie said, half an ear listening for the door. 'And David for a boy?'

'No.' The girl hesitated. She was breathing more easily now. There would be another contraction soon but just at the moment she seemed more comfortable than she had for some time. Perhaps the baby had shifted off whatever nerve it had been lying on. 'I thought, if you don't mind, I'd like to call him Graham. I mean, he isn't Graham's baby, we know that, but you've helped me such a lot – and it was always Graham I liked best. Would – would you mind that?'

'*Mind –*' Elsie began, but even as she spoke Jackie's eyes filled with pain again and she grabbed frantically for Elsie's hand. Elsie held her firmly, putting her other arm round her shoulders. 'Bear down, love. Bear down. It'll help you and the baby. That's it, you shout as much as you like, but keep bearing down. Oh, crikey, now what's happening?'

A gush of fluid had flooded out over the bed. Jackie cried out again and then lay still, her face suddenly white. Elsie looked at her in alarm.

'It's all right, love. It's just your waters broken, that's all. It won't be long now. Jackie – *Jackie!*' Her voice rose in a scream as the distorted body writhed again and then went into a violent convulsion. 'Jackie, stop it! You'll do yourself a damage. *Jackie* – oh my God, she can't hear me – what's happening? It shouldn't be like this, I know it shouldn't.'

The tortured body twisted once more and then fell still again. Elsie stared at her in terror. To her intense relief, she saw that the girl was breathing, though her eyes were closed and she seemed to be barely conscious. Then she heard the front door open and close, and voices downstairs. The heavy tramp of feet sounded on the stairs and Mrs Porrit was at the bedroom door.

'Oh, thank goodness you've come! I don't know what's the matter with her. She's definitely in labour – her waters have just broken – but she's having terrible pains and she's just had a fit of some sort. I *knew* there was something wrong, I knew it from the start. What is it? What's the matter?'

Mrs Porrit shoved Elsie aside and bent over the bed. She raised one of Jackie's eyelids and then passed her hands over the throbbing stomach. A small protuberance showed against the taut skin, as if the baby were fighting back with a tiny fist. Mrs Porrit shook her head.

'It looks bad. Here comes another one.' Jackie began to writhe and jerk again, her head stretched back and her back arched to push her stomach hard towards the ceiling. 'We'd better get her to hospital.'

'Hospital!' Elsie stared at her in dismay. You only went to hospital to have a baby if there was something seriously wrong. 'You mean the War Memorial? That's nearest.'

'Yes, but they're keeping their wards empty in case of casualties. She'll probably have to go out to Alverstoke, to the Children's Home – that's being used as a hospital. But we'll have to get the doctor round first, he'll be the one to decide. Can you get your hubby to run up the street and phone him?'

Elsie gave one more frightened look at the contorted body on the bed, and scurried down the stairs. Charlie was standing in the middle of the room, his thin frame taut with anxiety. Quickly, she gabbled out the midwife's message and he turned and ran out through the door. Elsie scrambled back up the stairs, tripping over herself in her panic. There was a strong smell of blood and urine and faeces in the small back room now. 'What can we do?'

'Not much, till the doctor gets here. You kneel down here, look, beside the bed, and keep hold of her hand. Talk to her. It'll help her to hear your voice. Have you got a kettle on? I'll go and get a bowl of water, clean her up before the next one comes.'

'But what is it? What's the matter with her?'

'It's to do with her blood pressure – it must have shot right up.' Mrs Porrit was already halfway out of the bedroom door. 'She needs to be in hospital, they've got all the stuff there to deal with it. But . . .' Her voice drifted back up the stairs, full of doubt. Elsie knelt by the bed as instructed and took Jackie's hand in one of hers. She laid her other arm around the girl's shoulders and held the shuddering body close against her.

'There, there,' she murmured soothingly. 'It'll be all right. It'll all be over soon and you'll have your lovely baby. Little Veronica Ann – what a pretty name. Or maybe little Graham.'

She closed her eyes, fighting the panic that rose in her breast. Was it tempting fate, to call this baby after her dead son? Could any baby survive the contortions such as the one that was now gripping Jackie's body again, wrenching her this way and that on the bed and forcing such dreadful screams from her throat?

It's not fair, she thought bitterly. It's not fair that she should suffer like this, just because of one mistake. And the man that did it to her – that GI who promised her so much and left her with nothing but misery and pain – he's got off scot-free. He'll go back to America and marry some other woman, and never even know what this poor girl's going through, all because of him.

Unless he's already dead himself.

Chapter Twenty-Nine

Although the normal Friday afternoon routine of sweeping and scrubbing and polishing the magazine floors with shellac had been observed as usual, everyone came in on Saturday morning for more overtime. They all knew that the Invasion – D-Day – must be happening soon and that as many munitions as possible must be made. The demand would be enormous, once the fighting began.

Sally seemed to be one of the few who were unaffected by the tension in the atmosphere. There had been another argument at home last night when Hazel and Val had called round to ask Kate to go to a dance with them. Some of the soldiers camping near Foxbury had cleared a space amongst the gorse bushes and got up a band and were inviting local girls to come along. 'It'll be a bit of fun,' Hazel urged her. 'And it'll be patriotic too, because they'll be going off to fight in France soon.'

It was quite the wrong thing to say to Kate, who had been awake half the night worrying about Brad and was still afraid that her jinx might send him to his death. 'Thanks, but I can't be responsible for any more men being killed,' she said, leaving them wondering whatever she meant. Sally, however, saw this as yet another obstacle to her longing to go out and have fun.

'Come on, Kate. If you go, I can go too. Dad won't let me out without her,' she explained to the others. 'It's stupid.'

'Even if we do go, we'll have to be back by half-past

nine,' Kate pointed out. 'It'll be hardly worthwhile getting dressed up.'

'It'll finish at ten anyway. Dances always do. Come on, Kate, please.'

But Kate shook her head and Sally flounced up to the bedroom and stayed there for the rest of the evening, refusing to speak to her sister when she came up to bed. She was still sulking next morning as they walked to work, although as they drew near the gates a small smile twitched her lips and there was a gleam in her eye.

'What are you cooking up now?' Kate asked suspiciously, but Sally shrugged and gave her sister an impudent glance.

'Wouldn't you like to know!'

Kate sighed wearily. 'For goodness sake, Sally, don't get into any more trouble. I know that look on your face – you're up to something.' She followed the direction of Sally's gaze and saw Mrs Sheppard walking a few yards ahead of them. 'I hope you're not planning any more silly practical jokes. This isn't the place for them, you know it isn't.'

'Who said I was planning a practical joke?' Sally began, but her words were almost drowned by the shrill whistle of the little train as it came down the track from Frater. Ned was in the driver's cab and he waved and shouted as the train drew near. Kate flapped one hand rather absently, too concerned with her sister to be bothered with Ned, but Sally gave a cry of excitement and jumped up and down, waving both arms. 'Hello, Ned! Hello! Hello!'

'*Sally*,' Kate began, but broke off, aware that the train was coming much faster than usual. There was only herself and Sally and a few others on the path now, with Mrs Sheppard marching in front. The narrow track ran right down the middle of the path and they all stepped aside, accustomed to its careful progress through the yard. To Kate's alarm, however, it didn't slow down as it approached the curve. Instead, it came even faster, Ned blowing the whistle shrilly, waving one arm and shouting at the top of his voice. Sally laughed and the other girls jumped away but Mrs Sheppard, her broad back stolid and indifferent, marched steadily on.

'What on earth is he doing?' Kate cried. 'He's going much too fast for that curve. Ned, you stupid idiot, you're not in a cowboy film now.' He was half-leaning out of the cab, pretending to shoot them as he went by. 'Oh, you fool, you stupid, stupid *fool*.'

The train was taking the curve. It leaned over perilously, with Ned hanging out of the cab too far to be able to drag himself back. His whoops of glee changed to yells of panic. The whistle seemed to be stuck, its piercing note painful to their ears. At last Mrs Sheppard looked up and stopped, staring frozen and open-mouthed as the train teetered to one side, tilted, and toppled over.

Kate and Sally screamed. The other girls flung themselves away from the train and fell headlong into the ditch that ran beside the path. For a moment or two, nobody could move; it was as if the scene had become a tableau, part of some ghastly carnival entertainment. The only sound was that of the whistle. At last that too faded and there was a horrified silence.

'Oh, my *God*,' Kate said, and began to run.

Elsie was late that morning. By the time Jackie had been taken to the Children's Home the night before, she had been almost unconscious, her body worn out by the violent convulsions. Elsie, told to stay at home and telephone for news at ten o'clock, had been almost beside herself with worry. 'I don't know what to do for the best,' she said to Charlie. 'Her dad ought to be told, he's her next of kin, but I don't want to frighten him. I mean, he's a miserable old sod and he hasn't done anything for her, but he's her dad when all's said and done and he must have his feelings. And he's not a well man. I just don't know what to do.'

'He ought to know,' Charlie decided. 'I'll go round there with you now, Else. It's not for us to decide what's best – we've just got to do what's *right*. Do that, and you'll usually be doing what's best anyway.'

Elsie agreed a little doubtfully, so they put on their macs and went out. The evening had settled into a steady drizzle and it was chilly despite being the beginning of June. The soldiers, camping in the streets, were sheltering under tarpaulin awnings rigged up against their vehicles and had lit stoves to keep warm. 'It might as well be November,' Elsie said. 'Talk about flaming June!'

Jackie's father was, as Elsie had half-expected, too concerned with his own welfare to worry too much about his daughter's. 'Well, she arst for it, didn't she?' he said when Elsie told him what was happening. 'I suppose that means you got to do my dinners for a bit longer. Well, I won't say I'm not grateful,' that'll make a change, Elsie thought, 'but it's not the way things oughter be, is it? A girl oughter be looking after her own dad. And I'll tell her so, just as soon she gets this over and comes back home again.'

Elsie gazed at him with distaste. He looked crumpled and dusty, like a large, battered doll chucked down in a corner and left there. He was an invalid, she knew, but that didn't mean he couldn't have a bit of a wash now and then and put on some clean clothes. She knew he had some, because she'd taken home a bundle of washing last week and Jackie had seen to it, ironed it beautifully, she had, and Elsie had brought it back. It surely wasn't too much to expect him to sort out a clean shirt to put on.

'I don't know as Jackie's coming home again,' she said, and he took her up sharply.

'Whaddyer mean, not coming home? Course she's coming home. Where else would she go, eh? Tell me that. I don't reckon that Yank'll be coming back for her, for a start. And no one else'll have her, not now she's damaged goods.'

Elsie took in a breath but before she could speak Charlie had butted in. As a rule, he left most of the talking to Elsie – he'd sometimes said that he didn't have much choice – so the sound of his sandpapery voice speaking out now surprised her into silence.

He stepped forward and addressed Herbert Prentice direct. 'Now, you listen to me, mister. Your girl's as nice a young lady as I come across in many a long day, and if you ask me, you don't deserve her. Nor do she deserve a father like you. What you ever done for her, eh? Tell me that! And what we come round to tell you is that she's having a rough time. The birth ain't going right. Anything could happen. My Else is right – she might not ever come round here again. She might not be *able* to.' He paused to make sure that Herbert Prentice understood what he was telling him. 'And what'll you do then, eh? How'll you get that past your conscience, if you've got one? You made her feel she couldn't stop here no longer, just when she needed you most. Why *should* she come back – even if she does get through this lot? Why, eh? *Tell me that!*' He turned to his wife and took her arm. 'Come on, Else. We'll leave this old misery to stew in his own juice, and good luck to him.'

They walked out, leaving the invalid in his armchair, wrapped in his moth-eaten old blankets, and let themselves out into the street. Elsie stopped and looked at her husband.

'Blimey, Charlie, you didn't half tell him! Wonder what he'll think of that, eh!'

'I dunno, love. I dare say it'll have all gone right over his head. People like that can't never see when they're in the wrong.' They walked on in silence for a few moments, then he said, 'I dare say you won't be going round there no more then.'

Elsie sighed. 'Oh Charlie, I dunno. I can't leave the poor old blighter all alone, can I? There's nobody else to look after him, and I do feel sort of responsible, what with us having his Jackie at our house. I expect I'll carry on.' She shook her head. 'You know, the worst of it is I'm not even sure he took in what we were telling him. About Jackie, I mean. Did he realise just how bad she is?'

'I don't think he wants to realise,' Charlie said soberly. 'He doesn't want to know anything bad any more. He's had enough of it.'

'We all have.' They were passing a telephone kiosk and Elsie paused. 'Got any pennies, Charlie? I want to phone up the hospital, see if there's any news. I know it's only nine o'clock, but surely they'll be able to tell us something.'

They went into the kiosk and Elsie dialled the number the doctor had given her and pushed in two pennies. After a while, a tinny voice answered and she pressed Button A to be connected. She asked about Jacqueline Prentice and waited for what seemed an age before at last another voice answered. Elsie listened and then put down the phone and turned to Charlie.

'What did they say? How is she?'

'Comfortable!' Elsie said with a snort. 'That's all the woman would say – comfortable. I ask you, did she look comfortable when she went in? The only time that girl will be comfortable is when she's finally had that baby and can have her body to herself again!'

'So when will we know?'

'I can ring up again in the morning,' Elsie said. 'Any time after eight o'clock.'

'But you're supposed to be going to work tomorrow, aren't you? You got to be there by seven.'

'Then I'll be late, won't I?' Elsie said with asperity. 'For once in me life, I'll just have to go in late.'

It was fortunate that there hadn't been any explosives on the train. The accident could have been even more serious if there had been, and many people might have been killed. As it was, three people were hurt, one of them very badly indeed.

Elsie arrived to find the laboratory in shock. A different chargehand was standing at the door, looking grim, and neither Sally nor Mrs Sheppard was anywhere to be seen. The faces of the women standing at their benches were pale and solemn, their voices muted.

Elsie took her place at the bench. Jean Sproggs was standing in Sally's place. She glanced at Elsie without speaking for a moment, then she said, 'I s'pose you've heard about the accident?'

'You mean the train? I saw it on the way in – all on its side. What happened? Was anyone hurt?' She felt a beat of fear. 'It wasn't Sally, was it?'

The woman nodded. 'She's bin took into hospital, her and Mrs Sheppard and that Ned Harrowbin. I dunno why they put him on driving the train at all, the bloke's only half there. Coming round the track about ninety miles an hour, he was, yelling and shouting like he was on the pictures, and then it tipped over and he was chucked out, and Ma Sheppard and young Sal couldn't get out of the way fast enough and got hurt. We're just waiting to see how they are. They say one of 'em's not going to pull through.' She lifted another shell on to the table and began to dismantle the fuse.

'Not pull through?' Elsie stared at her in horror. 'Oh, my God, that's awful. Which one is it? What about Kate –

Sally's sister? Does she know?' She put her hand to her head. 'I can't take it in.'

Jean Sproggs looked at her curiously. 'Kate was there – she saw it happen. She went over to the hospital with them. It happened just as we was going in the shifting room. Where were you, then?'

'I've only just got here – the girl I've got staying with me was took bad last night, she's had to go into hospital and I couldn't ring up till eight o'clock.' Elsie shook her head. 'They couldn't tell me nothing then. Said she's under control and *comfortable*. Well, she wasn't comfortable when she went in last night, I can tell you that.'

'She's having a baby, ain't she?'

'Yes, but we didn't think it was due till next month. Well, that's what the doctor said, but I don't mind telling you I've had me doubts all along. She didn't seem to know what her dates were and she'd got like the side of a house these past couple of weeks. Then the baby started to drop, and last night she—'

'That's enough chatter,' the chargehand said sharply. 'We've had enough delay this morning. The big push'll be in a few days and they're going to need a lot of munitions, so get on with it.'

The women fell silent and the work rate increased. They all knew that the Invasion must be soon. There was an air of readiness amongst the soldiers camped in the streets, as if they were prepared to go at a moment's notice. The harbour was full of ships, and through the entrance you could see more vessels massed outside. Because nobody was allowed out to the beach, it wasn't known how many more were in the Solent, but there were rumours of thousands of vessels, crowded so closely to-gether that you could walk to the Isle of Wight across their decks. When you thought of all those ships needing ammunition, not to mention the thousands and thousands of soldiers waiting to cross the Channel and the aircraft that were already flying over night after night to bomb the cities, you could see that places like Priddy's Hard were vital. However anxious the women were about their comrades, the work mustn't be allowed to let up for a second.

They were allowed a quick break for breakfast, and they immediately gathered round the new chargehand for news. 'Have you heard anything? How's young Sally, and Mrs Sheppard? What about the boy? There wasn't nothing wrong with him, he was just a bit simple. I know his mum. How did it *happen*?'

The chargehand shook her head. 'I don't know no more than you. We'll just have to wait till someone comes over from the office.' She glanced at Elsie. 'You're Mrs Philpotts, aren't you? There's a message for you.'

'For me? It must be about Jackie! What is it?'

'Here.' The woman handed her a slip of paper. 'You can't have no more time off, mind. You've already lost an hour this morning.'

Elsie read the words quickly. 'It says she's asking for me. Oh my God, that must mean she's worse. They wouldn't bother otherwise.' She stared, agonised, at the chargehand. 'It's the girl that's been stopping with me: she's in labour and she's having a bad time. They want me to go out there.'

'She your daughter-in-law? No relation at all? Well, I'm sorry but you'll have to wait till we knock off. Got any relatives in Gosport, has she?'

'There's her dad, but—'

'Well, they'll have let him know, won't they? He'll go out.' The chargehand looked at the big clock on the wall. 'Time to get back to work. You've had your break.' She scanned the anxious faces and her voice softened a little. 'I'll let you know the minute there's any news.'

The women returned to work, fear in their hearts.

Suppose all three injured people died. It had been said at the time that one was badly hurt and might not live, but they hadn't been told which one. Yet who knew but what the others might also be in danger? For Elsie, who was closer to Sally than most of them, the fear was even greater, and on top of that she had Jackie to worry about.

They wouldn't have sent her that message, only a few hours after she'd rung up, if there hadn't been some change for the worse. There was something seriously wrong with her and the labour wasn't going right. I'll go there the minute I knock off, she thought. But what about Sally and Kate and their poor mother? I ought to go round there too, see if there's anything I can do. But perhaps they're both at the hospital.

'Where did they take her?' she asked. 'Sally, I mean – and Ned and Mrs Sheppard, too. Which hospital did they go to? The War Memorial, or over to Pompey?' The War Memorial Hospital was only small and didn't take many casualties, but if they were hurt really badly there might not have been time to take them for the fifteen-mile journey round the top of the harbour.

'They took 'em in one of the lighters,' Jean Sproggs said, referring to the barges that transported munitions across to the ships in Portsmouth Dockyard. 'Must've gone to the Royal, I suppose, or St Mary's. I dunno no more than that, Else.'

It was time to go back to work. 'I'll have to go and see Jackie first,' Elsie said, rubbing her head so that her frizzy ginger curls turned into a bird's nest. She wound her turban round and poked them underneath. 'Oh, what a thing to happen! Everything comes at once. I won't even have a chance to nip out at dinnertime – and God knows what sort of a state she'll be in by this evening. If only we weren't so busy!'

The rest of the day dragged by. Elsie was on tenterhooks, waiting for a second message about Jackie, and the whole yard was anxious for news of the three who had been hurt. Mrs Sheppard was known to quite a few and Sally to some, but everyone knew Ned. His tall, gangling figure was a familiar sight mooching between the grassy hummocks with his mower and rake, or trudging along the roads with his wide broom, and they'd all followed his progress on the train, waving to him as he went by and yelling things like, 'Whoa, Trigger!' and, 'Hey, there's Injuns up ahead!' Some of them were feeling guilty about that now, wondering if their encouragement had caused him to get over-excited. They had a whip-round for all three of them, to send presents to the hospital, but until they knew how serious the injuries were no one knew quite what to do with the collection.

At last it was time to knock off. There was a rush for the office, where Mr Milner would surely have some news for them. He came to the door, looking grave.

'Some of the news is good, you'll be pleased to hear,' he began, and there was a collective sigh, partly relief and partly dismay. 'Mrs Sheppard wasn't badly hurt at all. She was pushed to one side and she's quite bruised, but that's all. She'll be back at work on Monday.'

'Is that the good news or the bad news?' someone near Elsie muttered, and there was some muffled laughter.

Mr Milner went on, 'Sally Fisher was quite badly knocked about, too. She's broken her arm and she's got some facial injuries, but she'll be all right.' He paused and looked at them over his spectacles. 'Sally's quite a little heroine. She's the one who pushed Mrs Sheppard out of the way, and probably saved her life. We have a lot to thank her for.'

There was a cheer. Elsie joined in, thankful that Sally wasn't badly hurt, but privately she doubted whether the girl was quite such a heroine as Mr Milner thought. There was something funny about this accident and the three people who were most closely involved, and she couldn't forget Sally's dark muttering that she'd get even with the unpopular chargehand.

Mr Milner waited for the noise to die down, then he said soberly, 'I'm afraid I can't give you such good news of the train driver, Ned Harrowbin. He was flung out of the train and it fell over on top of him. His legs were crushed and he has serious head injuries. He's in a coma at present and unless – *until* he comes round, the doctors won't be able to say just how badly he's been affected.' He looked at the assembled workers gravely. 'I needn't tell you how sorry we all are about this. Ned was one of our most popular workers, known and liked by us all. He was always cheerful and always ready to do any job that was asked of him.'

'Blimey, don't talk as if he's dead already!' Jean Sproggs exclaimed. 'While there's life, there's hope, ain't there, Else?'

'God, I hope so,' Elsie agreed, and the two women exchanged rueful looks. Mr Milner went on to tell the crowd where the three injured people had been taken – the Royal Hospital, in Portsmouth, the very one where Elsie's son Graham had been killed – and said that Mrs Sheppard and Sally were being kept in overnight and would probably be allowed home tomorrow. Then he sent them all home.

Elsie trooped out of the gate with the others. There was a buzz of excited chatter all about her but she couldn't bring herself to join in. The day had been too filled with anxiety, and it wasn't over yet. Sally and Mrs Sheppard might be all right, but Ned was hovering between life and death, and even if he recovered he might never be the same again. His brain hadn't been up to much before the accident – God knows what it would be like now! And on top of all that, there was Jackie.

I'll go straight to Alverstoke now, she thought, before I go home to tea. They'll let me in to see her, surely, specially since she's been asking for me.

At least she must still be alive, or surely they would have sent another message. Unless Jackie's father had gone to see her, and told them not to bother.

Mind you, Elsie thought, hurrying to catch a bus, some people might say it'd be the best thing all round if the baby just passed away peaceful now. What sort of a life was it going to have – and Jackie too, come to that – if it lived?

Chapter Thirty

Kate's first impression, as she ran forward to the scene of the disaster, was of Ned crumpled like a broken doll on the rough track beside the railway line, the lower part of his body trapped beneath the engine. There had been blood seeping from his thatch of hay-coloured hair, and she'd caught one horrified glimpse of a gaping wound in his skull before someone had pushed her aside and knelt beside him.

She'd turned her attention to her sister then. Sally was sitting beside the track, crying, shivering and holding one arm awkwardly. Her face was covered in blood, but she was obviously very much alive. Mrs Sheppard was there too, glowering and swearing, with blood on her face and arms, and her coat dirty and torn. Matron had arrived already and was giving them a swift examination. 'You'd better all go to hospital. There may be other injuries. Don't move that boy,' she added sharply to the first-aid worker who was kneeling beside him. 'He's got to be looked at properly before we can do anything for him.'

They had all grown used to seeing casualties. There had been enough during the many bombing raids, and especially the Blitz itself, for everyone to know more or less what to do. Someone had already sent for a doctor, and someone else had raced down to the Camber to arrange for the three to be taken over to Portsmouth by barge. It would be the quickest, most comfortable way for them. Three more arrived panting under a load of blankets, bandages and other first-aid equipment, and a bowl of hot water appeared from nowhere to wash the grazes.

Matron waved her hands at the crowd, ordering them out of the way. 'You've all got work to go to. You,' she pointed at Kate, 'you're this girl's sister, aren't you? You'd better stay for a while. I'll see if you can go to the hospital with her, in case she's allowed to come home. She oughtn't to travel on her own, not after a shock like that. What about this lad? Does anyone know where he lives? What about his parents?'

'I know him,' Kate said quickly, and gave directions for someone to go to his mother. 'She'll be frantic. She's a widow and Ned's all she's got. Oh, poor Ned.' She gazed unhappily at his crumpled body. 'He will be all right, won't he?'

'We'll have to wait and see, I'm afraid.' Matron went on giving orders and before long the doctor arrived and examined Ned before allowing him to be lifted carefully on to a stretcher. The three of them, with Kate scurrying alongside, were taken to the tiny dock and put aboard a lighter. From there, they would be taken to the hospital.

The rest of the day seemed to have been one long wait – a wait for the ambulance which had been called to take them to the hospital, a wait for the doctor to come and see them, a wait while Ned was taken away, still unconscious, to be X-rayed. They sat in an uncomfortable row on a hard bench. Sally had stopped crying but was shivering so badly that a nurse had draped a blanket round her shoulders.

Mrs Sheppard too was shocked and kept going over and over the accident. 'I never even heard it coming. I been a bit deaf just lately – my friend kept on telling me I ought to get my ears syringed out, they fill up with wax, just fill up with it. And then all of a sudden I felt someone push me hard in the middle of me back,' she looked at Sally, 'and I sort of fell sideways into the ditch, and then all of a sudden there it was, that whole bleeding engine on its side not two yards away, steaming and whistling like a bleeding dragon it was, and people shouting and running . . . I never even heard it coming, never heard a bleeding thing . . .'

The nurse came at last and took Sally away to be examined. Kate went with her, as much to get away from Mrs Sheppard as anything, and waited again in a bleak corridor while Sally was taken to an examination room, an X-ray department and then to some distant part of the hospital where she would be fitted with a plaster cast.

Nurses, doctors and patients went past in an unending stream, people came and sat beside Kate until their names were called and they too disappeared, and she was beginning to wonder if she would ever see her sister again, when a very young nurse with a frightened face came and told her that Sally was now in a ward and would be kept in overnight.

'Why? What's wrong?' Kate asked, alarmed by the girl's expression.

'Nothing. Well, a broken arm and some bruises and things. It's just a precaution, in case she's got concussion or anything. You can see her for a few minutes if you like,' the nurse added, her eyes darting nervously about the corridor.

'Yes, please.' Kate followed her guide through a maze of corridors, suspecting that they were actually lost at least three times, and realised that the girl was simply new and scared stiff of her responsibilities. This impression was reinforced when they finally arrived at the ward – she distinctly heard a sigh of relief – and saw the Sister bearing down upon them fiercely. The young nurse gabbled something and disappeared into the sluice, and the Sister fixed Kate with an eye like a basilisk's.

'Visiting time's not until seven o'clock.'

'My sister's just been brought in with a broken arm,' Kate said, standing her ground. 'I was told I could see her for a few minutes.'

'Oh, that'll be the young woman in bed three.' The Sister gave a begrudging nod. 'Very well, but for five minutes only, please. She's not to be upset.'

'I wasn't going to upset her' Kate began indignantly, but the Sister had already turned away. Kate glanced around and caught sight of Sally, sitting up in bed and looking rather pale. There was a lump the size of an egg on her forehead, and a purple bruise on one cheek. As soon as she saw Kate, she began to cry.

'Sally!' Kate hurried over. 'You poor thing.' She put her arm around her sister's shoulders. 'There, it's all right now. There's nothing to cry about.' She thought guiltily of Ned. Nothing had been heard of him since they had arrived and although Kate had tried to stop several of the hurrying doctors and nurses to ask how she could find out, they had either ignored her (mostly the doctors) or shaken their heads sympathetically enough but said they had no idea (mostly the nurses).

'Buck up, Sally,' she said, trying to push away the fear that Ned might be really seriously hurt. 'You're all right, except for a broken arm and a few bruises. You'll probably be able to come home tomorrow.'

'It was all my fault,' Sally wept. 'He wouldn't have done it if it hadn't been for me. It'll be my fault if he's killed.'

'Don't be silly. How could it be your fault? And he hasn't been killed. He just got a bump on the head, that's all.' She tried not to think of the sight of Ned, half-trapped beneath the crumpled train, his head a mass of blood. 'He'll be right as rain, and so will you.'

'It *is* my fault. I told him to do it. I *made* him.' She glanced sideways at her sister and her voice dropped to a whisper. 'I told him if he drove the train really fast past Ma Sheppard and frightened her, I'd get Dad to let you go to the pictures with him.'

'You did *what*?' Kate stared at her.

'Right, you've had long enough.' The Sister was approaching, her shoes clacking on the linoleum. She gave Sally a swift look and then turned accusingly on Kate. 'I thought I told you not to upset her.'

'I didn't.'

'Well, you'd better make yourself scarce before Doctor or Matron see the state she's in. Anyway, we're too busy for visitors now.' She turned back to Sally. 'We've got a nice surprise for you, dear. Your friend's going to be in the bed beside you. She's got quite a nice crop of bruises too, so we're keeping you both in for the night just to be on the safe side. Here she comes now.'

Kate and Sally both looked towards the double doors. They had opened wide and a trolley was being pushed through. On it, paler than usual but with her scowl as fierce as ever, lay Mrs Sheppard. Her face was even more bruised than Sally's, with a black eye and a puffy nose, and there was a bandage wound round her head and another covering one arm.

'There!' Sister said in a tone of deep satisfaction. 'Isn't that nice for you both!'

By the time Kate arrived back in Gosport it was too late to go back to work and she wanted only to go home and tell her mother about the accident. Win, dismayed but as practical as ever, immediately set about getting an early tea ready so that they could all go over and visit Sally in her hospital bed. George arrived home in time to have a quick wash and go with them, eating a sandwich on the way. 'You can have a proper supper when we get home,' Win told him.

The visit was peculiarly unsatisfactory. With Mrs Sheppard in the next bed, Sally couldn't add anything to her confession and conversation was stilted. The charge-hand was treating Sally with an awkward gratitude and Kate slowly realised that she thought Sally had saved her life. Sally herself could barely bring herself even to look at her old enemy, and Kate could see the guilt in her eyes. Serves her right, she thought unsympathetically. Perhaps this'll teach her not to play stupid jokes on people.

'What about Ned?' she asked abruptly, and saw what little colour there was drain from her sister's face. 'Have you heard anything? Has he come round yet?'

Sally's eyes filled with tears. Mrs Sheppard spoke up. 'Still unconscious, one of the nurses told me. They don't reckon much to his chances. Silly fool, he shouldn't have been driving so fast, could've killed us all. *I'd* have been a goner, that's for sure, if it hadn't bin for young Sally here, pushing me out of the way.' She gave Sally a nod. 'Got a lot to be thankful to you for.'

Sally turned scarlet and looked down at the bedclothes.

'What on earth do you suppose possessed the silly fool to do it?' George asked for the umpteenth time. 'Driving the train like a madman. Mind you, they shouldn't never have let a twerp like Ned Harrowbin do a responsible job like that. Criminal, that's what it was. It was bound to go to his head, not that there was much there to stop it.'

'He was a good driver,' Kate said defensively. 'He enjoyed doing it.'

'Enjoyed it a bit too much, if you ask me,' Mrs Sheppard said. 'Thought he was in some daft Western, yelling and shouting about bloody Indians. Well, he won't be allowed to drive it no more, he won't be allowed near it. That's if he don't kick the bucket and have done with it,' she added.

Sally gasped and Kate cried, 'Don't say that! He's not

going to die!' She saw her sister's agonised expression and felt a pang of sympathy. Feeling guilt over her foolishness was one thing, and she deserved it, but to feel that she had been responsible for Ned's death . . . 'He's *not going to die*,' she repeated forcefully, and prayed that it was true.

Sally looked at her with a desperate appeal in her eyes. 'Can you find out, Kate? Can you go and see him for me?'

'I'll try.' Kate got up and walked out of the ward. She had no idea where to go, but there was a nurse sitting at a table by the door and she looked up as Kate approached.

'Mr Harrowbin? He'll be in Ward Fourteen. On the next floor. But I don't know if you'll be able to see him . . .'

'That's all right. As long as I can find out how he is.' She walked quickly along the corridor. Hospitals were horrible places, she reflected, with their stark corridors and their revolting smell, consisting of everything you least wanted to smell mixed together and topped up with disinfectant. She hoped Sally would be allowed home tomorrow. It was that bump on the head they were most worried about, but she didn't seem to have been affected by it. She climbed the wide stairs, standing back to allow two porters to manoeuvre past with a stretcher on which lay a wheezing old man, and found the door to Ward Fourteen. Another nurse was sitting at an identical table, and she looked up as Kate approached.

'I'm looking for Mr Harrowbin. Ned Harrowbin. He was in an accident at Priddy's Hard.'

'Oh yes, the train . . .' The girl looked at her notes. 'He's over there, behind those curtains.'

Kate looked at her. 'D'you mean I can go and see him?'

'Yes, he's only got one other visitor.' The nurse looked at her with sympathy. 'Are you his girlfriend?'

'Not exactly, but I've known him since we were babies.' Kate hesitated. 'How is he? Is he conscious yet?'

'I'm afraid not.' There was genuine compassion in the girl's eyes. 'He's very ill indeed. Doctor's rather worried about him. His mother's with him now – do you know her too?'

'Yes.'

'Well, perhaps you can help her. She's very upset. And if she lives near you, you might see her home.'

Kate went over to the curtained bed, her heart thumping. She had another vivid flash of memory, seeing Ned's crumpled body and gashed head, and had to pause for a moment and brace herself before gently parting the curtains and peering through.

Ned's mother was sitting on a hard chair. Her face was puffed up with crying and she was holding Ned's left hand. It was about the only part of him that wasn't bandaged.

'Mrs Harrowbin,' Kate said softly, and Ned's mother turned. She recognised Kate and began to cry again. Kate came closer to the bed and put her hand on the woman's shoulder, gazing at the figure in the bed.

Ned was as thickly bandaged as an Egyptian mummy. He lay absolutely still, only his eyes, mouth and nose visible, with an array of tubes leading in and out of his body. There was a large, square frame in the bed over his legs, holding the sheets away from them. He was breathing heavily, but with each breath he gave a groan.

'Oh Ned,' Kate whispered. 'Oh, poor Ned.'

'He's bin like this ever since I come in,' his mother sobbed. 'They don't know when he'll come round. I heard someone say he could be like this for days. *Months*. I dunno what I'm going to do without him round the house. He does everything for me. And he's always cheery, always got a smile on his face. I dunno what I'm going to do.'

Kate squeezed her shoulder. There was nothing she

could say. She stood quietly, trying to give comfort through the physical contact between them, while tears poured down her own face at the sight of her friend, the boy she had known since they were in their prams, the boy she'd played with in the street, the boy she'd gone to see so many cowboy films with . . .

The boy she had gone out with. The thought struck her like a hammer blow and she almost staggered. It's the jinx, she thought in horror, staring at the helpless figure. It's not Sally's fault at all – it's *mine*. All this time I've known I had a jinx, and yet I still went out with Ned. I thought he didn't count. *I thought Ned didn't count*.

A deep sense of shame swept over her. Wasn't that what so many people had thought about Ned? Just because he wasn't as clever as most people, deemed capable only of simple, straightforward tasks like sweeping the roads or cutting the grass, just because he had simple tastes and would have gone to see the same cowboy film every night of the week if he could have afforded it – just because of all this, people had dismissed him as someone who didn't count. And she'd done the same.

Yet he *did* count. He was friendly and affectionate towards his friends. He was always willing to take on jobs that others didn't want to do. He looked after his mother, and he was always cheerful and optimistic. And he'd been so thrilled to drive the little train – a responsible job that he could do better than anyone had expected, a job he loved and was proud of.

Ned, I'm sorry, she thought, staring at him through her tears. I'm as bad as all the rest. It's *my* fault you're lying here, whatever Sally did. If I hadn't gone to the pictures with you so many times . . .

Her reason told her that it was impossible. But her heart told her differently, and as the nurse came to tell them it was time to go and she led Mrs Harrowbin out of the ward and down to the next floor to meet her own parents, it lay like a lump of lead in her breast. If Ned dies, she thought, it will be my fault. And if Ned dies, what about Brad?

If Ned died, there would be no hope at all for Brad.

Chapter Thirty-One

Sally watched her family leave the ward and was suddenly very lonely. She felt the sting of tears in her eyes and turned her face to the wall. If only they hadn't put Mrs Sheppard in the next bed, she thought despairingly. If only the chargehand wouldn't go on and on about Ned, how stupid he was, and – almost worse – about Sally herself and her supposed bravery.

If she knew the truth, she'd half-kill me, she thought wretchedly. And I'd deserve it. I even deserve being stuck here beside her in bed!

The gruff voice sounded in her ear. 'You all right, love? You've gone ever so quiet. Want me to call a nurse?'

Sally turned over and shook her head. 'I'm all right, thanks.' She looked guiltily at the bruised face. I never meant all this to happen, she thought miserably. 'What about you? Does – does it hurt much? Is your arm broken too?'

The woman shook her head and winced. 'No, well not much. Bit of a headache, and me eye's throbbing and me arm aches, but it ain't broke. Got a bad cut on it from a bit of metal, all jagged it is, and bits of stuff got stuck in so they had to pick it all out with tweezers. I daresay they were frightened of me getting lockjaw too; you can get that off roads when you gets a bad cut. Die from it, you can.' She gritted her jaw as if she was already feeling the effects, and Sally shuddered. Oh God, please don't let her die, she prayed. Please don't let me have murdered her as well.

'It's all right, though,' Mrs Sheppard added. 'Gave me an injection, they did, so I won't get it. Gave you one as well, did they?'

'I don't know.' Sally had barely been aware of what had been going on as she was treated. 'They pulled me about a lot and I didn't like getting my arm set much. I think they did give me an injection, but I don't know what it was for.'

'Lockjaw,' Mrs Sheppard nodded. 'I daresay that's what it was.'

There was a short silence. The nurses were busy bringing round bedpans to the patients who couldn't go to the lavatories on their own. Sally felt the colour run into her cheeks. The thought of sitting up on a bedpan here, beside Mrs Sheppard, was so embarrassing that she made up her mind that she'd get herself to the lavatory even if she had to crawl there. The chargehand looked at her again.

'I daresay you were pleased to see your mum and dad, and young Kate.'

'Yes,' Sally said, and then realised that Mrs Sheppard hadn't had any visitors of her own. 'Your – your hubby – is he away?'

'Dead,' the woman said briefly, and Sally coloured again and started to apologise. Her fumbling words were lost as Mrs Sheppard went on in her harsh, gravelly voice: 'He was at Dunkirk, see. Never come home. Missing, believed killed, that's what they said. So I had to come out to work, see. Got four youngsters to keep, didn't have no choice.'

'Four children?' Sally stared at her. She had never imagined the burly chargehand as a wife and mother. 'How old are they?'

'Eldest is twelve, youngest is coming up to six. Two years old when her daddy died, never knew him properly and can't remember him at all now.' Something very like a tear crept out of her blackened eye and slipped down

397

the battered cheek. 'But my Dorrie, she bin a tower of strength. She was only eight but she was a handy little thing and she turned to and helped me round the house like she was born to it. And when I got a job at Priddy's, and had to come out early in the morning, she was up same time as me and got the rest of them up and ready for school, washed their faces and give them their breakfast and everything. Proper treasure, my Dorrie is.' The bandaged head nodded.

Sally could find nothing to say. All this time she'd treated Mrs Sheppard with scorn and insolence, never thinking what the woman's life might be like. She'd been working at Priddy's Hard long enough now to know that the hours were long and exhausting, and that Mrs Sheppard must have worked extra hard to have been made a chargehand. She could also imagine, although only faintly, what it was like to go home worn out in the evenings and have to turn to and cook a meal for four children, to do their washing and look after the house. Even if you did have a twelve-year-old daughter who was as ready to help as Dorrie Sheppard sounded.

I don't do anything much at home, she thought guiltily. I wash up the supper things and help Mum when she asks me, but I don't do anything like as much as Dorrie does. I've never got Pete or Barney ready for school or given them their breakfast.

Mrs Sheppard must be tired out, all the time. And on top of that, she's been widowed. She's lost her husband and the children have lost their father, yet they've carried on. No wonder she's bad-tempered sometimes. It must all seem too much to bear.

Shame washed over her again as she stared at the broad, ugly face coarsened by hard work and grief and thought of the many ways in which she had tormented the woman. It's through me and my stupid ideas that we're here, she thought. It's me being selfish and vain and spiteful. I could have killed us all. I still might have killed Ned. Kate's right – it's time I grew up.

'I'm sorry,' she said, reaching out a hand. 'I'm sorry about your husband, and about the children – and about all the stupid things I've done. I'm sorry about the accident.' She swallowed hard. 'It – it was my fault, you know. I asked Ned to go too fast. I wanted – I wanted him to frighten you. I'm sorry now. It was a cruel, stupid thing to do and I'm really, really sorry.' She bit her lip and stared at Mrs Sheppard. 'I didn't save your life at all,' she whispered. 'I nearly killed you.'

There was a long silence. The young nurse with the bedpans was coming nearer. Mrs Sheppard drew her heavy black brows together and looked at Sally closely. Then she shook her head and said in a heavy voice, 'Well, I don't see as that matters now. You never meant it to turn out as it did. I can see that. And whatever the ups and downs of it are, you *did* save my life in the end. And who's to say young Harrowbin wouldn't have had an accident someday anyway? Accident waiting to happen, that's what that boy is, and always has been. I know his ma – my hubby used ter live next door to her. The times he's got into some sort of trouble, you wouldn't believe, but he always comes out of it all right. If he fell down a sewer he'd come up smelling of roses, that's what my old man used ter say.' She patted Sally's hand again and gave her a grin. 'He'll be all right. You don't need to worry about him. All those things I said about him before, you don't want to take no notice of them. That's just me. Always had too much gob for me own good.'

Sally nodded and smiled weakly. She was only half-comforted by the robust words, but she knew that some of what Mrs Sheppard had said was true. And the charge-hand seemed to have taken her confession with much more equanimity than she could have expected. At least I'm not living a lie, she thought.

'Come on, you two,' the nurse said, arriving at their bed. 'It'll be supper time soon. Do you want bedpans first?'

'No!' Sally exclaimed, climbing awkwardly out of bed with her arm held stiffly before her. 'I'll go to the lavatories. I can manage. I'm sure I can.'

Mrs Sheppard winked with her undamaged eye and gave the nearest thing to a cheerful smile that Sally had ever seen. 'If you can't, love,' she said, 'you just give me a shout, see? We're mates now, you and me. And mates help each other out.'

Not in this, they don't, Sally thought grimly, setting off down the ward. She was thankful that the air had been cleared, relieved that they were on better terms – but, however much she had learned in the last quarter of an hour, however much she had changed, she knew that she and Mrs Sheppard would never be 'mates'.

The Children's Home stood on a corner of the slope that ran up from St Mary's Church towards the top of Stokes Bay common. When Elsie got off the bus she found the village full of soldiers and from the glimpse she caught of the Solent she could see masses of ships gathering like clouds before a storm. It must be any day now, she thought, and wondered how it was possible that the Germans didn't know all this was going on. Surely all they had to do was send their planes over and they could bomb the whole lot out of the water.

She couldn't give too much attention to that, though. Somewhere in this big building, standing behind its high walls, was Jackie Prentice, fighting for her life and her baby. She found the door and hurried in.

'I'm looking for a young girl, having her first baby. Miss – *Mrs* – Prentice.'

'Up the stairs and first on the left. There's a maternity ward, she'll be in there.'

Elsie reached the top of the stairs and hung on to the banister for a minute or two, panting. She hadn't run so much for years. As a girl, she'd been slim and agile but she'd never got her figure back after Graham had been born, and was too fond of her food to try very hard. Even on wartime rations she still hadn't lost weight and, since Charlie said he loved her as she was, she wasn't bothered. Now, out of breath and with her heart going like a steam-hammer, she wished she could be that slim, agile young girl again.

The maternity ward was a few yards along the corridor. Elsie looked in and saw a row of beds, each with a woman sitting up feeding a baby. There was no sign of Jackie.

She caught sight of a nurse, bending over a cot at the far end of the long room, and puffed her way towards her. The nurse looked up and frowned.

'It isn't visiting time, you know. The babies are being fed.'

'Go on, I'd never have guessed,' Elsie said sarcastically, and then bit her lip. It wouldn't do any good antagonizing the woman. 'Sorry, only I've had a terrible day and I'm worried sick about my girl, Jackie Prentice. She was brought in last night. Started labour early and she was having fits, and they sent for me this morning only I couldn't get off work. D'you know where she is?'

'Mrs Prentice?' The nurse's face shadowed. 'She's in a room on her own, further along the corridor. I don't know that they'll let you in, though.'

'They better had!' Elsie said grimly as she headed back to the door. 'I didn't come all this way to be fobbed off.' But the expression on the nurse's face had frightened her. What was the matter with Jackie? Had the baby been born – and died? Her heart thudded.

The door to the small room was slightly ajar. Elsie could hear voices inside. She pushed gently and peered through the gap.

Jackie was lying on a high bed, moaning weakly. She was draped with a sheet and there was a towel knotted to the bedpost for her to grip when the pains began. Her ankles were fastened to a high iron frame and the end of the bed, her legs held wide apart. Clustered around her were three nurses and a doctor, talking in low voices. Elsie heard the words 'not much longer now' and she caught her breath. The baby hadn't been born yet, then. There was still hope.

One of the nurses glanced round and saw her. She said something to the others and came over quickly. 'You can't come in here.'

'But she's been asking for me,' Elsie said, refusing to move. 'I was sent for. I came the first minute I could – they wouldn't let me off work before. She's been living in my house, it was me that was with her last night when all this started. Elsie, my name is, Elsie Philpotts.'

'Oh, I see.' The nurse hesitated. 'Stay here for a moment.' She went back and spoke to the doctor. He glanced towards Elsie and nodded.

'All right. Doctor says you can come in for a minute or two, just to let her know you've arrived. She's been calling out for you all day.' There was a touch of reproach in her voice. 'I'm afraid the labour hasn't been going well at all,' she added quietly. 'Doctor's very worried about them both. She's had high blood pressure and then developed toxaemia, and it's brought on convulsions. And the baby's in an awkward position. We're doing our best, but . . .' She shrugged.

'But what? You mean she's going to lose the baby?' Elsie stepped forward quickly. The group round the bed parted to let her through and she bent over the swollen figure. 'Jackie, it's me. Can you hear me? It's Elsie. I've come. I'm sorry I couldn't get here before, they wouldn't let me off, but I'm here now. It's Elsie, Jackie. Don't you know me?' Her voice took on an edge of fear. 'Say you know me, duck. Say you know I'm here.'

The girl lay with her eyes open but unseeing. They stared blankly at Elsie's face and then began to fill with pain. There was swift movement behind her and the doctor spoke in a crisp voice. 'Stand aside, please.' She stepped back hastily and they took up their positions again. Feeling sick with anxiety, Elsie retreated to a corner of the small room and watched.

Jackie began to writhe and cry out. Her cries grew louder, became shouts and then screams. Two nurses gripped her hands, another stood at the end of the bed. The doctor was doing something under the sheet. He snapped out a word and the nurse handed him a pair of long forceps.

'Bear down!' he snapped. 'Make her bear down.' The nurses began to shout at Jackie, urging her to bear down, to push, to try harder. She can't, Elsie thought, watching with horror, she can't try any harder. The poor kid's been going on like this for twenty-four hours, she must be exhausted. She covered her face with her hands and then heard Jackie let out a high, piercing shriek. It was like nothing Elsie had ever heard before.

'That's it!' The doctor's voice was triumphant and the nurses all broke into a babble of encouragement. 'Gently, now. Let me lift it out . . . we've got to be very careful now. Don't let her bear down again . . . That's better . . . yes . . . here it comes. There!' He lifted the slimy, purplish, blood-streaked creature clear of Jackie's body and held it high. 'It's a boy!'

'Oh!' Elsie uncovered her face and stared in rapture. The baby lay motionless in the doctor's hands as if too exhausted to make any movement. The doctor turned it upside down and gave its bottom a light slap. The nurses watched anxiously.

There was no response.

It's dead, Elsie thought in panic. All that trouble and pain, and it's dead.

The doctor gave the baby a harder slap. It jerked in his hands and gave a cry. A weak, feeble cry, but definitely a cry. There was a general sigh of relief and the doctor handed the baby to one of the nurses.

'Get him into a warm cot. He's not out of the woods yet. And neither's this young woman,' he went on, turning back to the bed. 'There's a long way to go before I can feel happy about either of these two.'

The nurse carrying the baby came over to Elsie. 'You'd better come with me. There's the afterbirth to come yet, and she'll need stitches. The doctor won't want you here.'

'Just let me see her again,' Elsie begged, although she longed to go with the nurse and take a proper look at the baby who was now whimpering softly in her arms. 'Let me just talk to her for a moment or two first.' She went to the bed and looked down. Jackie looked exhausted but her eyes were focusing now. She recognised Elsie and gave her a feeble smile.

'Is it born? Have I had a baby?'

'You have, duck, and he's lovely. A little boy. Your little boy.' But Jackie's eyes were closing already. She's worn out, poor little scrap, Elsie thought tenderly, and she touched the girl's white cheek, then took her hand. It lay limply in her grasp. 'You'll see him later on, when he's had a bit of a clean-up. In a worse state than a mudlark he is now! And you need a bit of cleaning up yourself. But you'll be all right now it's over. And I'll come back and see you in the morning.'

Jackie gave a faint nod. 'Go and see my baby, will you?' she whispered. 'Make sure he's all right. Look after him for me.'

'Course I will,' Elsie said heartily. 'Course I'll look after him. So will the nurses. He'll be all right, don't you fret, my duck. And you'll be able to look after him yourself in a day or two. Think of that – in a couple of weeks you'll be out of here, and you can come home to Charlie and me – the two of you. Won't that be grand!'

'You'll have to go now,' one of the nurses said quietly. 'Doctor needs the room clear.'

Elsie nodded, gave Jackie's hand a final squeeze and tiptoed from the room. Outside, she followed her nose and found the nurse in a small washroom, giving the baby his first bath. Elsie joined her and gazed down at the small body.

'Is he going to be OK?'

'I hope so,' the girl said softly. 'He's quite big for an eight-month baby. She told us she was due in July, is that right?'

'We never really knew. I always thought she'd got her dates wrong. She got so big the last few weeks.'

'Well, perhaps she had. Her condition would have made her bigger than she ought to have been. And we don't know how it will have affected this little fellow.' The girl was handling the baby tenderly, washing him with care. He was quiet now, sobbing a little, and as Elsie gazed down at his tiny, screwed-up face she felt her whole heart go out to him. Oh, you dear little soul, she thought, you dear, dear little soul. You've *got* to be all right. You've *got* to live. We love you already, Jackie and me. You can't go and leave us now, when you've only just arrived.

'Do you know what she wants to call him?' the nurse asked. 'We might need to get him baptised.'

Elsie nodded. Her eyes were full of tears.

'She wants to call him Graham. That's the name she chose.' Her voice trembled. 'Graham.'

'I ought to go and see Maxine,' Kate said wearily as they got off the ferry, at just about the time when little Graham Prentice gave his first cry. 'She wasn't at work yesterday, nor today. I would've called in after work but there just wasn't time. I don't suppose she even knows about the accident.'

'You can go in on the way home,' Win said in a tired voice. Seeing her daughter in hospital, so badly bruised and with a broken arm, had left her feeling sick and frightened. She knew just how close Sally had come to death, and although she didn't realise how guilty her daughter was feeling over the accident she was also worried about Ned. She'd met Kate coming out of his ward, her face white and streaming with tears, and she'd been shocked. 'He's dying,' Kate had whispered. 'Mum, I think he's *dying*.'

'Are you sure you feel up to going to the Fowlers'?' George asked. He too was worn out, and he was hungry as well. He'd been thinking of suggesting getting some fish and chips on the way home. He wanted nothing more than to sink into his armchair with the hot battered fish and the greasy chips, soaked in vinegar and sprinkled heavily with salt, tipped on to a plate on his lap. He was anxious about Ned too – he'd known the boy since he was a nipper, and although he'd often dismissed him as a bit of a twerp he wouldn't want any harm to come to the lad. But mostly, he was tired and hungry and he was pretty sure Kate must be as well.

'Oh yes,' she said. 'I really feel I ought to go. She hasn't been herself lately and we're all wondering what's the matter. I won't stay long.'

'I'd come with you,' Win said, 'only there's Barney. We

can't leave him next door too long. It's past his bedtime already.'

Kate left them at the corner of Cider Lane and walked down to the Fowlers' house. She knocked on the door and after a few moments it was opened by Clarrie. They stared at each other for a moment, and then Kate, still not sure how things stood between Maxine and her parents, said uncertainly, 'Is Maxie in, Mrs Fowler? Only I need to see her. Something's happened at Priddy's. And I've been worried that she hasn't been to work the past two days.' A sudden dreadful thought struck her, and she stared at Clarrie with horrified eyes. 'She *is* still living here, isn't she? She hasn't gone off, after all?'

'Oh Kate,' Clarrie said in a stricken voice, and put out a hand to draw her inside. 'Oh Kate, I'm so glad to see you!'

She shook her head blindly, and burst into tears.

Chapter Thirty-Two

Maxine had known nothing of either the accident or Jackie's rush into hospital on Friday night. She'd woken up on Friday morning feeling sick and rushed to the bathroom, where she'd been violently ill. She'd gone on being sick all morning and it was obviously impossible for her to go to work. Clarrie stayed home from the dairy to look after her and they stared at each other fearfully.

'It's a baby, isn't it,' Maxine whispered. 'It's that morning sickness. Someone at work had it. She was ill every morning for months – had to bring a bucket to work with her.'

'It might not be,' Clarrie said, trying to sound convinced. 'It seems a bit early to me. You might just be having a bilious attack. Something you've eaten. You don't want to worry yourself, Maxie. It was only the once, after all.'

'How can I help worrying? It happened to you, didn't it? That was only once. Or was it?' Maxine stared at her mother, her old doubts suddenly resurfacing. 'It was only that bloke who jumped on you, wasn't it? You hadn't been with anyone else as well?'

'No! I've told you, Maxie, over and over again. I wish I *had*, then at least I'd know your father was – was someone I liked.' Clarrie's eyes flooded. 'Don't start that again, love, please. Haven't we got enough trouble?'

'Yes. I'm sorry, Mum.' Maxine reached out and touched her mother's arm. 'I'm so upset, I hardly know what I'm saying. I just don't know what I'll do if I'm having a baby.'

Clarrie was quiet for a moment. Then she said, 'You'll do the same as I did, I suppose. Look after it, bring it up, keep it. Me and your dad will help you, you know that.'

Maxine stared at her. 'Keep it? I couldn't! You know what people will say. And nobody will want me – *I* haven't got someone to marry me, like you did.' She bit her lip. 'Don't look like that, Mum. I didn't mean it the way it came out, but you know it's true. I don't know that I want to get married anyway, not after this,' she added.

Clarrie shrugged. 'I'm not bothered what people say. I went through it all myself, and they stop thinking about it after a bit. Something else comes along to gossip about and they forget. It's not as if you didn't have a home, Maxie, and you know we'll stand by you.'

Maxine didn't speak for a moment. Then, very quietly, she said, 'I don't know that I could keep it, Mum. I don't know that I could even bear to look at it. Every time I see its face, I'm going to think about Joey Hutton and what he did to me. It might even *look* like him! How could I love it, knowing where it came from? I just don't think I could.'

'Maxine, it's your *baby* – that's if you're having one,' Clarrie amended quickly. 'Of course you'd love it! Every mother does. You just can't help it.'

'It would be his baby too,' Maxine said. 'I don't think I'd love it at all. I think I'd hate it.'

When Clarrie brought Kate into the back room, Maxine was lying back in her father's armchair. She looked white and exhausted, and Kate stared at her in dismay. 'Whatever's the matter, Maxie? Are you ill?'

Maxine gave a short laugh. 'I wish I was.' She glanced at her mother. 'Have you told her?'

'No, love, of course I haven't.' She glanced nervously at Kate. 'We think we've got a bit of trouble.'

'A *bit*!' Maxine echoed. 'A lifetime of it, you mean.' She looked at her friend. 'You might as well know. I've been a fool. I've got myself into a mess and I think I'm expecting.'

'Expecting!' Kate sat down on one of the dining chairs. This was the last thing she had thought of, and yet she knew that Elsie had been concerned about the blonde girl. 'Oh, Maxie! Who – who is it?'

'Who d'you think? Joey Hutton, of course.'

'What are you going to do? Is he going to marry you?'

'No, he's not!' Maxine retorted. 'I wouldn't marry Joey Hutton if he was the last man on earth! I don't even want him to know.' She caught Kate's startled expression. 'He's a bastard,' she said viciously, and Kate heard Clarrie gasp. 'Well, he is, Mum, you know he is. And so's his baby,' she added dismally. 'So's his bloody baby.'

'*Maxine!*' Clarrie protested, but the girl ignored her. She addressed Kate again.

'D'you know what he did? Shall I tell you? He *forced* me. I didn't want to do it – well, I did to start with but then I changed my mind, I got scared and asked him to stop – but he wouldn't stop, he went on and on, he really hurt me, and then afterwards he said – he said—' Maxine was crying now, hard, painful-sounding sobs that seemed to wrench their way up through her chest, 'he said there was no point in telling anyone what he'd done because nobody would believe me. They'd say I'd asked for it. And they will, too,' she added mournfully. 'I know they will. I bet you do, for a start.'

'No, I don't.' Kate was gazing at her in dismay. 'Maxine, that's awful. When did this happen?'

'Nearly three weeks ago. And I didn't come on when I should have done, and I was sick all day yesterday and I

410

haven't been much better today. I haven't actually *been* sick, but that's only because I haven't had anything to eat. So that's two things. And that's the start of it. I *must* be expecting.'

'But isn't it called "morning" sickness?' Kate asked doubtfully. 'Doesn't that mean it's just in the mornings? My Cousin Betty had it when she was expecting, and she was always all right by dinnertime.'

'It can go on all day,' Clarrie said, sniffing and blowing her nose. 'It's usually over by three months, but I knew someone who had it every day, morning, noon and night, right up to the birth.'

'Oh my God,' Maxine said. 'Have I got to go on like this for another eight months?'

Kate looked at them helplessly. She didn't know what to say. She had come round to bring bad news, and they'd faced her with some of their own. 'You know I'll do anything I can to help,' she began hesitantly, and then faltered into silence. How could anyone help in a situation like this? Offering to knit little bootees wasn't what Maxine wanted just now.

Maxine was of the same opinion. 'Don't see what you can do, really,' she said and then, evidently thinking she'd sounded ungracious, added, 'Except still be my friend. I'm sorry I've been such a miserable cow lately, Kate.'

'That doesn't matter. I can see why, now. And of course I'll still be your friend, Maxine. So will we all – Val and Hazel and Janice and Elsie, and all the rest.' Kate chewed her lip for a moment, and then said, 'I ought to tell you why I came round. There was an accident at work this morning.' As briefly as possible, she recounted the story of the crash. Her two listeners stared at her, open-mouthed.

'Ned did that?' Maxine asked at last. 'But why? I thought he was so careful, driving that train.'

411

'He was. I don't know why.' Kate couldn't bring herself to repeat what Sally had told her. In any case, she hadn't had time to ask any questions. 'But he did do it, and now Mrs Sheppard looks as though she's gone fifteen rounds with Joe Louis and our Sally's got a broken arm and – oh Maxie, I think Ned's going to die!' She started to cry.

'*Die?*' Maxine whispered after a moment. 'Ned? Oh Kate, that's awful.'

Kate had covered her face with her hands. Tears streamed between her fingers and her shoulders shook. Maxine moved to sit beside her and put her arms round her. She held her tightly, murmuring in her ear.

'Kate, I'm so sorry. I know you're fond of him. Well, we all are. Poor old Ned. He didn't have an enemy in the world. Always got a smile on his face, whatever he's doing. I know he's a bit simple, but—'

'What does *simple* matter?' Kate burst out. 'Being clever isn't everything. It's being *good* that counts – being the sort of person that everyone likes and trusts, being the sort of person people are glad to see. Being cheerful and willing and hard-working – like Ned was. Oh, just listen to me! I'm talking as if he was dead already. Oh Maxine, if you could have seen him in that bed, all covered in bandages and with tubes sticking into him everywhere – it was just awful. And his poor legs, under a huge cage in the bed because it would hurt too much even to have a sheet touch them – what must it *feel* like? It must hurt so much. Poor, poor Ned. It must hurt him all over.' She began to cry again.

'And here's me going on about my own troubles,' Maxine said ruefully.

'Well, they are pretty bad,' Kate said, trying to pull herself together. 'I must say I wouldn't like to be in your position.'

'At least I'm not dying. And having a baby doesn't have

412

to be the end of the world.' Maxine forgot that it had seemed exactly that only half an hour ago. 'Look at that girl Elsie's taken in – Jackie Prentice. She isn't doing so badly.'

'I dare say she'd rather not be having it, all the same,' Kate said, and Maxine nodded in agreement.

Clarrie went out to the kitchen. 'I'm going to make a pot of tea. We could all do with a cup. And Maxine's dad will be in soon, he'll be gasping for a drink.' She ran the tap and Kate murmured to Maxine, 'Your mum doesn't seem too upset with you. Is – is everything all right now?'

Maxine gave her a rueful look. 'Well, it's got to be, hasn't it? I know what she went through now. I know what it's like. And she *really* didn't ask for it – some bloke just jumped out at her from the bushes. At least I was with someone I knew.' She paused and added reluctantly, 'In fact, I think I did lead him on a bit. He said we'd get engaged, you see, and I could go and live with his mum. But all the same, he ought to have stopped when I said no.'

'Maybe he couldn't,' Kate said. 'I've heard that men can't, not once they get to a certain point. I'm not making excuses for him,' she added hastily. 'He still shouldn't have said those things to you afterwards. Anyway, the main thing is, what are you going to do now?'

Clarrie came back with the tea. She set the tray down on the table and spoke with unaccustomed firmness.

'I'll tell you what we're going to do to start with. We're going to stop talking as if Maxine's definitely in trouble. It could have been just a bilious attack. And she's only a week or so late – that's nothing unusual, not after what she's been through. We'll wait a bit longer before we start to worry about it.' She handed Kate a cup of tea. 'There you are, love. Drink that. I've put some sugar in it – it's good for shock. You look as if you need it.'

413

'Oh, you shouldn't have,' Kate began. 'Not with your own ration.' But she drank the tea gratefully and Clarrie was pleased to see a little colour return to her pale cheeks. The two girls looked at each other.

'I'm sorry about the past few weeks,' Maxine said again, and held out her hand. 'We'll always be friends, won't we, Kate?'

Kate nodded. It was at times like this, she thought, that you needed your friends most of all.

'Yes,' she said. 'Always.'

There was a moment of silence. They smiled at each other and for a short while, although their troubles were just as bad, they felt at peace. Their friendship was restored and they felt they could face whatever happened next.

'I'd better go home,' Kate said at last. 'Mum's been nearly out of her mind over our Sally, and Dad looked as if he was out on his feet. They'll need me there.' She looked at Maxine. 'I'll let you know the minute there's any news. But I expect you'll be back at work Monday morning. I dare say your mum's right, and this was just a tummy upset.'

'I hope so,' Maxine said. 'I really do hope so.'

Kate went over to Portsmouth again on Sunday morning to fetch Sally from the hospital. The weather was still dismal and chilly for June, but looking out through the neck of the harbour she could still see the ships massed in the Solent. The air of waiting was everywhere, like the air of waiting for Christmas but a thousand times more serious. We're not waiting for presents now, she thought, we're waiting for death.

Her thoughts turned back to Ned. She had been thinking of him all night, and even when she'd slept he'd been in her dreams, both he and Brad, so mixed up together

414

that she scarcely knew which was which. All she knew was that the jinx had worked when she had least expected it. And that if Ned died, Brad would surely do so too.

Let Ned live, she prayed. Please let Ned live. And then, guiltily, but not just so that Brad will live too. Because he's *Ned*, and we all love him.

There had been no word from Brad that week. Every time a plane flew over, Kate looked up, wondering if he might be piloting it. Like a lot of people, she had learned to recognise the Allied planes – the British Spitfires, Hurricanes and Halifaxes, the American Liberators, Marauders and Flying Fortresses. She still didn't know what kind of plane he flew; there was something mysterious about his work, something he had never discussed with her and she knew better than to ask. All she could be sure of was that he was in danger, and that over the coming weeks that danger was certain to grow worse.

As she trudged through the damaged streets to the hospital, Kate wondered what it would be like to live in a world where there was no war. Where a boy and girl could court each other and fall in love without the spectre of death looming between them like a sickly shadow. Where you could write whatever you liked in your love letters, where you could walk in the countryside and laze on the beach and simply live your life in the knowledge that you and those you loved were safe.

She had been younger than Sally was now, when all this began. How old was she going to be before it finished, and would Brad still be alive at the end of it?

The cold fear of the jinx gripped her heart.

By the time Win had got the Sunday dinner ready, Sally and Kate were back home. Sally was ensconced in her father's armchair, her left arm in a sling and the bump on her head gone down but now a rich medley of purple, yellow and green. She was still pale and subdued, and it wasn't until after she'd finished picking at her dinner, with her food cut up into small pieces, that Kate was able to talk to her properly. George and Win had both gone over to the allotment, taking Barney with them, and the house was quiet. Sally lay back in the armchair, looking tired.

Kate looked at her. 'Sal, what you said in the hospital – about Ned. Did you really mean it?'

Sally opened her eyes. 'What d'you mean? What did I say?'

'You know – about getting him to drive fast to frighten Mrs Sheppard. Is that true? And did you really promise to get Dad to let me go out again, so he could take me to the pictures?' There was a silence. 'Come on, Sally, out with it.'

Sally sighed and nodded reluctantly. 'I can't get it out of my mind,' she whispered. 'It was meant to be a bit of fun, that's all. I thought if he just drove up close and blew the whistle to make her jump – that was all I meant him to do, honestly. I didn't know he'd go mad like he did, tearing along like he was in a cowboy picture. I didn't know he was going to crash the train.'

'I don't suppose he meant to crash it. He just got carried away. It was a daft thing to do, all the same.'

'I know. I just wanted to get my own back on her. I'd thought of a few other things too, all stupid little things just to tease her. That was all. I never meant anyone to get hurt.' The tears began to seep from her eyes. 'And now Ned's lying there and he still hasn't come round and they don't know if he ever will. Or what he'll be like if he does.' She covered her face with her good hand. 'Someone told me he could be like a – a vegetable. He could come round but not know who he is or be able to do anything for himself. And, Kate, that would be even worse than dying.

And it's my fault. It wouldn't ever have happened if I hadn't persuaded him to do it.' She shuddered. 'I'll never do anything like that again, Kate. I swear I'll never do *anything* as stupid and childish as that again.'

Kate looked at her. Sally had changed over the past few days, she thought. She looked older. Shock had taken some of the chubbiness from her face, leaving it thinner and more mature. The sulky pout that was so often on her lips had gone. Now she also seemed more vulnerable – more open to other people's feelings. She knew now that her thoughtless actions could bring terrible, unforeseen results.

'If Ned dies,' Sally whispered in horrified tones, 'you know what it'll mean, Kate. It'll mean I'm a *murderer*.'

Chapter Thirty-Three

By Monday morning there was still no change in Ned's condition. Mrs Harrowbin had been sent home on Sunday evening and had called in to tell the Fishers how she'd sat beside his bed all day, just holding his hand and talking to him. 'He can't hear me, but they say it does some good. The doctor said I'd got to come home now, though. He says I've got to get a good night's rest.' She sighed, looking defeated. 'I don't reckon I'll ever rest easy again, not knowing my Ned's like that. He looked like a little boy again laying there asleep.' She put her handkerchief to her face and sobbed.

Kate went to work feeling as though the weight of the world was on her shoulders. There seemed to be trouble and anxiety wherever she turned. It was a relief to catch sight of Maxine, walking just ahead of her.

'How are you feeling? Are you better?' she called out.

Maxine turned and gave her the ghost of a smile. 'A bit. I was sick a couple of times yesterday but this morning I don't feel so bad.'

'Perhaps you're going to be all right, then,' Kate said, and told her about Sally. 'She came home yesterday. She's got a broken arm and some bruises but she's OK apart from that. Mrs Sheppard came out too, she's a bit knocked about but the doctor says she can start work in a few days. She says Sally saved her life.' Kate grinned. 'They're best buddies now – at least, she thinks so. Sally was glad to get away from her!' She looked ahead. 'Look, there's Elsie. She wasn't at work either on Saturday. I was going to go round but never had a chance. Perhaps she had a tummy upset too.'

They hurried to catch up. Elsie turned. Her face was red with crying, and the two girls stared at her in alarm. 'Whatever is it? Is it Jackie? Has she had the baby?'

'Oh Kate,' Elsie cried. 'Oh, it's awful. I wanted to come round and tell you, but I was round the Children's Home all day yesterday and when I got home I was so tired out . . . And I kept wondering about your Sally and poor Ned. How are they? We couldn't get no sense out of no one on Saturday.'

'Sally's all right, just a broken arm. It's Ned we're really worried about. He hasn't even come round yet.' Kate described her visit to Ned and his mother's distress. 'I don't know what she'll do if he doesn't recover. But what's happened to you, Elsie? You look terrible. Is it the baby?'

Elsie shook her head. 'He's all right – a lovely little boy. Wouldn't cry at first and they didn't think he was going to breathe for a minute, but he's all right now, had a bath and looks like a little angel.' She was talking fast, gabbling out the words. At last she drew in a huge, shuddering breath and said, 'It's Jackie. She's really poorly. They haven't said so, but I'm not sure she's going to pull through.'

'*Elsie!*' Kate's hands flew to her mouth and Maxine gave a cry of dismay. 'But she was all right – she was only having a baby. How can she—'

'Lots of people die having babies,' Elsie said drearily. 'I thought all along there was summat not right about her. She was poorly all the time, you know, never stopped being sick, and she got so *big*. I thought her dates were wrong but the doctor said no, it was an eight-month baby all right. I'd have thought he was nine months myself, but they can tell by their fingernails or summat. Anyway, there he is, a lovely little fellow in his little cot – and there she is, too weak to sit up, and hardly seen him yet. It's pitiful, Kate, that's what it is.' She looked at them both, her face working. 'Pitiful.'

'Elsie, I'm so sorry. That's awful.' Kate scarcely knew what to say. 'What about her dad? He must be worried sick.'

'All Herbert Prentice is worried about is who'll get his dinner for him!' Elsie said bitterly. 'I tell you, Kate, I never met such a selfish, nasty man in all my life, and that's saying something. He wouldn't even have stirred himself to go out and see her if I hadn't got the news-paperman to take him out in his van. And he didn't seem all that sorry when he did see her. His own flesh and blood! If you ask me, his mind turned when they got bombed and he lost his missus.'

'Could I go out to see her?' Maxine asked. She had only met Jackie once, but now had a fellow feeling for the girl who had been abandoned by her lover and found herself in such trouble. She also felt somewhat guilty about her own jealousy of Jackie, when Elsie had offered the other girl the help that Maxine had needed – or thought she'd needed. I'm glad now that I didn't leave home, she thought. I might never have got back with Mum and Dad if I had . . . She asked Elsie, 'Will you be going out there tonight? I could come too, if you like.'

'Oh, would you? I'd be glad to have you with me. To tell you the truth, I get so upset when I see her. And that poor little baby, such a lovely little chap – it's cruel, that's what it is. Cruel.'

The people at Priddy's Hard shared their tension that day. Everyone was aware that D-Day must be close. 'They must be waiting for the weather to clear up,' they said, looking out over the grey harbour, thronged with ships.

'That's all that's holding it up now. They won't do anything while it's like this.' And they worked even harder to keep the torpedoes and shells passing through to the lighters, determined that, when the time did come, the ships would be as fully armed as possible.

The day's work was finished at last. Tired to the bone, they trudged out through the gates. Kate said goodbye to the others and went home, making up her mind to call in on Mrs Harrowbin on the way, to see if there was any news, even though she knew that Ned's mother would probably be at the hospital. Elsie and Maxine went straight out to the Children's Home.

The nurse met them at the door of the ward. She looked grave and Elsie's heart sank.

'I'm sorry. Mrs Prentice died an hour ago. She had a sudden haemorrhage.' The nurse gestured helplessly. 'There was nothing we could do about it. She was gone in minutes.' She looked at Elsie with sympathy. 'If it's any comfort, she can't have suffered.'

Elsie stared at her piteously. In the past few months she had become as fond of Jackie as if she had been her own daughter. Now she was gone, just like Graham. Now, once again, she had no one.

Beside her, Maxine was equally shocked. The idea of a young girl dying just because she had had a baby was a terrifying one. Poor, poor Jackie, she thought, and then: It could be me. It *might* be me.

'What about the baby?' she asked, and the nurse's face brightened.

'He's fine – a dear little chap. Taken to the bottle well, too. Doctor says he'll thrive, even though he had such a bad start.'

'And what'll happen to him?' Elsie asked quietly. She felt numb with shock, her throat aching but her eyes dry. It was so unfair. At least I was able to give her a bit of comfort these past few months, she thought, and thanked God that she'd taken the girl in and given her a home. 'What'll happen to that poor little baby now?'

The nurse shrugged. 'He'll go with the other children – they've been evacuated, you know. He'll be looked after all right. I expect they'll find someone who wants to adopt, unless his grandfather wants to keep him,' she added doubtfully.

'Herbert Prentice'll only be interested when the kiddy's old enough to work!' Elsie said sourly. 'Can we go and see him? And Jackie, too? I'd like to pay my respects.'

The nurse led them through the ward to where Jackie lay in a curtained alcove, covered with a white sheet. Together, they gazed down at the still, cold face, and Elsie reached out and touched the smooth cheek with one fingertip.

'Poor little girl,' she said softly. 'There wasn't an ounce of harm in her, you know, Maxine. Sweet as they come. It wasn't fair, what happened to her.' She straightened up. 'But then, life ain't fair, is it? We all learn that, sooner or later.'

Silently, they followed the nurse to the room where the babies were kept. There weren't many, for most women gave birth at home, and the Children's Home wasn't normally used as a maternity hospital. Of the half-dozen cots in the room, only three were occupied. Elsie glanced at them and then stopped.

'This is him. This is Jackie's baby.'

Maxine looked into the cot a little fearfully. She had never seen a really tiny baby before, and her mind was filled with dread at the thought that within a few months she too might be responsible for a scrap of life like this. She looked down, and then felt a strange warmth flood her body.

'Oh,' she said. 'Oh Elsie, he's beautiful.'

The baby was asleep. His initial redness gone, his skin was smooth, the colour of palest coffee that had been liberally doused with cream, and as translucent as finest china. He had dark hair, curled tightly over his head, and he lay with one minute fist tucked under his chin. As the two women gazed down at him he stirred and opened his eyes. They were a dark, chocolate brown.

'I thought all babies had blue eyes!' Maxine said in amazement.

'I reckon he must take after his father,' Elsie said quietly. 'Jackie never said much about him – only that he was an American GI. But I reckon that's who he looks like.'

Maxine thought of her feelings about the baby she might herself be having. She'd thought that if it looked like Joey, she would hate it. Yet this baby, even though he must, as Elsie said, look like his own father, had his own beauty and his own innocence. You couldn't blame him for what or who he was. You could only look at him and love him.

If I do have a baby, she thought, I won't hate him because he's Joey's. I'll love him. Because he's mine. And because he's who he is – himself.

A warmth stole across her heart as, for the first time in months, she realised that she was feeling at peace. With herself; with her parents; with whatever fate held in store.

She looked again at the baby. 'Has Mr Prentice seen him? Do you think he'll want to have him? I don't see how he could – a man like that. He can't look after a tiny baby.'

'No, he can't,' Elsie said with determination. 'But I could.' She turned to look into Maxine's eyes. 'Jackie was going to stop with me, you know. She was going to keep the baby, and Charlie and me were going to help her look after it. We were going to be a family, the four of us. Well, she's gone but that needn't stop us having him. You heard what that nurse said – they'll look for someone to adopt him. Me and Charlie can do that. I'm sure they'll let us – they'll be only too glad to find someone to take the poor little scrap. We can be his mum and dad.' She looked down at the cot again and touched the baby's cheek, as she had touched his mother's cheek a few moments before. 'Jackie wanted him called Graham,' she said softly. 'He'll be our second little Graham.'

Tuesday, 6 June dawned as chilly and damp as every other day for the past week. The clouds were low and the wind was blowing the waters of the harbour into grey, foam-flecked waves. Yet as the people came out into the streets they realised at once that something momentous had happened. They stood and stared, and then turned to each other with rising excitement.

'They've gone! The soldiers have gone!'

The vast Army camp that had filled the roads leading to the bay had disappeared. Overnight, the men who had been sitting with their vehicles, smoking, singing and cooking their meals on primus stoves, had vanished. The streets were empty once again and only on the main roads were military vehicles still to be seen, rumbling their way to the beaches where they too would embark on landing craft to be taken to France.

'It's D-Day,' Kate whispered as she stood outside the door. 'It's come at last.'

Her thoughts flew immediately to Brad, and even as they did so she heard the low distant roar of approaching aircraft. With everyone else, she turned her face to the sky, and gasped at the extraordinary sight.

The sky was black with planes, coming from some-where over the Hill. Yet there was something very different about these planes, for behind each one came another kind of aircraft – a massive, heavy-bellied machine with broad wings, that followed its leader as if tied on a leash. And then she realised that that was exactly what they were. They were tied to the planes that pulled them steadily through the sky. They were gliders.

This is what Brad's doing, she thought at once. He's towing a huge glider. Perhaps he's even a glider pilot. They're taking men and tanks and lorries across in gliders as well as on ships! She watched in fear and amazement as they passed overhead and were gone.

Her mother came hurrying out of the door.

'They've just announced it on the wireless! It's D-Day! The Invasion's started. They're taking thousands of tanks and things over by ship, and they're making harbours on the coast of France. That's what they were building out in Stokes Bay all that time! Mulberry Harbours, they're called. And the King's going to broadcast tonight at nine o'clock. We'll have to listen to that. Oh Kate, Kate, it's the Invasion – it's started at last!'

At work, everyone was buzzing with the news. They all had a story to tell, of how the tanks parked outside their homes had started off in the middle of the night, or they'd been kept awake by lorries rumbling past their windows. The ships that had been massed in the Solent had vanished like ghosts; the sky was filled with the noise of aircraft, going out to bomb the German defences or to lay protective smokescreens over the huge fleet of Allied ships. Nobody had ever known anything like it. Even Dunkirk hadn't been like this. Then, it had been a hasty, desperate effort to rescue the men of the BEF who were stranded in France. This time, it was an operation which had taken months – even years – to organise, and it was fuelled by the determination to win.

All the women at Priddy's Hard who had men in the Forces were waiting anxiously for news. Janice, whose fiancé would be on one of the ships, had forgotten her flirtations and went about her work with a white, drawn face. Hazel and Val were anxious about the Canadians they had met. Kate herself was in a state that was bordering on terror. She was desperately afraid for Brad. And she was almost as afraid for Ned.

Mrs Harrowbin had had no further news the night before. He had remained unconscious, not responding to anything she or anyone else said or did to him. The doctors said he was in a deep coma. He might come out of it, or he might not. If he did, he might be the same old Ned – but he might not. They simply couldn't tell.

'I'd like to go and see him tonight,' she said, 'but everywhere's so crowded with people, and Mum wants me home to listen to the King. I'll go round and see his mum straight afterwards, though. She'll be home by then.'

The day was a mixture of excitement and hard work. More news was arriving all the time and broadcast over the Tannoy system. The women worked even harder, driven by elation and a desire to provide 'our boys' with the ammunition they needed. As they hurried home again in the evening, they found an atmosphere of jubilation in the streets. The war was being fought at last on the long-awaited Second Front, and it was being fought to win. Nobody doubted that, from now on, the tide had turned in favour of the Allies.

With everyone else, Kate sat down by the radio at nine o'clock that evening to hear the King's broadcast. As she listened to his familiar, hesitant yet well-loved voice, she felt warm pride steal over her heart. They had fought this war for so long, and so hard; they had suffered blitzes, homelessness and evacuation; they had sent their men to war, so many to die. And there was still a great battle ahead, with more deaths and perhaps even more bombing at home. Yet nobody, listening to the King's quiet voice, could mistake the pride he felt in his country and his subjects, and nobody could help feeling that same pride. He's right, Kate thought, we will go on, and we will win.

Afterwards, she walked round to the Harrowbins' house, feeling quieter in her mind than she had for a very long time. There were still troubles to be faced – Jackie Prentice had died, Maxine might be pregnant, Ned was desperately ill – yet there was after all a silver lining to the cloud that had hung over them for so long. Elsie was going to take Jackie's baby and care for it as if it were her own, her 'second little Graham'. Maxine had begun to come to terms with what had happened to her and had been to church to make her own peace. But there was still Ned – and Brad. There was still the shadow of the jinx.

She came to the Harrowbins' front door and knocked. It was a small house, in a narrow street, with only two tiny rooms downstairs, a lean-to scullery and two bedrooms above. After a moment, the door opened and Ned's mother peered out. She was as small as her son was large, a skinny scrap of a woman with grey hair tied back and a tattered apron over her frock. Her eyes were red-rimmed, and sore with weeping.

'Kate. It's you.' There was a moment's silence and then she began to cry.

Kate's heart sank. She stepped into the narrow passageway and took the woman into her arms. 'Oh, Mrs Harrowbin, I'm so sorry. Is he worse? Has he come round? Or has he . . .' She couldn't go on.

She felt the grey head shake against her breast. 'It's not that. Oh, Kate, he opened his eyes this afternoon. He looked at me. He *knew* me, Kate! And he spoke to me as well. He said, "What happened to that bloody train? I tried to steer it round the corner and it wouldn't go!" He said all that, and then he went back to sleep. Proper sleep, the doctor said. And it means he's going to be all right. Oh

Kate, *he's going to be all right!* He's going to get better and be my Ned again!' She shook and heaved with the tears that had slowly collected inside her as she sat beside her son's bed and prayed, except that they were now tears of joy.

Kate held her and tried to understand what she had heard. Ned had come round. He had spoken and what he said made sense. More sense than Mrs Harrowbin realised, she thought, for it implied that there had been something wrong with the train itself, and therefore not his fault at all. And if it hadn't been Ned's fault, it wasn't Sally's either . . .

And if Ned lives, she thought, that means the jinx has gone! He isn't going to die, just because we went out together. And, hard on the heels of that realisation, came another.

If there was no jinx, Brad would live as well. He would come back for her, just as he had promised, and when the war was over they would go to Canada and start a new life together.

When she came out of the tiny house, the clouds had parted and there was a clear sky. She stood for a moment looking up and breathing the evening air, thinking of all that had passed.

Once, back in the early days of the war, Winston Churchill had described the winning of El Alamein as the end of the beginning.

Surely, she thought now, D-Day will go down in history as the beginning of the end. And then, at last, Brad and I will be able to dance again.

Chapter One

'Christmas is coming, the goose is getting fat,
Please put a penny in the old man's hat.
If you haven't got a penny, a ha'penny will do,
If you haven't got a ha'penny, a farthing will do.
If you haven't got a farthing – God . . . Bless . . . You!'

The voices rang out like bells in the crisp night air and Ruth Purslow felt her throat tighten as she saw Sammy's bright head gleaming amongst those of the other children gathered around the farmhouse door. It was three years since that first Christmas he had spent with her at Bridge End in 1941 – three years of a war that it had sometimes seemed would never end. Now it looked at last as though the Allies were winning. The D-Day invasion, back in June, had turned the tide and the enemy were being slowly beaten back.

'Let's hope this will be the last Christmas of the war,' her sister Jane Warren murmured in her ear. 'We've all had enough, even out here in the country. God only knows what they must be feeling like in towns and cities like Portsmouth and Southampton – not to mention London.'

'It'll end soon,' Ruth said. 'It's got to. And then the men'll come home and we can go back to normal.' But her voice trembled a little.

Jane glanced at her in the moonlight. 'And the rest of the kiddies'll go back home,' she said quietly. 'That's what you're thinking, isn't it? *Sammy*'ll go home.'

Ruth hesitated, then admitted, 'Well, I've got so fond of him. He's been like my own little boy these past three years. And he loves being in the country – he even talks like us now! I just don't know how he'll take to going back to a little street in Pompey. And there's that brother of his, too. He'll be coming out of the Army and goodness knows how they'll get on together.'

'Hasn't his dad said anything?' Jane asked. 'I thought you and he were – well, quite friendly. Hasn't he talked it over with you at all?'

Ruth felt herself blush. 'No, not really. Well, he hasn't been able to get out here much lately, what with all the work on the ships. He goes to sea a lot, you know. And it seems a bit early days to be – well, making any plans.' She felt her cheeks redden deeper and was glad of the darkness. Even so, she knew her sister was looking at her curiously. 'Your Lizzie will be glad when Alec can come home,' she added hastily. 'They'll be able to start their married life properly then. They haven't had much of it so far.'

'He's got to be let out of POW camp first,' Jane said grimly. 'And God knows when that'll be. Poor Lizzie's at her wits' end over it. And it seems so unfair – he wasn't even in the Armed Forces. It doesn't seem right that merchant seamen should be taken prisoner. Nor that their ships should be sunk.'

Ruth, whose own husband had been a merchant seaman, sighed. 'You know what they say – all's fair in love and war. And I suppose preventing supplies getting to us is just another way of fighting.'

The children were singing a different carol now. There were eighteen or twenty of them – largely village children, for most of the evacuees had gone home now that the bombing seemed to have stopped, but there were a few who, like Sammy Hodges, had stayed on for one reason or

432

another. Sammy's mother had died early in the war, leaving his father Dan unable to care for the boy properly, and since he still worked long hours in the shipyard Ruth had been only too happy to keep the boy with her.

'*God rest ye merry, gentlemen,*' the carol-singers warbled, '*let nothing you dismay.*'

The carol-singing was a feature of village life. It had been dropped in the second Christmas of the war, when everything had seemed so dark and dismal and the blitzing of the cities had begun, but started again in 1941 when Ruth and Jane and Lizzie had made up their minds to give Sammy Hodges a Christmas to remember. Almost everyone in the village had joined in, bringing back life to the dark lanes and the huddled cottages, and every Christmas Eve since then there had been a grand tour of the village, ending at the Knights' farm where they would be plied with mulled ale, cider and mince pies.

Even there, things had changed. Arthur and Emily Knight had aged during the past few years and the farm had been taken over by their son Ian. At first, it seemed that he would be allowed to stay at home, but as the war progressed he was called up and went into the Army while three Land Girls were brought in to work the farm under the direction of his wife Heather and Arthur. Eli, the stockman who had been on the farm since he was a boy, had hobbled out of retirement and together they'd kept the land worked and the animals tended.

'Heather'll be glad to see her man back,' Jane commented as they trooped into the big kitchen. 'She'll be able to hand over the reins and settle down to raising the family. Three kiddies are a lot to look after as well as running a farm.'

'I'm not sure she'll find it all that easy, just the same.' Having lived alone for so many years since her own husband had died, Ruth understood what it was like to have your independence. 'It seems to me she enjoys being a farmer. She might not want to go back to the kitchen – especially with her mother-in-law already there!'

Jane laughed. 'They won't have any trouble. Emily Knight'll be only too pleased to sit back. It's the natural way of things, isn't it – the younger generation taking over while the older ones take it easy. They'll all slot into place all right when Ian comes home, you'll see.'

Sammy came over and took Ruth's hand. 'Did you like the singing, Auntie Ruth? We've been practising for ages.'

'You don't have to tell me that! Even Silver knows most of the words,' Ruth said, smiling at the thought of her big grey parrot squawking them out in his creaky voice. 'He'll still be singing "See Amid the Winter's Snow" in the middle of July.' She gazed affectionately at the boy. He had changed so much since he had first come to her, a thin and frightened little waif, so dirty that she hadn't even known his hair was fair until after she'd bathed him. Now he had grown and filled out so that, while still on the small side for eleven, he was a sturdy little chap, his rosy face shining with confidence. The thought of losing him brought a pain to her heart.

Heather Knight arrived with a tray of steaming glasses. 'Mulled cider,' she offered. Her brow beneath the mane of rich brown hair was smooth despite the cares of war, her hazel eyes lively and her wide mouth smiling. 'Our own – we had such a good crop of apples. There's hot milk with honey in it for the children.'

'Just what we need on a cold night,' Ruth said, taking a glass. 'Have you had any word from Ian?'

Heather nodded. 'He'll be in Italy for a bit longer yet, but they're not putting up much of a fight now. I don't think their heart was ever really in it, you know. It was Mussolini, in cahoots with Hitler, who pushed them in.'

'Just think,' Jane said, looking into her glass, 'it could

be all over by this time next year and we'll be able to have a proper peacetime Christmas again. Things do seem to be getting more hopeful, don't they?'

'What's a peacetime Christmas like?' Sammy asked, and they all turned to look at him, startled. Ruth opened her mouth to say that surely he remembered Christmases before the war – he'd been five years old when it started – but then she recalled what his home life had been like and smiled at him.

'Not so very different from the ones we have now, really,' she said. 'But all the men will be home – Ben and Terry, and Alec, and young Mr Knight – and they won't have to go away again. And we won't have to think about bombs and air raids and the blackout. And there'll be all sorts of nice things to eat, things we haven't seen for years – bananas and coconuts, and ice cream – all sorts of things.'

There was a short pause. She glanced at the other women, knowing they were thinking the same as her. Then Sammy spoke the words that were in all their minds.

'And I'll have to go back to Portsmouth,' he said. 'I'll have to go back, because there won't be any need for me to be evacuated any more.'

When everyone had gone, trooping out into the cold night with laughter and a few snatches of song still on their lips as they wished each other a Merry Christmas, Heather Knight and her mother-in-law started to clear the big kitchen. There wasn't too much to do – Ruth and Jane and some of the others had already washed up the cups and glasses, and the plates were stacked in a neat pile to be rinsed. Once they were all put away, Emily went into the larder and brought out the big turkey, already stuffed and in its enamel roasting pan.

'This can go in the oven now. If it cooks slow overnight we can just fire up the stove in the morning and have dinner ready for twelve. Then everyone'll have the chance for a sit-down in front of the fire till it's time to see to the animals again.'

Heather nodded. The three Land Girls and Eli would all be joining them for Christmas dinner, and there would be Eli's widowed sister Clara who lived with him in the farm cottage, and Heather's own three children, Roger, Pat and Teddy. That would make eleven faces around the table. A nice number for Christmas dinner; though however many there were, she knew that the most important face of all – her husband Ian's – would be missing, just as he had been missing for the past three Christmases. But surely, if the war ended soon, as everyone seemed to think it would, he would be home for next Christmas. And then we'll be a proper family at last, she thought. For the first time, really, since he's never even seen little Teddy yet.

Ian had spent most of the war in Africa and Italy. Letters came infrequently, often months out of date, and in them he referred to letters Heather had written so long ago she had forgotten them. He asked constantly what was happening on the farm, whether the cows were giving a good yield, had there been many heifer calves born, how had the lambing gone, and he complained that she wasn't telling him the things he wanted to know. But Heather knew she had reported all these things faithfully, along with family news, and could only assume that some of her letters had got lost. And she was just too tired, after working on the farm all day, to write it all over again – it would all be out of date by that time anyway.

I can't wait to get home, he wrote. *The farm must be going to rack and ruin with just you and Eli and a few town girls to look after it. What do they know about animals and crops? I know you're doing your best, Heather, and you've got Dad to tell you what to do, but it needs a man around the place. Never mind – the minute this war's over, I'll be home and we'll soon get the place back on its feet.*

Heather raised her eyebrows a little as she remembered this. Born and brought up on a farm herself, she considered that she was making a good job of looking after this one. Mr Knight – 'Dad' to her – was old now and had arthritis, so couldn't do much more than advise. To begin with, feeling rather as if she were trying to steer an avalanche, she had turned to him almost all the time, but after the first few months her confidence had begun to grow. The sight of tiny points of green shimmering over the fields as shoots of new wheat she had sown herself pricked through the earth had been a real thrill, and the arrival of her first lambs almost as amazing as the births of her own babies. From then on, she had taken more and more control, and Arthur Knight had come out into the fields more to congratulate than to advise.

The Land Girls had been a tremendous help too. They lodged in one of the farm cottages and old Aggie Clutter had been glad to move in and look after them. She gave them breakfast and supper and the girls had their midday dinner with the family in the farmhouse kitchen.

'It'll seem strange when they go home,' Heather said to Emily now as the oven door was closed on the turkey. 'They're part of the farm. You wouldn't think they were the same girls as those townies who came here, scared stiff of the cows and cooing over the lambs as if they were cuddly toys!'

'You wouldn't,' her mother-in-law agreed with a chuckle. She went to the sink and pumped up some water to rinse her hands. 'But they've turned out real well. I must say, when I saw them I thought they'd be more trouble than they were worth – especially young Stevie with her gold ringlets and all. More like a film star than a farmhand, she was.'

'She can't help her looks,' Heather said, as if Stevie had been ugly rather than pretty. 'And it was handy that Pam and Jean already knew each other in Southampton. I did think Stevie might taken longer to settle in but when it turned out she knew the Budd family and some of the other evacuees – well, it seemed to make it easier. I suppose it must help if you're in a strange place, to see a few familiar faces about.' She sighed. 'I'll be sorry to see Stevie go back to Portsmouth, I really will.'

Stevie and Heather had hit it off right from the start. The other two were nice enough girls, and they all worked well together but, to Heather, Stevie had become more like a sister.

'That won't happen for a while yet,' Emily said, wiping her hands on the roller towel behind the door. 'I know everyone's talking as if the war'll be over soon, but you never know what dirty trick that Hitler might have up his sleeve.'

Heather nodded. There'd been a lot of talk lately about 'secret weapons' and bombs even bigger than the ones that had already been used by both sides. You couldn't take anything for granted.

When Ian comes home, we'll work the farm together, she thought as she began to set the big kitchen table for breakfast. The older kiddies are more or less off my hands now and Teddy'll be at school in a couple of years – I'll be able to show him all the changes there've been and we can plan what we're going to do next. All these hardships will be past then, and we can look forward to a happy future. It'll be different – I don't suppose he realises how much things have changed here, especially for women – but it'll be good. And the main thing is, we'll be able to share it all.

It had been so long since she had been able to share anything with her husband.

Jane, Lizzie and Ruth walked back down the lane together. Jane's husband, George, had slipped back early to make a final check on the animals and Sammy was walking ahead, putting his feet down very quietly in the hope of seeing a badger. The three women linked arms and sauntered along in the moonlight, talking softly.

'Another Christmas,' Ruth said, with a little sigh. 'It doesn't seem possible that a war can drag on so long. D'you realise, this is the *sixth* since the war started? Six Christmases of war! A lot of the kiddies don't know anything else. They've grown up with bombs and air-raid warnings and their daddies away fighting, and they don't even know that life can be different.'

'And some of them will never see their daddies again,' Lizzie said in a sombre voice. 'Some men never even got the chance to *be* daddies.' Her voice cracked a little.

Ruth took her arm quickly. 'Lizzie, I'm sorry. I didn't mean to upset you. Me and my big mouth! I should've known better than to remind you of Alec, especially after having such a nice evening.'

'You didn't remind me. There's not a minute goes by when I don't think about him. I just live for the day he comes home again. Thank goodness I've got my nursing to keep me occupied.' Lizzie drew in a deep breath and turned to her mother. 'Is there anything else to do for dinner tomorrow, Mum? Don't forget we've got company.'

Jane laughed. 'I'm not likely to forget, with you reminding me every five minutes! But just in case you think I can't count, there'll be eight of us – you, me and your father, Ruth and Sammy here, and Dan Hodges if he manages to get over from Portsmouth, and the two Americans. Not a crowd, but enough to make a bit of noise and give young Sammy a party.' She hesitated, then added, 'It may be our last chance to do that.'

There was a small silence. Lizzie glanced at her aunt but before Ruth could speak, there was a cry of excitement, quickly hushed, from Sammy and they all stopped. He tiptoed back to them and even in the moonlight Ruth could see that his face was glowing with delight. 'I saw one, Auntie Ruth! I saw a badger! He came out of the hedge and ran across the lane – I saw the stripes on his face. I knew there was one here!'

'There's a sett in the woods,' Lizzie told him. 'You went to see it with Ben last time he was home, didn't you?'

'Yes, and Ben showed me the track he makes coming over the bank and across the lane. It's his own path. But I didn't know what time he'd come. He doesn't come out until very late, Ben said.'

'In that case,' Ruth said, taking his hand, 'it must be very late now and time for us all to be in bed. Come on, Sammy. You know who's coming tomorrow, don't you?'

He glanced up at her and for a moment she thought he was going to tell her scornfully that he didn't believe in Father Christmas any more. But then his smile broke out and he gripped her hand tightly and said, 'Dad! Dad's coming tomorrow, for Christmas dinner. And I've got a present for him.'

'Which still needs to be wrapped up,' Ruth said, walking on briskly. 'Come on. You won't see the badger again tonight – he's probably three fields away by now, scared out of his wits by all the noise we're making. Let's get home and make sure everything's ready for tomorrow. It's Christmas again and we're going to give your dad the best Christmas he's ever had!'

The best Christmas he's ever had? Lizzie thought, as she and her mother turned away up the farm track. Well, I don't begrudge Dan Hodges his Christmas, even if he is an odd sort of a bloke. But I wish I could be saying the same about my Alec. I wish I could be giving him the best Christmas he's ever had.

As it was, she knew that he probably wouldn't be having any sort of Christmas at all, hundreds of miles away in a German prisoner-of-war camp.